"A gloriously entertaining plunge into the ultracompetitive world of youth sports and the lengths we go to for the kids and games we love."
—*New York Times* bestselling author KJ Dell'Antonia

"How much raw emotion can one writer put into a story? Kathleen West shows us in her luminous new novel, *Home or Away*, set in the competitive world of youth hockey in Minnesota, known as the State of Hockey."
—*St. Paul Pioneer Press*

"West captures the kid hockey scene with blade-sharp precision."
—*Star Tribune*

"A sincere and thoughtful study of dedication and sacrifice."
—*Publishers Weekly*

"This nuanced, heartfelt novel exploring abuses of power in sports will appeal to fans of Hannah Orenstein's *Head over Heels* and Alena Dillon's *The Happiest Girl in the World*." —*Booklist* (starred review)

"An excellent, deeply layered story that explores how ambition, hope, and dedication impact the choices people make, the secrets they hold close, and the lies they tell themselves and others. It's also about powerful women supporting each other, friendship, parenthood, marriage, attraction, sexual harassment, and the all-encompassing world of high-level youth—and Olympic—sports." —*Kirkus Reviews*

Praise for *Are We There Yet?*

"A breezy yet affecting read filled with struggle and hope." —*People*

"Filled with witty charm, humor, and family secrets." —*Woman's World*

"Fans of Liane Moriarty of *Big Little Lies* fame will love *Are We There Yet?*, a heartfelt and thought-provoking drama about the trials and tribulations of modern suburban motherhood."
—*Working Mother*

"Kathleen West's latest novel, *Are We There Yet?*, tackles the struggles of parenting with unflinching honesty.... Alice's picture-perfect life seems to disappear overnight, leaving her with no choice but to embrace the mess."
—PopSugar

"*Are We There Yet?* perfectly captures the friendships we form when our children are little, and the often painful ways they shift and change as our kids grow up and into their own identities. I fell headfirst into this novel, and I didn't want to leave."
—Julie Clark, *New York Times* bestselling author of *The Lies I Tell*

"A sparkling, page-turning take on modern motherhood that reminds us, in the most entertaining way possible, that the illusion of control can be blinding. A family drama full of surprises and plenty of heart, *Are We There Yet?* will give you all the feels. I loved it."
—Jamie Brenner, author of *A Novel Summer*

"With crisp prose, a compelling cast of characters, and a storyline that will immediately strike a chord with parents (as well as anyone who's spent time around tweens and teens), *Are We There Yet?* hits all the right notes. Kathleen West's latest is at once a clear-eyed portrait of the challenges of our fast-paced, technology-obsessed society and a heartfelt and empathetic examination of motherhood. Highly recommended."
—Camille Pagán, bestselling author of *Good for You*

"An astute and witty look at the ties that bind us and the events that can undo them. *Are We There Yet?* is a nuanced take on contemporary parenting bursting with warmth and heart."
—Julia Whelan, author of *Thank You for Listening*

"A timely, engaging story about modern parenthood and familial angst told with graceful insight, witty humor, and more than a few deliciously page-turning twists. Kathleen West has delivered a novel full of heart and soul."
—Lisa Duffy, author of *My Kind of People*

"*Are We There Yet?* is a sharp-eyed but generous novel, filled with a vivid cast of characters. Despite their flaws, you can't help but root for them as they grapple with their competitive urges, family secrets, and some very lewd graffiti. I laughed out loud and got really nervous about someday having tweens of my own."
—Laura Hankin, author of *One-Star Romance*

"With a wide cast of perfectly drawn characters, *Are We There Yet?* is a sharp social commentary wrapped in an engrossing family drama. West brings her trademark wit to a romp through the savage hallways and phones of junior high students. Where are the (well-meaning but neurotic) adults, you ask? Behaving just as badly as their tweens. I could feel my hair graying with each new blunder—to anyone raising a teenager in the age of social media, I salute you."
—Stephanie Wrobel, *USA Today* bestselling author of *The Hitchcock Hotel*

Praise for *Minor Dramas & Other Catastrophes*

"A wry, engaging debut."
—*People*

"Just as good as Liane Moriarty's *Big Little Lies*."
—*Kirkus Reviews* (starred review)

"Fans of *Where'd You Go, Bernadette* will flip for this clever, drama-filled debut novel."
—*Woman's World*

"A smart and delightful story of entitlement, friendship, and overparenting, with page-turning twists galore. West writes across lines of class and generation with grace and ease. A bighearted debut."

—Bruce Holsinger, author of *The Displacements*

"As intriguing as it is timely. West provides a funny and shocking glimpse into American parenting through the lens of an out-of-control stage mother who has lost all sense of boundaries."

—Amy Poeppel, author of *The Sweet Spot*

"A cutting and witty examination of modern parenting that excels in suburban relatability, West's debut novel will pique the curiosity of fans of Maria Semple's *Where'd You Go, Bernadette*." —*Booklist*

"Helicopter parenting and high school politics at their worst—and funniest. A smart, fast-paced, and deliciously entertaining debut!"

—Meg Donohue, *USA Today* bestselling author of *You, Me, and the Sea*

ALSO BY KATHLEEN WEST

Minor Dramas & Other Catastrophes
Are We There Yet?
Home or Away

MAKING FRIENDS CAN BE *MURDER*

KATHLEEN WEST

BERKLEY
New York

BERKLEY
An imprint of Penguin Random House LLC
1745 Broadway, New York, NY 10019
penguinrandomhouse.com

Copyright © 2025 by Kathleen West
Readers Guide copyright © 2025 by Kathleen West
Excerpt from *Home or Away* copyright © 2022 by Kathleen West
Penguin Random House values and supports copyright. Copyright fuels creativity, encourages diverse voices, promotes free speech, and creates a vibrant culture. Thank you for buying an authorized edition of this book and for complying with copyright laws by not reproducing, scanning, or distributing any part of it in any form without permission. You are supporting writers and allowing Penguin Random House to continue to publish books for every reader. Please note that no part of this book may be used or reproduced in any manner for the purpose of training artificial intelligence technologies or systems.

BERKLEY and the BERKLEY & B colophon are registered trademarks of
Penguin Random House LLC.

Book design by Nancy Resnick

Library of Congress Cataloging-in-Publication Data

Names: West, Kathleen, 1978- author.
Title: Making friends can be murder / Kathleen West.
Description: New York : Berkley, 2025.
Identifiers: LCCN 2024025583 (print) | LCCN 2024025584 (ebook) |
ISBN 9780593335536 (trade paperback) | ISBN 9780593335550 (ebook)
Subjects: LCGFT: Detective and mystery fiction. | Novels.
Classification: LCC PS3623.E8448 M35 2025 (print) | LCC PS3623.E8448 (ebook) |
DDC 813/.6—dc23/eng/20240617
LC record available at https://lccn.loc.gov/2024025583
LC ebook record available at https://lccn.loc.gov/2024025584

First Edition: June 2025

Printed in the United States of America
1st Printing

The authorized representative in the EU for product safety and compliance is Penguin Random House Ireland, Morrison Chambers, 32 Nassau Street, Dublin D02 YH68, Ireland, https://eu-contact.penguin.ie.

To my mom, Miriam Williams,
who loved these characters from the beginning

CHAPTER ONE

April 1, 2023

By the time the group met up for the long-anticipated yarn-bombing, Sarah had netted four new personal training clients via The Sarah Jones Project Instagram account. Not bad for the brainchild of a kid she'd met in her first week after moving to Minnesota.

"It's gonna be fun," Sarah had told her grandmother on the phone that morning, "and only a normal amount of weird."

"Your profile on the 'gram was nice," Grandma Ellie had said. Of course, Ellie approved of Sarah's unconventional stab at making friends in a new city. Ellie had always believed in "the fates."

The fates struck quite a lot when your name was as common as Sarah Jones—emails meant for other women who shared both monikers, multiple rewards customers at the local bookstore, alumni news that had nothing to do with you from your midsize university. Mistakes and misidentification abounded.

So it had been both surprising and not when three days after Sarah had arrived from Vermont and started as the director of personal training and running at LifeSport Fitness, she'd gotten LinkedIn and Instagram DMs from a girl with her same name. But, on purpose this time.

"It's the fates!" Ellie had said, and Sarah could only agree. She'd felt giddy when she'd driven to a meet-up of fellow local Sarah Joneses that week. The group had met twice already when she joined, and they'd been so welcoming. Brian, Sarah's ex-fiancé, had warned her it would take months to find community halfway across the country from home. But there she was, about to meet four women—well, three women and one seventeen-year-old kid—all with the same name. And in the month she'd spent with them since, The Sarah Jones Project had built a social media following. Sarah's client list was growing. There would certainly be more after they "bombed" the iconic eastern cottonwood in Crosby Farm Regional Park. The *Pioneer Press* had sent a reporter, a woman young enough to be on her first assignment, after the group had sent in a tip. Lucky for all of them, it seemed like a slow news week. A group of same-namers could make the local section.

"Remember," Sarah Patrice Jones, age sixty-nine, shouted to the group from her crouch near the tree's trunk, "stretch the fabric and simple stitch!"

Sarah—"Thirty," the group called her, as they all went by their ages so as not to be utterly confused—smoothed a double-stitched section of crocheted yarn in robin's-egg blue over a low branch and smiled at Seventeen. "This is the best," she whispered.

Seventeen beamed. "I know. I can't believe this is my 'punishment.'"

Sarah giggled. The group had begun because Seventeen had made several public and unfortunate social media blunders. The Catholic nun who directed the Upper School at Seventeen's Sacred Heart Academy had mandated a positive social media endeavor as part of a rehabilitative disciplinary proceeding.

"Is this right?" Forty-Four asked, pulling another swatch across the trunk.

Sarah held her hand over the part of the seam she'd been sewing and peered at Forty-Four's work.

"Obviously not!" Sixty-Nine piped in. "I measured precisely. We all did, remember? Or were you taking a selfie at that particular critical time?"

Thirty and Forty-Four exchanged a glance, and Thirty-Nine spoke up, her words muffled around the thick yarn needle she'd stashed in the corner of her mouth. "We have a social media presence to maintain," she said. "Forty-Four and I are the only same-named teachers who regularly wear matching outfits in the nine-state area!"

"So I've heard," Sixty-Nine said, repositioning the yarn square.

Sarah grinned as she stitched. "It's an odd group," she'd told Grandma Ellie about the Sarahs, "but they're also funny. And they're nice! You'd have to be, right? To even entertain something like this?"

Sixty-Nine, in addition to being the crochet master, had retired in the last year from corporate law and also ran a moderately popular *Murder, She Wrote* recap blog. Thirty-Nine and Forty-Four taught elementary school in neighboring rooms. And Twenty-Seven, Sarah's closest friend in town, was halfway to a PhD at the University of Minnesota in sociology. "Here for academic interests," she said when she'd shown up to The Sarah Jones Project a week after Sarah.

"It seems like destiny, right?" Twenty-Seven had said. "A whole club of me? A group devoted to having the most common name in the world?"

Seventeen had peered at the newcomer's state-issued ID at her first meeting. They couldn't have imposters, the kid insisted. That would "dilute the appeal of the project."

"It's not even the most common name in the state." Seventeen handed the license back to Twenty-Seven with an eyebrow arch. "James Johnson, for instance. James Smith. Both occur more per capita."

"But, you know what I mean, right?" Twenty-Seven had smiled at the other women. She was gorgeous, long brown hair settling perfectly over her shoulders. "When people tell you you're the seventh Sarah Jones they've met or something?"

Seventeen had looked suspicious, but then she came out with the group's own origin story. "There was another one on my basketball team," she admitted, "but she's horrible and she spells it wrong."

"No *h*?" Twenty-Seven had asked. But Seventeen's dopple-namer was even worse.

"Uh-uh," she had said. "Sera*fina*."

"Good lord." Twenty-Seven had chuckled a little, and Thirty noticed her sparkling white teeth and the sideways *S* on her necklace. "So she's S-E-R-A? She's not invited, is she?"

"Absolutely not." Seventeen had put down her Starbucks and crossed her arms. "I'm a purist." She rolled her eyes toward the ceiling, thinking the statement through. "But in a good way."

And now, here they were, performing their culminating task. They hadn't talked about what was next for the group, but they'd all agreed on a spring break after the yarn-bombing, during which Seventeen would rehab her AP Bio grade and the others would do whatever things normal adults did. The Sarahs swirled around the cottonwood, each with her own tote bag. The reporter from the *Pioneer Press* stood close, scribbling notes between questions like, "How many Sarah Joneses have you all met in your lifetimes?" and "Why yarn-bombing?"

"It's whimsical!" Seventeen said in response. "An intergenerational endeavor with positive public appeal." She'd rehearsed that one.

"Are we still on for lunch after this?" Twenty-Seven whispered to Sarah as they smoothed out a cable-stitch section.

"Totes," Sarah said. They'd go to their usual spot, a café across from her Minneapolis apartment, just a building north of the one her mother had lived in when she'd moved to the city thirty-five years before. Sarah liked to look up at the third-story window she imagined had been her mother's, liked thinking about Ainsley taking Sarah's father back there after they'd been to a play at one of the city's many tiny theaters. The fates had taken Sarah's mother from them back when Sarah was a sixth grader, but Ainsley had shared countless stories about her time in Minneapolis. Even though Brian had been sure the entire endeavor would be filled with woe, Sarah hadn't regretted moving to Minneapolis even one time, especially once she and Twenty-Seven became virtually inseparable in their first month of friendship. "Meant to be," Ellie had said. "Your mother would be proud."

And as she looked at the tree, its girth covered with fiber, Sarah agreed. Ainsley would have loved this as much as she'd loved making god's eyes with her daughter's Girl Scout troop, as much as she'd loved collecting lines of poetry in spiral-bound notebooks.

"It's frickin' gorgeous!" Seventeen said from the base of the ladder Sixty-Nine had climbed to stitch the final sections. "The colors! They're magical!"

"Let's not get carried away," Sixty-Nine said, her hiking boot thunking the bottom rung. Once they were all earthbound, the six Sarahs and the reporter walked across the wood-chip path that ran next to the cottonwood. The colors they'd chosen—the swatches of blue, lavender, goldenrod, and kelly green—checkerboarded over the bark, the tree's knots poking through here and there. The branches telescoped toward the sky.

Seventeen sighed, her hands clasped over her heart as if in prayer. "It worked."

"It's gorgeous." Sarah squeezed Sixty-Nine's shoulder. The oldest Sarah had both fists on her hips and tears in her eyes. The tree *was* oddly moving, an explosion of color in the midst of the spring-brown woods.

"It's weird in a truly great way," Thirty-Nine agreed. "My first graders are going to love this." She turned her back and took a selfie, Forty-Four ducking in with her matching Liston Heights Elementary sweatshirt.

"Get by the tree," Seventeen said, herding them all and handing her phone to the reporter. "Take our photo?"

Sarah ran a hand over the trunk before she turned back toward the camera. Twenty-Seven's arm looped around her waist. Sarah tipped her head against her friend's, felt the warmth of her cheek next to her own.

Sarah couldn't know as she smiled that nothing about this group was really as it seemed.

CHAPTER TWO

Video Transcript Recorded by Sarah Jones, Age Seventeen

May 29, 2023

Hello. I'm reading to you from the extensive narrative I've written (and may one day publish) about the events of spring 2023 and how they relate to my endeavor called The Sarah Jones Project. I'll start by saying I never expected it to go this far. Technically, after the yarn-bombing in the park—which, I might add, was covered by both the Minneapolis and St. Paul papers, as well as a couple dinky local publications—I'd executed my duties and been excused from my purgatory.

I allowed a spring in my step as I walked into Sister Mary Theresa's office that Monday during study hall, our usual meeting time, knowing I would no longer be on probation. This was it: no more punishment, no more guilt, no more confession.

When I made the first Instagram account and posted the offending memes, I didn't realize all of it would lead to this. And, perhaps for liability purposes, I should say that this video is not sanctioned in any way by Sacred Heart Academy. They don't even know about it. Well, I think they don't.

Hi, Sister. I swear my heart is in the right place.

That morning after the yarn installation, Sister had the *Pioneer*

Press open on her desk. There we were in full color, a multigenerational group of friends, arms around each other in front of the tree. I couldn't believe how well it turned out—how actually beautiful the tree looked, the squares interlocked like some kind of magical 3D quilt, the limbs snaking into the sky like a creature out of Greek mythology.

"Can you believe how it turned out?" I remember asking Sister. I pulled out my phone to show her some of the other photos we'd taken, including close-ups of the stitches and colors.

"I suppose this is an acceptable use of your cell phone." Sister sounded serious, but I could see a smile at the edges of her mouth. She isn't as tough as she wants everyone to think.

Just being honest here, Sister, as you have so diligently taught me.

The articles, the publicity, the clicks on social sort of proved that my project—to create a "whimsical internet extravaganza designed to bring an intergenerational group of women together to explore authentic friendship"—had actually worked. The *Pioneer Press* piece began with the lede, "A seventeen-year-old girl with an unusually common name has built an uncommon community." How much more perfect could you get?

Sister grinned at me and said, "You've done it." Remember, before The Sarah Jones Project embarked on Season Two, *everyone* thought it was a great idea. "You've created something meaningful and shared it." Sister smiled wide, and she rattled the Starbursts around in her habit pocket until she found two yellows, my favorite, and tossed them like dice on the table.

"So, I can have a clear record?" I asked.

"I'll clear the suspension," Sister said. "I'll write your college recommendation personally. People"—she raised a finger, and I said the rest with her—"can grow and change."

I hadn't considered then what would happen to the Sarah Joneses next. We hadn't talked about disbanding or anything, but Sarahs Thirty-Nine and Forty-Four were busy with teaching. Sixty-Nine had her crochet club and the blog she couldn't shut up about. Thirty and Twenty-Seven were, like, best friends, which annoyed me because Thirty had become sort of a big sister to me, plus my AP Bio tutor. But, I was a kid. I was supposed to have friends my own age. After the meme debacle that had landed me in Sister Mary Theresa Probation, I still had a lot of work to do on that front.

That was why, when I got an Instagram DM from @Rubyyyyyy_13, I was so quick to respond. I have the DM right here. It says, "When I first heard about you, my nanny and I agreed you were socially awkward and weird."

I mean, what a start, right? But those descriptors are both sort of accurate. Maybe I'm awkward. And weird. But at least I'm socially aware? Ruby went on: "But now I've seen the tree, and it does actually look sick. And, you're kind of famous. I can't believe my nanny got to do that. She's Twenty-Seven, btw."

I knew that, too. Twenty-Seven's boss was also a Sarah Jones. That's how they met. But her boss? She had like a big-time job with all kinds of crazy public responsibilities at the Minneapolis branch of the actual Federal Reserve. As Twenty-Seven put it (and as I definitely did not repeat to Sister Mary Theresa because we don't say the *h*-word), there was not a "snowball's chance in H-E-double-hockey-sticks" that she would join the group.

But her nanny signed right up! And now, I was fielding messages from actual teenagers who were interested in my work. In *me!*

"Are you taking new members?" Ruby asked next. "I mean, I know I'm not named Sarah Jones. But are you going to yarn-bomb again?"

I thought the group was sort of over. Like I said, I'd done my penance after "bullying" Serafina Jones. Everyone was happy with the elevation of their public profiles. Sixty-Nine had texted to say she had a new sponsor for the *Murder, She Wrote* blog. Sister was happy with both the results of the project and the positive press. She even let Sacred Heart's director of communications put me on the school's main Instagram account, which seemed ironic because I was getting famous for making bad choices.

But I did want a new friend my own age. And I couldn't afford to lose the Sarah Joneses. My whole social life revolved around them.

"New non-Sarah members for Season Two?" I wrote back to Ruby. "It seems like a good idea."

How was I to know then that everything would be so different just fourteen days later? I couldn't have known that Ruby and I and all the Sarahs would be thrown together for another, higher-stakes project. Investigating a murder! Can you believe it? It's not like murder and yarn-bombing have much in common, right?

I swear to God—Father, Son, *and* Holy Spirit—none of this was premeditated.

CHAPTER THREE

April 3, 2023

"You must be Nightingale," Supervisory Special Agent in Charge Vance said. "Welcome to Minneapolis." George's boss motioned him into her office but didn't look up from the folder in front of her.

"Thank you." George coughed and was suddenly conscious of holding his spine uncomfortably straight as he had at academy graduation.

"I understand you're a unicorn?" She flipped the file shut. Her eyes flashed with the familiar intensity of the training agents at Quantico, same as the game makers in Hogan's Alley, the ones who, without warning, transformed a faux fraud interrogation into an active robbery simulation. George let his hand graze his holster, remembering.

"Unicorn?" George hadn't heard the term in the past four months of training.

"Minneapolis was your first choice." She blinked at him. George had ranked the fifty-six FBI field offices in his first week at Quantico. The special agent in charge had told the trainees the bureau average was hovering around five or six, meaning most recruits ended up in their fifth- or sixth-choice city. George had briefly considered writing Minneapolis in the fifth spot, but he'd been disabused of attempting to game the FBI bureaucracy. During the interview process, an HR specialist had asked him why he'd purchased bulk Nerf ammunition in May of 2019 and then also to explain a moving violation he'd incurred a week after he'd gotten his driver's license in 2008. There'd been a deer in the road, though before the stone-faced specialist had mentioned it, George hadn't thought about the swerve in ten years.

Nothing got by the FBI, George learned. The ammunition, he'd told them, was for Camp Birdsong. Nerf tag was among the favored evening programs at the summer camp the Nightingales had run for four generations, at least for four generations until George abandoned ship. And from his first moments as a trainee, George had learned that however slow, methodical, and seemingly inefficient the FBI could be in charging cases, he shouldn't test them.

"Yes, ma'am," George said to his new supervisor.

"I appreciate your following protocol." Vance cracked a smile. "But I despise being ma'amed. You can call me Vance." She planted her palms on the desktop. "Or boss."

"Gotcha," George said, the word one of his father's favorites. The staff at camp had made T-shirts one summer emblazoned with it. George still had his, a hole in the right armpit.

"We're putting you on the fraud team," Vance said now. "As you know, squad assignments aren't permanent. You're replacing Haverford."

"No one could replace Haverford," George said. Gerald Haverford had been special agent in charge in Minneapolis for more than twenty years, a tenure unheard-of. During that time, he'd closed dozens of high-profile cases.

And he'd left perhaps the highest-profile case of them all unsolved.

"Well, certainly a thirty-two-year-old junior special agent with zero field experience couldn't replace Haverford," Vance said. George felt his eyes bug, but his boss laughed. "No," she shook her head. George caught sight of a small scar near her right temple. "I'm saying this wrong. I'm thrilled to have you, and I'm not looking for a new Haverford. He's just the reason we have an opening."

"Am I . . ." George was afraid to ask. He wanted to solve Haverford's leftover case, join *that* task force.

"You're on the fraud team," Vance said again.

"Fraud," George repeated.

"I'm handing you a case developed by a Chicago police detective. She sent it over to us because the perp crossed state lines."

George looked at the file on the table, but Vance shook her head. "This is your personnel file, Nightingale. Camp Birdsong, eh?" She tapped her fingers on the manila. George judged the file's thickness. Maybe twenty pages? It had to be his academic and field records from Quantico (equally stellar), a summary of his application process, and what else? Psych eval? The copy of that fifteen-year-old moving violation?

"You probably know it is—was—a family business," he said about the camp.

"Yep. And you get high marks in interpersonal relationships because of it." They'd focused on this during his interviews and in training. George had always been good at making friends, winning over kids and counselors. People confided in George. They trusted him. This quality would be useful to the bureau.

"A few years down the road, your profile is a good one for an undercover assignment." Vance echoed the assessments George had garnered in training. If he cleared cases and notched solid performance reviews, he'd have a shot at the competitive advanced training academy for covert agents. "Until then," Vance continued, "you'll develop informants. You'll need one for your first case. It's small-time fraud—and closable. Give the Chicago investigator a call. Possible connection to narcotics, too. Keep me posted."

Narcotics was a separate team, one George had even less interest in than fraud. He wanted violent crime and major offenders. Vance pointed toward the door. "You'll find the file on your dashboard."

George walked back to the cubicle assigned to him, logged into his terminal, and scanned the file, which included notes from the Chicago detective and from an analyst in the Minneapolis office who'd done the initial FBI review. It was an imposter scam. A woman used an alias—the same name as her target—befriended her, got close enough to steal documents and glean passwords, and then pocketed a sizable sum from the target's savings. The Chicago detective had passed the file to the city's district attorney, who'd sent it back for lack of evidence. There wasn't enough to charge, though it seemed obvious that Gabriella Johnson, the suspect, was guilty. They'd need the nitty-gritty, the bank records, the account numbers, the call log. George's job would be methodical, but more or less straightforward—watch, document, close. And, he hoped, take one step closer to major crimes.

George made notes on a brand-new steno pad. Most recently, Gabriella Johnson had disappeared from Chicago and then used an ATM card in Hudson, Wisconsin. *A mistake?* The STAR system, a complex evidence aggregator used by the bureau, identified a known license plate the following day on a Toyota Camry before her trail went cold twenty miles from St. Paul. All signs pointed to the Twin Cities metro area, right in George's new jurisdiction. He picked up his handset and dialed Chicago.

"Detective Sutton," the woman said.

"Detective Sutton," George repeated. "This is Special Agent George Nightingale from the Minneapolis Field Office of the FBI." George's shoulders slumped with relief. He'd gotten through the title without choking on it.

"Gotcha," Sutton said, and George couldn't help thinking the word was a sign. "You must be calling about the Johnson investigation?"

"I've just been assigned the case and need the lay of the land." *Lay of the land?* It was something else George's father always said.

Sutton sighed. "We almost had enough for a charge, and then she skipped town. Totally messed with my clearance numbers."

"Sorry to hear that." There'd been talk of clearance rates at the academy, the pressure to solve cases. Both the public and the legislative branch expected miracles.

"I'm glad you're taking it up," Sutton said. "It's small, but it's personal. Johnson gets into these women's lives."

"Women?" George scrolled the documents. He'd read about just one victim, a Grace Smith who was out fifty-four thousand dollars, the entire sum of her trust fund, stolen with her own credentials and wired to an account that no longer existed.

"Yeah," said Sutton. "I'm not sure about this, but I have a hunch."

George knew intuition was everything. It had saved him in Hogan's Alley. He'd seen the surprise robbery coming. He'd garnered a note about "exceptional suitability" in his file.

"Right," George said. "Can you tell me about the connected cases?"

"So, there's another file with a vic named Annabeth Silver who reported a theft," Sutton said. "Similar amount and similar circumstances. Also a trust fund. Inheritance." George could hear Sutton flipping pages.

"At first she gave us a bunch of intel—her friend had been

threatened by someone. The friend, who I am ninety-five percent sure was Gabriella Johnson, discussed needing to go into hiding."

"Silver didn't give the name?" George thought about the camp kids who ended up on the office porch in trouble, clearly upset, but not quite willing to implicate their cabinmates. George had felt the same way when his Quantico roommate popped a ZYN pouch on an off Friday night, the academy strictly drug-free. George wondered if it was a test to see if he'd prize loyalty or protocol. He'd chosen the former, and none of the trainers ever mentioned the incident.

"My partner took the call," Sutton said. "There were tears. Silver said the thief was a close friend. A colleague. I did a little research, and it's the same woman. Gabriella Johnson, a former teacher who left her job suddenly about two and half years ago."

"We don't know why she left?"

"No. Silver said something about a threat, but there were no details. In the end, she wouldn't cooperate. Didn't press charges. Didn't give us the bank details."

"She chose loyalty," George said.

"Johnson seems good at ingratiating herself, good at making friends," Sutton said. "She might try it again in Minneapolis."

"Do we know how she targets people?" George would use STAR, find the car, triangulate the cell phone data. She likely used burners.

"Grace Smith said they became friends shortly after her mother died last year. She showed up at her Pilates studio and said she was new in town. A lie, we know, because of Annabeth Silver. And it seemed like a miracle to Grace—the real one—to have a new friend with the exact same name."

"Same middle name, too?" George asked.

"Not sure," Sutton said. "But here's what I think. She'll show up with an alias, but the alias will be a really common name. It'll be the same name as her next target. She had Grace Smith picking up packages for her."

"What was in the packages?" George asked. It wasn't a bad idea, having someone else run suspicious errands. The network of CCTV cameras George would access to try to pinpoint Gabriella's location would have fewer hits.

"Not sure. Smith never opened them."

"Drugs?" George asked. Vance had mentioned narcotics.

"Could have been, but I think stolen goods."

"Was there anything missing at Grace Smith's house?"

"Yes," Sutton said, "and from Silver's. Heirloom jewelry in both cases."

"Sale records?" George had moved to page two of his new notepad.

"Nothing definitive," Sutton admitted. "We didn't have the resources to check the antiques circuit, but you're the FBI."

Except George had no idea how to check the antiques circuit. "Thanks," George said. "This has been really helpful."

"The best photos we have are in the file," Sutton said by way of goodbye.

George dabbed his brow with the cuff of his dress shirt and pulled up the images of Gabriella Johnson. The first was a school photo, a young teacher with long, brown wavy hair. She was pretty with light sparkly eyes, plastic clear-framed glasses, and a button-down shirt. The photographer had caught her on the verge of a laugh.

The next picture was a blurry selfie provided by Grace Smith. The two women's faces pressed together at the cheeks, and Gabriella looked somewhere above the camera. It wasn't a lot to go on, but STAR should produce at least a few hits.

George put his hand in his pocket and felt the edges of Henry

O'Neill's old Pokémon cards, omnipresent in his wallet. A small-time multistate fraud with just a few victims wasn't what he'd hoped to investigate, though he'd hardly expected to profile his friend's abductors in the first week on the job.

Solving the Johnson case, presenting it airtight to the appropriate prosecution team—this type of success built on itself. He would move closer to the O'Neill Task Force one step at a time.

CHAPTER FOUR

April 7, 2023

George couldn't believe the efficacy of the FBI's STAR system. Especially now with AI, it seemed a miracle that anyone got away with crime. The system aggregated biometrics, financials, and IP addresses. Thus, it took George only five minutes on his first day to get an updated license plate for Gabriella Johnson's Camry. From there, he tracked her movements day-to-day. He had her at a Minneapolis Starbucks twice, at the University of Minnesota on four days, and at a place called the Miller School on three separate afternoons. By Friday, it was time to tail her in person.

The website for the Miller School, one of those fancy college-prep institutions, had high-resolution drone footage on the home page and, buried in an FAQ, quoted a $35,000 annual tuition bill.

STAR pinged Gabriella there from 3:10 to 3:45 on Monday, Tuesday, and Thursday that week. *Car pool line*, George thought. *Let's hope she works Friday.* As he parked the unmarked FBI Charger in the back of the school's lot at 2:45, the queue was already six vehicles deep. George breathed, excising his nerves. He'd done practice fieldwork at Quantico, but this was his first true investigative mission.

At three, a steady stream of parents and nannies joined the line. Most of the cars were luxury—not a few Teslas and Rivians—but

George felt a jolt each time a Camry arrived. Finally, he got a bead on a dark blue one. He adjusted his binoculars. The woman in the driver's seat wore a ponytail and sunglasses. Two teenage girls got in the car on the curb outside the main entrance.

He sparked his engine and made his way to the exit. George tailed the Camry for fifteen minutes until they parked in front of a stately Tudor on one of the Minneapolis lakes. He pulled over two houses down and watched the trio disappear through the front door.

He opened his Notes app and double-checked the address. This house had come up on STAR, too. According to county records, the mortgage holders were Caden Campbell and Sarah Jones, the latter a common name if George had ever heard one. He remembered Detective Sutton's hypothesis about Gabriella's next move.

George scanned the windows, saw nothing, and then drove away. He arrived at the field office at 4:15, with enough time to finish his paperwork and update Vance at the close of his first week. This new intel on Johnson was solid progress, and his fingers tingled a little as he ran background on the homeowners. Sarah Jones was chairwoman of the Minneapolis branch of the Federal Reserve. A huge job. The potential payout for a con artist nanny could be significant.

George coughed lightly as he knocked on Vance's doorframe.

She looked up and half smiled. "You made it through your first week."

"I did." George nodded. "And I made some progress."

"Update me." Vance pushed her reading glasses onto her head.

"I ran the Camry data with facial recognition, and I found Gabriella Johnson in three places," George said. "At the University of Minnesota, at a Starbucks just outside of downtown, and at the Miller School."

"The fancy private one?" Vance squinted at the ceiling. "So, she's a nanny?"

"Check," George said. Vance had gotten it so quickly, a reminder of his beginner status.

"And the university?" Vance mused. "What's that about?"

"I think her cover is that she's a student," George said. "That's my working theory."

Vance blinked. "Good."

"Oh!" George had forgotten to lead with the best part. "I found a third victim, I'm pretty sure." This was the break.

Vance clapped her hands. "Tell me."

"We started calling precincts in the Midwest, and I got a hit in Peoria." George and an intern had divided larger-city police departments and described Gabriella Johnson's MO. An unsolved fraud case, they told the detectives, involving a woman with an unusually common name. Catherine Anderson in Peoria had met someone with her same name at the café where she worked on her dissertation. It had seemed like the best kind of serendipity until Anderson's inheritance evaporated.

George matched up the timelines and interviewed the vic. She and Johnson had known each other for three months.

"Three pretty intense months," Catherine admitted. "My therapist has been helping me unpack it."

The woman described the way Gabriella had once asked for a Wi-Fi password and presumably had seen where Catherine kept a list of her log-in credentials. By the time the transfer went through, Gabriella had disappeared.

"This is good, Camp Counselor," Vance said. "Some good old-fashioned elbow grease almost always leads to something. Lesser investigators call it luck. Good ones see serendipity as the reward for covering all of your bases."

George smiled. He couldn't help it.

"And now what about Minneapolis?" Vance asked. "Have you determined the new target?"

"The owner of the house where she's a nanny," George said. "It's Sarah Jones. She's the chairwoman of the Minneapolis branch of the Federal Reserve."

Vance's eyebrows shot up. "That job must pay a lot?"

"Check," George said. "Plus the husband's family is fourth-generation in the Twin Cities. Father and grandfather were named partners at a local law firm. Country club memberships, international travel, the works."

"Family money." Vance bit her lip. "What I wouldn't give for a little of that."

George's camp salary had included the house his grandparents had built next to Lake Whitehook. But he'd chosen a lateral move, moneywise, into national security. He'd picked one kid—Henry O'Neill, whose kidnapping had never been solved—over the hundreds that flocked to Birdsong every summer.

"I'm pretty sure the woman I'm following is the same one who offended in Chicago and Peoria," George said. "The timelines, the aliases, STAR—it all lines up. Can we arrest her?"

Vance shook her head. "I wish. Wouldn't that be great? Pick up a case a police detective already worked, dot a couple of i's, and notch a clearance?"

George blushed. Naivete was a familiar embarrassment he'd faced at Quantico after being a lifelong expert on everything from archery to latrine maintenance at his last job.

"The DA in Chicago said no charge, and the Peoria case also fizzled. We need everything buttoned up." Vance lowered her glasses again and glanced at the terminal, a signal this conversation had run its course. "Follow Johnson, both literally and online. Document. When she transfers the money from the target this time, get the wires immediately. Make it airtight. It has to stick in federal court."

"Airtight," George repeated.

"Make it undeniable. Watch it happen. That's how we do fraud." She clicked her mouse. "This is a good one. Relatively low stakes. Few victims. One suspect."

George felt a swell of hope. The Gabriella Johnson case seemed like a sure thing.

CHAPTER FIVE

April 11, 2023

"What do you mean you have to cancel?" Sarah tapped her pencil against the desk at LifeSport. She glanced at the clock in the upper right corner of her computer screen.

"I have to pick up this package at a FedEx store in Liston Heights and then be back at the U for a meeting with my advisor." Sarah could picture Twenty-Seven, her face serene except for a telltale wrinkle on the left side of her mouth. "The timing's too tight."

Sarah scanned the fitness floor. Her eleven o'clock, a seventy-six-year-old racewalking champion, lunged in the stretching area, executing her warm-up fifteen minutes early, as prescribed. Sarah loved a rule-follower. Joyce, the walker, gave her a thumbs-up as she switched to leg swings.

"Let's get creative," Sarah said, hungry already for the wood-fired pizza lunch they'd planned.

On the phone, Twenty-Seven laughed.

"What?" Sarah asked.

"It's just, I've known you for like a month, and already I know you'll do anything for pizza."

A warmth rose in Sarah's chest. In fact, Twenty-Seven knew a lot more than her affinity for pizza. Just a week after they met, Sarah had invited her for dinner at the new apartment. It had been a good excuse for Sarah to get the living room together, buying a new rug, arranging her crystal collection on the bookshelf, placing her most energetic hunk of rose quartz directly in front of her favorite picture of her mother. The photo had been taken just a couple of blocks from their respective postwar buildings, in front of the iconic cherry-and-spoon sculpture ubiquitous on Minneapolis postcards.

When Sarah had uncovered the photo in a box at Grandma Ellie's house, just ten days before she'd imploded her relationship with Brian, it had seemed like a sign. There had been a lot of those over the years. Sarah kept a list of them in her day planner, on a page near the back labeled "LRFM," for Little Reminders from Mom. An important one had been the heirloom teacup she'd broken during a five-year-plan meeting with Brian. He'd said the words "three children," "birthing tub," and "organics garden" in quick succession, and she'd shattered the cup. Everything had gone quickly after that, and now she was here in Minneapolis, hankering for pizza with her new best friend.

"I don't have a client between noon and two," Sarah said, "so I've got some extra time. What if I grab the package for you?"

"You need ID—" Twenty-Seven started to laugh.

"What?" Sarah asked as Joyce dutifully moved into cat-cow.

"It's just, I was about to say you need to show your ID to get the package, but of course, you *have* ID. We have the same name."

Sarah smiled. LRFM. Everything was working out. "Send me the address. I'll fraudulently grab the package and meet you near the U for yummy, yummy bread and cheese."

"Are you sure?" Twenty-Seven asked. "I don't want to be a pain."

Sarah thought about the broken teacup, the shard of glass she'd stepped on, the blood she'd seen drip onto her kitchen floor, and then her characteristic faint. That had been a pain. This? Doing a favor for a real friend and then going out for lunch? This was an absolute delight.

"You're a godsend," Twenty-Seven told her.

In the end, the errand was a thrill. The package wasn't for her, and yet it was. She showed her ID, and the disinterested clerk handed over a small square box. When Sarah placed the package down at the restaurant, Twenty-Seven had already grabbed a table and ordered Sarah's usual, a straight-up margherita pizza with a side salad and a Mountain Dew.

"I still can't believe you drink that crap," Twenty-Seven said, pointing at the Day-Glo liquid.

"Moderation in all things." Sarah grinned.

Twenty-Seven opened her tote bag, slid in the package, and started to grill Sarah about her favorite topic: potential suitors at the gym. Sarah hadn't told her yet about the early-morning guy in a Dartmouth T-shirt with a curl of hair that fell just above his left eyebrow.

"You don't want to date gym bros," Sarah said, thinking of that guy in the squat cage.

"I don't," Twenty-Seven agreed. "But we're talking about *you*."

CHAPTER SIX

April 11, 2023

Vance had told George serendipity catalyzed these types of cases, and it didn't get much better than a group of Sarah Joneses led by a high school kid whose fifteen minutes had begun when they yarn-bombed an eastern cottonwood that sat at number five on the list of St. Paul's most iconic trees.

"There are seven newspaper articles!" George exclaimed aloud to himself in his cube. The photo of Gabriella Johnson in front of the tree wasn't perfect—sunglasses and hair in her face. But, just like in the school parking lot, he was pretty sure.

And that "pretty sure" had led him to the Tudor and the chairwoman of the Federal Reserve. This photo of the yarn-bombed tree—it was quite beautiful, actually, the limbs like gloved fingers reaching skyward—could garner him an informant. And once again, camp counseling had prepared George for the job: he knew what yarn-bombing was. He'd even been in a knitting club at Birdsong for a session, sitting by a lonely first-time camper who'd been afraid to put her face in the lake.

"Can you believe this project and the coverage it got?" George asked Vance at his next check-in.

"Must be nice to have time to meet up and plan an art project." Vance gestured at her computer, toward the filing system that held the twenty-odd cases she was carrying, not including the O'Neill Task Force. In the beginning, that kidnapping assignment, George's childhood friend at the center, had been a full-time job for basically the whole office.

Still, they hadn't solved it.

Vance scanned the article about The Sarah Jones Project on George's bureau-issued phone. "Assume you've been to the group's Instagram?"

He had, and he'd run each of the Sarahs through STAR. "It's a group started by a teenager, and it seems to be supervised by a nun at her high school? Something about 'whimsical connection'? And do you know who just popped up in the DMs, asking to join?"

"Who?" Vance clicked something on her terminal.

"Ruby Campbell," George said. "The daughter of the Fed chair. She left multiple new comments, all coming in after the newspaper articles ran."

"Teenagers read the newspaper?" Vance asked.

"The paper plugged the story on Instagram. Six women with the same name wrapping a tree with yarn? Total clickbait."

"Was it?" Vance pulled her glasses down. The meeting was almost over.

"Yeah. Highest engagement on a post from the newspaper this week."

Vance rolled her eyes. "We don't care about climate change or peace in the Middle East. But a tree wrapped in textiles?"

"So," George began. He tapped his fist on his chest, willing his heart rate to slow. "I'll need an informant, right? You mentioned that? One of the Sarah Joneses in that group?" He cleared his throat. "If Gabriella's in the group, there's gotta be a second target there."

"You need a CHS," Vance said. Confidential Human Source. Informant. George relaxed. He could do this. He was a unicorn, an award winner, and he'd graduated with special honors.

"I'm guessing this is a boon for Johnson, right?" George tried not to sound too excited. "She already targeted the chairwoman of the Federal Reserve, and now, just her luck, a group of women also with the same name?"

"It does seem serendipitous." One of Vance's favorite words. He noticed things like this—people's preferred candy, whether they wore a particular pair of pants on a certain day, a pattern to their lunch ordering. It had all felt superfluous until he'd joined the FBI. He didn't necessarily believe in fate, but the job really did seem made for him.

George held still. His boss was thinking. She'd give him the go-ahead. He'd been flawless so far. The investigative work, the new lead on the Fed chair, the third victim. This case would clear in record time.

"One of them has to be another mark," George continued. "If I find that one, I can watch the transfers up close. We'll have everything we need."

"Which Sarah Jones are you thinking?" Vance asked. "The grandmother?" George saw the beginnings of a smirk.

"Actually, the personal trainer is the one I think would be easiest."

"This one?" Vance pointed at the picture. "The young blond who looks like she keeps in shape?" Now, there was definitely a smirk. And an eye-roll. George didn't want to embody unflattering stereotypes. But really, he had more reason to meet with a thirty-year-old fitness enthusiast than with a middle-aged elementary teacher or a grandmother with a blog.

"She's a marathoner." George willed himself not to blush. There'd been more than one class at Quantico on keeping one's cool, minimizing the physical symptoms of stress. "And I already joined the gym where she works. The LifeSport in St. Louis Park?" It was closest to George's apartment and just minutes from the office. "I think I've seen her at the fitness desk, actually. Early mornings." More good luck.

"Uh-huh." A narcotics special agent appeared at the door.

"I'll make an appointment with the fitness trainer?" George prompted.

"Okay," Vance said, already on to the next thing, "but then, frequent updates. Constant."

George grinned. He'd thought he'd break his father's heart when he told him he was leaving Birdsong for the bureau. He'd let down literal generations of Nightingales and perhaps forfeited the family land. But this? A closable case and a viable informant? He was in the right place.

CHAPTER SEVEN

Video Transcript Recorded by Sarah Jones, Age Seventeen

May 29, 2023

Let me back up. If I'm being honest, and I swore to my mother, Sister Mary Theresa, and the Blessed Virgin that I would be completely honest going forward, none of this would have happened if Serafina Jones hadn't just waltzed her way directly onto the Sacred Heart varsity basketball team.

"I'm Sera Jones," she'd said at the first day of summer workouts a year ago. She'd stood with her feet spread, like she belonged exactly right there at center court in the Mother Mary Gymnasium.

My jaw dropped. Because *I'm* Sarah Jones. And, I'd been at Sacred Heart forever.

"I'm a junior transfer," Serafina continued. "Small forward." She'd cut her T-shirt off at the shoulders, and her triceps had that annoying ridge of definition that only comes with excellent genes and a zillion dips.

"What a funny coincidence!" Coach Patterson pointed at me. "We've got a Sarah Jones already."

The new one gave a little nod. "Right," she said. "I saw that online." I thought of the photo of me on the team website, my bangs swooped sideways, as usual. My measly stats in a table below the marginal photo. I'd averaged only 1.7 points per game in my sophomore season.

"But, I'm Sera*fina*," the new girl said, emphasis on the latter half. And then she spelled it. "I go by S-E-R-A."

I'll be honest. I disliked her immediately. Something about the condescending arch in her eyebrow. By the time basketball tryouts officially started in October, I pretty much hated her.

You're probably already thinking it, so I'll confirm that the problem was jealousy. S-E-R-A broke the curve in AP Bio. Her three-point shot was epic. Four girls who'd ignored me since middle school had cried about how much she meant to them during the friendship circle on junior retreat. In the third week of school, my homeroom teacher—the woman is supposed to be my advocate!—asked if I wouldn't like to start going by my middle name, to minimize the confusion of having two Sarah Joneses in the same class.

"No, thank you," I'd told her as I'd wiped at a mustard stain on the belly of my white uniform button-down. "I was here first." And I had been. My mother had enrolled me at Sacred Heart in the same month my father had left her more than a decade before. She thought the nuns would be a good influence.

Since Sister Mary Theresa taught me the Glory Be and the Ten Commandments *and* was horrified when I confessed the honor code violations that have led to this very video, I suppose my mother was right.

But back to Serafina Jones. It's not like I'd never met another Jones. There were six separate and unrelated Jones families at Sacred Heart. Jones, I'd learned in a "Jesus Loves Me" project in third-grade religion class, was the fifth-most-popular surname in the entire country. There were nearly two million American Joneses according to the US Census, and even more in the UK. We were everywhere, and presumably, Jesus loved us all.

And Sarah? It's not exactly a unique first name, though it was my grandmother's, and Serafina's parents named her thusly because after having four baby boys, they felt their darling double-X was an angel. Seraphim, you know? Like from the hymns?

But more importantly, and intimately related to my own unfortunate outcome, that basketball position Sera announced herself for on the first day we met? Small forward was supposed to be mine. I'd waited three years for Astrid Nilsson to graduate. I'd been in the gym every damn day. I'd sat on the bench, rapt and cheering during postseason. Coach P and I had talked about my future as a Sacred Heart Phoenix. We both pictured me in the starting five.

And if I'd been there and fulfilled that destiny? I never would have created that Phoenix Wenis basketball Instagram. I never would have made those TikToks. I never would have alienated Alli and Ali. And, I wouldn't have needed the Sarah Joneses.

That's why I'm saying it started with Serafina. It's accurate.

Also, if I hadn't totally skewered Serafina on Instagram, Sister Mary Theresa and my mother never would have hatched the idea for a "social media project with positive impact." And while I wasn't wild about being punished at all, I guess I was grateful that there was a way to keep my record clean. And The Sarah Jones Project was all my idea, inspired by the very thing that had gotten me in trouble in the first place: having a ridiculously common name. I told Mom and Sister that TSJP would be a "whimsical internet extravaganza designed to bring an intergenerational group of women together to explore authentic friendship." I started a new Instagram with heartwarming content of me hanging out with other people—reasonably well-adjusted adults—who share my name.

Now, we all know things went haywire after the cottonwood. But remember, it's documented: in the beginning, we all liked the idea of TSJP. My mom the advertising exec said it had "undeniable story appeal and also tapped into a post-pandemic need to belong." It was a good idea, even if things got murderous and complicated.

CHAPTER EIGHT

April 18, 2023

"So you're not dead, then." Sarah's ex-fiancé didn't sound overly relieved.

"I'm not dead." After eleven a.m., Sarah would have hit "decline" on Brian without thinking too hard about it, but the guilt she harbored for ending their engagement held more potency in the morning.

"I got a Google alert." Brian snuffled. "A Sarah Jones in Minneapolis just died? Last night?"

"What?" Panic flared, but then Sarah remembered all five of the Sarah Joneses she knew had checked into the group chat at ten the night before. Everyone had been home, or at least it had seemed like it. Seventeen had sent a roundup of the last of the yarn-bombing coverage. They'd all replied, anchored by Sixty-Nine's assertion that the project was among her greatest achievements in retirement. The woman had been retired for only sixteen months.

"I hadn't heard about the death," Sarah said to Brian. "How freaky." She needed to check in with her friends again.

"Well, it just seemed like the decent thing to do," Brian said. "To call, you know."

"Thanks," Sarah said. "I'll talk to you—"

He was gone already, the hurt palpable in the sudden silence. But Sarah didn't have time to second-guess breaking up with her childhood sweetheart. Instead, she fired off a quick text to the TSJP group chat. I have a session with a new client in 15, but have you seen the news? I guess a Sarah Jones died? 27, I really hope it's not your boss. Sarah felt a chill. A dead Sarah Jones would have to be prominent to make the news. None of her friends was famous.

The Federal Reserve chair Sarah, though? The mother of the teenagers Twenty-Seven was always talking about? She would be famous enough. *Those poor girls.* Sarah heard stories about Ruby and Lula most days.

"Morning." Sarah looked up, startled. It was Bryce, the CrossFit instructor, his spandex tank stretched across his six-pack. He waved but didn't slow down to chat. Most of the employees at LifeSport seemed a different breed of "wellness professional" from the ones in Vermont. Sarah had felt out of place from the moment she started her managerial position, though she was, as her new supervisor acknowledged, supremely qualified. Even in boutique gyms, not many personal trainers came complete with master's degrees in genomics, EMT certification, and six years' experience.

LifeSport was no Ace Blickson's Center for Fitness, her gym back east. Her clients there had been senior citizens who wanted to take a few strokes off their golf games and bored work-from-homers who needed a midday destination. Yvonne, for instance, had booked Sarah every Wednesday at twelve thirty, and all she wanted to do was lie in corpse pose beneath the yellowing photo of the gym founder, a 1970s NFL Hall of Famer, with his most famous quote, "Might as well die ripped."

Sarah basically agreed with Ace's sentiment. After all, she ran six days a week and had even dropped into Bryce's CrossFit extravaganzas, though being fit hadn't helped Sarah's mother. Nineteen years after the fact, Sarah still remembered Ainsley in tree pose just hours before she died. Being limber didn't prevent placental abruption and severe blood loss.

Sarah's phone buzzed, and she thought it must be Twenty-Seven texting back, but instead it was the automated system reminding her of a new client. She reached into her pocket and held the tumbled hunk of gabbro, a rock of mottled purple and black inclusions she'd chosen that morning from her inherited crystal collection, a tradition when she met new clients. According to her mother's scritchy handwriting, the stone would ground Sarah, aid her in problem-solving. It had worked thus far. Her boss was impressed with her growing roster, and the Run Club attendance was up 15 percent over the past month.

"Supremely qualified," Sarah whispered to herself. She put her phone down and clicked into the scheduling system to review the profile for her seven o'clock. *George Nightingale*, she read. Thirty-two years old. Much younger than her average client and also male. Most of the men chose Bryce or another of the heavily muscled, Y-chromosomed trainers. But in the "fitness goals" section, George had written, "Fast debut marathon." Sarah would be the obvious choice for that.

In fact, besides her unconventional premed training, the primary reason Sarah had landed the LifeSport job was her experience in running. She'd recently run a three-hour-and-ten-minute personal record in the marathon. She'd also coached fifty-six Boston Marathon qualifiers online. LifeSport needed a more robust running program. Sarah felt like she was born to make that happen, or certainly more born for that than for bringing Brian's three future children earth-side in the plastic home-birth tub he'd shown her online before she'd dropped the heirloom teacup, cut her foot, and fainted.

Sarah read the rest of George Nightingale's intake form. He'd posted a reasonably fast 10K and ran five days per week. That was a lot to work with. Still, a guy with this profile would typically print a program from a website and take it from there. A little suspicion crept in behind Sarah's initial excitement. There were plenty of weirdos who thought female personal trainers would be their ticket to some kind of twisted sex-fantasy fulfillment.

The end of the form read, "Anything else you want your trainer to know?"

George had written, "I picked Sarah Jones because her bio says she can run a 3:10 marathon."

The time had technically been 3:10:42.

"I've got a lot of runner friends," George went on, "and I don't want to embarrass myself. I'll be badgered mercilessly unless I give this a decent shot."

Okay. Sarah liked him already. George didn't sound like a sex-crazed lunatic, but she'd verify before he arrived. She finished typing "George" in the Google search bar just as the tall and broad-shouldered guy with a charmingly crooked smile and a Dartmouth T-shirt strode up to the fitness desk.

LRFM. The one cute guy she'd noticed in the gym so far was her new client.

"Good morning." *It has to be him, right?* She peeked over the desk, looking for running shoes. *Check.* Sarah felt her shoulders relax. "Can I help you?"

He raised his arm in an adorable half wave. "I'm George Nightingale. I have an appointment with—"

Sarah clasped her hands together, a gesture of hers that Grandma Ellie said reminded her of Ainsley. "You're my seven o'clock."

"Yes, sorry. I'm early." *Is that a blush at the base of his ears?* He rocked back on his heels, boyishly nervous.

"A man after my own heart." Sarah wished she hadn't said "heart," but George was smiling, thick curls falling over his forehead toward his deep brown eyes.

"So." Sarah clicked her favorite fuchsia-ink ballpoint as she led him to a high-top in the lobby. "You're on your way to a debut marathon, and you don't want it to be mediocre."

"That's right." George resumed that crooked smile. "I've got a lot of fast friends, and I can't be the worst. Actually"—he squinted at her and paused—"not even in the middle."

"Gotcha." Sarah despised mediocrity. "Tell me about your most recent road race."

A wrinkle appeared in George's forehead just beneath the largest of the curls. "10K," he said. "I do the same one every August, so it's been a while."

"Finishing time?" She'd read it on the intake, but she'd verify. "Just so I can get an idea of where we're starting?"

George cleared his throat. "Thirty-seven flat." Those forty-two seconds on her marathon time gnawed at Sarah again.

"Six-minute pace." She shifted in her seat, trying not to smile too widely. When Sarah had announced she was moving to Minnesota, one of the many arguments Brian had made against it was that it would take her months to build back her client base. But George wasn't even the first potential three-hour marathoner on her new roster.

George pulled a buzzing phone out of his pocket. "Excuse me. Work thing." Sarah's gaze drifted politely over his shoulder to one of dozens of televisions mounted on the LifeSport walls. A news anchor looked gravely at the camera.

Before he could hang up, Allison marched through the lobby with a phone pressed to her ear. "No, she's *here*!" The boss's tone was exasperated. "I'm looking at Sarah Jones right now. She's right here in front of me." Allison whisper-shrieked, "I'm telling you, she's not dead! She's. Right. Here." Then she thrust the phone toward Sarah. "Good lord," she said. "This woman doesn't sound like a grandmother, but she says she's yours, and I think she's delusional."

"I'm so sorry," Sarah said. "Grandma?"

"Oh my God, it *is* you." Ellie sighed.

"Grandma? I'm at work, what's going on?"

"Have you watched the news?" Sarah squinted at the chyron on the TV in the lobby.

"Sarah Jones," she read there, realizing it was national. "Yeah. Brian called earlier. But it's not me. I'm here, and I'm fine. I'm not famous enough for my death to land on the news."

"Thank goodness. I mean, not about not being famous," Grandma Ellie said, "if that's what you want."

"I'll call you back, okay?" Sarah put the handset on the table and bit the inside of her lip. It was weird. She knew five other Sarah Joneses in town already. But now, another one of them was dead? Just miles from where the group of them met? From where Sarah worked? Sarah felt goose bumps rise on her forearms as the chyron read, "Foul play."

"Okay?" George asked.

Sarah blinked. "I'm sorry," she said. "It turns out I'm having a weird morning. Someone with my same name died. And . . ." They both stared at the television. "It might be murder?"

CHAPTER NINE

April 18, 2023

"Change of plans?" George had whispered into the phone as Sarah, sitting across the table from him, looked politely away.

Vance sounded matter-of-fact, as usual. "Who could have predicted one of them would die? It's not Johnson's MO." Sweat dampened the back of George's neck.

"Are you thinking it's unrelated?" George whispered. "A coincidence?"

"Seems unlikely, doesn't it?" George heard papers shuffling in the background on Vance's end. He wished he could be in the field office, if only to see what happened when news of a homicide broke. His simple fraud case had suddenly become infinitely more complex.

"Anyway," Vance said, "I just wanted to tell you to stay the course. Same plan. We'll talk when you're back."

His supervisor hung up, and George rolled his shoulders. He felt off-balance. FBI training had prepared him for uncertainty. The whole job was reactive, everything inherently unpredictable. But still, this was his first case, his first time on the fraud team, his first crack at developing an informant, and now suddenly they were in the middle of a high-profile murder investigation that had, in the first hours, garnered national media attention. He had to regroup, and fast. George kept his phone to his cheek for an extra second after Vance ended the call.

The dead woman's body had been discovered just hours prior to his appointment with Sarah Elizabeth Jones from Vermont. And the FBI hadn't gotten any kind of head start. They'd been alerted to the situation at the same time as the news media.

"I'm so sorry for the interruption," Sarah said when George put his phone down. "That was my grandmother." Sarah's grandmother was Elizabeth McKenna Montague, George knew. She also lived in Vermont. "I just moved here a couple of months ago, and now this." She pointed at the television where the story had run. "Grandma demanded proof of life."

"Wow." George's heartbeat thrummed all the way down to his fingers. He hadn't been this nervous in any of the Quantico training scenarios, not even in Hogan's Alley. "You're new in town?" He choked out the question.

"I'm getting the hang of the long *o*." Sarah bopped the tip of her pen against her clipboard as she imitated the stereotypical Fargo accent. She was a pro. She dealt with jittery first-time clients every day. "And you're among the first of my new clients who's looking to run a three-hour marathon." She grinned.

Sarah seemed so happy that George felt a surprising shiver of guilt for his duplicity. There was something about her demeanor that made him want to confide in her, and he had to fight the impulse to blurt his entire ruse: that he'd booked the appointment after Gabriella Johnson had shed her previous identity and begun targeting the exact Sarah Jones who'd just died.

When he had told his sister, Bea, what he could about the case, she had balked at the idea of George being undercover. This was a reasonable concern, as he'd failed to stay hidden in every elementary school game of hide-and-seek.

"Not undercover," George had explained. "I'll be myself at Life-Sport. Sarah will be in a position to share certain information. At some point, I'll tell her I'm FBI." He wasn't clear on when this would be.

"That's a flipping fantastic idea," Bea had said, "as lying comes so naturally to you. Last year, you disclosed Grandpa's Christmas check on your 1099."

But George's assignment with Sarah was to win her over, to engender her trust. George could do this, even if he held back a bit of the truth. He already had some credibility. He was a legit member of the gym. He'd worked out here before he'd even known who Sarah was.

"Let's do some basic testing." Sarah bounced on the balls of her feet, her calves rippling, as she led George to the fitness floor. He demonstrated his single-leg squats, his balanced glute bridges, his hip stability. George knew he was in good shape. "Impressive," Sarah said after he'd deadlifted to failure at three hundred pounds. She slapped him on the shoulder, and George felt goose bumps down his arms. He'd spent at least an hour looking at photographs of Sarah, but her adorable freckles were more pronounced in person.

On several of the televisions around the gym, news stations ran photos of the dead Sarah Jones. As they walked to the treadmill, they both stopped to read the closed-captioning. "Impressive woman," Sarah said, as the news listed her degrees from Stanford and Wharton.

"Probably can't run a 3:10 marathon, though," George deadpanned. Sarah laughed, and he felt relieved to have recovered from the rocky start.

"Maybe her position as Fed president, Ivy League education, and presumed candidacy for US Senate made up for her inability to sustain a 7:15 pace over twenty-six miles?" Sarah pointed at the treadmill. "We'll end it here for today," she said. "Just a quick progression, okay?"

George pressed the acceleration button on the machine. He wondered what Vance was doing back at the office, how the negotiations about jurisdiction with the local cops were going, whether there was a joint task force to investigate the murder yet. George shook his head as he made it to eight miles per hour. He would focus on Sarah's last test. He would develop the informant, impress Sarah with his top-notch aerobic capacity. Vance had told him to be an ideal client. After today, Sarah should look forward to his visits.

Not that it was hard to connect with Sarah. She was clearly a natural with people, too. She was nerdy-funny, like him. She even blushed at her own ridiculous puns ("Shall we take the LUNGE, so to speak?" "Are you INCLINED to work harder?"). She would have been an excellent counselor at Birdsong. The kids would have collected dumb jokes to tell her and mobbed her at dinner. George blinked back an image of Sarah in a red lifeguard's swimsuit.

At the end of the hour, after he'd wowed her with his quick recoveries and overall core strength (he'd seen Sarah mark a couple of columns on her clipboard with exclamation points), she said she looked forward to seeing him the following week. "I mean, assuming you think we can work together?"

George recognized the query as the pivotal moment. He'd passed Sarah's first test. He could see the tension in the grip of her pink pen, the way she'd bitten the inside of her lip, creating a divot just above her chin. She wanted him to say yes, and George was ready. George understood people's instincts, supported their goals, saw the best in them. At camp, he'd delivered high fives and encouraging notes. Here, the stakes were higher. The body discovered at the base of the Hennepin Avenue Bridge that morning could very well signify that Gabriella Johnson had escalated from fraud to murder and the case had lost its predictability factor.

"I mean, I think we can work together." Sarah's brow had furrowed, and George regretted his pause.

"It feels right," he said. Sarah's eyes shone.

"Awesome." She turned back toward the fitness desk. There was something between them, he thought. A spark. But then, they were both just doing their jobs. "I'll have your training plan ready next week. We have to talk about weights, too, and maybe some preliminary race plans?"

A few days ago George's marathon had been a ploy that he and Vance had dreamed up, but after this hour with Sarah, George thought he might as well actually do it.

"In between now and then, run another thirty-five miles total this week?"

"I'm in," George said, grinning. He'd also bump into her in the meantime, putting in a few of his miles on a treadmill here, aiming for maximum exposure.

"Can't wait." Sarah grabbed her phone from her shorts pocket. "Whoa," she said. "This has been blowing up. Apparently Grandma Ellie isn't the only person who thinks I might be dead." She tapped. "But I'm not dead." They both burst out laughing at the ridiculousness of the statement. George wasn't sure if developing her as an informant would be easier or harder because she was objectively so delightful. "There are a lot of us Sarah Joneses, you know?" she asked when she caught her breath. "Well, you probably don't know. There are more than six thousand people with my same first and last name in the United States. More in the UK."

"Really?" George felt a zing of opportunity. This was his job, after all, to catch a con artist and probably murderer, not to flirt with his first informant. "Have you met any of them?"

"This is fascinating, actually." Sarah shoved her phone back in her pocket. "And also kind of weird." George watched her face as she caught sight of someone over his shoulder. To his disappointment, her eyes brightened every bit as convincingly as they had when she'd greeted him that morning. Sarah was likely everyone's favorite personal trainer, just as George had wooed all of the people who came to his camp.

"Be right with you, Alice!" Sarah called.

"What's weird?" George pressed.

"Oh." Sarah held out her hand to shake his. "I know a bunch of other Sarah Joneses, actually. A bunch of these texts are from them. We're *all* not dead, as it turns out. Well, except for the one who *is* actually dead."

George cocked his head, willing her to continue.

"The same-name group is a teenager's high school project." She opened her hand toward the waiting client, inviting her over. "We knew about Fed Sarah, but she wasn't one of us. It's complicated. I'll tell you next week?" And then she spoke a little louder. "I've got to get busy crushing it with Alice."

Sarah had already alluded to Gabriella Johnson, though she didn't know it. And, she'd already agreed to tell him more. That was all as it should be—better than he'd expected. More alarming to George was the warmth between them. The undeniable charge he felt. If she weren't poised to be his informant, George would call Bea and ask for advice on how to non-creepily ask his new trainer on a date.

CHAPTER TEN

April 18, 2023

Are you okay? Sarah texted Twenty-Seven after her eight a.m. There was a break in Sarah's schedule, time enough to wade through the forty-eight messages that had flooded her phone. Sarah had processed the reality that the dead woman was indeed Twenty-Seven's boss while she put George through his paces.

I wouldn't say okay, Twenty-Seven typed back. I'm in the living room with the girls. They're lying on the couch with their feet touching. Neither of them has said anything for twenty-four minutes. I'm timing.

On the morning Ainsley had collapsed, there'd been the ambulance, the pool of blood that she could still see and smell. Years later, there'd been the myriad blood-induced faints during her EMT internship, the catastrophic two weeks that had led her to abandon her lifelong dream of medical school. Doctors, as it turns out, can't hit the deck every time they prick a finger.

Are the police there? Sarah asked.

Yes.

Do you have to talk to them?

Yes, Twenty-Seven wrote. We all do. I should, right?

Sarah breathed. She and Twenty-Seven had talked almost every day for the last couple of months. Twenty-Seven had shared endearing and funny stories about the kids. The girls each kept a bag of candy in the center console of Twenty-Seven's Camry. Sarah pilfered from the stash whenever she sat shotgun.

Is there a cop in the living room with you? Sarah had seen enough police procedurals on television to know everyone needed a lawyer.

Yeah. Twenty-Seven sent a picture. Sarah could see her friend's feet in Nike socks and the officer in profile, a woman in uniform who looked about sixteen years old herself. A family liaison or something. Idk. Everyone's crying. I'm crying. They told us not to leave until we'd each given a statement.

I'll come over, Sarah wrote. I'll cancel my eleven o'clock. Text the address. She hadn't known Twenty-Seven that long, but she adored her. People didn't know what to say in times like this. But Sarah did. She was good in a crisis.

That's so nice, Twenty-Seven said, but I think maybe not. The girls. Idk.

Sarah stared at the giant ceiling fans spinning over the elliptical machines. Whatever you need.

I'll keep you posted, Twenty-Seven wrote. We might do nail polish. Is that weird?

Sarah thought of the tarot cards she and Grandma Ellie had pulled in the hours after, the two of them huddled under one of Ellie's quilts. Along with Three of Swords, which symbolized heartbreak, they'd turned over the Sun and the Wheel of Fortune. It had seemed like both a cruel joke and also a little glimmer. Sarah couldn't have predicted it back then, but there'd been lots of moments of happiness to come in her life, including a total full-body peace when she lay in her new bed in her Minneapolis apartment. Things would, more or less, be okay. Eventually.

The whole thing is horrible and sad, she wrote back. Do whatever you need to do.

Sarah clicked into The Sarah Jones Project text thread and read the back-and-forth from the other women. They'd finished the yarn project. There'd been talk of a "reunion" dinner to look through some social media shots of the tree. Sarah had exchanged texts with Seventeen's mother, assuring her that she'd continue tutoring through the May 10 AP Biology exam. But now, there was a whole slew of new texts, all expressing shock that "one of them" had plummeted from a bridge, only to be discovered by a group of hobby joggers on their predawn jaunt earlier that day.

This seems like something we should be talking about, Sixty-Nine wrote. Not that I'm looking to get into the true crime space. Saturated is an understatement! But, this? It's, like, us!

Thirty-Nine sent a photo with a magnifying glass—something from her classroom, no doubt.

Forty-Four said, I'd be open to a Season 2 . . .

Sarah couldn't help smiling, despite the distress she knew Twenty-Seven was feeling. It did seem like a reality show, this group. Grandma Ellie had started a scrapbook with the yarn-bombing coverage. "I know you're not supposed to print Instagram," she'd told Sarah the previous weekend, "but there are a few apps that make it easy."

It's 27's boss, Seventeen said in the chat. ARE YOU OKAY?

And those girls, Sixty-Nine wrote.

Twenty-Seven hadn't replied. It would be overwhelming to participate in what was basically a virtual coffee date, where the entertainment news of the day was playing out in front of her friend in the form of broken teenagers wilting on a sectional.

Meeting tonight, Seventeen said after no one had replied for a while. I have a message from a special guest, a non-Sarah who wants to be part of, or at least adjacent to, our group. It'll be fine.

Sarah clicked on her computer. Although she tried to avoid morbid curiosity as a personal practice, she supposed she needed to know some details about the death. The news reports had said the woman had been found at the base of a bridge. Could she have fallen? Did she drink? Did someone with a big job like that regularly get death threats?

In the hour before her next appointment, Sarah settled in for some research, starting with the two biggest local papers that had covered the Crosby Farm tree project, and then moved on to the local public radio station. All of them had prominent news articles, and Sarah made notes in her journal.

The biography of the dead woman matched in each of the sources: very impressive academic resume, lifelong Minneapolis resident except for when she'd been at school, married to a college professor, two teenage daughters. The death was listed as "suspicious" on the public radio website. The *Star Tribune* reported that "police suspected foul play." Sarah's hand shook as she copied the phrase into her notebook. Finally, she checked the *Pioneer Press*. That was where she found the most ominous quote of all. It was from the dead woman's sister, someone named Gretchen Jones. "The police won't say it yet, but we all know. Sarah was definitely murdered, and I expect a full, widespread investigation."

As she finished copying that quote her phone buzzed. Twenty-Seven. They're saying murder. Sarah held her breath as the reply ellipsis popped up immediately, indicating that she was still typing. I'm talking to the police detectives now.

Don't do it was Sarah's first thought, but what she typed was a much tamer, Thinking of you.

I can't believe this, Twenty-Seven wrote back. But I'm pretty sure I'm the last person who saw her. I mean alive. Should I admit that?

No. I'd just answer the questions and not say anything extra, Sarah typed. To be safe.

Minneapolis Police Department Interview with Sarah Christine Jones (aka Twenty-Seven)

Detective Present: Suzanne Barter

April 18, 2023

Suzanne Barter: Can you state your name, please, for the record?
Sarah Christine Jones: I'm Sarah Jones.
SB: Same name as the deceased.
SCJ: That's how I got the job with the family, actually. The job board at the university listed the contact person as Sarah Jones, and I don't know. It felt sort of meant to be. I mean, now it seems … I don't know …
SB: Take your time. It's a shock.
SCJ: My God. The girls. I can't believe it.
SB: What is your relationship like with the girls?
SCJ: We get along great. It's a good job. I mean, I like them. They're easy.
SB: And the deceased's husband, Mr. Campbell, says you've been employed with the family since the start of second semester?
SCJ: Their regular nanny is studying abroad in Hungary. I'm here for the term.
SB: Uh-huh. And what were you doing last night? Whereabouts?
SCJ: Well, I think you already know this, right? From talking to the family? I had my regular biweekly dinner with Sarah. We went to the Mill City Café as usual.
SB: You and Sarah went out to dinner every other week? She seems pretty busy for that kind of commitment.

SCJ: She said it was her way of keeping tabs on the kids. Her job is obviously intense. They've always had a nanny, full-time before the kids got to middle school. She always says—said—that the caregiver was like a third parent. It seemed over-the-top at first, but...

SB: And what were these dinners typically like?

SCJ: Well, Sarah was pretty regimented. It made sense with her work. There was a set agenda, and she wanted me to come with notes. It was a fifteen-minute check-in on each of the girls, academics, social life, extracurriculars, observations. She cared. She was so professionally successful and also a decent mom.

SB: So, it was a thirty-minute dinner?

SCJ: And then it was chitchat. That's what she called it.

SB: Like, socializing?

SCJ: Yeah. Chatting. Hanging out?

SB: You mentioned you thought she was a decent mom.

SCJ: Yeah.

SB: Just decent? Not good?

SCJ: No, I didn't mean that. She was good. I meant that she tried hard even though she had a really busy job.

SB: And the girls, they got along with her?

SCJ: As much as any teenager ever gets along with her mom?

SB: And was there anything different or out of the ordinary about this week's dinner?

SCJ: Well, it was late. She got delayed beforehand.

SB: We're following up on that. She got hung up at the house?

SCJ: I'm not sure exactly. She just texted and pushed it back.

SB: Where were you when that happened?

SCJ: I was at my apartment.

SB: Alone?

SCJ: I live alone. I'm pretty new in town. Here for school. I transferred.

SB: From?

SCJ: From a small school in Illinois.

SB: Okay, so the dinner was late. What time did you leave the restaurant?

SCJ: I think 9:30?

SB: And were the two of you drinking alcohol at dinner?

SCJ: I had a cocktail, and Sarah had a couple of glasses of wine.

SB: Typical for her?

SCJ: More or less.

SB: I'll need you to be precise, please. Was a couple of glasses of wine typical for the deceased, and is that how much she actually drank last night?

SCJ: Do you have blood alcohol levels or whatever? You'll test, right? I can't remember exactly what she ordered, but Sarah liked wine.

SB: We're waiting on the coroner's report. Did she use any other drugs, do you know?

SCJ: Drugs?

SB: Other substances you're aware of?

SCJ: You think the chair of the Federal Reserve uses street drugs? The woman was considering a run for Senate.

SB: We're covering all our bases, Ms. Jones. Can anyone verify your location after dinner?

SCJ: Like I said, I live alone.

SB: No neighbors or anyone you interacted with?

SCJ: Is that a problem?

SB: When did you last see the deceased?

SCJ: We said goodbye outside the restaurant.

SB: You didn't drive together.

SCJ: Not this time. Because of the work delay I mentioned.

SB: Do you think Ms. Jones was safe to drive?

SCJ: Like because of the wine?

SB: Right.

SCJ: Sometimes she liked to stroll after dinner. That's what she called it. A stroll. She might have done that. That might explain...

SB: Explain what?

SCJ: Well, wasn't she on the bridge?

SB: Did you see Ms. Jones on the Hennepin Avenue Bridge?

SCJ: No.

SB: You sure about that?

SCJ: Excuse me?

SB: Can you just confirm for the record, where exactly were you when you last saw the deceased?

SCJ: On the sidewalk outside of Mill City Café.

SB: Near the front door?

SCJ: On the corner. I parked a couple of streets over.

SB: Why so far?

SCJ: I'm not good at parallel.

SB: Hmmm.

SCJ: Are there other witnesses? Anyone see her?

SB: We're still canvassing.

SCJ: But not yet?

SB: Right now, you're the last one to have seen her alive. We'll need your full cooperation and your assertion that you won't leave the state until the case is closed.

SCJ: What?

SB: You have to stay in town.

SCJ: I don't have any plans to leave.

SB: Don't make any.

CHAPTER ELEVEN

April 19, 2023

This felt different, the so-called emergency meeting the night the news broke, hours after Twenty-Seven had dropped the bomb that she'd been the last person to see the dead woman alive. Sarah pulled on a black long-sleeved T-shirt and realized the look was funereal.

The first time she'd gone to one of Seventeen's meet-ups, she'd felt giggly. There'd been a charming LinkedIn message, the suggestion from the teenager that Sarah might need some "non-spandex-wearing friends" since she worked in a "fancy gym," which had made her laugh out loud.

That first day, Sarah had made the mistake of telling Brian about TSJP when he called to ask how she was settling in.

"You're joining a cult for people named Sarah Jones?" he'd said.

"Not a cult." Sarah remembered putting her index finger on the hunk of selenite she'd placed on the windowsill of her apartment. Her mother had written that the crystal was good for "resetting energy."

"The founder is calling it 'a whimsical social experiment,'" Sarah had told Brian.

"Sure," he huffed. "It's a whimsical experiment until someone takes a knife to your femoral artery."

Sarah shivered even as she remembered the comment. It seemed ominous that he had predicted violence among the group. Sarah felt shaky as she turned into the drop-off lane in front of Seventeen's building. She'd become her ride to meetings, in addition to her tutor.

But Seventeen flopped into Sarah's waiting car, casual. "You should really keep your doors locked when you're idling," she said as she buckled up.

Sarah gave her side-eye. "You're welcome for picking you up, young lady."

"Not even Sister Mary Theresa calls me 'young lady.'" Sister had become one of Sarah's favorite topics of conversation—the nun who'd approved the social media project rather than insisting on a letter in the kid's file, the nun who kept Starbursts in the front pocket of her habit next to her rosary beads. "Sister says hi, by the way."

"Did she love the coverage of the yarn-bombing?"

"Duh," Seventeen said. "They even put me on the main Instagram account. And you'd be proud, I did *not* point out the irony of being Instagram-famous for making bad choices on the same platform."

"I need to meet Sister. She does like me, right? I'm her favorite one of us?"

"She thinks you're cool and appreciates that you're tutoring me..." Seventeen trailed off.

"But?" Sarah prompted.

"But," Seventeen said, mirth in her voice, "I did have to tell her about Twenty-Seven's prettiness."

Sarah rolled her eyes. Twenty-Seven was objectively gorgeous. She had brown waves that bounced mesmerizingly around her shoulders, perfect eyeliner, a slightly upturned nose, and what seemed like a zillion pairs of trendy earrings. It would have been annoying if she weren't also one of the kindest, most genuine women Sarah had ever met. "She's a perfect friend," she'd told Grandma Ellie.

Sarah turned in to the Starbucks parking lot. Given that tonight's agenda was a corpse, she might have preferred an establishment with a liquor license, but there was the issue of their teenage founder.

"Hey," Sarah said, remembering Seventeen's promise of a surprise visitor. "Who's joining us? It's not like you to accept new members. No offense, but you're kind of—"

"Vain and exclusive?" Seventeen deadpanned.

"I wouldn't have put it that way," Sarah said.

"Let's just say I'm raising the stakes." Seventeen hopped out, the cuffs of her Sacred Heart sweatpants dragging on the sidewalk.

Inside, Sarah found Twenty-Seven at the counter waiting for her decaf latte. She snaked an arm around her friend's waist and squeezed. "Are you okay?" Sarah asked, knowing the question was inadequate.

"I had to talk to the police," Twenty-Seven whispered.

"Was it awful?"

"It was awful." Sarah could smell Twenty-Seven's shampoo. She used Herbal Essences, a blend that reminded Sarah of junior high. If only she'd had a friend like Twenty-Seven back then, she might not have needed to rely so heavily on Brian in middle school. But there was no point in imagining what-ifs. She was here now, and it seemed right. Better than almost anyone, Sarah knew how to provide support in a horrible time.

"What did the police say?" Twenty-Seven's drink came up, and

Sarah steered her back toward the cash register, where she'd place her own order for chamomile tea. Twenty-Seven tipped into her a little, not wanting to stand on her own. Sarah was familiar with this kind of feebleness from the end of high school cross-country meets, her teammates' limbs like noodles as she helped them hobble back to the tent. Sarah had never been the one to crumble, always holding a little bit of her energy back just in case.

"They said—" Twenty-Seven whispered, so quietly that Sarah could barely hear. "They said I shouldn't leave town."

Sarah felt her hand tighten on Twenty-Seven's forearm. "Wait, what?" Her breath caught, and she recognized the feeling as fear. "Are you a—"

"I know," Twenty-Seven whispered again. "It's like I'm some kind of..."

"Suspect," they said together.

In the back room, they all settled around the same table in their usual spots, with Seventeen at the head. "Let me state the obvious," their leader said once everyone was seated and Forty-Four was sucking down a monstrous Frappuccino with a two-inch haystack of whipped cream on top. "One of us has died. And the police think it was murder."

Despite the stress of the arrival and Twenty-Seven's revelation, Sarah fought to keep from smiling. Seventeen was generally hilarious without trying.

"No shit." It was Sixty-Nine. Her glasses had slipped down her nose and she peered over their rims. "I can't believe how many people texted, wondering if it was me. As if my death would make the news, even if I were found in the middle of a walking path by a gaggle of joggers."

"It wasn't in the middle of the path," Seventeen said. "In fact, that's why I think she wasn't found until this morning. There's a shadow there, and some kind of utility box."

"How do you know about the shadow and the utility box?" Forty-Four asked. She and Thirty-Nine were taking sketch notes—a mix of icons and drawings and words—on the opposite pages of a notebook, as usual. After each meeting, they posted a picture of their work to their TwinTeachersInThirdland Instagram account along with a matching outfit selfie. Tonight they were sporting merch from Sixty-Nine's blog, pink T-shirts with the iconic Jessica Fletcher quote, "I may be wrong, but frankly, I doubt it."

"I don't want to brag," Seventeen said, "but I have an inside source."

"Does this have to do with your surprise visitor?" It was Twenty-Seven, who still looked pale and slumpy.

"Yes. It's sort of serendipitous, actually. That means lucky?"

"Duh," interjected Sixty-Nine.

"I got a DM from her after the yarn-bombing. I agreed to let her come to the meeting because of a connection to our names."

"A connection to our names?" Sarah squinted at Seventeen, suspicious.

"You'll see," Seventeen said, "and I think recent events indicate that we should renew ourselves for a second season. Who better than us to investigate the murder of one of our own?"

"It's super weird and creepy that one of us is dead." Sarah felt immediately embarrassed about the simplicity, the obviousness, of her comment, as if *she* were the high schooler.

Sixty-Nine turned toward her. "You mean the fact that we started meeting three months ago as a group of Sarah Joneses to help this yahoo escape academic ruin"—she jacked a thumb at Seventeen—"and then we had our fifteen minutes of fame, and now just two weeks later one of us is frickin' dead?"

Tears suddenly and surprisingly threatened at Sarah's eyelids. *A mother dead.* "In a nutshell." Sarah's voice was thick. "It feels like it means something." Tears flooded Twenty-Seven's eyes, too.

Seventeen cleared her throat. "So, what I'm trying to say is, we investigate. We solve this."

Thirty-Nine coughed a little as she put her cup down. "We're not police. We don't have skills."

"But we do have an inside track." Seventeen tapped her foot, her running shoe poking out beneath her oversized sweatpants. "We've got the dead woman's nanny." She pointed at Twenty-Seven, who swallowed hard. "You still work there, right? You have access to the house? You overhear things?"

"I'm not comfortable—" Twenty-Seven started to say when another teenager appeared in the doorway. She wore wide leg jeans and Adidas three-stripe sneakers. A tangle of necklaces fell over her gray sweatshirt.

"Ruby," Twenty-Seven said. She was on her feet, and Sarah's jaw dropped. She'd spent the day reliving the aftermath of Ainsley's death. This girl was living her own nightmare, her own first day. Sarah wanted to stand up, too, to pull Ruby in to her.

"Hi," the girl said. "I'm Ruby Campbell."

"Oh lord, you poor thing." It was Forty-Four. "I read about you online. Are you okay?" She waved a hand in front of her face and shook her head. "What a stupid question, of course you're not. What can we get you?" She was up, her marker abandoned in the middle of her notebook page, a line half-drawn. "Thirty-Nine, get her a hot chocolate." She said with a snap at her partner, the noise of it ending with an extended finger.

Thirty-Nine looked confused. "Okay, but who—"

"It's the daughter of the deceased Sarah," Sixty-Nine hissed, answering for all of them, and then she turned to Seventeen and spoke normally. "What is she doing here?"

"I asked to join," Ruby said, her voice clear. Her face looked flat somehow, even with the sparkly eye shadow Sarah could see from across the room. "I sent Seventeen a message before this happened, but then? Well, we've been messaging. The police have nothing—"

"Nothing?" Twenty-Seven asked, her voice higher than normal. "They have nothing? And, honey, how did you get here?"

Ruby rolled her eyes. "Certainly you've heard of Uber? And you've never called me 'honey' ever. Let's not start that."

"See?" Seventeen said. "The police have nothing, the family wants—"

"How do you know they have nothing?" Twenty-Seven asked.

"You know they don't." Ruby stood still in the doorway. "The best they've got is that you were the last one seen with her," Ruby went on, her voice a little louder. "They said it to my dad like it meant something, but what the hell? You were basically her best friend. She talked about you all the time, what a godsend you were. It's not like you pushed your BFF off a bridge!"

"Sit down." Seventeen pulled a chair out next to hers and Ruby stumbled into it. Sarah's breath felt shallow.

"Your BFF?" she whispered to Twenty-Seven, whose tears had spilled over. Sarah put her hand on Twenty-Seven's back, forcing away the pang of jealousy. The girl's mom had died, and Sarah was worried that Twenty-Seven might have two best friends? Still, she'd barely mentioned her boss in any of their conversations over the past several months. All of her stories were about the girls.

"I definitely didn't push her," Twenty-Seven choked out.

"Right," Ruby said, "so, that's why I'm here. You guys—women—are good at stuff. You got attention for the yarn art or whatever. You have followers. I know true crime is a thing."

"But, Ruby, we're just a group of random people with the same name." Sixty-Nine looked serious, professional even, and Sarah could picture her negotiating a deal over a boardroom table.

"And I'm just a kid," Ruby said, "watching my mom's case get massively bungled." She didn't sound like a kid, Sarah thought, but then again neither did Seventeen. Maybe kids sounded different now.

"See?" Seventeen told the group. "We have a purpose. Sister Mary Theresa might even say it's ordained or whatever. We need to help one of our own."

"We're going to investigate a murder?" Twenty-Seven gasped. Sarah reached over and grabbed her hand, rising above the petty BFF jealousy.

"I don't think we can actually investigate murder," Sarah said.

"You're wrong." It was Thirty-Nine, on paper the least likely of them to think amateur sleuthing was a good idea. "Forty-Four and I spend all day telling kids they can make a difference in the world. If the police are already messing up, it's our civic duty."

"Amen," said Forty-Four, writing "civic duty" in her notes.

"It's up to us," Seventeen said to Twenty-Seven. "Unless, of course, you want to get arrested for the crime."

CHAPTER TWELVE

April 20, 2023

Vance poked her head into George's cubicle. "Come with me." She walked out before he could answer.

George wiped the crumbs of energy bar off his cheek as he followed her, his hair still wet from the gym. He'd run four miles on a treadmill at LifeSport hoping to see Sarah. She hadn't been there, but he'd waved at the supervisor, who seemed to recognize him. The encounter was good for his credibility, a fact he'd documented in his paperwork and uploaded to the system.

"Where are we headed?" George caught up to his boss near the elevator banks.

"It's time to interview Caden Campbell." Vance jabbed a finger into the lobby button and straightened the lapels of her blazer as the door closed.

"The husband of the Fed chairwoman." George started sweating again in anticipation of his first real interrogation. "We worked out jurisdiction?" "We" was an overstatement. The FBI field office operated on a need-to-know basis. Special agents—George still couldn't believe this was his title—didn't discuss their duties at the water cooler. The segmentation wasn't unlike the organization of Camp Birdsong, George thought, as he followed Vance to the black Charger. At camp, the swim dock instructors were the only ones who ran the sauna; the archery specialists, the only ones with keys to the arrow shed. When George had been promoted to assistant director, a whole world opened up. Suddenly, he could access camper health documentation, staff performance reviews, and tax statements. None of it had been relevant to his previous position as marina director. Before George's promotion, his father had been the one who kept all of the minutiae in his head. The guilt of his familial abandonment dogged George the entire year it had taken him to complete the FBI application process.

"It's not a real thing to apply to the FBI," Paul Nightingale had said the first time he'd mentioned it. His dad had looked up from his spreadsheet, and it was only via the minuscule arch in his eyebrow that George could tell there was humor in his response.

"It actually is." George had tipped his phone toward Paul so he could see the official seal in the upper corner of the recruitment page. "And there's a shortage of qualified candidates at the moment with the prevalence of domestic terrorism and police violence..." He trailed off as his dad clicked into the next cell on his spreadsheet. Paul Nightingale cared about white extremists as much as the next guy, but without George, the family business would no longer be in the family.

George owed his dad a text, he realized as he got in the car with Vance. He could ask how hiring season was starting out, something he'd always helmed in the past.

Vance pulled out of the parking lot of the suburban 1970s-era office building and headed toward the Tudor. "What's the coroner saying?" George asked.

"Scuffle before the fall." Vance clenched her teeth. So far, George had never seen his boss relax. In that way, she was a little like his dad. "She didn't jump," Vance continued. "Maybe pushed, maybe slipped, but someone else was there. Of course, it's possible it wasn't Gabriella. She's never been violent in the past, so this would be a major change in behavior. I'm advocating for a task force, but the politics at Minneapolis PD are a bear."

Would he get to be on a task force since he'd already started investigating Gabriella Johnson?

"You got around the Minneapolis cops for access to the husband?" George finally asked again. Vance kept her hands at ten and two.

"There was a call from the White House."

The dead woman had been an assistant cabinet secretary. This was more pressure: national-level oversight on his first fraud case. As thieves went, Gabriella Johnson was no Bernie Madoff. George hoped to have her charged within three months, to move on to the next thing, perhaps to get transferred to abductions. He'd planned to talk to Vance about it after he aced his first test.

George reached into his pocket and ran his finger over the top of his wallet, where he felt the soft and fraying edges of the Pokémon cards. His father had known from the beginning that the FBI decision was about his friend Henry O'Neill, who had gone missing. "Becoming a police officer is not going to change what happened back then," he'd said.

"It's a twenty percent acceptance rate," George had told his dad, changing the subject. He'd rubbed a palm over his biceps, the vein there sinewy from a month of boulder placement and dock installation. He knew very well he could score ten points on the pull-up section of the FBI fitness test. "I figure it's gotta be tougher for the program I'm interested in. Still, it's just like Dartmouth." Acceptance there had been a long shot, too, but George had clicked the portal, and the digitized green confetti on the screen had matched his father's Birdsong staff polo. "And I've got the coding background," George said, "plus basic Arabic. That puts me—"

They were interrupted then by the repeated dinging of the food truck's reverse alarm. "Dammit," George's father said. "I didn't rearrange the freezer." He'd taken off running toward the dining hall and preempted George's first attempt at quitting.

Vance pulled up in front of the beige stucco house with a turret. A crew of gardeners worked the front yard, scraping the remains of last year's leaves out of the damp flower beds. A dried hydrangea bloom floated across the path that led to the front steps.

"He knows we're coming?" George asked.

"He does." Vance hurtled herself out of the car.

Before they could knock, a teenage girl with a cat-ear headband opened the door. "Are you the feds?" she asked.

Vance flashed her badge. "Jane Vance." George startled. No one had used her first name in the weeks since he had been at the field office. "This is George Nightingale." She stuck out her hand, but the kid turned around without shaking.

George kept his head on a swivel as he walked through the hallway. At least half of the information he could glean was from observation. At Quantico the schedule was regimented, the instructors supportive but exacting. Instead of archery and windsurfing, there'd been firearms training, lectures on law and civil rights, tactical planning and simulations. George had done it all with a gray T-shirt on, "Nightingale" stenciled on the back. There'd been high fives and whispering after lights-out. George had earned special honors in long-distance running and academics. If it wasn't also life-and-death, it could have been the summer he'd finished his American Archer award and captained the four-day canoe trip down the Crow Wing River.

"Here." Their cat-eared escort pointed at an oversized sectional.

A haggard man with bed head—the husband, Caden Campbell—sat at one end, a pile of manila folders in his lap. At the other, another teenager lay under a Pendleton blanket, her eyes closed but not sleeping. The built-in shelves opposite the couch had professionally organized memorabilia in each section, a soccer trophy nestled against a piece of paisley porcelain, a pile of hardcovers topped with an antique teacup.

Vance transformed her body language. Her steps shortened, her shoulders rounded. "Mr. Campbell?" Her voice was the softest George had heard it. The prone kid fluttered her eyes open.

"This is Jane Vance," Cat-Ears said. George assumed from the accessory that she was the younger daughter.

"The police were just here," Campbell said.

"Thanks for having us. I know this is a horrific time." Vance pointed at an upholstered chair near the coffee table. "Mind if I sit?"

The man nodded, and George disappeared into the corner. From his vantage, he could see the kitchen over the back of the couch, the surface of the refrigerator cluttered with magnets and photographs. The cat-eared girl wandered out there.

"Is it okay if I ask you a few questions?" Vance glanced at the kid under the blanket. This was Campbell's opportunity to ask the minors to leave.

"We'll tell you whatever we can," he said. "The girls have heard everything so far. I called my friend in the psych department at the college. She said there's no use trying to shield them when everything is in the paper. Sarah was always a public figure..."

He trailed off. George watched the couch kid, her hair half covering her eyes, the blanket touching her lower lip.

"What do you know about your wife's whereabouts on Monday evening?"

"I told the police this," Campbell said. "She had her usual dinner with our nanny. She liked to know the nannies well, said it—" He put his folders on the couch next to him and leaned over, his elbows on his thighs.

"She said it was her way of 'triangulating' on us," the couch girl said. "She always needed help taking care of us." The tone was flat, resentment—an indictment—in the statement.

Campbell blinked. "We've had careers," he said. "Hers got bigger, obviously, the stint in Washington, and then the girls came along."

"And interrupted her political rise," the girl said.

"Ruby." It wasn't a warning exactly. And now George knew that the couch girl was the older at sixteen. The girl in the kitchen, then, was fourteen-year-old Lula.

"Your mom was a really important person," Vance said. "I bet it's hard to have this tragedy all over the news."

Ruby's blanket moved up and down as she shrugged. "At least my teachers are taking a break on the homework."

"They go to the Miller School," Campbell explained. "It's intense."

"Intense for Ruby." It was Lula, who'd drifted back into the room with a Coke. George registered some surprise. This seemed like a no-soda kind of house. "*I* like school." Lula lifted her chin.

"I like it, too, asshole." Ruby blew the hair out of her face.

"Okay." Vance kept her eyes on Campbell. It was George's job to take in everything else. "So, she had dinner with the nanny, as usual."

"Not as usual," Ruby said. "It got pushed back because of something at work. That's what you need to think about. That work thing. Or, whom she was meeting *after* dinner."

Vance nodded at the girl, acting like it was totally normal that she remained prone, the blanket pulled resolutely up to her neck.

"Got it," Vance said, making a note. She looked at the dad. "When was the last time you heard from her?"

"We exchanged texts at about 5:15." Campbell nodded at the phone on the coffee table. "I checked for the police. You have access to their files, right? She said she'd be home before ten."

"Nothing odd about the messages or the timing?"

Campbell shook his head and sniffed. "I wish I had said something else. Something real."

"Your daughter mentioned work. Were there conflicts there? Enemies?"

"Work was always contentious, but it's banking policy," Campell said. "The arguments are academic."

"She didn't express concern about any conflict at work?" Vance pressed.

"Nothing out of the ordinary at all."

"Except the Senate run," Ruby said. "*That* was different."

"That was different," Campbell allowed.

"Did Sarah express any concern for her safety?" Vance asked.

"That's just it," Campbell said. "No. Not at all. Things were going well, overall."

"And how was the relationship between your wife and the nanny?" Vance flicked her eyes toward George, and he clicked his molars together.

"Sarah? Oh, they were both named Sarah. Actually, same first and last name, as coincidence would have it. Sarah—my wife—loved her."

"Has she been with the family for a long time, then?" Vance asked.

"No, actually." Campbell half-heartedly lifted the papers on the table in front of him and let them flutter back down again. "She started in the last week of January. Our regular nanny is studying abroad. It was always going to be a short-term thing."

Lula sat on the arm of the sofa next to her sister's head. "But she doesn't feel like a sub," Lula said. "Whatever happened, it wasn't her."

"And your whereabouts last night around nine p.m.?" Vance sounded casual, but George knew she was anything but.

"The girls and I had dinner, and then we were here. We were here when—" He closed his eyes, and Ruby sniffled.

"Take your time," Vance said, looking at her notebook. And then, she lowered her voice to just above a whisper and pressed on. "Was there anything unusual going on in your wife's life?" Vance asked. "Any conflicts with friends that you were aware of?"

Campbell shook his head. "I keep trying to think of the magic clue, but everything was normal."

Lula slurped her Coke. Ruby breathed out, ruffling the blanket over her mouth.

"Do you have other family in town?"

"Sarah's sister, Gretchen, lives in Woodbury." It was a suburb of St. Paul, a good thirty minutes from where they sat now. "We don't see them often."

Vance bit her lip. "But I've read in the press that Gretchen is sure the death involves foul play."

"We all think that." It was Ruby again. She'd lifted her head off the pillow, and as George watched, let it fall again. "Because, think about it, right? What's the alternative? That our mom jumped?"

"Like, on purpose?" Lula added, her lip attached to the Coke can.

Vance nodded, unrattled. "That makes sense. Is there anything missing among Sarah's things?"

"The police asked me that, too," Campbell said. "I don't think so?"

"But she lost her necklace last week," Ruby said.

"Which necklace?" Campbell turned, surprised.

"The necklace," Ruby said. "The one from Gran."

Vance cocked her head and waited.

"She hadn't mentioned it to me." Campbell blinked and put his hand on one of the folders. "I can start an insurance claim," he muttered, "but that won't get it back. She must have been devastated."

"It's valuable?" Vance asked.

"Well, yes"—Campbell closed his eyes—"but that wouldn't have been it." Lula slid off the side of the couch and walked to the shelves where George stood. She grabbed a photo from its spot next to an abstract sculpture. In it, a smiling Sarah Jones stood in a black suit, an ornate necklace hanging in the V-neck, a large yellow diamond at its center. Younger versions of Lula and Ruby stood on either side of their mother, their heads resting against her torso. Everyone looked happy. Lula walked the photo over to Vance and tipped it toward her to show the necklace.

"Beautiful," Vance said. "Did your mom have any idea what had happened to it?"

"She didn't tell us," Ruby said. "But we know who did it."

"You do?" Vance's voice was steady, though George's heart thudded.

"We do *not* know." Lula stamped her foot and dropped the photo on the wood floor. Everyone but Vance winced. She leaned over and grabbed the picture. The glass had cracked in the corner.

"Girls," Campbell whispered.

Ruby pulled her blanket up over her nose again. "I should say we know who *Mom* thought did it. But, she was wrong."

Lula's face had gotten redder as she stood in the center of the room. George had worked with enough kids to know her anger would soon volcano out of her. At Birdsong, George would have leapt into distraction mode, handing her a friendship bracelet kit or a jump rope. But now, he held still.

"It wasn't her!" Lula's eyes blazed, and she half crushed her Coke can. "Ruby, God!" The soda sloshed onto the rug. George surveyed the room like a lifeguard on the swim dock, checking the viability of each person present. Campbell's thighs had tensed. He was ready to leap up, to rush to his frothing daughter. "We promised!" Lula shrieked.

Vance had reached one hand out to Campbell's biceps, an attempt to steady him, to keep him from interrupting. Ruby's body hadn't moved at all. She watched her sister from beneath a veil of hair.

"Mom thought it was Aunt Gretchen," Ruby said, flatly. "She thought she'd been in the house, like alone."

"Gretchen?" Campbell asked. Lula's explosion fizzled. As if nothing had happened, she walked back to the couch and sat on the armrest.

"The aunt in Woodbury?" Vance confirmed.

Ruby freed an arm from her side and pushed her hair off her forehead. "She and our mom hate each other."

Something was off, George could feel it. "Gretchen" wasn't what Lula thought Ruby was going to say.

"Hated," Lula said. She uncrushed her can, the pop echoing in the silent room. "They hated each other."

"You know what?" Campbell stood up. "I think that's enough for now. You understand. We need—" He dipped his head to his palm. "We need some time. And, I've been thinking—couldn't this have been random?"

Vance gave the widower a long look before she signaled George. "Only ten percent of homicides are random, and her purse was found with her. It wasn't a robbery."

Campbell let out a shuddery breath. The shoulder bag had been pinned beneath the dead woman's torso.

"We'll be in touch," Vance said.

At least, George thought as they walked to the door, Caden Campbell understood that there would be more discomfort, more prying. When he'd been a child, George had expected the Henry O'Neill case to be solved imminently, by the end of an hour-long television show. Instead, the line of investigators stretched on and on. And Henry was still in limbo.

This was different, George told himself, in that Sarah Jones's body was found at the bottom of the bridge where she fell, not even twelve hours afterward. There were plenty of unknowns about how she'd gotten there, her bones broken and her skull cracked, but no mystery about where she'd actually landed. The family had immediate, if horrific, closure.

Whereas Henry was still missing. George felt his jaw tighten as he put his hand on the passenger door of the Charger. Henry O'Neill and Sarah Jones were both dead. It would go on forever. They'd continue to be dead next week, next month, in twenty years. The finality of it still surprised George.

Vance buckled her seat belt and hit the ignition in one smooth movement. Experienced agents practiced an easy efficiency. Their feet struck the ground faster than the newly commissioned, their glances over their shoulders in traffic timed perfectly with their lane changes.

"Did you catch that?" she asked.

If it was a test, it was an easy one. "You mean, did I catch that Ruby did a one-eighty?"

Vance nodded, her eyes narrowed beneath her sunglasses.

"She wasn't going to say 'Aunt Gretchen,'" George said. "That was pretty clear."

"The girls planned ahead," Vance agreed. "They alluded to a promise."

George remembered Lula shouting at Ruby, furious at her for deviating from whatever they'd plotted. "Whom are they protecting?" he asked.

"The nanny?" Vance said. "Campbell was clueless, though. Ruby and Lula were running the show."

George remembered Lula skulking in the kitchen, helping herself to a Coke while Ruby lay catatonic on the couch. There was no attempt at politeness on anyone's part. Campbell seemed more or less oblivious to their movements. It was hard to judge people's motivations, though, in the early stages of grief. They behaved all kinds of sideways. George knew this from watching his classmates back then, from seeing Henry O'Neill's father in the cereal aisle, stalled in front of a jumbo box of Honeycomb. And there was his teacher, recycling the extra copy of each assignment she made for the rest of the year, as if she couldn't quite believe Henry's desk would remain empty.

"How do we get the girls to tell us what they really think?" George asked Vance.

"We go back," Vance said. "If not tomorrow, then the next day. We wait for more reports from forensics, including the bank stuff. We have more fodder and dig a little deeper. We hopefully make headway on a task force. The MPD have already interviewed a bunch of people, including your nanny. She could be the person the kids are protecting."

She'd said "we," and then "your." George tried not to smile. "And in the meantime?"

"Don't you have another fitness training appointment?" Vance grinned, the littlest flash of sarcasm in her tone. Had he given away his attraction to Sarah Jones the trainer? George blushed. He was supposed to learn about Gabriella from Sarah, to be close enough to see the con artist's machinations, to gather the evidence as Sarah dropped it.

George thought about Sarah Jones at the gym, her grandmother, her fast marathon. And then, the crime scene photos of the dead Sarah's neck, her hand limp in a drying slick of blood.

"Fraud to violent crime," Vance said. "Not a bad first month, Nightingale."

Group Chat of The Sarah Jones Project

April 20, 2023

69: This is going to be awkward, but it occurred to me last night, and I think we have to get it out of the way.

44: I wonder if it's the same thing 39 and I were thinking at lunch . . .

17: Enough with the suspense. Out with it.

39: Are you texting at school? I'm sure the nuns don't allow that.

17: Shhh. Mrs. O'Leary has gone round the bend talking about the foreskin surgery alluded to in the Maccabees or some shit. She won't notice.

69: So, I was thinking, we should ask . . . 27, do you know what happened to Dead Sarah? We should probably call her Fed Sarah? Less morbid? Anyway, I've watched enough murder shows to know, sometimes all you have to do is ask, and the person who might have accidentally done something . . .

44: Yep. That was our thought. 27, you were the last one seen with her. Did you do it?

27: Wait, what?

30: Guys. Come on.

69: We have to ask the question. It could have been an accident, she could have been drinking.

44: You could have gotten angry. A slip? A wrong move?

17: Well?

27: I can't believe you even have to ask!!!! NO. It wasn't me. We left dinner, and I went home.

69: Did anyone see you when you got there?

27: You sound like the police.

69: Wait, you got interrogated by the police?

27: We all did. Or, the family gave statements. It wasn't an interrogation.

44: And you're not family.

27: I don't know what to tell you. Is this for real? No, no, no. I didn't do it.

30: Ok, let's give it a rest.

69: I had to ask. Moving on. I'm looking at the network of CCTV cameras near the bridge. They won't have it on video, I don't think. What's your address again? Maybe they can catch you coming home or whatever.

17: We're like real investigators!

69: I know. Who would've thought that my Murder, She Wrote recap blog would have been so undeniably practical!

30: We'll talk about all of this at next week's meeting. We're meeting next week, right?

17: Right.

30: 27, we believe you. We're on your side.

27: Sure. Thx.

CHAPTER THIRTEEN

April 25, 2023

George woke in the early dark covered in the same old sweat. He gasped, the breathlessness familiar as he blinked away the eyes that seemed to glow up at him from a hole in the floor. He hadn't seen Henry this way, in the moments between sleep and waking, since he'd been commissioned at the FBI.

"He's not here," George whispered. He pulled his T-shirt away from his torso and felt its dampness.

George swung his legs over the side of the bed. He let his feet press into the floor, the wood surface solid and slightly cool in the spring morning, not at all like the moss-covered logs he'd scrambled over as they'd searched for Henry, his missing friend. He'd followed his dad through the woods back then, trying to avoid the smaller branches snapping back from the upright trees. George put his hand on his cheek in the spot the white oak twig had whipped into his face that morning.

"Focus," Paul had said. There had been no apology for not holding the branch. George remembered pressing his fingers over the scratch when he'd gotten home. There had been no sign of Henry in the Birdsong woods or anywhere else. His mother had smoothed antibiotic ointment over the wound as he dozed off, tucked in a sleeping bag at the foot of his parents' bed. He'd stayed there in their room until the beginning of sixth grade, when his parents had insisted on a "fresh start," which had meant that George and his sleeping bag moved down the hallway outside of Bea's door.

In his condo alone, George blinked hard and then focused his vision on his toes, his adult-sized toes. This wasn't about Henry, it was about the dead Sarah Jones; the task force that he'd just been assigned to; the meeting room in the basement of the Minneapolis Police Department; his informant, who would now be providing information on murder rather than fraud. George had lucked himself into a promotion of sorts.

Forty minutes later, George waited for Sarah at LifeSport. He was early for his training appointment, so he took a mat and rolled himself down onto his back, his hands stretched above his head. Vance had been clear: he was to work this side of the case for the morning. No distractions or notifications. After checking his usual news sites and the TSJP Instagram account, which had been uncharacteristically quiet, he'd left his phone in the locker room and reviewed his plan to weave their conversation toward the other Sarah Joneses.

"Another early bird," Sarah said, standing over him. "I like it."

"Well, I am a Nightingale," he said.

She looked confused and then her eyes crinkled. "Right," she laughed. "Duh. And also you're a night owl. Allison told me she saw you at least once on the treadmills in the evenings. Did you get your miles in? Running after work?"

"Thirty-six miles," said George. She'd said to do thirty-five.

"Above and beyond." She dropped down next to him.

"Just one extra mile." He sat up. "So you'd know I was legit." *Too flirty?*

Sarah half smiled, her left eyebrow arching, flirty herself. "I had no doubt. What do you do? I mean for work?"

"I'm in national security." His heart fluttered. This was it. He was supposed to tell her. She'd be a willing informant.

"Like the CIA?" She laughed. "NSA? I sound like an idiot. Do real people even have those jobs?"

"I'm FBI." George's cheeks reddened. It felt like bragging. "It's a real job. But, I'm new to it." *What a doofus.*

Sarah's eyes bugged. "Well, this is a new one! I've trained a couple of cops and also a private eye, but never a real agent. At least not that I knew of." She stepped back, palms up. "It's sometimes a secret, right? I can't wait to hear about it while you warm up." As she led him to a treadmill, George noticed the definition in her calves, the strength of her hamstrings. *She* was legit.

At the machine, Sarah cranked up the speed. "An easy jog," she said. Sarah's every movement on the job was practiced, a contrast to how clumsy George felt in his. Sarah was Vance in mesh shorts, rocking back on her heels next to the machine, totally in her element.

"So, FBI." Sarah hugged her clipboard. "You're telling me that's a real thing."

"Indeed. But mostly, it's an office job."

"No fieldwork? No thick files on Minneapolis-area personal trainers?" She leaned in, inviting a faux confidence. Of course, George did have a file on her—her and the other Sarah Joneses—not that he was about to tell her that now.

"I'm in my first couple of months on the job, actually," George admitted. "I'm on the fraud team." That was still true, the task force notwithstanding.

"Fraud," Sarah repeated. "So not murder? Remember the last

time we were together, when my grandmother thought I'd been murdered?"

George saw a twinkle in her eye as she remembered the chaotic misunderstanding. But then again, murder was more exciting if you didn't have to look at it up close.

"I do," he said. "Actually, coincidence—" He and Vance had discussed this part. "My supervisor is looking into that case. We got appointed to a special task force."

"That seems good! But is the murder fraud related?"

"My boss is on a different team as well," George explained. He wouldn't go into details. "Anyway, it's early days in the investigation."

"No leads?"

George shrugged and increased his pace. He might as well sweat from exercise, in addition to nerves. "What do the other Sarah Joneses have to say about it?" *Casual.*

"Our meeting was a little more exciting than the usual." She went on for a couple of minutes about letting go of the yarn-bombing agenda. George asked some questions, pretending not to have read all the coverage about the eastern cottonwood and its geometric sweater.

Sarah finally hit "stop" on the treadmill. "Should I tell you about our murder investigation while we do some explosive stuff?"

George grimaced. "Is that really necessary for a fast marathon?"

"We've gotta get stronger. A three-hour marathon is no joke." He followed her to the free weights. She handed him twenty-pound dumbbells. "Reverse lunge with knee-up." She demonstrated, her form immaculate and her quad rippling as her shorts inched toward her hip. "Ten times on the left with good running arms." She held her own at ninety-degree angles for him to emulate. "And then we'll switch."

"So, has your group solved the murder yet?" George prompted before his breath got away from him.

"Wait," she said. "You for sure know more than I do. Shouldn't we start with you?" Sarah winked, and George almost lost his balance.

"The existence of the investigation isn't a secret," George said, "but some of the details are. So, maybe we start with the Sarahs."

"We don't know anything for sure. None of us are in national security." Sarah shrugged, rising on her toes a bit, and then bouncing back down. "But, we had a surprise visitor at our meeting, which was actually kind of intense." She shook her head, and her ponytail whipped over her shoulder, a few strands catching on her collar. "Somehow, Seventeen, our founder—we go by our ages, right?—became friends with the dead woman's daughter, Ruby, on Instagram."

George froze for a second and then recovered. The information flowed quicker than he had expected it to. "Wow," he said, aiming for nonchalance and lowering back into a lunge. "That *is* intense." George knew they went by their ages because he'd read every Instagram post and story highlight on the TSJP profile, but to Sarah he said, "Clever hack with the ages." It was.

She nodded. "Yeah, and actually my friend, also Sarah—she's Twenty-Seven—is Ruby's nanny. So there are two strange connections to the family in our one small group." She blinked. "Three, I guess. Because of the names, too. Seventeen is right—it really does seem like we're supposed to be investigating. Like, fate. Don't stop those lunges," Sarah said. "I'm looking for big-time fatigue." George's brain went into overdrive, processing her news about Ruby joining their meeting and also trying to exceed her strength-training standards.

"Why did Ruby come to the meeting?" George asked, slightly winded now. "Is that allowed? Since she's not a Sarah?"

"It's an emergency," Sarah said. "So I guess it's fine. Plus she just showed up, and then she told us—" She squinted at him. "Wait."

"What did she tell you?"

Sarah led him to a box for jumps. "Are you here for professional reasons?" she asked. "Like, you need my information?" She laughed, an explosion of giggles prompting her to bend at the waist. "I'm sorry," she said. "Can you imagine? Me? Working with the FBI?" George held his breath and watched her think, stalling while he swiped his neck with one of the gym's scratchy towels. "But you made your appointment *before* she died, and I'd seen you here before that, so . . ."

"A big coincidence," George said, wincing a little into the towel at the lie, "but maybe now that I'm here, we can help each other?"

"Seriously?" Sarah pointed at the box. "Now you're doing box jumps alternating with push-ups. Start with five and then we'll ladder down." She clapped as if she were a football coach and then added, "Why would the FBI need help from a group of amateurs?"

He started jumping and gulped for breath as he spoke. "We don't have the last person to see the deceased alive and also the woman's daughter at our disposal."

"Wait," Sarah said, "you know about Twenty-Seven's dinner with Fed Sarah?" *Fed Sarah*, George thought. *Better than Dead Sarah.*

"Of course you do," Sarah continued as he finished the first set of jumps. "I'll join you for the push-ups. Nose to mat, okay?" She smiled at him as she matched his elbow bends.

Sarah hopped up, tapped the box, and George jumped. They didn't speak again until he'd finished the micro-set of one box jump and they'd both taken to their knees after their one push-up.

"So, Twenty-Seven and the dinner," she said again. "She's not actually a suspect, is she? Because she's totally awesome and not, like, murderous at all. Ruby was worried about her being investigated." Sarah tapped her foot as George caught his breath. "Oh, and good job on the workout." She gave him a cheesy thumbs-up. *Pure camp counselor.*

"Are you in?" George asked, pushing his damp hair off his forehead. "You'll be my informant on the case?"

"I'll think about it," she said. "It seems like it might be mutually beneficial." She grinned then, and he noticed the way her front teeth turned in slightly toward each other, an adorable imperfection.

And then suddenly, without thinking too much about it, George blurted an invitation: "Do you want to go for a run sometime?" It was off script. But they'd need more time if he was going to dig further. And also, Sarah looked so cute, strands of hair escaping her ponytail, her name tag slightly askew above the LifeSport logo on her shirt.

"Date or training session or, like, you grilling me about my Sarah Jones friends?"

George blushed. He tipped his head back and forth, not sure how to play it. He finally raised his palms in a shrug.

"Date." Sarah answered her own question.

George wasn't sure Vance would sanction it, but he felt his chest swell.

"And," she continued, "if it becomes a conflict, like if the date doesn't go well, I'll transfer you to Allison." She pointed at the training desk. "She's good, too."

After he'd finished his squats and some single-leg stuff, she handed him her card and wrote her cell number on the back. "Text me," she said. "Or whatever." And then she winked again.

George grinned all the way back to the locker room and had taken his phone out of his bag to enter her number when he saw his dad's text. Ran into Andrew O'Neill. Told him you're with the feds and he wants to talk. Ok?

Andrew O'Neill. George still remembered his skewed collar at his son Henry's service. A service with no casket. A memorial with no certainty.

I'm on the fraud team, George texted back. No point in mentioning the murder to his parents yet.

That's a no, then? An immediate text response from his dad was rare. Paul must have been holding the phone.

No, said George. I mean yes. I'll talk.

Group Chat of The Sarah Jones Project

April 25, 2023

27: I know we're investigating a murder, but excuse me, everyone! Alert! Alert!

44: My class is at PE. Spill. And quick.

39: Yeah, it's been a crappy day in the 3rd grade and it's breaded fish for lunch, so things aren't going to get any better on this front. Hit me with the murder news.

27: I said it's NOT murder, but. . . . [a photo of an embarrassed-looking 30 with one hand covering part of her face]

69: I'm working on a new post, so no more suspense-building: let's hear it. This blog doesn't run itself.

27: Where's 17?

44: She's probably in pre-calc.

69: School has never stopped her from texting before. But, oh, that's the strict teacher, right?

39: Come on! Silent reading is almost over and I've got two kids rolling around on the rug. I have like 30 seconds, tops.

27: Ok! It's this: 30 has a DATE! With a client!

69: OMG.

39: Is that, like, ethical?

MAKING FRIENDS CAN BE MURDER

30: It's fine. And, there's something cool about him I'm going to tell you at the next meeting.

44: Not now? And also, photo.

30: It's a first date! I haven't taken any pics of him yet.

39: Have you heard of google? What's his name.

30: No.

69: Not even a surreptitious photo while he's like, pumping iron? Come on!

39: What are you going to do for your date? Last question . . . my usual suspect just took his shirt off.

27: What kind of classroom are you running over there?

44: Not an easy job. What's the date?

30: It's a run.

39: Oh, barf. It's exercise???? FR????? Ok, gtg. Send pics.

69: When Ginny and I started dating, we'd do normal things like go to a restaurant or a museum.

30: Maybe we'll do that someday!!!!

27: Guys, she's totally blushing.

17: Wait! You're texting during the school day? Without me?

CHAPTER FOURTEEN

April 26, 2023

"I can't believe I had to ask again," Twenty-Seven gushed over the phone. "Thank you *so* much."

"Of course!" Sarah bit off a hunk of protein bar.

"You're sure you have time over your lunch break to pick up the package?"

"Totally." Sarah held the phone between her ear and her shoulder and jotted a reminder in her notebook. "It's only two miles from here." She wanted to ask what was in the package, but it seemed insensitive to pry, what with the funeral that morning.

"I know it's a weird request," Twenty-Seven said, "but it worked last time. I really appreciate it."

"No, it makes sense. And I hope you're okay." Sarah winced. It was a stupid thing to say. Of course her friend wasn't okay. The murder case hadn't been solved; the police had no evidence except the fact that Twenty-Seven was the last to be seen with the dead woman. And now she had to support two teenagers as they mourned the violent death of their mother.

"It's so heartbreaking," Twenty-Seven said. "I hate to admit it, but it's hard for me to even look at Ruby and Lula, thinking about their future."

"They'll be okay." They wouldn't be, Sarah knew, not completely.

Sarah had stashed some high-energy crystals in her pockets in the girls' honor that day, hunks of amethyst, rose quartz, and amazonite. She felt them clicking together as she picked up the package for Twenty-Seven. Sarah felt like she was channeling George when she sauntered through the doors of the UPS Store, doing a little something spy-like. Although maybe the comparison to George wasn't quite right. He was solving crimes, and she was committing one. *Is it a crime to pick up someone else's package?* It certainly seemed like fraud. She thought about texting George to ask, but decided against it. He'd perhaps feel compelled to prosecute. It would be a bummer to have to cancel their first date because of an arrest.

Got it, Sarah texted Twenty-Seven after she'd stashed the heavy square box in the center console of her car. Felt like a secret agent or something.

You're the best. Twenty-Seven punctuated the text with a heart-kiss emoji. Let me know if I can return the favor!

Sarah wondered when she might need someone to pose as her, to retrieve something, to sign something. Her life wasn't that exciting.

When do you want to pick it up? Sarah asked.

Can I swing by this evening?

I'll be home by 6:45. Or, if you want it earlier, feel free to come by LifeSport. Sarah had a full docket of training appointments in the after-school hours, the busyness a Little Reminder from Mom that everything was actually okay in her new life.

That would be amazing, Twenty-Seven responded. I'll stop by on the way home from my research site. Twenty-Seven was assisting in some kind of school study, impacts of social-emotional interventions? Something like that.

Looking forward to seeing you later, Sarah typed. Hugs. Back at the office, she loaded the file on her three-thirty client. Sam was a fifty-two-year-old mother of three teenagers who wanted to beat her youngest in arm wrestling at the family's Labor Day picnic. Sarah had to do some specialized research in wrist strengthening.

Later, she sent Sam away with sore forearms and was nearly finished putting her four-thirty client through her single-leg Romanian deadlifts when she saw George near a treadmill. Sarah waved, a ripple of excitement zinging down her arm. George increased the speed on the treadmill and started jogging, his pecs straining the fabric of a 10K race T-shirt.

It wasn't until her third client, a marathoner in her sixties, hit the foam roller cooldown that George finally finished running, and Sarah simultaneously felt her phone buzz. I'm here, the message from Twenty-Seven read.

Be right there, she texted back. With only a slight detour around the step mills, she'd run into George on the way to the desk. As she strode toward him, she felt her pulse rev. George took a swig from his matte-black water bottle and grinned at her. Sarah's breath caught. If he were a cartoon character, a sparkle would have glinted off his canine tooth. "Hi," she breathed. "Were you doing the 5K pace reps I wrote for you? How were they?" She bit her lip and caught sight of Twenty-Seven over his shoulder.

"Good! But, I have to say, I felt a little demoralized by the skills of your senior citizen," George said. "With the back squats? What was that? Eighty pounds?"

"That woman is a state age-group half-marathon champion," Sarah admitted. "Come this way?" She tipped her head toward her desk, where Twenty-Seven waited. As he turned, his forearm brushed hers. "Did you leave work early?" Sarah asked. "You were here before five."

"Are you going to tell on me?" George asked.

"Nope," she said, "especially not since you were doing your workout. I've gotta support that kind of dedication. Plus"—she smiled at Twenty-Seven as they approached—"doesn't your job, like, require fitness?"

"That it does." He noticed Twenty-Seven waiting for them. "I'm sorry"—he lowered his voice—"am I making you late for another session?"

"Not at all." Twenty-Seven was dressed in ripped jeans and a coral-colored V-neck. Casual, for a research site visit. "This is a friend. It's Twenty-Seven. Sarah. My best friend. In Minnesota, I mean."

But Twenty-Seven had quickly become her best friend, period. It had been the intensity of not knowing anyone else in town plus the excitement of meeting someone just perfectly aligned with her way of being, not to mention her name. *Fate*.

"Sarah!" she said to Twenty-Seven. "This is perfect timing!"

Twenty-Seven raised her eyebrows in acknowledgment of George.

Sarah gave the subtlest nod and mouthed, "I know, right?" She almost giggled. This was the best coincidence. Sarah couldn't wait to talk later with Twenty-Seven about George's objective hotness. Brian had been handsome, too, but in a skinny, nerdy way. He didn't stop anyone in their tracks. George's abs, on the other hand, which Sarah had seen once or twice while they worked out, just might.

"This is George." Sarah introduced them. "A client."

Twenty-Seven stuck out her hand, the nails perfectly pink. "Nice to meet you," she said. "I'm Sarah."

"Is this one of the others?" George seemed delighted.

"A Sarah Jones, yes." Sarah opened her desk drawer and grabbed the package. She wouldn't say anything about the errand. No need to actually test the legality of the pickup. She handed it across the desk.

"You're a lifesaver," Twenty-Seven said. "And," she tipped her chin down, "are we famous? He knows about The Sarah Jones Project?"

George piped in. "I was here when the news of the Sarah Jones murder broke."

"My grandmother called," Sarah said, "thinking I was dead. And," she said to George, "this Sarah—we call her Twenty-Seven—is the one who knew the kids." Twenty-Seven's face fell, the sparkle immediately out of her eyes. "Knows," Sarah corrected. "Sorry. That was insensitive." She felt dizzy, interspersing banter with sympathy.

"You're the nanny." George's mouth gaped a little. "Can I give you my card?" He felt the pockets of his workout shorts, but they were empty.

"George is investigating the murder," Sarah said to Twenty-Seven. She'd planned to tell the whole group about George's job at the meeting that week. She'd deliberately kept it off the group chat, wanting especially to see Sixty-Nine's face when she uttered the syllables F-B-I. But now, her two worlds were colliding right in front of her. "He's FBI," Sarah said. "Isn't that crazy? I planned to tell you all on Mon—"

But before she could finish, Twenty-Seven had taken several steps backward. "Thanks again for this." She held up the package. "And," she looked at George over her shoulder, "it was nice to meet you."

CHAPTER FIFTEEN

April 28, 2023

"News," George said to Vance during their two-minute daily check-in. "I met Gabriella Johnson in person."

"Oh, excellent." Her tone was flat, but Vance was stingy with praise. "Excellent" thrilled him.

"There was a package," George said. "Sarah the trainer gave it to her."

"A package?" Vance curled a lip. "And you didn't find out what was in it?"

"No. It wasn't the moment to ask." The only choice had been to play it cool. George continued, "Our Sarah introduced Gabriella to me as Sarah, too. One of the Sarah Joneses."

"Excellent," Vance said. That was two "excellents" in one check-in. "And how did Gabriella react to that? To you? Did you give her your card? She's talked to the police, but we'll need to talk to her as well."

"I did, but she retreated"—George frowned—"as soon as Sarah told her I was investigating the murder."

"You shared your affiliation?"

"Yep," George confirmed. "I told Sarah I was FBI at our last session. You were right." He smiled. "She was fascinated."

Vance rolled her eyes and looked back at her terminal. Her collar was crisp, but her nails were chewed and her cuticles raw. "Use that ignorance, Nightingale," Vance said. "As soon as people find out that being an FBI agent means working ridiculous and unpredictable hours and generally feeling like a giant failure for not fixing everything, they're less enamored."

George shrugged. "I'm already a giant failure for not taking over the Nightingale family business."

It was the first personal revelation he'd made to his supervisor. She gave him a sidelong glance but didn't bite. George was grateful. He hadn't premeditated the divulgence. "Do you have another personal training session scheduled?" she asked.

"I asked Sarah to go for a run." It had been a bold move. But he knew from experience that inaction could be at least as dangerous as impulsivity. He'd sat next to Henry's empty desk for those last months of fifth grade without doing anything to find him. It was like everything he *could* do—play baseball, get good grades, eventually graduate from an Ivy League—was swallowed up by not being able to go back to the day Henry disappeared. George could still feel his fingers flex around the handlebars of his bike, remembered pulling his green hoodie over his head and lending it to his friend.

Vance frowned for a second. "Date? Or training session with Sarah?"

"That's exactly what she asked." George peered at the picture of Vance and her partner she'd tacked to the wall behind her terminal. They wore matching hot-pink T-shirts and stood in front of Cinderella Castle at Disney World, their kids in front of them. He couldn't picture his boss on Space Mountain or posing with Mickey.

"And what did you say?" Vance was a master interrogator: utterly calm, nonjudgmental. In fact, she gave George the impression that she was only half listening. Later, though, if she'd wanted to,

Vance could provide a full transcript of their conversation. She'd shown him these records of other chats, with police or witnesses.

"I hesitated," George admitted, "and then she said 'date.'" It was factual. George didn't need to tell her about the butterflies in his stomach.

"It's ambitious, Nightingale." Vance breathed out. "In general, we don't date our informants."

George pictured Sarah's swinging ponytail, her easy smile, her fluid push-ups. He hadn't dated anyone since college, really. It had seemed more important to focus on the future of Birdsong, and then, for the past two years, on the bureau. "So . . ." George shifted his weight from his left hip to his right. He'd cancel if she said to.

"Go ahead," Vance said, "but"—she turned toward him, and he felt exposed by the clarity of her brown eyes—"don't let it get serious. And now, since the funeral is over, let's go back to the Campbell Joneses this afternoon. The police have talked to Aunt Gretchen twice. The sisters had a contentious relationship with her, but Gretchen has an alibi. We've got to follow up on that, too."

"We could compel Gabriella Johnson to sit down with us," George offered.

"We need all of the evidence lined up first. She's a flight risk, obviously. I'm guessing she's still in town in part because of whatever's in the packages, and then maybe she's got another target in the Sarah Jones group. It's your job to cross all those t's."

He walked back toward his own station with, in spite of himself, a little spring in his step. The case had turned into an important one. Vance wouldn't trust him with it unless he was doing good work. He wasn't one for overcelebration, but George had a sanctioned date with Sarah Jones, a Gabriella Johnson sighting, a second interrogation with Caden Campbell, and, in—he checked his watch—four minutes, a call with Andrew O'Neill. It was a good day at the office, even if he had omitted the O'Neill appointment from his check-in with Vance. It was an informal chat, he told himself. And it wasn't as if he could admit that he planned to pry into the most public and embarrassing cold case the field office had ever handled. Vance wouldn't find that to be "excellent."

George held his phone until the time flipped to the exact minute he said he'd call his friend's father, and then dialed. Before it even rang once, Andrew picked up.

"Is this your office phone?" the man asked.

"No," George said. "I'm in the office, but I'm on my cell."

"Fair." George wasn't sure what Andrew meant. There was a pause, and George could hear him breathing.

"What can I do for you?" George's cheer drained away. Andrew's grief oozed off him like sludge. People said parents never got over losing a child.

"You have no idea how long I've waited to have someone on the inside," Andrew said. "To be honest, I never pictured you as an investigator."

George felt his shoulders tense. He wouldn't describe his relationship with the man as close. He saw Andrew once a year at the Henry's Hope 10K, and sometimes at the anniversaries of the disappearance. There were vigils. At the beginning, those had been cathartic, and then later, a burden. He held the requisite candles, the wax dripping first on the paper shields slid over the tapers' ends, and then, when Andrew's speeches went into their eighth or ninth minute, onto the pad of his thumb. "My parents and I always assumed I'd take over at Birdsong," George said.

"People have to go their own way." Andrew coughed. "And Henry would have liked this. It's a childhood fantasy, you know? Police? FBI?"

"Did Henry ever talk about what he wanted to be when he grew up?" George slumped a little. It wasn't what Vance would have asked. He didn't sound like someone who could crack a twenty-two-year-old mystery.

"He did talk about that." Andrew laughed, a welcome levity. "Last I heard, he was torn between a fireman and a zookeeper." Henry had drawn penguins and lions in the margins of his math worksheets at school. Zookeeper checked out. George flipped to a clean page in his steno pad and wrote "zookeeper" at the top. "Believe it or not," Andrew continued, "he never wanted to go into dentistry."

Andrew had his own dental practice, Smiles by O'Neill, the irony of the cartoony grin on the sign painful for the whole town.

"I can picture Henry in the lion's den," George said, and then second-guessed himself, hoping the image didn't conjure the kidnapper.

Andrew didn't seem rattled. Like George, he must have spent part of every day imagining that attacker. "I've pictured Henry in a khaki outfit and a sort of safari hard hat many times. But, you know, he probably would have changed his mind."

"Probably," George agreed. "I mean, I did." George felt his phone pulse against his cheek with an incoming text. He didn't check. "It's always nice to talk to you, Mr. O'Neill, but is there something specific you were hoping I could do for you?"

"There is." The definitive statement made George nervous. He couldn't deliver anything specific. "I've been over all the evidence that I can get, including a few files I'm not supposed to have. I don't want to go too far into it, but when Haverford retired, he handed over some records." Haverford had said in a well-publicized, and ill-advised, interview that his biggest regret in his forty-year career was not solving Henry's case. "And I'm sure—" Andrew continued, "and between us, Haverford agrees—that the trail goes cold in the Birdsong woods."

"What?"

They hadn't discussed it afterward, but the Birdsong woods, his family's land, had only been searched during that one week, the initial days after Henry was taken. The publicized theory had been that Henry had been put in a boat. George always imagined him on the point to the west of camp, the green hoodie ripped and his face streaked with dirt.

"We can't search the woods again without a warrant," Andrew said.

"What?" He'd never heard about a warrant. George tried to imagine losing a child, what would stop him from searching wherever he wanted to, wherever his intuition told him to go.

"Did you ask my parents?" The Birdsong woods were theirs and George's grandfather's. If Henry's dad had called the office to ask for permission, George hadn't realized it.

"The Nightingale family has been reluctant to provide continued access."

"That surprises me." George tapped his index finger on his desk. Could his dad have been thinking about the preservation of the natural habitat? Disruption of the summer program? There were liability concerns, of course, involved in keeping camp kids safe.

But what about Henry?

George's phone pulsed again. "Can I send you this case material?" Andrew asked. "The files Haverford procured?"

"Yes." It was the only answer.

"Do you have a personal email?"

"I do." George recited the address.

"It's on its way," Andrew said. "Will you call me when you've had time to review it?"

"I will. And Mr. O'Neill," George said, "thanks for reaching out. I think of you all the time." George blinked at his desk. He felt his voice thicken on the last word, and though, in general, tears didn't scare him, he wasn't sure that special agents generally cried in their cubes.

"That's why I'm calling you," Andrew said. "I know you've never forgotten."

George would look at the files when he got home, sometime between his run and his before-bed IPA. He'd already read every official report and every article he'd ever found.

"I'll be in touch." When they'd hung up, George checked his texts and, in spite of the stress, smiled when he saw the messages were from Sarah.

Looking forward to tomorrow! she wrote. And, just an FYI, I don't want to run faster than 8min miles, so we can for sure talk.

George would be happy to take it easy.

Her second text read, I have so many questions for you about Fed chairwoman Sarah Jones, so buckle up. This one made George tense his shoulders again. There was only so much he could say, and also, he was the one who was supposed to be asking questions.

HENRY O'NEILL CASE FILE

Crow Wing County Sheriff's Office Interview with George Nightingale, Age Ten

Investigators Present: Deputy Stephanie Granger and Deputy Theresa Conaty
Also Present: Sylvia Nightingale, Mother of the Minor Witness

April 16, 2001

Stephanie Granger: Are you comfortable, George?
George Nightingale: What?
SG: Warm enough? Do you need anything to eat or drink? I know you've got your mom here next to you. That's good, right?
GN: Good?
Theresa Conaty: George, we're going to ask you some questions about your afternoon with Henry, okay?
GN: Okay. I have to do this, right? If I do it, will you find him?
SG: We're going to work together to find him. The more information you can give us, the easier it will be for us to bring him back.
GN: Okay.
SG: Thanks, George. Let's go back to the afternoon. You and Henry left school together. Is that right?
GN: We rode bikes to the park. We had money for a blue Icee. Well, it could have been any color Icee. It's just, Henry likes blue.
SG: Who gave you the money for the Icees?
GN: I had it in my savings jar. Like, from my allowance.

MAKING FRIENDS CAN BE MURDER

SG: And you were going to share with Henry?

GN: It would have been pretty mean, don't you think? To get one only for myself? It's not like they cost that much. Seventy-nine cents for any size.

TC: I bet you got the big ones, didn't you?

GN: Yes. That's okay, isn't it, Mom?

SG: She's nodding yes. Of course, that's okay. So, when you and Henry were riding bikes, did you see anything unusual?

GN: No.

SG: No people that seemed different? Anyone different in the gas station?

GN: There was a guy in a baseball hat. He seemed mad he had to wait for us. Henry couldn't click on the top of the cup, you know? I had to help him.

SG: This guy, did he say something to you? Theresa, note that for a follow-up with the Holiday store attendant.

GN: He said, like, "Hurry," and then maybe something else? We tried to hurry.

SG: Did you see that guy later?

GN: No.

SG: Did you notice what kind of car he had?

GN: No. I'm sorry! I don't know!

TC: It's okay, George. Let's move on. Did you see anyone else?

GN: I didn't know all the people we saw, but we did see Principal Green from school.

SG: Oh really? Was she at the gas station?

GN: No, she came to the park.

SG: Was she alone?

GN: No, she was with her kid. She's in first grade.

SG: Okay. Good memory, George. And then, after you left the gas station, what did you do?

GN: After we drank the Icees, we rode around. We took the big hill on that street by the school.

TC: On 5th?

GN: Is that the street by the school? If you go down fast, your stomach feels like it's on a roller coaster.

SG: That sounds fun.

GN: It was okay, but then Henry fell.

SG: He fell off his bike?

GN: Yeah. He does that sometimes. He wants to be a good biker, but he's not.

TC: Are you a better biker?

GN: Most kids are better. I'm not trying to be mean.

TC: It's okay, George. You're doing really well.

GN: But you haven't found him yet!

TC: I'm going to give you a tissue, okay? Just a little more. [*Muffled negotiations with the parent*] Yep, Mrs. Nightingale, we know. Just a little more.

SG: So, after Henry fell, what did you do?

GN: I said we should ride to his house. It's not far from there. He lives in town, near the dentist's office. His dad is a dentist.

SG: Did Henry think that was a good idea? To go home?

GN: No. He wanted to, like, wipe the blood with a leaf, but he was crying, and I thought we should get a Band-Aid.

SG: Were Henry's parents there when you got to the house?

GN: Henry only has a dad. His mom died. Don't you know that? She died when he was born. Everyone knows that. He never met his mom.

TC: It's okay, George. Yes, Deputy Granger misspoke. We know about Henry's mom.

SG: Was Henry's dad there, then?

GN: Yeah.

SG: Was he worried about Henry's knee?

GN: He was kind of mad. Not that mad. But he said Henry shouldn't be falling now that he's almost in middle school.

TC: And then what happened?

GN: Then we got a Band-Aid and Dr. O'Neill said he'd drive me home.

SG: Did he put your bike in the back of the car?

GN: Yeah. He put Henry's bike in there, too. He said they could practice some hills by my house. We have some bike stuff—like obstacles and stuff? Because I live at a camp. And there's a big hill. Bigger than the one at school.

TC: That's right. Camp Birdsong. I went there when I was a kid for a school trip.

GN: Kids do that every year.

SG: Did you see anything on the way home?

GN: What do you mean? I know the way, the roads and stuff. I could even bike it if I had to, but my parents say I'm not old enough yet. There are crazy drivers.

SG: Your parents are smart. When you were driving with Dr. O'Neill, did you see anything out of the ordinary?

GN: Henry and I were looking at Pokémon in the back seat. [*crying*]

TC: What are these tears about, George?

GN: Henry . . . Henry really loves Pokémon.

SG: When you got to your house, what happened?

GN: I said I would help him practice, but Dr. O'Neill said it was okay, and then my mom said it was time for dinner anyway.

SG: And you didn't see anything else? No one? Nothing?

GN: I'm trying.

TC: I know, George. It's okay. Did you see anything?

GN: I remember Henry was wearing my sweatshirt still, but I let him take it. There was a little blood anyway, on the sleeve. From his knee. And then he biked down the road.

SG: And where was his dad?

GN: Behind a little bit, talking to my mom in the driveway.

SG: Did Henry turn back into camp? Like, where you keep the bike obstacles?

GN: [*crying*] I stopped looking.

TC: It's okay. Mrs. Nightingale, do you remember how long it was before Mr. O'Neill got in the truck?

Sylvia Nightingale: It couldn't have been more than five minutes. And then he drove down the road toward the bike trails.

SG: We'll interview you separately, so George can be finished for now.

GN: Is it true?

TC: Is what true, George?

GN: Am I the last one?

SG: What do you mean, kiddo?

GN: My sister says I'm the last one who saw Henry alive? Is that true?

TC: We hope not, George. We hope he's still alive.

CHAPTER SIXTEEN

April 29, 2023

Sarah lined up amethyst, moonstone, rose quartz, and smoky quartz on her dresser as she pawed through her pile of running tights. The most flattering were the black compression ones with a zipper pocket for her phone. The most striking were pink with an abstract flower print.

Black, she decided, for straightlaced FBI agent George. When she pictured an agent, it was navy, black, and those iconic bright-yellow letters on the backs of their rain slickers.

How did a nice guy like George end up in the FBI? And where did he keep his gun during their training sessions? She'd googled it and discovered that agents typically packed heat at all times. But if there'd been a firearm on his body, Sarah would have noticed. It wasn't like George came to LifeSport in baggy sweats.

Sarah added "Why the FBI?" to the list of topics she'd written on a sticky note and plunked on her dresser. Her first conversation-starter ideas had been pets and favorite ice cream flavors. But George's FBI origin story might be slightly more interesting.

In addition to planning ahead for scintillating conversation, Sarah had checked the weather sixteen or seventeen times in the last twenty-four hours. It looked like the NOAA, European, and

North American models had all settled around forty-four degrees and sunny. Not bad for running, but not great for being outside without a heavier jacket.

Sarah picked a newish light blue pullover and a pink ear band. They could end their run near the two-story converted-firehouse coffee shop just down the street from her apartment. There was a two-top on the second floor near a gas fireplace. She'd cruise through her memorized sticky note of topics and garner as much information as possible about the Fed Sarah murder investigation to report back to TSJP so they could follow up on any new leads. And then, when the conversation had run its course, she could offer to give George a ride home. He was running to meet her, covering all of the miles she'd prescribed for him that weekend.

At precisely seven minutes before their designated meeting time by the cherry-and-spoon sculpture, Sarah left her apartment. Her hands shook as she locked the door, and she compulsively opened it again, checking for who knows what. Her Garmin showed her heart rate at 120 beats per minute, typical only if she'd already warmed up with an easy mile.

Sarah understood her extra nervousness, as this was her first date in Minneapolis. And she hadn't dated anyone back in Vermont besides Brian. She and Brian hadn't really even had a first date. Lock-in night at Montgomery Junior High hardly counted, though they had swapped spit behind the second-floor stairwell. After that, it had always been Brian. She was thirty years old and hadn't even kissed anyone else. Her nerves nearly pulled Sarah back to her apartment door, but then she saw her mother in her mind's eye, her happy smile in that framed photo, her iconic love story. Sarah couldn't procure happiness like that if she wasn't brave like Ainsley had been.

As she ran toward the sculpture, Sarah wondered if she'd kiss George after the run. His mouth would taste like the mint she'd smelled on his breath during their sessions. Despite the cool temp, Sarah could already feel warmth in her cheeks when she crossed the intersection in front of the sculpture garden. The place was mostly empty on this cool morning. For a second, she wondered what she'd do if George stood her up. He wouldn't, would he? He was in the FBI, for goodness' sake, and therefore a serious and reliable person.

Before she could give it a second thought, she saw him loping in front of the giant cobalt rooster sculpture. It hadn't been there in her mother's day, though the garden had. Things changed, Sarah knew, which was all the more reason to seize every moment. She hadn't been doing that in Vermont.

Sarah waved as she ran toward George.

"Look at that!" George said when he got close. "We timed it perfectly. I was worried."

"I realized we didn't think about the coffee when we made this plan." Sarah wasn't sure how to broach her idea of driving him home.

"Yeah," George said. "I thought of that on the way over. I figured I could Uber if my stomach got too sloshy. Or—"

Sarah giggled. "Or, I could drive you."

"I thought of that, too."

Sarah pointed toward the bike path that led to the Mississippi River. They'd run in the direction of the bridge under which Fed Sarah was found. Sure, it gave the date a bit of the macabre, but also, the other Sarahs would expect her to take advantage of the situation.

"On our way to the River Road?" George asked.

"Minneapolis really does have the best places to run," Sarah said.

"I'd imagine that Vermont is picturesque for the marathoner?" They'd settled in next to each other, their strides in sync.

"It's hilly." The Minnesota Twins stadium rose before them, its scoreboard visible above the wall. "But it's nice to see city stuff."

"Are you a baseball fan?" George asked.

"Not really," said Sarah. "So slow."

"Seven innings too many for you?"

"It's nine, isn't it?"

George guffawed. "I can't believe I said that. I played Little League and everything. My dad is huge on the Twins. He listens to all the broadcasts on gigantic headphones while doing work around camp." He put his hands over both ears, showing the size.

"Camp?" Sarah planned to take a drive up to her mother's camp that summer, to look at the lake that had meant so much to her. She'd mapped it. It would take three hours, and there were charming rentals nearby. She could even take a boat on Lake Whitehook, retrace Ainsley's canoe trips based on her notebooks.

"We own a camp," George said. "Well, my parents do."

"You worked there?" She flashed on George in red lifeguard swim trunks, and then on George with a camp polo and cargo shorts. Sarah's entire frame of reference about summer camp was from movies. Her mom had always talked about sending her to sleepaway camp, but then she'd died. It had never seemed right for Sarah to leave for the summer again.

"For the most part, I was marina director," George said. "I pulled water-skiers and rescued canoes in the wind. Repaired windsurfing equipment. That kind of stuff. I still work there sometimes. My parents need me to put in the docks in a couple of weeks."

"You have time for that with your new job?"

"What is time anyway?" George mused, and Sarah laughed again.

"This is a dumb question, but do FBI agents work nine-to-five?" Sarah's watch beeped, showing a first-mile split of eight minutes and twenty-four seconds. Easy enough to talk. "Pace okay?" she asked.

"Good for me," George said. "And yeah, we work forty hours per week unless something big happens. Which is often. Otherwise, there are shifts. All that jazz."

"Does the Sarah Jones murder count as something big?"

"One hundred percent," George said. "I got named to the task force and everything." He seemed proud.

"Task force?" Sarah asked. "Sounds fancy."

"It just means we share information and coordinate tasks with the Minneapolis Police Department."

"Have you seen the transcript of my friend Twenty-Seven's interview with the police?" Sarah blurted. She held back from saying that she'd thought Twenty-Seven should have secured a lawyer.

"I have." Sarah tried to judge George's expression, but it appeared flat from the side.

"It's ridiculous, right?" Sarah asked. "Certainly she's not a suspect?"

"I'm not supposed to say a ton," said George.

"But I'm your official informant!" Grandma Ellie, who'd hooked Sarah on Agatha Christie as a kid, had been thrilled with the title. Sarah's father, the stalwart family physician, had been less enamored of her involvement in a law enforcement investigation. Sarah couldn't help feeling he was always a little disappointed in her. They'd planned for her to join his practice.

But then, her failure had been so swift in the physician internship. After she fainted the first time, she and Brian had brainstormed solutions. There'd been cognitive behavioral therapy, exposure therapy, repeated self-flagellation, and even hypnosis. But, in the end, everyone agreed: someone who couldn't remain conscious at the sight of blood couldn't actually complete medical school.

The personal training certification had taken only weeks, given her premed coursework in biology and physiology. She finished the master's in genomics as a consolation.

"You are a Confidential Human Source," George agreed, using official terminology. "It's in the paperwork and everything."

"So you can tell me what you thought of the interrogation. Was it an interrogation? What's the difference between that and an interview?"

"One seems friendlier?" George smiled.

"And what else do I get to know?" Sarah thought about the amazonite crystal on her dresser, good for luck and overall success. She could enjoy George and also make investigative progress.

"I'm thinking." George picked up his pace a little, squinting.

Sarah reviewed what she already knew. "Twenty-Seven and Fed Sarah had dinner as usual. That was a standing date."

"Fed Sarah," George repeated. "I like that."

"Better than Dead Sarah?"

"Indeed," George agreed. "Anyway, yes, they had dinner, but it was later than their usual dinner, which was interesting to the police. And"—he looked up at the cloudy sky, considering—"I will say that it does seem like your friend and the deceased were very close."

"You know what's weird?" Sarah blurted again. "I've heard that they were best friends a couple of times now, and I didn't know that. And I feel like Sarah and *I* are very good friends." She dug a fingernail into the pad of her gloved thumb and felt her cheeks warm. Her jealousy felt junior high, embarrassing like the lock-in with Brian. "How could your best friend have another best friend you didn't know about?"

The two of them approached the path next to the Mississippi and Sarah veered right. They'd see the Hennepin Avenue Bridge in just a couple of blocks. "Maybe there's stuff she doesn't tell you?" George's voice was soft.

Sarah knew Miranda rights from *Law & Order*. Anything you say can be used against you. The things she said now could be used against Twenty-Seven. That was the point, after all. Sarah was George's informant. She let a pause open as they both ran faster, and then she remembered her sticky note with conversation starters. This semiawkward moment was why she'd written those out.

"Soooo." She let her arm bump against his. "Let's go back. Why'd you join the FBI?"

"To solve the crimes." It was matter-of-fact, a prepared answer.

"Why?" she asked. Lots of people had the inclination to do something that matched an elementary school fantasy like becoming a police officer or a lion tamer. Not that many people actually did it.

"Something happened when I was a kid," George said, his cheeks flaring. "Um, this is kind of heavy?"

"I can do heavy." It was a benefit of having a dead parent. She had practice dealing with the worst.

"Okay." George took a couple of deeper breaths and rolled his shoulders. "When I was in fifth grade, my friend Henry was kidnapped."

"Holy shit! That's so traumatic!" Sarah slowed down, but found herself a few steps behind George right away, shocked.

"We can keep going," he said, but he pulled the pace back.

They were quiet for a beat while Sarah thought of a follow-up question. Just when she had it, George spoke again. "He's still missing, which means, well—"

"He's dead," Sarah said. "I'm sorry."

"Almost certainly," George acknowledged. "Probably within the first few hours. But no one knows for sure."

"Wait. This sounds familiar." Sarah had a vision of her mother at the dinner table—a taco, of all things, halfway to her mouth—talking about a missing child near her summer camp.

"It was national news," George said. "There have been literally thousands of tips over the twenty-two years since he's been gone. They go through the Minneapolis FBI field office."

The dinner memory of her mother was new, not one of the several that Sarah regularly replayed. She looked around it a little bit, to see what Ainsley was wearing. Sometimes, if she tried hard enough, she'd get the color of a sweater or a wisp of a hairstyle.

"Henry," Sarah said, after a moment.

"O'Neill, yes," George said.

"Was he riding his bike down a dirt road? With other kids?"

"Alone, but yeah. Dirt road." Sarah glanced over, but George looked calm. She could see a couple of freckles on his cheekbone above his stubble.

"Some women detectives?"

"Yes!" George did stop then. "How do you know that? The two county cops were women. They got skewered in the media when they didn't solve it."

"I can't believe I know this." Sarah readjusted her headband. "My mom said it happened just a half mile from the camp where she'd worked. She loved it there. I think it's the whole reason she loved Minnesota so much. I guess, if you think about it—"

"Wait! Your mom worked at Birdsong?"

That was a memory Sarah didn't have to work hard to access:

Ainsley in a holey Birdsong T-shirt at the breakfast table every weekend. The dot on the *i* in "Birdsong" was a nest with a tiny robin's head sticking up.

"You know it?"

George put a hand to his cheek. "That's my camp," he said. "That's the camp my family owns."

Text Messages between Sarah Elizabeth Jones and George Nightingale

April 29, 2023

Sarah: That was so fun. Thanks again.

George: I still can't believe your connection to Birdsong. I called my mom immediately.

Sarah: You did? In an official FBI capacity? 🙂

George: Yes. Purely professional, Jones.

Sarah: Well, I don't want to jeopardize my status as an official agent of the FBI.

George: You're not an official agent of the FBI.

Sarah: Says you.

George: Exactly. That's on the record.

Sarah: I think we both know the truth. That there's no way you could possibly be a successful agent of the FBI without your partner.

George: You're my informant.

Sarah: Your confidential human source. Do you have a partner?

George: I have a supervisor.

Sarah: When do I pick up my .45?

MAKING FRIENDS CAN BE MURDER

George: We will not be issuing you a firearm.

Sarah: Says you!

George: Okay.

Sarah: What are you doing now?

George: I'm having my before-bed IPA.

Sarah: Just one?

George: I prefer not to get in the habit of drinking alone. Seems bad for FBI business.

Sarah: Wish I were there, but I've got an early client.

George: Joyce the racewalker?

Sarah: Nope. It's a high school runner who wants to get swole before Algebra starts at 8.

George: Can I confess something?

Sarah: Is it about murder?

George: That's a negative, Ghost Rider.

Sarah: You're confusing me. Are we naval aviators or law enforcement?

George: National security.

Sarah: Oh, right. Well, anyway, what's your confession?

George: I chickened out in the car. I should have leaned in.

Sarah: #obviously

George: You could have taken over. It's on you, too.

Sarah: I guess we'll just have to see each other again in order to accomplish a kiss?

George: ASAP

CHAPTER SEVENTEEN

Video Transcript Recorded by Sarah Jones, Age Seventeen

May 29, 2023

It turns out Sister Mary Theresa wasn't super pumped about having the school attached to a murder investigation. "This is the end of the project," she said. No nonsense, as usual. She followed up with, "Sacred Heart is not getting involved in an ongoing criminal proceeding."

"So?" I asked, winking. "Does this mean I'm on my own?"

"It means we expect you to suspend the project. You've done your duty." She planned for those to be her last words on the matter, but I didn't let her off the hook so easily.

"It's murder, Sister," I said. "It's literally people's lives."

And that's when her face did the same thing I'd seen when she confiscated a vape pen from the second-floor bathroom. There was a grayness to her skin and a sharpness to her jaw. But I hadn't ever vaped in my whole life. Still haven't.

"Don't tell me about murder," Sister said.

"Okay?" I didn't understand. It's not like being a member of a contemplative religious order made you an expert on homicide.

Sister pulled her cross along its chain. "Have I ever told you what I did before I came to Sacred Heart?"

"You did something before you came to Sacred Heart?" Is it terrible to say it had never occurred to me that Sister had a life outside the convent?

"Well, I didn't spring from the forehead of the statue of Mary in the courtyard." Sister rolled her eyes and popped a cherry Starburst.

"Okay," I said. "Spill. What did you do?"

"People don't know this," Sister said, "and you're not that good with secrets."

I leaned forward, curious. "I'm different now," I said. And that was actually true.

Sister cleared her throat. "I was a police officer. A detective."

If I were in a cartoon at this point, my jaw would have hit the table. "Nuh-uh," I said.

"Indeed, I was." Sister lifted her chin, not making eye contact. "And here's what I know: murder is exciting unless you have to look at it up close. And I don't want that for you." She checked the clock on her desk. "In fact, I forbid it. No more TSJP. Not when we're talking about homicide."

I had a million questions, obviously, but Sister scribbled me a pass and held it out with finality.

"More later?" I asked, hopeful.

She didn't answer.

And then, though she was clearly serious, I went ahead and circumvented all of her wishes for me. Which is to say, I snuck around and lied and also conducted a massive Google search about Sister's police history. We'll get to that later.

Now, I'm going to tell you about the first of the illicit TSJP meetings. Forbidden by an actual conduit of the Holy Spirit, but also, still on my calendar.

Twenty-Seven was late, which was unusual. But Ruby was

there, a fact I regretted as soon as Sixty-Nine began explicating her suspicion of Ruby's dad. "In my research," she said, sounding official, "I went for the husband. Don't they always start there?"

By "they" she meant investigators. I'd thought of it, too, obviously. I'd looked it up on the Bureau of Justice Statistics website. A full 34 percent of female murder victims were killed by their intimate partners. Yes, that's a ridiculous and depressing number, and something my generation will definitely tackle. But for now, it's just a fact of the case.

"Ruby, you don't have to be part of this," I said, proud of my newfound ability to address emotions. I *had* learned something from TSJP.

"She's right," Sixty-Nine added. "That was insensitive of me to jump right in there without—what does your generation call it? A trigger warning?"

But Ruby was stone-cold. She shoved her entire cake pop in her mouth and let us watch while she chewed. And then she said, "I'm here to solve my mother's murder. She took a header from a bridge. I'm ready to delve into the darkness."

Ruby meant business.

"I appreciate that, sweetheart," Sixty-Nine said. "But, even so, your dad doesn't really seem like a murderer."

Thirty picked it up there and was partway through a detailed history of Caden Campbell's education, including the titles of several of his papers on the Old Testament, when Forty-Four pointed at the door. "There she is."

We owled toward the Starbucks entrance and watched Twenty-Seven lurch in. I can still see the walk. It wasn't her usual, which was quick and efficient, sometimes with a TV-perfect hair flip over her shoulder. It was, well, like Frankenstein's monster. Or how my mom heaved around the living room after she'd done an especially hard Zumba video.

We stared at her until Sixty-Nine stood from her chair. "Are you wasted, or do you have a load in your pants, or what?"

"I'm just late." Twenty-Seven's voice sounded different.

"Oh, she's totally drunk," Ruby said, crossing her legs. She's younger than I am, but even she knew. Then again, my experience with alcohol is pretty much limited to a couple of swallows of Mom's Chardonnay at dinner. The taste, to be honest, is not exactly appealing.

"You're blitzed," Sixty-Nine said as Twenty-Seven sat down in a chair and tipped her head toward the ceiling.

"It's not appropriate in front of your nanny charge!" Thirty-Nine pointed exaggeratedly at Ruby.

"It's not like I haven't seen it before," Ruby said. "She and my mom have guzzled wine in front of *The Bachelor*."

"You watched *The Bachelor* with her, too?" Thirty looked hurt.

Twenty-Seven ignored Thirty's question and burst into what's commonly known as an ugly cry. Her face smooshed up. Her cheeks pressed in against her nose, which spewed snot. "I have a reason," Twenty-Seven snuffled.

Ruby sipped her drink, as if this were all totally normal. Trauma must do weird stuff to people.

"Deep breath," Thirty cooed as she rubbed Twenty-Seven's back. Sixty-Nine sat close to them, one of her hands over Twenty-Seven's.

"Shhhh," Sixty-Nine said, a little spit projectile landing on the black table in front of her.

"What's going on?" Thirty-Nine whispered to Forty-Four. "Did I miss something?" I shook my head. This was all very sudden and more than a little bit alarming.

"It's okay," Thirty was saying.

But, I mean, was it? The woman had basically imploded. Where there used to be perfectly drawn eyeliner and spiffy outfits, we now had a puddle of saliva and a cloud of stench that I now know must have been booze.

"It's not okay," Twenty-Seven wailed. We were in the back room of the Starbucks as usual, but she was loud enough that patrons on the other side of the doorframe turned toward us.

"Shhhh," Sixty-Nine said, louder and more spittily.

"Nothing matters." Twenty-Seven dropped her head into her arms. "It doesn't matter if they hear me."

Thirty's hand went slowly up and down Twenty-Seven's back, the band of her sports watch sometimes catching on Twenty-Seven's sweater, at which point she lifted her wrist a little and kept rubbing in the same cadence.

"What are you talking about? Of course it matters." This was Forty-Four.

"He's dead." It was a wail again, and Twenty-Seven started to rock back and forth while keeping her forehead on the table.

"No," Ruby said, still not a trace of emotion. "*She's* dead. My mom was a she."

Everything was so awkward and terrible that I wished for a minute I had followed Sister's orders and canceled the meeting.

"Who's dead?" Thirty whispered.

"Oscar," Twenty-Seven said.

"Who?" Sixty-Nine asked.

"My brother."

The crying went on from there, but the bottom line was, the guy was dead. Ruby texted me while we sat there.

"This is super weird," she wrote. "And that's saying something."

I nodded at her aggressively, and the two of us let the adults take it from there.

I'd like to say that my hesitancy to get involved right then was a sign that I knew something wasn't quite right about Twenty-Seven's outburst. But it's easy to take credit in hindsight.

Text Messages between Sarah Elizabeth Jones (30) and Gabriella Johnson (27)

May 1, 2023

30: Please text as soon as you can.

27: I'm okay.

30: Oh, finally! I've been worried. You left the meeting hours ago.

27: I've been . . . well, just weeping really.

30: Can I come over? It would be easy. Or, you can come here? I'm not sure you should be alone.

27: I am alone.

30: But, you're not. I'm here. 🖤 🖤

27: I appreciate that.

30: What do you need? Food? Coffee? A cozy sweater? I've got all of that. Come over!

27: I'm in bed. I think I might fall asleep.

30: Don't take this the wrong way, but did you take something?

27: Whiskey. My brother's favorite.

30: No . . . Ambien or whatever? I want you to be okay. I don't know that much about drugs.

30: Sorry. That was insensitive.

27: I'll be okay. Can we talk tomorrow?

30: First thing? I'll text you.

27: I'll text you. ₂z^Z

CHAPTER EIGHTEEN

Gabriella Johnson

May 3, 2023

It took a while to find the trust fund.

There was a rhythm to this, Gabriella knew after so much trial and error. She started with warm hellos, then the little drop-ins. Then she relied on the fledgling-but-intense friendships. Sometimes, like with Grace Smith, the jackpot dropped in her lap, requiring nothing but time and good humor. Other times, the payday entailed a little more finessing, some sleuthing, a dose of luck, and a bit of her soul.

In Minneapolis, where she'd moved the previous fall, it seemed easier at first. She'd scored the nanny job. She'd found the necklace. But the mission—that was how she thought of it, like she was Tom Cruise in an action film—had gotten murky.

"I'm out," she'd written to Oscar after she'd sent the stolen necklace to her contact. "Close enough." He hadn't responded, which was unusual. There was typically a coded message, a hint of where he was headed next. But this time, nothing. Gabriella even rebooted the burner phone and shook it a little like their father used to do with the faulty television remote. She'd stay in Minneapolis until she heard from him.

And though she hadn't talked to him, she could still hear

Oscar's voice in her head. "There's another mark right in front of your face," he said. And he was right. Seventeen had convened the whole group of them. It seemed crazy not to join, as the chances of another mark in the group were high and she'd already adopted the identity. They could get the full amount they wanted without Gabriella needing to go to another city, to find another name. Sarah Jones was meant to be.

It was convenient that Gabriella could hear Oscar's voice, because without him she was on her own. It wasn't like she could go back to Annabeth. She'd trashed that friendship, just like she'd trashed ones with Grace and Catherine. She'd do it next with Sarah. Still, Annabeth had been the worst. Gabriella had wrenched her Camry onto the shoulder and sobbed on the drive from Chicago to Peoria after that first con, the money her friend had inherited from her grandmother ferreted away in an old, dormant account with Gabriella's father's name on it. She'd replayed Annabeth's startled and furious accusations over and over again.

How could she have done it?

It had been incremental, each betrayal damaging but not catastrophic—forty-dollar cash-back transactions at the grocery store, the lifted ATM card, the fives she'd slipped from Annabeth's pockets. Dozens of little things her best friend didn't notice until she finally did.

Gabriella hadn't done it on purpose, but when the choice had been Annabeth or Oscar, she really didn't have any options. In their childhood, Gabriella had preserved her safety over and over again by being the "better child." She'd amassed a longer and more impressive resume while Oscar concurrently failed math, while he'd gotten arrested for tagging some rando's garage with graffiti, while he'd washed out of college for the second time.

Gabriella had aced the test that was the Johnson family, making it to adulthood relatively unscathed. She hadn't done shit for her brother.

Instead, Oscar had taken the brunt of a brutal upbringing for both of them. And now? Now that he was really in trouble, she owed him more than ever. She was his only way out, and that was through Annabeth and Catherine and Grace and the Sarahs.

As she got dressed in joggers and a light pink sweatshirt, Gabriella replayed the grief scene she'd staged at The Sarah Jones Project meeting. It was a reprise, and it felt as true as ever. It was easy to tell people Oscar had died. He was always a hairsbreadth from it, and now it had been four weeks without any communication. The grief was accessible and liquid, right beneath whatever veneer she'd established. She wasn't a pathological liar.

Still, Gabriella felt a little guilty remembering the way the wholesome Sarah Joneses had eaten it up. Not that Sarah Elizabeth Jones from Vermont was the suspicious type. Befriending her was the easiest job ever. It had been the medical school failure, Gabriella surmised, that made her so approachable. Sarah Thirty wasn't living her first-choice life. She was a fitness trainer to stay-at-home moms, not a physician. She was always looking for a little glitter.

Gabriella was fantastic at sprinkling it. She'd been an expert at making people feel special since elementary school when she'd first needed an extra half sandwich at lunch or an invite to the cool roller-skating party. All those times when it would have been impossible to reciprocate.

On the Wednesday morning after she had poured out her grief about Oscar, Gabriella brought a pair of oat milk lattes to Sarah's apartment. They'd been texting almost constantly, Sarah asking questions about Oscar, sharing memes, and comparing favorite episodes of *New Girl*.

"Thanks for being my friend," Gabriella said, holding the latte for Sarah out in front of her like a shield.

"Are you kidding?" Sarah reached her arms around Gabriella and held her gently, trying not to spill the drinks. "You're helping me start over. I feel like our friendship is meant to be." Gabriella smiled into Sarah's shoulder. "Meant to be" was something Gabriella always provided.

Sarah led them both to her kitchen table. In the middle sat a small Chinese money plant in a bright-yellow pot and a rough hunk of green aventurine, both symbols of prosperity.

"I'm so sorry about your brother." Sarah squeezed Gabriella's forearm. "I know I've texted that, but I wanted to tell you in person again, too. It's horrible." Sarah let go. She was good at empathy. Most of them were, as they were all marked by loss. Grief was like lye. Barriers people built over the years dissolved a little bit under its potency, providing cracks through which Gabriella oozed.

"To be honest, the death has been coming for a while," Gabriella said. "Now, it's so final." She let her voice get thick at the end of the statement, but kept tears at bay. She needed to be okay *enough*, while also being sad, the perfect blend of relatable and fragile.

"I know what you mean. It keeps coming back." Sarah looked over her shoulder at her perfectly quirky bookshelves with the mix of crystals and novels and knickknacks. Gabriella could see the photo of Ainsley Jones there, the one with the sparkling smile.

"I thought maybe we could do something a little silly," Gabriella said, "to take my mind off things."

"Yes?" Sarah grinned.

Gabriella knew she would agree to the makeover. Sarah was just like Annabeth, the kind of person who said yes to new adventures—a cross-country move, a random group of Sarah Joneses to join, a new friend with a dead brother.

"I think you're going to love this." Gabriella unzipped her sling bag and removed an eye shadow palette. She pointed at the ottoman on which Sarah kept her tarot cards. Sarah sat in front of the tray, hands in lap.

"It's like a sleepover," Sarah said, eyeing the makeup. "Except, like a sleepover in the movies, not like the real sleepovers I attended."

Gabriella smoothed the glittery shadow onto Sarah's eyelid. "Hang on." She grabbed a charcoal pencil. "Look up." Sarah tilted her whole head back, her chin pointed straight at the plaster ceiling. Gabriella guffawed.

"What?" Sarah asked, her neck gooselike as she gazed skyward. "Can I look back?"

"Yes, weirdo." Gabriella had called Oscar that name when they'd been in middle school. Their mother had hated the moniker, but it made both kids laugh. "You need to look up with your eyeballs," she said to Sarah, "not your whole head."

"Oh." Sarah's giggles erupted, and Gabriella joined her. "I'm sorry," she said. "It's probably bad to laugh like this when you're in the middle of a grief bomb."

"This is exactly the vibe I was hoping for," Gabriella said. It was true. "Oscar suffered for such a long time. He and I hadn't seen each other in more than a year." That was true, too. This was what people didn't understand about her: she lived a mix of authenticity and hyperbole. It was mostly real, until she had to deviate.

"I'm sorry." Sarah put her hand on Gabriella's knee.

"It sucks." Gabriella shrugged and then smiled. "Now look up. Like, with your eyes." Sarah did it, and after one false start, Gabriella had executed a perfect casual liner. Sarah's blue eyes sparkled.

"I want to see," she said.

"Not yet." Gabriella reached an arm out to keep her from standing. "Mascara."

She slicked on two coats and then pointed down the hall. Sarah leapt up, a human golden retriever headed for what Gabriella knew to be an immaculate bathroom.

"Pretty, right?" Gabriella glided across the living room to the end table she'd clocked near the door, the repository for mail. It was the beginning of the month. She hoped there would be a statement.

"You did a cat eye!" Sarah exclaimed.

Gabriella snorted. "It's called 'kitten' because it's so small."

"Oh my gosh, I don't even look like myself!"

Gabriella flipped through an energy bill, a card from someone with spiky handwriting who lived in Vermont—the grandmother—and then the statement from Fidelity, already open. She folded that envelope and slipped it into her bag.

"How did you make it look special, but still sort of normal?" Sarah called from the bathroom. "Can you video yourself doing it next time?"

"Come out here," Gabriella said, "and we'll do a touch of bronzer."

"This is so lucky." Sarah jogged back to the ottoman. "I feel like a beauty friend was exactly what I needed."

A beauty friend was exactly what everyone needed. Gabriella had discovered this ages ago, when she first consulted on Annabeth's beach waves. She'd been perfect and adaptable ever since.

"Especially since you have the adorable FBI guy?" Gabriella had initially panicked about that development. But trying to leave in the middle of the homicide investigation would only make her look worse and invite chase. And, this could be the last chapter in repaying Oscar's debt for good. If she stayed the course, it would finally end. One more time. One more evasion.

"He's a client," Sarah said. "But we almost kissed!"

"You sound like you're in junior high." Gabriella giggled.

"I feel like I'm in junior high," Sarah agreed. Her freckled cheeks went pink.

Later, after they'd had lattes and Gabriella had cried a little more about Oscar, she finally went back to her empty rental. She unsheathed the Fidelity statement and puffed her chest when she saw it: a lump sum from the dead mother. Families did this sometimes. They bypassed the living spouse and put any life insurance funds directly aside for children. As Sarah was the only living child, she'd likely been the sole beneficiary. And it was all in there: enough for Oscar, enough for the end.

It didn't appear that Sarah had even touched the fund. Maybe she would have for medical school, but Gabriella knew how that plan had turned out.

The bottom line was $865,000.

Eight hundred and sixty-five thousand dollars.

Gabriella pictured Oscar's shaggy hair, his dingy mattress in the corner of the last shitty apartment she'd seen, the hollow eyes. She saw her father's hairy knuckles, red as they gripped Oscar's forearm. This money would end it. Oscar had supposedly been clean for months; he could pay his debt, buy a new identity, and move somewhere warm and safe. The money would do the same for her; it could erase her past.

Gabriella reached under the couch for the flat box she kept

there, a few fashion magazines on top of a burner phone she replaced every couple of months. I've got it, she typed to her brother. She waited, but there was nothing. We're so close. It's almost all over.

And the moment she was about to collapse again in relief against the back of her camp chair, she saw Dead Sarah's crumpled form. She bit her lip so hard she tasted blood.

If only, she thought, as she did most days. If only she could go back.

Group Chat of The Sarah Jones Project

May 4, 2023

30: I don't think we should keep murder-related secrets.

69: It's 5:47am.

30: I can't sleep, and I didn't want to keep it anymore. The last meeting came off the rails a little with 27's brother 🤍, and I meant to tell you.

39: Coffee and Wordle. I'm ready.

30: Ok, so you know my date 27 texted you about the other day? The client?

69: Would not forget that. My whole life is basically vicarious. Devote several hours a day to a fictional detective and her iconic and highly treacherous fishing village.

39: But you do a good job writing about that show. I had totally forgotten about it before I met you.

69: I appreciate that.

44: OMG, HOW WAS THE DATE? I can't believe we didn't get to that!!!!

30: We were v busy. So this is what I have to tell you: George, my date, is in the FBI.

69: The FBI? Is that a real thing? Real people walking around on the street in Minneapolis are in the FBI?

30: That's what I said.

44: Omg, that's super sexy beyond BELIEF. Did he show you his gun? 🥒

39: Take it easy, there's a minor in this group chat.

69: She's sleeping.

30: Anyway, his office is investigating the murder. I told him we were investigating, too. He wants me to be his INFORMANT.

44: But maybe you don't want to tell him everything we know.

39: But we don't really know anything.

30: We do know that 27 didn't do it.

69: Let's not inflate our own importance here. We're a school project.

44: School projects rock! I've devoted my life to school projects!

69: Still, it's not like we're real crime solvers.

39: Neither is Jessica Fletcher, but she does it!

69: That's an excellent point.

30: Ok, that's the big news.

44: In addition to being law enforcement, was he insanely sexy?

30: Talk to you later. 😉

17: NEW RULES: No texting before 7am when I'm sleeping, and no texting during school hours! Come on, people.

CHAPTER NINETEEN

May 4, 2023

"So, update me on your Sarah," Vance said as she and George drove to the Campbell-Jones residence for take two.

George felt a flutter in his stomach, which he tamped down in the name of professionalism. "There's a bizarre coincidence," he said. "Sarah's late mother, Ainsley, was a counselor for three summers at Camp Birdsong in northern Minnesota. That's our camp."

"Huzzah!" George startled at her exclamation, but Vance kept her hands at ten and two, utterly calm, as if she hadn't just invoked Ren Faire speak. "Serendipity is so important in investigations like this one," she said. "It takes a little magic, right? To get the big break?"

"You sound like Sarah." Vance was the epitome of textbook, all dotted i's and crossed t's, whereas Sarah had drawn the High Priestess tarot card that morning and texted him the photo. Apparently the card meant he might have secrets, which he denied.

Vance gave him a self-satisfied glance. "Doing everything right—following protocol, filling out the paperwork, and minding the basics—that's what leads to the breaks. It feels like luck or magic, but it's the result of grunt work."

The same was true in his old life at Birdsong. George cleaned the cabins, repaired the equipment, tightened the fishing wire, and all of a sudden, kids gained confidence and made friends.

"You did a good job picking your Confidential Human Source," Vance said. "An inroad is the reward."

"I'm worried the personal trainer is also a target," George continued, "because she also has a deceased parent. That's the link, right? Inheritances?"

"Trainer Sarah has a dead parent?"

"Her mother." He'd found the obituary for Ainsley Montague Jones, who'd died from complications of pregnancy. The blurb listed a sister, too, the unborn child. "And Fed Sarah, too. Her mother died two years ago during Covid," he reported, "but there is no note about cause of death in her obituary. As far as I can tell, the burial was private."

"Do both Sarahs have wealthy fathers?"

"Personal trainer's is a family doc in rural Vermont. Fed Sarah has generational money on both sides."

"Trust funds?" Vance asked.

"Working on it." There'd be an account, or other assets like the missing necklace in the family photo from the Campbell-Jones living room, the one that had started the argument between the girls the last time the agents had been there.

"And has Sarah said anything salient about Gabriella? Any operable intel there?"

Sarah had dialed George the previous day on the way home from the gym.

"It's awful," she'd said about Gabriella's supposedly dead brother. After they hung up, George found an Oscar Johnson with a long criminal record filled with drug charges and misdemeanors. He worried Vance would lift the whole case, mostly solved, and hand it to narcotics.

"Yeah," George said as Vance zipped into a spot in front of the stately Tudor. "Gabriella mentioned a dead brother. Supposedly recently dead, but I couldn't find any verification of that."

"You could tell Sarah about the lie. Might flip her," Vance said. George had thought of this. He'd wait for the right moment, for a time when Sarah had a piece of information George really needed. This calculus contributed to a growing stone of guilt in his gut. Sarah's smile was so genuine, and he was using her. It made him nervous that he really liked her, too. What if he had to choose between the case and his feelings for her?

"Something else is bugging me," George said. Vance shoved the gear shift into park. "Why did Gabriella suddenly turn violent? I mean, assuming she's responsible for the Fed chair's death? Should we be worried about other targets?" *About Sarah.*

Vance thumped the steering wheel with the heels of her hands. "It's troubling," she agreed. "But we're not sure yet, and if Gabriella *is* the killer, then it was almost certainly in the heat of the moment." George knew those murderers were highly unlikely to reoffend. "Let's watch and wait," Vance continued. "And in the meantime, let's do this." She pointed at the house.

The door opened before they knocked, and there stood Lula again, the fourteen-year-old, and this time the cat ears on her headband were glittery and rainbow-colored. The whimsical accessory contrasted her hostile expression.

"Hi, Lula. I'm Jane Vance," Vance said. "And—"

"Yeah." Lula opened the door wider. "He's George Nightingale. I remember. Hard to forget a guy whose name belongs in a Dickens novel." George smiled at her. Very few eighth graders he'd met made mention of nineteenth-century British lit.

"I'm surprised you remember us." Vance slid past the teenager. "It's been a hard time."

Lula shrugged as she followed Vance back to the family room. "You're the first FBI agents I've ever met."

"Are we what you expected?" George asked, as Campbell came into view, sitting at a table near the dining room, his upper body rounded over his computer.

"I guess?" said Lula.

Vance cracked a smile. "FBI as glamorous as it seems on TV?"

"I never thought it was glamorous." Lula slouched toward her dad, her pink flip-flops thwacking against her feet.

Campbell stared at the screen. "I'll be right with you," he said.

"Working on something related to your wife?" Vance leaned toward the computer, but Campbell jerked it out of her sight line.

Lula sidled up next to George as he took his spot near the bookshelves where they'd seen the necklace photo. It had been moved, that photo. He scanned the living room.

"You're like the sentinel?" Lula whispered, though everyone could hear. "Is it your job to monitor? And are you looking for that picture?"

"What picture?" George glanced at Vance.

"The one with the necklace," Lula said. "My dad gave it to the insurance people. Right, Dad?"

"The necklace?" he asked. "Yes, I gave the photo to the adjuster. We have a policy." George studied the man's red-rimmed eyes, the bags beneath them more pronounced than they had been. "Is it important?"

"Not sure," Vance said. "But we have a few follow-ups for you, if you're willing."

Lula leaned into George and whispered again. "You guys are smarter than the Minneapolis police, right? Like FBI is a step up?"

"Not really?" he whispered back. "It's just different. We work with them."

"They seem dumber," Lula said, and George stifled a snort.

Vance kept her eyes on Campbell. "Can we talk about your wife's relationship with her sister?"

"Aunt Gretchen?" Lula scoffed. "Sorry," she muttered, "'relationship' is a stretch. They pretty much hated each other, especially since Gran died."

Vance peered at Campbell. "Have you been in touch with Gretchen?"

"Of course." He folded his hands over the top of his computer case. "And with Sarah's father, though he's out of it."

"An understatement," Lula whispered to George.

"Does your father-in-law understand what happened to Sarah?" Vance maintained a warm tone, sympathetic.

"He does in the moment," Campbell said, "and then he forgets again. I've only talked to him twice since . . ." he trailed off, and Vance waited. "Gretchen will be the point person now. For his care. Which makes sense."

"Is she a good caregiver?" Vance asked.

"I mean, he's in a home," Campbell began. "Both of the parents were in a nursing home."

Lula piped in. "Aunt Gretchen was always late and never knew the names of the nurses. It wasn't fair, was what Mom said." George knew a bit about unfairness. He put his hand in his pocket and felt the edges of Henry's Pokémon cards between his credit card and driver's license. George was here; Henry had been gone for more than twenty years.

"Did you go with your mom, Lula? To visit your grandparents?" Vance turned her body toward the girl.

"On Thursdays," Lula said. "When Ruby has cello."

"What are you talking about?" George felt Lula stiffen beside him as Ruby walked in, but he resisted the urge to look over, not wanting to insert himself in the charged sister energy. The girls were clearly fighting.

"We're talking about Grandpa," Campbell said, a sigh tacked on to the end of the admission. "Not really about you, Ruby. They"—he raised a hand and gestured at the agents—"were asking if Lula went to visit the home with Mom."

"And!" Lula rocked forward on her toes, almost shouting. "I said I did, or I do. On Thursdays." Ruby gritted her teeth.

"It's true," Campbell said. George couldn't read anyone's tone.

"Ruby"—Vance turned to the older sister—"did you want to visit your grandparents also? Is that what this is about? You seem angry."

"I did go visit them sometimes. At least, I was there the most important time," Ruby said. "The last time."

"Ruby," Campbell said. "Don't let your anger make this worse."

Ruby's face flamed. "Don't let my *anger* make it worse? How could I even do that? She's dead! My mother dove off a fucking bridge two weeks ago!" The air went still, but Ruby kept shouting. "Her head cracked open on the pavement, and then she *died*!"

Campbell collapsed in on himself, his forehead almost touching the computer keyboard. Lula, next to George, opened and closed her fists.

"She didn't dive off a bridge," Campbell's voice choked. "We've been over this."

Ruby drew up again in a second gust of anger. "Right!" Her syllable hit George in the chest. "It was"—she put both hands out now and wiggled her fingers as if casting a spell over something—"muuurrdder. And that group of Sarahs has, like, way more information on what happened that night than the stupid FBI does."

George and Vance made eye contact for a split second. Campbell crossed his arms over his chest. "I don't think it's healthy for you to go to those meetings."

"You're in TSJP?" George asked, off script. He'd known she'd messaged Seventeen, but Sarah hadn't told him she'd been at the meetings. *Why not?*

"You know about it?" Ruby asked.

"We do have Instagram," Vance allowed.

Lula's breath came in puffs. "Are you okay?" George whispered to her. He felt her head nod against his arm. She'd moved closer.

"This is difficult for you," Vance ventured. "And we'll get back to the Sarahs, but are you saying you don't think your mother was murdered? Do you think she—"

Ruby sparked again. "Took a header onto the sidewalk to avoid being my mother anymore? Or to screw Aunt Gretchen? Or to give double middle fingers to Dad? Or to frame our nanny? Do I think she did this to herself?"

Nobody moved. George felt his breath catch. In interrogation class, they were taught to love an outburst. The energy could shake something loose, knock free a secret, unknot a thread.

"Any details you have to share are important." Vance backed away from suicide. "Even little ones. Let's start with Aunt Gretchen. Your mom and your aunt had been arguing?"

"Understatement," said Lula, louder.

"They always had a contentious relationship," Campbell said. "They especially hadn't gotten along since, like Lula said, their mother died."

"Which was in . . ." Vance prompted, though she knew.

"In 2021," Campbell said. "Covid."

"It wasn't Covid," Ruby spat.

"Ruby." Campbell slid toward the edge of his chair.

"What do you think happened to your grandmother?" Vance trained her eyes on Ruby.

"I don't think—" Ruby raised both hands to her head and pulled a bit of hair from each side of her ponytail. "I know." She'd tipped from teenage sarcasm to something else, something close to collapse.

"What are you talking about?" Campbell stood, knocking a glass of water onto the table. Vance reached over and lifted the laptop, but he took it out of her hand, letting the water breach the lip of the table and stream onto the rug below.

"I'm tired of keeping her secret." Ruby pulled more hair. "She made us promise, but it didn't get us anything! It got her dead! She's dead!"

Vance remained placid, whereas George felt like he'd stuck a finger into a light socket.

They waited, and then Lula exploded, catching the energy from her sister. "Tell them!" she yelled at Ruby, her cheeks red. "Tell them!" Though she was talking to Ruby, Lula spun toward George and slammed both hands into his chest.

George lost his breath. He reached back to steady himself against the shelf, and his hand grazed his Glock.

"Ruby, what is this about?" Campbell was out of his chair now.

"You don't know anything, Dad." Ruby pulled more hair from her ponytail and started crying, a bubble of snot expanding and contracting at the base of her nostril. "How can it always be that you don't know anything?"

"What do you need to say?" Vance put a hand on Ruby's shoulder.

"Tell them!" Lula screeched. She dropped to her knees in front of George and her headband tipped forward. Campbell sank back onto the couch.

"Tell them," Lula whimpered.

The voltage receded, and Ruby spoke. "It was May 4, 2021," she began. "Exactly two years ago, which seems like a sign, actually. Mom went to visit her parents. It was a Thursday. I was supposed to have cello, but it got canceled."

"So, we both went." Lula walked toward the middle of the room. "We took our temperatures and did the screening. When it happened with Gran, we were supposed to be at the vending machines, but we didn't have enough change." She faltered, choking. "We came back. It was my idea to sneak up. To just be funny. To surprise her."

"What did you see?" Vance asked.

Ruby spoke. "We—I—I opened the door super quietly, and Mom didn't hear us, and she was—" She looked at her little sister.

"We saw the pillow over Gran's face," Lula said. "Mom didn't turn around."

"And then I closed the door because what else was I supposed to do?" Ruby sat on the floor, spent. "Lula and I waited in the hallway."

Lula looked at George, her glittery cat ears shining in the sunlight. "And then Grandma was dead," she said. "So, maybe we're not sure about my mom, but my grandmother's death was for sure a murder."

"Did you tell your mom what you'd seen when you came back?" Vance asked.

"Later," Ruby whispered. "At the funeral."

"At the reception," Lula clarified.

"She begged us not to tell anyone else." Ruby shrugged. "Can you imagine? A US Senate candidate who killed her own mother?"

"You're doing great," Vance said, her voice filled with sympathy. "This is hard, and you're doing great. Have you told anyone else?"

"Aunt Gretchen knows," said Lula. "She asked me. I didn't tell her exactly, but she knew already."

"Shit," Vance said when they got back in the car. "We're going to have to call the MPD about the grandmother. More for the task force. And we're going to have to talk to Aunt Gretchen ASAP."

George flashed on an image of Fed Sarah standing over a twitching elderly woman, her flexed fingers spread over the pillow as her mother gasped on cotton and goose down.

What would it feel like to actually kill someone?

He'd inadvertently skewered a squirrel at the archery range, the arrow pinning it to the ground a foot or two in front of the target. Blood had seeped from its mouth into the fur on its cheek. George hoped Henry O'Neill had died as quickly.

"What do you do about murder when the victim and the perpetrator are both dead?" George asked.

"It'll be up to the county attorney." Vance shrugged. "I don't think there will be any obstruction, though." She pulled out onto the road and flipped her sunglasses down. "Family privilege. They're allowed to keep quiet." George felt Lula's hands against his chest, the desperation before the kids expelled the information. Ruby and Lula had been carrying the secret of her grandmother's murder—the actual images of it—for two years.

When they were back at the office, George left Vance to the murder, and he took on the missing necklace. In order to cash in, Gabriella would need to sell it. He checked all the usual sites without any hits.

Big day at the Campbells, he texted Sarah. Has Ruby mentioned anything about her grandmother?

Sarah's reply came immediately. He glanced at his watch: 2:36.

She must not be with a client. No? The grandmother hasn't been part of it. Should I ask?

Better not, George said.

A drink after my last client? Sarah asked. 7:18ish?

He grinned at his phone. I can't possibly make it before 7:19, he wrote.

See you at the Block?

Done. He'd stay at the office until then, maybe dig through some files on the grandmother, review the transcripts from the initial interviews with Caden Campbell and Gretchen Jones.

Minneapolis Police Department Interview with Caden Campbell

Detectives Present: Alli Faricy and Mark Schmid

April 18, 2023

Alli Faricy: Thanks for sitting down with us. I know this is a shock.

Caden Campbell: I can't believe this is happening. It seems unreal.

AF: That's a common reaction to violent death. I'm very, very sorry. We're going to get some preliminary details taken care of, so we can proceed with our investigation. Does that sound okay?

CC: Anything to help.

AF: The girls will be okay with the nanny?

CC: They love the nanny.

AF: Let's start with any enemies you know of. Had Sarah fought with anyone? Had she received any threats?

CC: No, nothing like that. The usual office politics. People really liked Sarah, in general. She's always been easy to get along with.

AF: We're aware she considered a Senate campaign.

CC: Yeah. Early stages of that. Talks with party officials. But nothing had been decided. The election was—is—a year and half away still, and we hadn't agreed . . .

AF: Were you in favor of her Senate candidacy?

CC: What? What does that have to do . . .

AF: It's important for us to understand the full context.

CC: Of course, I was supportive. We've spent most of our marriage planning around her career.

AF: Some husbands might resent that.

CC: Resent is the wrong word. I'm a feminist. I have two daughters! I just—

AF: Yes?

CC: I just thought with the girls in their teen years, maybe we just didn't need the scrutiny a Senate run would bring into our lives. But that didn't have anything to do with last night. It couldn't have. We hadn't even really talked about it.

AF: Did you keep secrets from your wife, Mr. Campbell?

CC: What? No! That's not what I meant.

AF: What were you worried the scrutiny would uncover? Had either of you had an affair? Financial problems? I heard there was something questionable at UVA? Were you asked to leave?

CC: Did Gretchen tell you that? Of course she did. She doesn't know the whole story. Sarah knew. We were fine.

AF: I know these questions are sensitive, Mr. Campbell, but they're also critical.

CC: There's nothing. Nothing we were hiding—nothing I was hiding, anyway.

AF: Details will likely come out, and news outlets are already reporting. Now's a good time to share.

CC: Sarah and I don't have secrets. We're a normal married couple with normal married issues. But there's nothing I can think of.

AF: Based on our interview with the restaurant staff, it's looking like her blood alcohol is going to be elevated when toxicology comes back. Did your wife have an issue with drinking?

CC: She had a high-stress job. She coped. You know what? That's enough for now, I think. I need to be with my daughters.

AF: Your daughters and the nanny.

CC: Yes.

AF: We'll have to do this again. This is just the start.

CHAPTER TWENTY

May 4, 2023

Sarah, well-practiced in the maneuver, changed out of her sports bra and into a real one without removing her shirt, all in the parking lot of the Block. George had only seen her in athletic attire; it wouldn't kill her to show up in a top not specifically designed for sweat. Twenty-Seven would be proud that she also slicked on a coral shade of lip gloss. Sarah wished she could re-create Twenty-Seven's eyeliner, but there wasn't time for a YouTube tutorial. The whole point of this rendezvous with George had been a casual after-work drink. And maybe she'd score a little intel to share with TSJP at their next meeting. Sarah wasn't sure how Ruby's grandmother figured in, but she was important enough for George to text about.

In between that exchange and showing up for this date, she'd asked Twenty-Seven about the grandmother. George had said not to, but Sarah's loyalty was first to her friend.

Hey, she'd written, just tell me to back off if you don't want to think about this, but just in case you're up to it, do you know anything about Ruby's grandmother? Anything suspicious there?

??? Twenty-Seven had replied, an unusually short and cryptic response.

Just something George asked, Sarah said. Sorry. Insensitive.

Twenty-Seven wrote back, No, it's okay. She died during Covid. That's all I know.

Sarah gave the text a thumbs-up and changed the subject to her drink with George. Twenty-Seven responded with three pink double-heart emojis.

She and George ordered spicy margs and guacamole, and Sarah began with the shop talk. "Should we compare investigation notes?"

"I thought you'd never ask." George grabbed two chips.

"First, what's the deal with Fed Sarah's mother? That seemed important."

George wrinkled his nose. "The girls had some information about her death that they were upset about."

Sarah studied his face. He must have skills in deception, right? Or, like, covertness? That must have been part of his FBI training. Sarah tried to discern his tells. "Like, the death was suspicious?" she asked. "I heard it was Covid."

George sipped his drink. "So you asked?"

"Didn't we agree to help each other?" Sarah asked. "In an official capacity?"

"Um." George looked skyward and Sarah nearly melted at his adorableness. "I feel like what happened is that you agreed to help *me*. And the FBI. As a Confidential Human Source in an official investigation. I'm not sure I agreed to help the group of random Sarahs."

Sarah grinned. "Maybe that's my new band name." She scooped some guacamole, holding the loaded chip in front of her mouth. "A Group of Random Sarahs." She crunched, and then through the corner of her mouth said, "But I think you mean the multigenerational friends joined together for whimsical extravaganzas." Sarah giggled, knowing she hadn't captured the original phrasing quite right.

George laughed, too, and Sarah realized he didn't very often. It was deep and seemed to envelop his whole torso. "I don't think that's quite the description I read on the Instagram page."

He'd read the Instagram page. "So you're stalking us?"

"We call it 'due diligence' at the bureau," George said.

She rolled her eyes. "Anyway, the grandmother."

George tipped toward her and lowered his voice. Sarah matched him, their faces close enough to see that the brown of his eyes deepened toward the perimeter of his irises. "The Campbell girls think there could have been some foul play," he said. "But that's not consistent with the coroner's report."

"What did the coroner's report say?" Sarah whispered.

"Covid," George sat back, suddenly more serious.

"And what does the coroner's report say about Fed Sarah?"

"That's mostly classified," George said, "but the newspapers will report an elevated blood alcohol level. Over the legal limit. No street drugs." Before Sarah could follow up, the server arrived.

"Taco order?" Sarah asked, hoping she and George could turn their drink into dinner.

George nodded and added a second margarita.

"I assume you asked Twenty-Seven about the grandmother?" George asked.

"Yeah, but she didn't seem to know anything."

George shifted in his seat. "How's she doing?" he asked, not making eye contact. "You mentioned her brother died?"

Sarah shrugged, guilty again, for making Twenty-Seven's personal life FBI business, and also for enjoying herself while her friend grieved.

George blew out a breath.

"What?" Sarah asked.

"I'm deciding whether I should tell you something." By the set of his jaw and the way all traces of laughter evaporated, Sarah knew he'd already decided. How much of this whole date was calculated? The second margarita? The question about the grandmother? And now this apparent hesitation? She was good at reading people. You had to be, in her line of work.

"What is it?"

"Oh!" He startled, and it seemed genuine. "I forgot. I actually have two things! The first is kind of cool." He pulled his phone out of his pocket and his eyes sparkled in the low light.

"What?" Sarah snuck a glance at his screen, but he pulled it back and grinned.

"Wait one sec. I hope this is okay. It's a change of subject, to say the least." He tapped a few times on his screen and then handed the phone over.

Sarah recognized her mother's curly fly-aways first, and then the signature toothy grin. She'd thought she'd seen all the photos of Ainsley she'd ever get to, but here was a new one! "It's my mom." She smiled at him. "Where did you get this?"

"We have an extensive archive at Birdsong." Sarah zoomed in on her mother's rosy cheeks, the crinkles at the edges of her eyes, and then scrolled down. Ainsley wore her Camp Birdsong sweatshirt and held a floating canoe in place with a sandaled foot. Sarah could see the chipped pink polish on her big toe.

"She looks super happy."

"I hope it's okay I asked my parents about her." George looked sheepish. "They usually remember people, especially the multi-year counselors. My mom says Ainsley was on staff for two or three summers?"

"Three." Sarah touched George's forearm. "Thank you so much for checking," she said. "I love seeing a new photo. It's like a little piece of an investigative file, you know? A little thread I've never pursued."

"I get it," George said.

"You said you had two things," Sarah said. "Was the other one about Fed Sarah?"

"Yeah, but wait on that." George attempted a serious expression, but his dimple looked mischievous. "Let me finish the Birdsong intel." The server arrived with their drinks and tacos. George thanked him and continued. "My mom said Ainsley—is it okay if I call her that?"

Sarah nodded. "I've always loved her name."

"Beautiful," George agreed. "My mom said she was the first Ainsley she'd ever met."

"That makes sense. The name rose sharply in popularity in the 1990s, right around the time I was born."

"You do a lot of name research?"

"With a name like Sarah Jones, you get jealous of uncommon ones. When my Grandma Ellie chose Ainsley, there were only two of them per million US births. Ellie said she'd read it in a book as a man's name and had thought it sounded both magical and sturdy."

"That's lovely," George said.

It was. Ainsley had definitely been magical, and then not quite sturdy enough.

George opened the Notes app on his phone. "Okay, so my mom said Ainsley loved the camp marina."

"No doubt." Sarah licked salt from the rim of her glass.

"And she was good with the little kids," George continued. That checked out. Her mom had led Capture the Flag on the playground in their town. She'd chaperoned a school field trip to the Lake Champlain Nature Museum. If she'd lived until Sarah was in high school, theirs would have been the hangout house. People liked to be around Ainsley.

"She was definitely good with little kids," Sarah said. "But weren't all of the counselors?"

George shrugged. "Sometimes they're better with teenagers. And one more thing: my parents are pretty sure her whole cabin had lice. The nurse must have missed a case on arrival, and then, before they knew it"—he swirled a finger like a tornado—"full infestation." Sarah giggled.

"At least she thinks it was Ainsley," George said. "She did admit the lice might have been an Audrey from another year." Sarah picked up the oozing carne asada taco, crumbles of cotija dropping to her plate.

"I think she did have lice," Sarah said, her mouth half-full. "She checked me religiously when I was a kid. Said she was forever scarred by a past lice experience, so this must be it. Although my dad saw lice all the time in the clinic. I assume she checked him, too."

"He's a doctor?"

"Family medicine." Sarah thought about her old dream, the white coat. She'd wanted to be a doctor even before her mother died, but then afterward, it had seemed like a calling, helping people.

"And finally"—George tapped his phone with a flourish—"my mom said Ainsley had a memorable and ridiculous—that's my mom's word, not mine—affinity for Tater Tot hotdish."

"Oh, I *know* that's true." Sarah snorted. "There was a song she sang every time she made it."

"I know the song!" George hummed the tune, and Sarah saw her mom in the kitchen in Birkenstocks and baggy shorts. "Wait, she made the hotdish at home?" George asked. "It's a little disgusting for regular rotation."

"No kidding. With the ground beef and the condensed cream of mushroom?" Grandma Ellie had made it once after Ainsley died, and then they'd let it go, along with a vile something Ainsley had called Chunky Jell-O.

"Don't forget about the limp green beans in there!" George lifted his glass, as if toasting them.

"My dad hates green beans. Isn't that weird? So she served them on the side."

"That was accommodating."

Sarah smiled. "My mom was a really nice person." No one had ever contradicted that assessment. "You can tell, right?"

George opened the phone again and zoomed in on Ainsley's face, just as Sarah had before. "You can totally tell."

If they hadn't been sitting in the middle of a restaurant, Sarah would have leaned in for their first real kiss right then. She couldn't wait to text Twenty-Seven after their date. Even without kissing, they'd leveled up. "Oh," Sarah said, remembering, "you had something else to tell me. Case related?" She'd want to report that to her friend, too.

George nodded. He wiped his mouth with the back of his hand. "It's about Twenty-Seven."

"Hit me," Sarah said.

"I checked on the brother," George said.

"Oh! I got the impression Oscar's death was drug related?"

George shook his head. "Oscar, as far as we can tell, is not dead at all."

"What are you talking about?" Sarah felt a disorientation, not unlike the wooziness that came when she saw blood.

"I'm saying, Twenty-Seven has a brother. That part is true." George swallowed. "But he's not dead." He gripped his margarita. "She lied. Why would she lie to you?"

Text Messages between Sarah Elizabeth Jones and George Nightingale

May 4, 2023

Sarah: Sweet moves there, Nightingale. Mission accomplished.

George: Are you texting about our first kiss?

Sarah: Too weird?

George: Nah. You're good. I can do weird.

Sarah: So you ADMIT you think I'm weird.

George: In a really good way. I like your weird.

Sarah: And it's not like you're the most totally normal person in the world. You had pet ferrets growing up.

George: Ferrets aren't that weird.

Sarah: Beg to differ. I looked them up, and they pretty consistently rank fourth or fifth on lists of smelliest pets, near marmosets.

George: What's a marmoset?

Sarah: A monkey.

George: Ok. Well, I don't have pet ferrets or monkeys now.

Sarah: Thank god because I was hoping for a tour of your condo sometime soon.

George: We'll see what we can do.

CHAPTER TWENTY-ONE

Video Transcript Recorded by Sarah Jones, Age Seventeen

May 29, 2023

What I did next served only to drive a wedge between Thirty and me—and also at first between Ruby and me—even though I did it in good faith. Well, sort of good faith. I'm not claiming to be a saint. Though I'm hoping writing this account and recording these videos of it after the fact will help set the record all the way straight. That, and perhaps help spring the innocent Sarah Jones from the slammer.

Here's what happened: Thirty and I had ramped up our AP Bio tutoring in the week before the exam. I arrived at her apartment on the Sunday before the test to review photosynthesis. We didn't typically do Sundays, but the frequency of TSJP murder meetings had us scrambling for extra hours. And when I got there *George from the FBI* was sitting at Thirty's little Formica kitchen table. I'd never seen George in person before, and let me tell you, I got the appeal immediately. Dude is handsome. Wavy brown hair that falls onto his forehead, dark eyes, slightly crooked smile, broad shoulders. And here I was, too scrawny to be small forward on the Sacred Heart Phoenix basketball team.

"Don't worry, Sarah," he said when Thirty let me in. "I'm not going to interfere. I'm on my way out." He smiled, and yeah, once again I totally got it. It was like a promo for *The Bachelor* in there.

"You know me?" I have to admit, I was flattered.

"Duh," George said. "I've seen you on the TSJP Instagram." He grinned, and then he *complimented* me. The guy is suave. "I like what you're doing with that account."

I couldn't really speak as he left, but Thirty scooted past me to grab her spare copy of *Campbell Biology* and jostled me out of it. It was then that I noticed the perfume. In all the times I'd seen Thirty for tutoring or at TSJP meetings, I'd never detected a scent. It was light, not at all like my grandmother's musty floral crap. I tipped my head and stared at her, and that's when I also noticed the mascara, and I think some kind of natural-looking blush.

"You smell nice," I said, suspicious.

"Twenty-Seven gave me some perfume."

And I was jealous, okay? Thirty and Twenty-Seven were at the gift-giving phase. They probably lounged on each other's couches while discussing topics not related to AP Bio.

"Does she give you a lot of stuff?" I tried not to sound desperate.

"This was a thank-you for picking up another of her packages." She pointed toward the door, where a padded envelope sat on the end table. "Her mailbox situation really makes it difficult."

Twenty-Seven had mentioned this before, the fact that packages tended to disappear from her mail room.

"Have you told the FBI guy about the packages?" I asked, fishing.

Thirty sat down. "Pass me the master study guide," she said, dodging.

"Hmmm." I handed it over, the first couple pages covered with her pink gel-pen check marks. "So, that's a no." Thirty didn't bite and instead ran her pen down the list of topics in the photosynthesis section. I kept pressing. "Why couldn't Twenty-Seven pick up her own package this time?" I asked.

"Something about Ruby and Lula, I think?" Thirty flipped to some diagrams of organelles, arrows indicating mitochondria and glucose.

"Ruby didn't say anything to me about that." We weren't as close as Twenty-Seven and Thirty, but we exchanged a couple of snaps most days. "But you know what she did say? That her mom thought Twenty-Seven had stolen something."

"What?" Sarah asked.

"Jewelry," I whispered.

Thirty cocked her head. "Does Ruby think she did it?"

I rolled my eyes. Just like Thirty, Ruby thought Twenty-Seven walked on water. "No," I admitted.

Thirty shrugged. "Do you want to study or what? You're usually the taskmaster." That was true, mostly because I felt like my time with Thirty was so limited, and she was basically my last chance at a four on the AP exam. After a full year in the lab with Sister Angela, plus all those extra credit sessions, I felt I deserved it.

"I'm almost ready to study," I said, "but has Twenty-Seven said anything else about her brother?" I had started some internet research on Oscar. I couldn't find any Oscar Joneses that seemed like the right one. And I definitely hadn't found any obituaries. Suspicion was setting in. "How's she doing?"

"She hasn't said much." Thirty's voice was even, but a flash of something—frustration?—wrinkled her brow before she smoothed it again. She tapped the textbook. "But let's study. I feel responsible for your grade."

"One sec," I countered, pushing my luck. "What's in the package?" I pointed at the padded envelope.

Thirty put both hands flat on the description of light-dependent reactions. "You think I opened her private stuff? Isn't that like a felony?"

"Maybe not when you impersonated her to go get it? Isn't *that* a felony?"

She went to flip through the chapter again and the pad of her index finger caught on one of the shiny pages and sliced her skin. Classic paper cut. "Ow!" Thirty said. She immediately put her finger into her other palm and squeezed.

"Ouch," I echoed, standing. "Want me to get you a Band-Aid?"

"Um." She opened her palm, and I could see a smear of blood on both her finger and her other hand. "Oh, shit," she said, and then immediately slid to the floor. She put her head between her knees. Whatever technique this was, it was too little, too late, and she tipped over on her side in a faint.

That I recognized. Girls went down all the time in mass at school—pale faces, the sheen of sweat, the whole business. Thirty had mentioned fear of blood before. I didn't realize it was so extreme. I ran for the kitchen, the roll of paper towels. *Cold compress*, Sister Mary Theresa would say.

It was at the last second that I made a detour. I was headed back to Sarah with the damp cloth when I veered to the table by the door.

Okay, yes, I took the mysterious padded envelope and shoved it in my backpack.

It was snooping, for sure. It was an action born of jealousy and immaturity. But, it also cracked open the case. Before you go thinking I just totally *stole* the package, I didn't. While Thirty was waking up and after I'd wiped her hand and put on a Band-Aid, I took the envelope to the bathroom, peeled open the adhesive as unobtrusively as I could, took photos of each of the pages inside, and then did my best to reseal it.

Was it a perfect job? Absolutely not, but I returned it before Thirty was back at the table and sipping water. We dove into photosynthesis as if nothing had happened.

Group Chat of The Sarah Jones Project

May 10, 2023

30: 17, let us know how the AP exam went as soon as you finish!!!

17: It's over. No one cares except for you, though.

69: I care!

44: AP Bio is no joke. Proud of you.

17: Really?

44: Yeah, everyone always says it's the hardest AP.

39: Who's everyone?

44: I've just heard, okay?

30: Well? How did it go? Did all the work pay off?

17: You know what? I actually think I did okay. Maybe not a 5, but . . .

30: Passing is 3!

17: Sister says to aim high.

69: I love Sister Mary Theresa.

17: OMG, I can't believe I forgot to tell you this! But guess what I found out? Guess what Sister's job was in another life?

30: Like, she did something before the convent? Was she a personal trainer? 😂

17: NO. She was a POLICE DETECTIVE. Can you even imagine?

44: Wow. Have you asked her about our investigation?

17: Um. . . .

27: Are we all attaching ourselves to law enforcement now? 30 has the FBI, 69 has Jessica Fletcher, and now you have a policewoman turned prayer enthusiast?

17: Got a problem with that?

69: I feel like it seems like fate. We're gonna solve this! I'm sure of it!

30: ✌️ Good job on the test, Kid!

CHAPTER TWENTY-TWO

Gabriella Johnson

May 11, 2023

"You're so much nicer than I am," Gabriella said when Sarah agreed to carpool as long as they also picked up Seventeen for that evening's TSJP meeting.

It was true: Sarah Elizabeth Jones of Vermont was unquestionably nice. Also, she was genuine, curious, and optimistic, all convenient characteristics for a mark.

Sarah believed the best about people, even about Gabriella Johnson, her new best friend, Twenty-Seven.

"I'll be there at 6:37," Gabriella said. Sarah laughed at her precision and then hung up. Gabriella collapsed into her foldable camp chair, the kind grandparents hoofed to the sidelines of youth soccer games.

But not her grandparents and not to Oscar's games, at least not after he failed to make the cut for JV soccer during his sophomore year. He'd come home from the announcement with a tiny Ziploc of something slipped to him by a senior captain, and within a month or two, everything had changed.

Gabriella had trained herself not to think about where her brother was, on whose insect-infested mattress, in what needle-ridden apartment. The deposits into the bank account in their father's name were enough. In order to save him, Gabriella had altered her entire moral code.

It was enough, right? Would she hear from him soon?

The last time Gabriella had seen Oscar, his face had been jagged, his cheekbones like cliffs, and his jaw razor-sharp. A cut oozed next to his right eye, and a new scar jutted from his eyebrow, about a quarter of an inch from the one she'd given him with a Matchbox projectile in an elementary school rage. He'd compelled her to meet up that night at a dive near O'Hare to outline the crisis that later led her to Peoria, to Kansas City, and now to Minneapolis. The ice in their glasses had rattled as the planes flew overhead.

That evening had ended in a breathless panic and a loaded suitcase. Oscar needed money. He couldn't tell their mother, not that she'd be inclined to help him again, not after paying for rehab twice over. Gabriella hadn't been inclined to help, either.

But he'd said "please" with a desperation she'd never heard before. And Gabriella owed Oscar. And once he told her how much the drug people demanded, she knew exactly how much it would cost to make their childhood up to him. This was her tax for escaping their home, for pushing him into the line of fire when the top blew on their dad's moods. It was $250,000.

A quarter of a *million* dollars.

"I don't have—" she'd said that night. But Oscar had interrupted her by pushing his phone across the table. The photo showed Gabriella teaching in a blue gingham dress, the third graders sitting cross-legged on the rug in front of her. It had been taken the previous Wednesday by someone on the playground. The image hadn't made sense to her.

"How?" She enlarged it, stared at the profiles of her kids, their little chins pointed up at her.

"They know who you are," Oscar had said. "The people, they have guns. They said they'll shoot up your school."

Gabriella and her class had practiced the drills enough times, hiding in closets and barring the door. "Who are *they*?" she asked. Luke, the apple-cheeked kid who dripped sweat on his desktop after every recess, sat in the foreground of the photo. There'd been a gun within shooting distance of Luke? Of all of them?

"I did some dealing in the last year, okay? It's cartel people." She slid the phone back. "I think if I were dead, it might end it," her little brother said, his eyes clearer than they had been all night. "I'm willing to give that a shot. I can't be better, anyway. I keep screwing up. I'm everything Dad said I was—"

"No." Thank God Gabriella's voice held.

Now in her empty sublet, she needed to finish the whole thing. The money went into and out of the accounts she'd set up. And Sarah Elizabeth Jones was the very last one she'd have to con.

When they pulled into Seventeen's roundabout, the teenager frowned, unaccustomed to Gabriella's occupation of the passenger seat. "Sorry," Gabriella said when Seventeen got in the back. "I'm crashing your car pool."

"It's okay," Seventeen said. "We're all going to the same place, and anyway I can't wait for this." Her enthusiasm bubbled over. "I've been playing it cool, but my God! We have so much to talk about." Gabriella tensed. She'd hoped the Oscar revelation would distract them, at least for a little bit.

Thirty giggled. "Are you excited about my official relationship with the FBI?"

Gabriella turned toward the window. Some of the trees, just that week, had started to bud. "I can't believe you met someone in the FBI." Gabriella was surprised her level of fraud had reached the federal radar, but then again, George was a rookie agent.

"I know, right?" Thirty said. "But he found me because he wants to run a fast marathon, and now he thinks I can be helpful."

Gabriella hated to deflate her, but then again, Sarah was her last one. "Wait," she said. "When did he first meet you?"

"You sound suspicious," Thirty said. "But he joined the gym back in January. I'd seen him there a bunch of times before his first appointment. *That*," she added, "was on the morning after Fed Sarah's murder."

"So, what kind of information does he want?" Gabriella tried to keep her tone light. "Because last time I checked, they had almost nothing on the murder." She paused here, knowing the kid wouldn't be able to resist breaking in.

It only took a second. "Except they think it's you!" Seventeen said.

"But I could be helpful there," Thirty said. "Since we know it's not you."

"Seems a little risky," Gabriella said. "People have a way of twisting things."

"Do they?" Seventeen asked as Thirty turned in to the Starbucks parking lot. "I was going to ask you, actually, about the necklace? Ruby mentioned a missing necklace the FBI was interested in? She said the police think you stole it, but she doesn't believe them."

"Necklace?" Gabriella echoed. The photo of her wearing the necklace, the one in which she wore little else, the one she'd sent to Caden Campbell, flashed in her mind's eye, as did his reply. She'd saved his photo, obviously, as insurance, but now?

Maybe Campbell would decide that rumors of infidelity were nothing compared to the gravity of a dead wife?

No, Gabriella thought. He wouldn't. Not over the necklace.

Thirty thousand dollars was nothing for a family like the Campbell-Joneses. It wouldn't make a single difference in their everyday lives.

"I've read a bunch of articles now," Seventeen continued, as Thirty pulled into her usual parking spot. "The police are under pressure because they haven't solved it." Seventeen was so different from Ruby, so much more industrious. So much... weirder. "I've perused basically the entire FBI website," Seventeen said, words spewing rapid-fire. "I've listened to podcasts. I think I've figured out as much as it's possible to figure out as an outsider. And I'm not even supposed to—"

She swallowed the sentence. Whatever she'd been about to say, she wanted to keep private. Gabriella grabbed at the dangling thread.

"What?" she prompted. "What aren't you supposed to do?"

"Oh, it's nothing," Seventeen said.

"How's your mom feeling about the project? Are you back on track for college recs?" Gabriella pressed.

"Yeah," Seventeen said, but she hesitated. *Lying*. Gabriella had gotten good at detecting it, a benefit of doing it so often herself.

"Who's that nun in charge of you?" Gabriella kept at her. "Sister Mary Theresa, the former cop?"

Thirty laughed, a tinkly, optimistic sound that contrasted with Gabriella's interrogation. "I love that woman."

"Really?" Gabriella wanted to ask whether she'd met her, but decided to stay on Seventeen. "And what does Sister think happened to Fed Sarah?"

"What does Sister Mary Theresa think happened to her that night on the bridge?" Seventeen asked. *Stalling*.

"Right." *Watch your tone. Light, but firm.* "Does she think it was the husband, like Thirty-Nine and Forty-Four do?" It had been a relief that the two of them were so focused on Campbell. The others had started researching Aunt Gretchen, another boon for Gabriella.

"To be honest," Seventeen said, "Sister hasn't said what she thinks."
Truth.

"And your mom?"

"Um . . ." Seventeen looked out the window.

"Wait." Gabriella had it. "They canceled the project, didn't they? You're not supposed to be here."

Seventeen coughed.

"Yes!" Gabriella said. "TSJP seemed like a good idea when it was teaching you about friendship and shit, but now that the project is an actual corpse, it doesn't seem so whimsical? I've noticed our Instagram has gone dormant."

"I don't want to talk about it," Seventeen mumbled.

"We're here now," Thirty broke in, opening her door. "We can deal with Sister later, yeah?"

Inside, Sixty-Nine was already at the head of the table. Forty-Four looked forlorn at the other end, probably because Thirty-Nine was uncharacteristically absent. Seventeen removed her file folders from her backpack. Gabriella sipped her usual decaf with cream and two Splendas.

"Okay, let's start." Seventeen's hands looked a little shaky as she spread photos on the table. "I have a big discovery, spurred by Ruby."

"Is Ruby coming?" Sixty-Nine asked.

"Not tonight," Seventeen said. "Cello lessons. Her dad says it's time for some normalcy." She rolled her eyes. "As if that's going to be possible ever again."

The women huddled toward the printouts, and when Gabriella realized what the pictures showed, she nearly choked.

"What am I looking at?" Forty-Four leaned over and snapped a pic. "For Thirty-Nine," she explained. "She had to go to soccer practice, but she didn't want to miss anything."

Seventeen carried on. "What you're seeing here is a yellow diamond pendant, an heirloom from Fed Sarah's side of the family."

"It's gorgeous," Thirty said, picking up an image. Gabriella wanted to tear the paper right out of her hand. "Was it her mother's?"

"Bingo," Seventeen said. Gabriella focused on breathing slowly through her nose, cool air in, warm air out, as she'd learned in Pilates with Grace. "And"—Seventeen lifted her hand like a priest giving a blessing—"the necklace is *missing*! The family has filed a claim."

"Well now!" Sixty-Nine clapped her hands together. "Isn't *that* a breakthrough! How much is the necklace worth?"

"Enough for a motive?" Thirty piled on. Gabriella's head felt heavy.

Seventeen glanced at her notes. "Appraisal was twenty-seven thousand in 2017."

"That is a *lot* . . ." Sixty-Nine said hesitantly.

"But," Forty-Four broke in, "would you kill someone for twenty-seven thousand? I mean, not *you*, but . . ."

"Would anyone?" Thirty bit her lip. "What can you buy with $30K anyway?"

"It might not just be about the necklace," Seventeen said, and Gabriella found herself nodding.

"Even if it's not the whole motive," Thirty said, "this is amazing. When did they file the claim, do we know?"

"Four days after she fell," Seventeen said.

"That seems significant, right? The timing?" Thirty caught Gabriella's eye and then turned back to the kid. "How did you find this?"

"Yeah," Gabriella said, trying to echo Thirty's excitement. "Where'd we get this?"

Seventeen grinned at Gabriella, and suddenly, she didn't look so young. She'd bullied Serafina Jones, after all. Seventeen's impulsive, unkind behavior had brought them all together in the first place. At least Gabriella's duplicity was ultimately altruistic.

"I came into possession of some auction documents. The disappeared necklace is about to be on the docket at a jewelry fair on the East Coast."

Oh, shit. It was the envelope, Gabriella realized. The one Thirty had picked up for her at the FedEx store near LifeSport. The seal had looked a little funny, but she figured it had been damaged in transit.

But now she knew. The kid had opened it. She'd stolen the documents. She knew about the auction. And—Gabriella bit hard on the inside of her cheek—she knew that Gabriella was involved.

"Auction documents from Ruby?" Thirty asked.

"These came from someone else." Seventeen stared at Gabriella, a little smile at the corner of her mouth.

I have to say something. Gabriella's phone buzzed. *Or, I have to go.* "Hang on," she said aloud, grateful for the excuse to look away. She didn't recognize the number, but the photo, she did. It was her brother against a cement wall, a damp spot near his right thigh. His cheek was bruised and blood dripped from his lip.

Time's up, the text message said. Final payment due in ten days.

Minneapolis Police Department Interview with Gretchen Jones

Detectives Present: Alli Faricy and Mark Schmid

April 19, 2023

Alli Faricy: I'm so sorry, Ms. Jones. I know this is a shock.

Gretchen Jones: How does this even happen?

AF: Let's start from the beginning. Do you know of any enemies or threats your sister was facing?

GJ: There's one thing you have to know right away. That's why I called you. I found photos.

AF: Photos?

GJ: There's a family heirloom missing, a necklace. The girls asked me about it.

AF: You mean Ruby and Lula? Are you close?

GJ: Yes—well, no. Not as close as I'd like, but I got a text from Lula asking if I'd seen the necklace.

AF: And then you found photos of the necklace?

GJ: Yes. In my sister's closet. They had—

AF: You were in your sister's closet? When?

GJ: Well, I was there on Monday.

AF: On the day your sister died?

GJ: Yes.

AF: Was your sister with you?

GJ: No. I was just—I used my key.

AF: Did you often visit her house when she wasn't there?

GJ: No, never. It was just the necklace.

AF: Okay.

GJ: Listen, my sister and I didn't get along. But I didn't do anything to Sarah. I'm devastated that we didn't have enough time to fix—I never imagined—but also, I found photos of the nanny with the necklace.

AF: In the closet?

GJ: Yes. Have you questioned her? I've never met her in person, but she seems too good to be true.

AF: Respectfully, how do you know? By your own admission, you and Sarah don't get along, and you're not close with the girls. And now you're telling us you broke into the home on the day of the murder.

GJ: Oh come on. We both know that's not what I said.

AF: Clear it up for us?

GJ: You know what? I'm going to call the family attorney, actually. But in the meantime, look for some nude photos. The nanny in the necklace. God. The incompetence. It's just like on television.

CHAPTER TWENTY-THREE

May 16, 2023

George's legs hovered eight inches above the mat, his hands behind his head, ready for another V-up, when Sarah asked about the necklace. "Are you guys looking at a yellow diamond? I mean, in the case?"

George's limbs collapsed. Sarah had already put him through treadmill intervals and squat jumps. Just the day before the appointment, he'd looked again at all the evidence taken from the house and the initial interviews with the family members. The girls and the sister both mentioned the necklace. And now Sarah, too.

"Nope," Sarah said, snapping her fingers at him. "You're a professional. You can report on the investigation while also working your core."

George hit four more Vs but didn't say anything until he finished the set. He scanned the fitness floor. They had a decent radius to avoid eavesdropping. "There's a necklace, yes." George hugged his knees. Sweat dripped from his elbows.

"And?" Sarah grinned. She handed him the towel she'd slung over her shoulder. "What about the necklace?"

George smiled back. "How long have you been waiting to spring the necklace on me, Jones?" George thought back to the warm-up, the rest intervals on the treadmill. She could have mentioned it anytime, but instead peppered him with questions about his favorite Italian foods, animals, and travel destinations.

Sarah's eyes sparkled. "I was gearing up for the big reveal. I know it's your job and stuff, but I thought you'd want to know the Sarahs are"—she leaned toward him and whispered—"on top of it."

"Or," George tipped his head, "were you just waiting to mention it until you'd worked me into a vulnerable state of exhaustion?"

"I have an important job here at LifeSport and a trainerly reputation to uphold," Sarah said. "I can't just skip right to my ulterior motives." She pushed her index finger into his shoulder.

"Smart," George said.

"So?" Sarah prompted. "The necklace is really missing, and it's really a thing?"

"We've heard of it." George nodded. "We're looking for it." He omitted his failed searches and Vance's vaguely disappointed queries over the last few days, plus the alleged nude photos that no one could find. "How does TSJP know about the necklace?"

"It's a little crazy." Sarah glanced at her watch, still running his workout. "We had a TSJP meeting the other night, and"—she paused—"well, I don't know how many details you want about the silliness that entails..."

George smiled. Of course, he wanted—needed—every detail he could get about how the meetings went. "I like that group," he said. "It's like a TV show or something. Intrepid investigators led by a plucky teen."

"Right." Sarah rolled her eyes. "A plucky teen and her unflinching biology tutor. Anyway, Seventeen had some photos." She glanced at her notebook and then pointed at the mat. "Plank variations."

They went from those to hip mobility, and then finally, when George finished the workout, he fished again about the necklace. "Where did Seventeen get the photos of the necklace? From Ruby?"

Sarah frowned. "Actually," she said, "I'm not sure if we got that far."

George and Sarah strolled back toward the fitness desk, where she'd presumably meet her next client. "Why? What happened?"

"Let me think." Sarah tapped her chin. "Well, it was weird."

"Like how?"

"I'm not sure how much to say," Sarah said.

"Because?" George sucked in his stomach, hoping to stop the butterflies there.

"Well, because I'm worried that what I'll tell you will make you suspicious, and I know Twenty-Seven didn't do it."

"Even though she lied about her brother?" George tried to match her seriousness.

"Did she actually, though? Is that for sure?"

"I've got him on camera in Eau Claire, Wisconsin, on Thursday."

"On camera? That's a thing?"

"CCTV. There's a system."

"In Eau Claire? You're sure?"

George considered how much to say. "Maybe ninety-five percent?"

Sarah shook her head. "Well, she still didn't kill Fed Sarah. I'm also ninety-five percent."

"Then maybe it won't hurt to tell me what happened at the end of the TSJP meeting? The more information I have, the faster I can close the cases."

"Cases?"

Shit. "Oh," he said, feeling his head shake a little. "I just meant the case. There are so many stakeholders—"

"But you said 'cases,'" Sarah said, hands on her hips. "What else are you investigating besides the murder?" He watched as her mouth dropped slightly open. A thinking face, he'd learned.

"I've got a couple of irons in the fire." He hoped he sounded light.

"But..." Sarah waved at her next client. "Is there something else besides the murder? Your first appointment was scheduled before Fed Sarah died. Did you..."

"I'd seen you here," George began. It was true. He'd been attracted to her bright smile, the spring in her step. He didn't find out who she was until after he'd noticed her. "Serendipity," he said.

Sarah smiled a little, which relieved George. "But you definitely said '*cases*.'"

"I'm working on more than one." George put his hand on her elbow, willing her not to pull away. "But only one of them has to do with you. And how lucky am I?" George asked. "It's *you*."

Now Sarah blushed. George grinned at her. "Plus your mom. It's meant to be. What do you call it again?"

Sarah shrugged. "LRFM," she said.

George put an arm around her shoulder and squeezed, hoping it wasn't too forward. Her hair smelled nice, he noticed. *She* was nice.

And she was also the next target of Gabriella Johnson. It had to be the reason Gabriella was still in town. The previous target, he remembered as Sarah pulled away and he longed to keep holding on to her, had plummeted from a bridge and smashed her head open on the bike path.

CHAPTER TWENTY-FOUR

May 18, 2023

"Wait just one second." Twenty-Seven's eyes gleamed as she raised her gin and tonic for a toast at the café. "George said what?"

Sarah had suggested drinks with Twenty-Seven for two reasons: to ask a few questions about Oscar and also to make sure she was okay. Instead of riding home with Sarah and Seventeen from the TSJP meeting, Twenty-Seven had left suddenly, claiming to have forgotten "something for Lula," and Ubered away.

Sarah had texted Twenty-Seven later and had only gotten a thumbs-up emoji response to her check-in.

Sarah coughed, questioning whether she should backpedal, to keep George's plural slip—"cases" rather than "case"—to herself. But then again, why would it be wrong to share? Twenty-Seven had been nothing but loyal and perfect as a friend.

Too perfect?

"He said 'case*s*,'" Sarah said again, going for it. George's explanation of his word choice had made her feel better at first, and then worse. He was precise and highly skilled, and maybe, she realized, trained to manipulate *her*. "He said 'cases' instead of 'case.'"

Twenty-Seven looked confused, but not suspicious. "You think he's investigating two cases?"

Sarah shrugged. "He told me that 'the more information I could give him, the faster he'd solve the cases.'" She used air quotes. "But there should only be one case. And then?" Sarah sipped her gin and tonic and looked out into the sunshine.

"And then what?" Twenty-Seven asked.

Sarah studied her friend's face for some kind of clue, some hint that she felt one way about the revelation or another, but it was open as usual.

Sarah dove in again. "I just started to think about the dates, is all. I'm his trainer, but he wants information. I thought it was about the murder, but that happened on the day of our first appointment, and then he said 'cases,' and I just started to wonder if maybe he had already found me for some other reason. You know? It's possible?"

Twenty-Seven's phone buzzed, and her brow furrowed as she swiped at it.

"Everything okay?" Sarah asked.

"Totally," Twenty-Seven said, though her face had clouded.

"Family?" Sarah hadn't pried at all about Oscar. If he was dead—she felt a pang of guilt for doubting it—it would obviously overwhelm Twenty-Seven. Sarah remembered the arrangements that had taken over their lives when Ainsley and the baby had died—a double funeral, photos, cousins from out of town flooding the Hampton Inn near the Kroger.

"What?" Twenty-Seven blinked at her.

"I was just wondering if you had a bunch of arrangements to make?" She pointed at the phone. "For Oscar? You haven't mentioned..."

Twenty-Seven stared at the ceiling. "It's complicated."

"Now that I'm thinking about it," Sarah said, "I've kind of dominated our friendship with my own issues. You can totally share."

Twenty-Seven twisted her glass on the table, moving the coaster in a slow circle beneath it. "My dad is kind of a psycho," she said. "We're waiting to plan the funeral until some things settle down."

"Things?"

"Honestly, it's a lot and it's messy." She sighed. "I'll tell you more later."

"Can I ask you one more thing?" It was the gin emboldening Sarah. "How did Oscar die, exactly?"

A silence opened, and Sarah wondered if she'd pushed too hard.

"There were drugs," Twenty-Seven said, finally, "but he didn't overdose. It was an accident."

Sarah leaned forward, put her elbows on the table, but Twenty-Seven changed the subject.

"Do you think Fed Sarah's death could have been an accident?"

Sarah thought back on the coroner's findings as reported in the news. Fed Sarah hadn't jumped. George and his team were looking for a perpetrator. There was the mystery of the later-than-usual dinner, which Twenty-Seven had never explained beyond some kind of hang-up at the Fed. There were signs of a struggle. And now, there was the family necklace, which hinted at financial motive. George had confirmed that. How could the death have been an accident?

"I don't think so?" She watched Twenty-Seven, a new suspicion bubbling. "Like, between the missing necklace and her different-than-usual work schedule? Doesn't it seem like something was up?"

"But the person up there might not have *meant* for it to happen." Twenty-Seven pushed her hair back and sat up straight. "We haven't found any enemies. No one wanted Fed Sarah dead. Maybe it was all an accident." Against her will, Sarah imagined Twenty-Seven on the bridge, watching Fed Sarah fall to her death.

"Does it matter if it was an accident?" Twenty-Seven's pensiveness troubled Sarah. When Twenty-Seven was on, she was all the way on—gorgeous and charming and sparkly. Maybe the lows were equally consuming? Her friend half collapsed against the café wall.

"Doesn't it?" Twenty-Seven asked. "I think it matters." She took a deep breath, her pink blouse expanding around her belly and then deflating again. "Like, philosophically. And maybe legally?"

"But those girls." Sarah sipped her drink. "Their mom is still dead."

Twenty-Seven wiped her eye with the back of her hand, leaving a smudge of black liner above her cheekbone. "I know. I just—" She crumpled a little more, her head close to the table. "I guess I just want everything to be okay for them."

Sarah's phone buzzed. She waited to grab it until she was sure Twenty-Seven was finished speaking. "We all want that," she said, and as she read the text from George, she felt herself grin.

"Gotta be George," Twenty-Seven said, peppier. "You're blushing."

Sarah's stomach flipped. She'd never felt this kind of romantic flutter, never counted down the hours until she could see someone again. Meanwhile George was texting about Birdsong. I'd love to show it to you someday, he'd written. Maybe when I put the docks in for my parents in a week or so?

"What's George saying?" Twenty-Seven asked.

"He's inviting me to his family's camp," Sarah said.

"An overnight?" She sat up.

"Quiet," Sarah laughed. "It'll be a chance to walk in my mother's footsteps. Not like a romantic getaway."

"Sure," Twenty-Seven said, eyes rolling.

"It's so weird that George's family owns that camp. We have so many magical links."

"The connection to your mom is really amazing."

"Yeah," Sarah admitted. "It's like my mom is standing over my shoulder and just, like, waving a wand. I've never felt this kind of serendipity, ever. From finding the apartment, to meeting you..."

Sarah felt herself blush. She hadn't meant to confess how much Twenty-Seven had meant to her, how having a friend who didn't know every version of her and every detail of her life story had helped her start over.

"I get it," Twenty-Seven said. "I hope this doesn't sound weird." She spun her glass again. "I *also* feel the magic. I did have a head start here in Minneapolis, but I've moved around a lot. There aren't a lot of people who really know me, and then Oscar—"

Sarah held her breath. As soon as Twenty-Seven said "Oscar," she froze again, clamping her mouth shut. Tears flooded her eyes. It wasn't like she hadn't cried in front of Sarah before—there had been the total meltdown at the TSJP meeting—but something about her body seemed different this time, her limbs heavier, everything slower.

"What?" Sarah leaned across the table and grabbed her hand. "You can tell me."

"I don't really like talking about it," Twenty-Seven said. "I don't know why I said anything."

"Well, maybe it was your subconscious? You're ready to get real and take this friendship to the next level?" She infused her tone with a little lightness, an invitation.

"I wasn't the best sister to him." Twenty-Seven's voice was quiet but clear. "I let him take the brunt of everything at home. I was better at escaping."

"You were a kid. You're not responsible," Sarah said.

"But I'm not a kid now," Twenty-Seven said, "and I am responsible now."

"What do you mean?" *Responsible for what?* "Like, you're trying to make something up to him?"

"Yes," Twenty-Seven said. "I owe him."

Sarah alternated between looking at Twenty-Seven and away, trying to be empathetic and also to give her some privacy. "But," she finally said, when it was clear Twenty-Seven had retreated, "I can see how you might feel like you owe something to him. But now you can let that go, right? Since he's gone?"

Twenty-Seven's eyes went wide. *Fear?* It didn't look like the sadness she'd been displaying for the last several minutes, anyway. She was on her feet in another second, her pink bag flung across her chest.

"Are you leaving?" Sarah asked. "We could have another round."

Twenty-Seven said, "I'm really sorry. I'll pay you back for the drink. I'm sorry I derailed us. I can be so self-centered." She whacked herself in the shoulder, a strange self-flagellation, and then ran out of the café.

Sarah didn't have time to even push her chair back and follow before her friend was already on the sidewalk outside.

Group Chat of The Sarah Jones Project

May 19, 2023

27: Ladies. I've been really up and down. Grief is crazy.

69: Absolutely. When Chester died, I could barely watch Jessica for a week.

17: Isn't Chester your cat?

69: I'm just saying, I empathize.

27: Well, this is my way of apologizing. I know I've been weird. I left the meeting. And then, I kind of stormed out on 30 yesterday, too. I'm just feeling, like, out of sorts.

30: It's okay. Totally understandable.

17: Can I just ask? Was it something about the necklace? Because that seemed to really bother you?

27: It's hard to investigate a murder of a person I actually knew and really liked, and also to mourn my brother.

17: Can you send us the obit for Oscar? Sister Mary Theresa wants to do a novena.

39: What's a novena?

17: Nine days of prayer. I searched online for the obit, but I can't find it.

30: Did Oscar live in Eau Claire by any chance?

69: Also, the necklace... has anyone told you we found the auction site? Looks like it's selling for 37K? 17, did you text Ruby like we said?

27: Could we not? Like, text Ruby? I feel like she has enough going on.

17: You would think that.

69: ????

17: Sorry. I didn't mean that. I haven't texted her yet. But the obit?

27: I'll see what I can find.

44: Hang in there, everyone. Murder is stressful. We've gotta stick together.

17: Or what?

30: 17, I'm gonna text you separately. ♡

CHAPTER TWENTY-FIVE

May 19, 2023

George didn't really have time to do the docks, but he knew how grateful his parents would be for his help. It was a nice intermediate step between full-on camp participation and abandonment of the family business.

When he'd called after work the previous week to confirm he was coming, his dad had picked up on the first ring. He sounded happy, and George realized that Paul hadn't for a while.

What had been keeping him down? Was Paul bugged by spring maintenance? Enrollment? Hiring? They'd all lived by the Birdsong rhythms for so long.

"Listen," George and his dad had said at the same time, and then they each laughed.

"Go ahead." George had felt his heart pounding in his throat. There had never been a time—not on the high school football team, not at Dartmouth, not even at Quantico—that he felt as nervous as he did when he was about to disappoint his dad. Lately, his feelings for Sarah created a similar disquiet. His affection for her was overtaking his desire to use her evidence in the case.

"Hey," his dad had said, "I know you don't have time with your new job to help me redesign the dock system. It's okay."

George's shoulders sagged. "Dad." He should have felt relief, but it was a different sensation. Regret? Nostalgia? *A big fat combo*, as Sarah might say. "I'm coming up."

"You don't have to do that. Bea's not free, either, as you probably know." George had examined each syllable for a hidden guilt trip, but his dad seemed sincere. "It's time for your mother and I to start dealing with the fact that the future of Birdsong is outside of the Nightingale family. And I'm not saying that to make you feel bad. I'm saying it because it's true. And really, George, it's okay. We've got several experienced staff here, and Owen has even drawn up a pretty good-looking dock configuration."

George had put his hand on his forehead and squeezed his temples. He'd wanted this outcome, right? But at the same time, sadness welled up in him. "Dad—"

"No," his dad had plunged on. "I'm okay. We're all"—he trailed off and then came back strong—"okay."

"You're right that I don't have time." George had sat up straight again. "But I've realized that I'm not ready to give this up quite yet." It was true. He'd told Sarah about his upbringing, all the random skills he'd developed. He couldn't stand the idea of Owen, the new boys' assistant director, doing the dock redesign. Nobody knew the topography of the lake bed like George did, the wave patterns, the realities of a busy marina running seven activities at once. No one knew better, and Owen was especially green. George had pictured his dad's bony ankles sticking out between his wet suit and his water booties, fixing and refixing Owen's mistakes.

"And what if I wash out of the FBI?" George had blurted. There hadn't been any indication of potential failure, but who knew? He was as green as Owen. "And," George had added without thinking too much about it, "I miss you guys." When he sniffed, the threatening tears had shocked him.

"Are you okay, Georgie?" It was his mother. George had laughed, coughing a little. He should have known she was listening. His parents hardly did anything apart from each other.

The tears had vanished as George chuckled. "Maybe investigating murderers is getting to me."

"You said you were in fraud," his mother had said. "Of course, I can't believe you're in law enforcement at all."

"National security," George and his dad had said simultaneously.

"And there's just one fraud-related murder." It seemed weird to say the words "just" and "murder" in the same sentence. He'd flashed on the photos of the dead woman, the pool of murky blood around her crushed skull.

"It just seems like a dangerous job is all," George's mom had said. "You carry a gun all the time."

"Mom." George had smiled. "You raised me on a literal rifle range."

"Okay, but not with pistols!" She was right, though there was an entire safe filled with .22 rifles.

"I'll see you guys next Friday night." It had lifted his spirits as he imagined the spring dampness of the assistant director's cabin, the smell of pine and snowmelt, the cool green pillowcases against his cheeks. "Oh, and can I bring my friend Sarah?" They'd say yes, of course. They'd be thrilled. When Bea married Tilly, they squealed about the expanding Nightingale clan for weeks. Not that George and Sarah were getting married.

"Ainsley Montague's daughter?" his mom had trilled.

"Yeah." Sheepishness crept in, and George had hurried on. "It's not serious—I mean, we're barely dating—" They weren't supposed to be dating at all. "Sarah wants to see the place."

"The more the merrier!" his mother had sung.

George had blushed. "Just don't get too excited."

"We're always excited to see you, Georgie," Paul had said.

"Thanks, guys. I'll see you next week. I mean, Sarah and I will see you Friday."

At work that week, his trip confirmed, George found the courage to ask Vance for the official O'Neill files. One less secret. Still, he wasn't particularly surprised by his supervisor's answer: "We don't join the FBI to solve our own problems or to avenge personal vendettas."

"I know, it's just—" George didn't know how to explain to his boss, who radiated calm competence, the reality of the memories of an empty desk in his fifth-grade classroom, the recurring nightmares, the community-wide before-and-after: safe, and then perpetually threatened.

George looked at Vance, willing her to understand without him saying anything, but she kept her eyes on her workstation, serene as ever.

"It's just, he was in my class in elementary school." George's voice was quieter than he wanted it to be when he said it. "I was with him when..."

"You think I don't know that?" Vance blinked up at him.

"You know that?"

Vance was thirty-eight years old. She'd been a teenager when Henry disappeared. She wasn't from Minnesota. Nebraska, she'd said when George had asked, and then she'd wiped the horizon with an open palm. "Wide-open sky."

"You think you can join the Federal Bureau of Investigation and not have us find a hit on your name from one of the biggest cases we've ever failed to solve?" George could see the hint of a smile in her cheek. "Frankly, I like it. It's personal for you. You're more likely to stay."

George fought his memories again, of his Huffy ten-speed, the muddy tracks leading into Birdsong Woods, Andrew O'Neill looking at him desperately, willing him to remember anything helpful from that afternoon.

George coughed. "I guess, now that you put it like that."

Vance pulled a key out of her breast pocket and efficiently opened her lower file drawer. She handed George a crisp manila folder with his name on the tab. "That's you," she said. "You can read it here in my office. But go fast. We've got other things to do."

George paged through his own application materials, interspersed with commentary on his interviews and grades. Although he knew, obviously, that the bureau was thorough, his eyes bugged at a report from an interview with his principal at Pine River High School. He'd left most of that life behind when he'd gotten to Dartmouth. He hadn't stayed in touch with anyone, having more in common with the other kids in New Hampshire. And then of course he'd had his one serious relationship with Hazel, who'd come to work at Camp Birdsong in the gap between her college graduation and her Peace Corps assignment in Guatemala, and who was also named in the FBI file. They'd interviewed Bea, who'd mentioned her.

It had been easy to love Hazel. And she was always going to leave. He'd known from the beginning, from their very first kiss on the road outside of his family's property, that on October 7, 2016, she'd fly to Guatemala City and be gone for two and a half years.

Hazel had not been a long-term commitment. Was the same now true about Sarah? He'd know her intensely, and then charge Gabriella for fraud and manslaughter, and everything would be over? He would get a new file, develop a new informant, stop his workouts at Sarah's gym and their runs through her neighborhood? What would happen to Sarah after Gabriella was behind bars? What did he *want* to have happen to her?

"Faster," Vance prodded him, reaching over and tapping the file. George flipped through his medical record, his scores from the physical fitness test, instructor comments from Quantico. ("Focused," "Driven," "Sharp.") His psych eval. "Some evidence of rumination and disassociation when discussing the O'Neill kidnapping."

Of course. He'd nearly forgotten about that conversation. The process of being assigned to the field office had taken nearly a year, but there were records of every step. He felt silly now, thinking that Vance wouldn't know. He wanted to leave the office, take a break, but felt that would only confirm whatever trepidation she might harbor about his well-being. He flipped a few more pages without really reading them before stopping on a transcript.

He felt his breath catch. Vance tipped her head but didn't look.

"Interview with George Nightingale, age 10." The interviewers this time, unlike the first conversation with the county detectives, had been Haverford and someone named Summerhill. George couldn't picture their faces, only their blazers, their badges in little wallets. The feds had come in afterward, after the local cops had failed to turn up anything.

Haverford and Summerhill had entered the Nightingale living room, just like George had interloped at the Campbell-Joneses. George had shown the agents his Pokémon card box. He hadn't told them, or anyone, about the cards he'd slipped from Henry's school cubby that week, the ones he still carried in his wallet today.

George remembered wanting desperately to provide the correct answers to the FBI. If he could crack the code, remember the perfect detail about the cars in the gas station parking lot, maybe Henry would appear as if at the end of a video game with confetti and a celebratory jingle.

But that didn't happen. The car he'd seen had been blue *or* green. The man's pants had been gray *or* black. Henry had disappeared, and George hadn't.

In the office, George looked up. Vance's attention remained on her screen. He wondered if someday the Campbell girls would read the transcript of their interview with him, if Ruby would regret telling the feds that their dead mother was a murderer. George himself had written a report about the interrogation, in addition to Vance's. He was part of their lives now, like Haverford and Summerhill were part of his.

He thought of Sarah Elizabeth of Vermont then, with her white-blond hair and quippy witticisms and optimism about people and fate and goodness. What would she say about him after this was over? He wanted to be more than a name on a report for her.

"You ready?" Vance held her hand out for the file.

No, George thought. His feelings for Sarah swirled through him. He was allowing—encouraging—her to get closer and closer to Gabriella, a con woman they all knew would try to steal her trust fund, to make her feel like a fool and a dupe. *And maybe to harm her? Like she did Fed Sarah?*

George handed the file back and hoped his face looked neutral, professional.

"I've got two docs for you," Vance said. "I'm questioning my judgment, but I like you."

She handed an envelope to him, pulling it from under her keyboard.

"You like me?" George asked stupidly.

"My last two trainees got transferred to Yuma." Vance shrugged. "You're not going to."

"I'm not?"

"No." Vance stood and walked ahead of him. "You're made of sturdy stuff. Let's go." She glanced over her shoulder and caught George looking at the envelope. "You can read that when you get back. Let's focus on Aunt Gretchen. The police confirmed her alibi via cell tower, so we finally got her and her lawyer to agree to a solo interview."

FBI Interview with Gretchen Jones

Agents Present: Jane Vance and George Nightingale

May 19, 2023

Jane Vance: Thanks for being so flexible about this. I know you're busy.
Gretchen Jones: My sister was murdered. What could be more important? And the police wasted like two weeks determining whether I was a suspect. Crazy.
JV: You've been sure from the start that Sarah's death was foul play.
GJ: My sister was completely devoted to her daughters. We were both devoted mothers, especially after . . .
JV: Take your time.
GJ: Our mother wasn't . . . suited for motherhood, really.
JV: Can you say more about that?
GJ: She was highly critical. Mean, sometimes. Nothing we did was good enough. You know the type? Sarah responded by studying constantly. More and more degrees and accolades.
JV: And you?
GJ: Oh.
JV: Agent Nightingale is going to hand you a tissue.
GJ: You just keep those in your pocket?
George Nightingale: Goes with the territory.
JV: Can you tell us about your mother? How you responded to her parenting?
GJ: I felt like I had to just be totally present and supportive for my

daughter. I quit my job. I was the classroom mom, the car pool organizer. The whole thing.

JV: How did Sarah react to that?

GJ: I . . . I regret this so much. We just couldn't see eye to eye. She told me I was wasting my intelligence. That I owed the world something. That my choices were antithetical to feminism.

JV: That would be hard.

GJ: Then I told her that bonding with her nannies wasn't the same as actually being a mother. I'm sorry. [*sniffling*]

JV: You had a falling-out?

GJ: You could call it that. Over the years, we just got more and more . . . distant. I let things go with Ruby and Lula and didn't visit or go to their events. I never meant . . .

JV: That sounds difficult.

GJ: You never think you're going to lose your chance, right? It always seems like sometime in the future, things could change.

GN: Things can always change.

GJ: Well, not now. She's dead.

JV: Can we talk about that night? We have some questions about her activities and about a necklace.

GJ: Our mother's necklace. It's gone, right? Ruby texted.

JV: The girls think you might have taken it?

GJ: Me? Oh, no. Oh, God. Things with the girls must be worse than I thought if they'd ever imagine I'd steal from them.

JV: What do you think happened to the necklace?

GJ: Her nanny took it. The photos? You don't have the photos?

JV: What photos?

GJ: I told the police. I found photos—nude photos?—of the nanny in the necklace. On the afternoon she . . . Speaking of, I think we need to consider why her dinner was so late that night.

Her and the nanny? Another Sarah Jones? Is that actually her name? They were at least an hour and a half late for their usual dinner. What was going on before that? What happened at work?

JV: We've checked with everyone at work. It was a typically busy day. There was nothing extraordinary. But I need to ask something else. Something sensitive.

GJ: Sensitive? My sister plummeted from a bridge. I'm *in it*, Agent Vance.

JV: The girls—Ruby and Lula—they told us some details about how your mother died.

GJ: My mother? She got Covid in the home. It was horrible.

JV: Did you visit her near the time of her death?

GJ: A few days before? What does this have to do with Sarah's murder?

JV: I'm sorry. But Ruby reported to us that she saw your sister hold a pillow over your mother's face. The girls' interpretation was that she killed her.

[*silence*]

JV: Gretchen? Agent Nightingale is going to hand you a cup of water.

GJ: Thank you.

JV: How does that assertion strike you?

GJ: I don't doubt what Ruby said. The girls are good. Sarah made sure of that. They don't lie. They wouldn't lie to the police.

JV: But?

GJ: I'm just hoping that somehow she's wrong. Mistaken. Could it be? I suspected, but...

JV: The girls were in a great deal of distress. We didn't ask too many follow-ups, and frankly, we're more focused on solving the murder of your sister.

GN: Can I ask? Why are you hoping the girls are wrong?

GJ: It's just . . . if they're right, things were so much more broken than I thought. Sarah was so much more lost than I thought.

JV: Your mother, though. She was . . .

GJ: Very difficult, yes. It was complicated.

JV: Gretchen, where were you on the evening of April 17?

GJ: The police already know.

JV: The more you tell us, the more likely it is that we can arrest the person responsible. It's hard to predict which details are critical. We solve this, and your family can heal. It sounds like you want that. You want a relationship with the girls.

GJ: On the seventeenth at the time she usually goes to dinner with the nanny . . . wait. You must have talked to her assistant. What does her calendar show for the hours before the dinner? Why does it say she was running so late? Or what did the nanny say about that?

JV: We'll get to that, okay? But first, can you answer my question? Where were you?

GJ: You would have this on security cameras if Sarah and Caden ever bothered to reconnect their system. The cable company inadvertently chopped some wires a few years ago, and as I understand it, they haven't gotten around to . . .

JV: Your whereabouts, Gretchen?

GJ: At dinnertime, I was at Sarah's house. Sarah wasn't there. I thought she was at dinner, their usual schedule.

JV: You maintain you were at your sister's house alone?

GJ: I was. And my alibi checks out for time of death. I'm trying to help you.

JV: Us, too.

GJ: Usually, Caden takes the girls for dinner that night as well. Or they order takeout. Anyway, both cars were gone.

JV: And?

GJ: I have a spare key.

JV: Do you often go to your sister's house when no one's home?

GJ: I've only done it once before. Right after Mom died. I swear. I'm not a creeper. It's just that we don't talk. Not even after our mother died.

JV: What were you looking for this time?

GJ: The necklace. Ruby had texted, asking if I'd seen it. I was sure it was there somewhere. You don't just lose a thirty-thousand-dollar necklace.

JV: How do you know the value of the necklace?

GJ: My mother was a very manipulative person, Agent Vance. You knew the value of everything. You knew exactly how many dollars you were worth.

JV: And Sarah was worth more than you were? Is that what you're saying?

GJ: When it served Mom, yes. Other times, no. Let's just say, it's not entirely our fault that we don't—didn't—get along. Oh, God.

JV: What did you find in the house that night?

GJ: Well, not the necklace.

JV: But something?

GJ: Photos. In the closet—you've seen it? It's not like you can really call it a closet. It's the size of my daughter's bedroom.

JV: Can you describe the photos?

GJ: Nudes. Of their nanny. Selfies she took in the vanity mirror. Oh, God. Topless and wearing the necklace.

JV: Connect the dots for me here.

GJ: I can only think she sent them to Caden? Something must have been going on between them.

JV: Has Caden been unfaithful in the past?

GJ: Sarah would never tell me if he were. But before, before everything got so ugly and complicated, there was a student at the university. His research assistant. There was a big fight, an ultimatum. And then a year later Lula was born and they moved back here, and I never heard my sister say anything about it again.

CHAPTER TWENTY-SIX

May 25, 2023

Vance was on her phone to the task force immediately when they got into the car after the interrogation. "Can you bring in the nanny? And have the phone records come back? Calls the evening of the seventeenth? And why didn't the file include the photos? That was a serious miss."

George was glad someone else was responsible for the gaffe.

"Got it," Vance said finally. "Can you upload a copy of that to the file? Thanks." She hung up and zipped out of their parking spot.

"So, she's not the killer," George said. "But being in the house alone makes you wonder. Did she do that a lot?"

Vance nodded. "I wondered that, too, and whether she ever ran into anyone there."

"The nanny," George asked. "Gabriella."

"I'm bringing Johnson in. I can't wait any longer, even though we might miss the transaction. And now that Gretchen's eliminated as a suspect, we have to seriously question whether Gabriella would snap again, whether anyone else is in danger." George felt a lump in his throat. *Sarah.* Plus, Vance had said "I." His boss was going to interrogate Gabriella without him. He wasn't sure how hard to push. He'd gotten lucky so far, permission to establish an informant and assist on interviews with the family.

"You can't come," Vance said, confirming his fears. "But it's not because you're not good. It's because of the trainer. Gabriella knows you, knows you're—what are you doing, exactly? Are you dating Sarah?"

George remembered now how he'd grabbed Sarah's arm when they'd discovered the Birdsong connection, the magical coincidence that Ainsley Montague had spent several summers in the place George had been born. "We've been on three dates," George said. "I wouldn't say we're..."

"But *she* might think you are." Vance glanced over her shoulder and merged into the fast lane.

"Probably," George agreed, remembering their kiss in the parking lot of the Block, the citrus smell of her hair.

"So," Vance said, "you can't be with me when I interrogate her friend for the first time. You know what? I'm going to have one of the Minneapolis detectives do it with me. They were there in the beginning. It'll feel a little more routine."

George felt slightly mollified. At least Vance wasn't calling up someone else from the field office; no one else from fraud or narcotics would join the Jones task force, at least not this weekend. The docks, he remembered. He could keep his promise to his dad and go up north. He wouldn't have to cancel for the interrogation. That was something.

Back at the office and sidelined temporarily from the Jones case, George reviewed a couple of tips the office admin had passed along to him. Nothing urgent, though he flagged a potential pyramid scheme for future review. He glanced at his backpack, the O'Neill files stuck in the pocket meant for a laptop. He could offer a little time to Henry, take advantage of his relegation. As he flipped through old interview transcripts, the fact that his father was interviewed didn't surprise him, but reading it gave him a chill nonetheless.

HENRY O'NEILL CASE FILE

FBI Interview with Paul Nightingale

Agents Present: Gerald P. Haverford and Howard R. Summerhill

April 20, 2001

Gerald P. Haverford: Good evening, Mr. Nightingale. I want to thank you for coming in. I know this has been an incredibly stressful time.

Paul Nightingale: Anything to help.

GPH: I'm glad you feel that way.

PN: Of course I do. I think the whole town—well, this has been unimaginable. And after Andrew's wife died? My God.

GPH: Indeed. Mr. Nightingale, let's start with some basics, if that's okay with you. As you know, time is of the essence, so we're going to dive right in. Where were you on the evening of April 15, 2001?

PN: Me?

GPH: If you would.

PN: Well, our staff had the night off. We'd just said goodbye to the Our Lady of Peace group...

GPH: Our Lady of Peace?

PN: The school group that had been at Birdsong that week.

GPH: You're open in the spring? It's not just a summer thing?

PN: We do outdoor education for five weeks in the spring.

GPH: And you have out-of-town staff here for that program?

PN: Bare bones, but yes. Our year-round staff plus two.

GPH: We'll need their names and contact information.

PN: Of course.

GPH: And, so, sorry—your own whereabouts the evening of the fifteenth?

PN: I was in the office. The camp office. Uh, on the property, obviously.

GPH: What were you doing?

PN: I finished up the paperwork from the session, and then I was placing the food order, and ... well, there's a checklist of things that have to happen, and I was motivated to get it done. Weekend off and everything.

GPH: Can anyone verify your presence in the office that night?

PN: Not sure. Maybe the timestamp on the food order? Sylvia, my wife, she was dealing with the kids that night. I mean, our own kids. I usually do the closing stuff. Gordon and Heath—those are the seasonal staff—they had the night off, as I said. I'm trying to remember what Cara was up to that night. But she didn't come into the office.

GPH: Cara?

PN: She's our year-round AD. Uh, assistant director.

GPH: You'll give us her information as well.

PN: Yes.

GPH: Let's see if we can get an email confirmation or timestamp on the food order. But in the meantime, let's switch gears. What do you remember about your son George's whereabouts on Friday afternoon?

PN: I don't think I'll ever forget this now. My God, you know?

GPH: What happened on Friday, Mr. Nightingale?

PN: George had a playdate with Henry. I'd dropped him off with his bike in the morning. The two of them were going to bike to Henry's house after school. It's close—well, you probably know that already. They got a ride from Henry's house back here after the playdate.

GPH: We've traced the route, yes. The boys came back here, and then your son saw Henry bike into Birdsong Woods. That's what you call this land here?

PN: We do. Well, my grandparents were the ones who started that. They began the camp in 1924, so we've been here—we've been in the community . . .

GPH: Take your time. It's difficult.

PN: I just can't believe this kind of thing would happen here, at this time, with George so . . . I'm just shocked. I'm sorry.

GPH: Here's a tissue. And then, if you would, Mr. Nightingale, the boys that evening?

PN: Did you ask George?

GPH: We'd like to hear what you know about it.

PN: Well, I only know what I've heard from George, and then from Sylvia. She saw them when Andrew dropped George off.

GPH: Go ahead.

PN: George said they wanted to ride some hills? We have a bunch of bike trails.

GPH: George said Henry needed the practice.

PN: Henry's a great kid, but he's not what we'd call athletic. His dad always seemed to hate that . . . the year they did kid-pitch, Andrew hated that Henry couldn't throw from first to third . . . I'm sorry. I'm off track. What?

GPH: When they went around the bend here at camp, Henry was alone on his bike?

PN: That's what George said. He watched him ride away.

GPH: And the woods in question? Where Henry would have ridden? Those are behind the camp office?

PN: Right.

GPH: And you didn't see or hear anything while you were working? You never saw Henry or his bike? Or anyone on the property who didn't belong there?

PN: No. I wish I had more. I told the Crow Wing detectives this, too. I wish I could help.

GPH: So do we, Mr. Nightingale. So do we.

CHAPTER TWENTY-SEVEN

Video Transcript Recorded by Sarah Jones, Age Seventeen

May 30, 2023

By this time, you can probably see that things were starting to go off the rails. It's not like I didn't know that. When I finally confessed everything to Sister Mary Theresa (not until school got out this week, obvi, because then she wouldn't be able to control my *every* move), she asked me when I knew things had gone too far.

This is one of the skills Sister and I worked on after my junior-year implosion: more self-awareness, more self-preservation, more of being a real and reasonable person who can definitely maintain baseline friendships and also attend a moderately selective American college or university, please GOD.

And I did improve, I'm sure, even though two Sarahs are currently in jail and I'm implicated on many levels.

It's just not *all* my fault, and the thing I'll now tell you about Twenty-Seven? I knew it was bad. I knew I was far, *far* out of my depth, and perhaps beyond the saving powers of the Virgin Mary when it happened.

The week after I laid out the necklace evidence and found the final selling price, though not the repository of the funds, Twenty-

Seven texted me. It was Friday. She wanted an emergency one-on-one get-together.

Twenty-Seven had almost never texted me. Yes, I'm clueless and self-destructive about some things, but I can actually tell when people dislike me, and Twenty-Seven had never been a huge fan. Ruby confirmed my intuition when she told me over DM how Twenty-Seven described me back in the beginning: "Weird and socially awkward."

It was that description that had delayed my telling Ruby about the necklace sale. Would I open a wound, telling her that her nanny had stolen her heirloom necklace? How much loss could Ruby handle? I was waiting for all of the evidence to line up to share my most damning findings, so she wouldn't be able to dismiss me, to think I was just weird.

Twenty-Seven's text read, "Meet up at the Dunn's near Mill City Museum?" The coffee shop was one I visited a lot, an easy walk from our loft, and also blocks from the site of Fed Sarah's fall.

"Did you mean to text me?" Just double-checking.

"I meant you," she wrote. "So, coffee?"

"I guess?"

"Coffee," Twenty-Seven texted next. "Now." Just the two words.

And though she's not the boss of me, my curiosity overpowered the tiny bit of trepidation I felt. I told my mom I was going to get a little exercise. Risky, yes, as we have a gym in the building, but I took a flier on the fact that the end of the fiscal year loomed. Mom was busier than usual, and she'd let her guard down. She wasn't so focused on my direct supervision, especially since Sister Mary Theresa had officially set me free.

At the coffee shop, I didn't bother ordering anything before I headed to the table where Twenty-Seven sat by the window, the light accenting her highlights. Or lowlights. Whatever. She looked fabulous, which was predictable but a little bit annoying. Meanwhile, I'd left the house in capri leggings and a running shirt.

When I sat down, Twenty-Seven just stared at me for like a full minute. My heart fluttered the same way it did when I was called to Sister's office. Usually, I ran through my potential transgressions as I waited for her to list my sins. But with Twenty-Seven, I *knew* what I'd done. I lifted my eyebrows and shrugged a little. This was Twenty-Seven's meeting. I had the right to remain silent.

She held eye contact while she sipped her coffee.

Just when I was about to crack, she spoke. "I think you know why we're here."

This was a classic Sister Mary Theresa tactic. I'd learned over time that it was always better to play dumb. Otherwise you end up confessing to, for instance, copying Ella Arthur's chemistry homework, when Sister is only about to bust you for out-of-uniform shoes.

"I'm happy you invited me?" I said.

Twenty-Seven laughed, and as she tilted her head back I could see the sparkly stuff she sometimes put on her cheekbones.

"You're happy I invited you?" Twenty-Seven asked. "Oh, that's *total* bullshit."

I looked around for eavesdroppers, but the coast was clear. "It is?"

"You know exactly why we're here."

"Are you, like, mad at me?" I sounded ridiculous, even to myself. But she was trying to get me to admit to stealing the envelope, to finding the photographs, to tracking down the necklace in Connecticut. And I was definitely sticking with the out-of-uniform shoes.

Meanwhile, my stupid question seemed to physically impact Twenty-Seven. She choked on her coffee, and while her swearing hadn't attracted attention, her coughing did. The cutest of the employees walked over and asked if she was okay. Her demeanor totally changed as she dabbed her tearing eyes with her napkin and waved him off.

"Wrong tube," I explained, but the guy barely looked at me.

Eventually, Twenty-Seven took another sip and recovered enough to say, "*Mad* at you?"

It was killing me not to say more, but I waited. See? I have learned something from TSJP. My patience is, like, through the frickin' roof.

She sipped again. She couldn't accuse me of stealing the FedEx envelope unless she also copped to lifting the necklace.

"You little shit," she said eventually, and my eyebrows spiked toward the ceiling. Twenty-Seven continued. "This is all a joke to you, right? This is, like, literally a school project, but there are people's actual lives at stake." Her anger intensified. A little spit bubble landed on her lip, hovering on the sheen of her gloss.

"Lives at stake?" I asked. "Like whose?"

I knew what I was doing. There was one dead person, Fed Sarah, and she wasn't part of our group. But there was one person *in* our group, Twenty-Seven, who knew her, and now, with the necklace, was capitalizing on her death. I'd gone from light suspicion to feeling pretty certain Twenty-Seven was at least adjacent to the bridge that night.

Twenty-Seven let some silence open, so I continued. "Fed Sarah never answered my email inviting her to TSJP. She wasn't in the group. *We* didn't cause her death. So, whose lives are at stake?"

Twenty-Seven laid both hands flat on the table, and for the first time, I noticed a tiny tattoo on the inside of her left middle finger. "Hope," it said.

"What are you saying?" It was a hiss and, frankly, not at all hopeful.

At this point, my voice started to sound thin, but I kept at it. "I'm just saying that I didn't do anything. I am doing a project for school. You agreed to be a part of it. And now? You're freaking out."

I'm not sure why I was baiting her except that I had this idea that she would admit something. Pretending you don't understand subtext is Obnoxious Teen 101. You just act like you have no clue about normal interactions and patterns of communication until an adult blows their top. Twenty-Seven's volume stayed the same for this next part, but the rage in it ramped up to a ten out of ten. Even in my worst moments, Sister Mary Theresa had never gotten to a ten. But then again, she spent at least half of her day in actual contemplative prayer. That creates force field levels of self-control.

Next, Twenty-Seven leaned toward me and squinted so hard her perfectly manicured eyebrows were like an inch closer together than usual. "You little bitch," she said. "You know exactly what you did and what you took and what you're threatening."

"Threatening?" I asked.

"Listen," she said. I can assure you, I *was* listening. I was a mix of fascinated and terrified. I listened so closely to every word because I knew I had to go home and take notes immediately, that if I got any detail wrong, people wouldn't believe that this woman who appeared so perfect all the time was actually part banshee. I wished I had thought to record the conversation. Still, I remember. Twenty-Seven said, "You have no fucking idea what you're dealing with."

My mouth dropped open.

"If you don't back off," she said, "if you don't keep your fucking mouth shut about whatever the fuck you think you know, I will—"

I honestly felt like I was in a movie, and I can't believe what I said next. I whispered it, but I put it out there, and it was perhaps the definition of "ill-advised," given the fact that I was now pretty convinced I was sitting across from an *actual* murderer. "What?" I asked. "You'll throw me off a bridge?"

The table rocked off its legs then. Her coffee sloshed onto the floor. She knocked her chair over. The most attractive barista again began his trek from the counter, but Twenty-Seven was through the door and down the block before he got there.

The guy looked at me like the mess was my fault. "Sorry," I mumbled. "She, um, had a little episode."

And after that?

After Twenty-Seven, who was not a Sarah Jones but actually a Gabriella Johnson, implicitly threatened my life and dropped her facade? I knew we were *very* much off the rails. But still, I stayed on the gosh-darn train.

CHAPTER TWENTY-EIGHT

May 26, 2023

"You're going on a weekend getaway with the new man?" Grandma Ellie practically shrieked. "I should have known! I pulled Ten of Pentacles this morning!" Sarah had waited to call home about the trip to Birdsong. There were so many strange details: her suspicion that George had targeted her before Fed Sarah had died, her growing skepticism about Twenty-Seven's brother, the strange tension between Seventeen and Twenty-Seven. It felt like too much to explain to Ellie. But, in a classic LRFM, she herself had pulled a Ten of Pentacles that morning, too.

"You want to know something weird?" Sarah asked.

"Don't even tell me," Ellie said. "I knew it! You pulled that card, too! This could be the one, kiddo!"

Sarah felt herself grin, but she also rolled her eyes. "Let's not get ahead of ourselves."

"He's taking you to that camp! That's another sign. Your mother absolutely *loved* that place. Maybe you'll see her up there!"

Neither of them, despite a litany of attempts, not unlike Sarah's own quest to become blood-tolerant, had ever had a supernatural visit from Ainsley. "Maybe," Sarah said. "But, let's not hold our breath."

That afternoon, George pulled up in front of Sarah's building for their trip to Birdsong exactly as her Garmin switched from 4:29 to

4:30. This guy was nothing if not punctual. Brian had been reliable, too—one of the few things the men had in common. Sarah couldn't be with anyone she couldn't count on. It was a side effect, that one therapist thought, of having a parent die in front of her. She overvalued reliability.

But George was so much more than reliable, as evidenced by the fact that Taylor Swift's *1989* played as she buckled herself into the front seat. And George had tucked a bag of Haribo gummy bears, another favorite, into the cup holder. A thrill rippled through Sarah, a rush of joy she attributed to both being with George, whom she was liking more and more ("Too much?" Twenty-Seven had asked her via text earlier that week), and the impending reality of actually walking in her mother's footsteps at Camp Birdsong. Soon, she'd see Cabin Red-Tailed Hawk, the dining hall, the nature center—all these places that were part of Jones family lore.

But how could she be thinking of George in a serious way when they hadn't even spent much time together? When their relationship was official FBI business? Sarah tried not to think about the complications, to let the Ten of Pentacles magic back in.

"So," George said after they'd gotten on the road, "I guess we should address the elephant in the Civic."

"Ha." Sarah glanced over her shoulder at George's navy duffel in the back seat. He'd tucked a pair of well-worn running shoes, not the newish ones he generally wore to their sessions, on the floor beneath it. "And what's that? The fact that you and I both know I'm fully unqualified to help with designing a new dock system?"

"You'd be surprised about that," George said. "I've installed docks with far less-skilled staff. But I do have high expectations given your supreme physical fitness. You are, in fact, a professional."

Sarah popped three gummy bears at once and then tried to say, "Are you nervous about introducing me to your parents?"

George laughed, and his cheek wrinkled adorably. He'd spent a lot of time outside. He looked young, but Sarah could see a preview of his older face, too, the lines already drawn. "Not nervous," he said. "And this is a special camp skill you might not have predicted, but I'm excellent at understanding people with their mouths full. Just try having a full meal with ten campers aged six to sixteen."

Sarah swallowed the candy. "You're not nervous because I'm so naturally charming and likable?"

George reached over and squeezed her hand, and she felt her cheeks flush. "That's undeniably true, but also my parents are just very good at meeting people. It's their business, right? Connecting and seeing the best in everyone? They're like"—he paused and cocked his head—"*camp* people."

Ainsley had been a camp person, too. "My mom, also," she said. "She liked everyone. Well," Sarah qualified, "she didn't like *everyone*, but she seemed to get them. People really liked *her*."

"Tell me again what her job was?"

"Writer," Sarah said. "Pretty much the opposite of what I do." Sarah had tried to follow her dad into his profession, yes, but she had never harbored any creative ambition like Ainsley had, except solving problems like how to make people in their forties run faster marathons. "And my mom was obsessed with spiritualism."

"Spiritualism?"

"Crystals and tarot and communing with the dead." Sarah grinned. She loved seeing people react to this interest, and she peeked sidelong at George, whose eyes had narrowed a little.

"Well, I'm okay with that, of course!" George gave a thumbs-up, and Sarah laughed.

"You seem supercool with it." She leaned back in her seat, aware of a full-body happiness.

"It's just that, in general," George qualified, "the Nightingales—well, also the FBI—are more focused on the physical rather than, like, the meta."

Sarah nodded, still smiling. "Most people are. My dad, too."

"Nightingales concern ourselves with water levels and wind speeds and mosquito concentrations. Less, like, *vibes*." He moved his hand off the wheel and let it undulate like it was riding a wave.

Sarah laughed again. "Fair," she said. "Good to know."

"Not that I'm not open!" George looked over for a second again. She tried, but couldn't really take her eyes off his profile, the deep wrinkles at the corners of his eyes, the smile line on his cheek. "Um, have you . . ." George trailed off, and then redoubled. "Have you talked to your mom since she died?"

Sarah stared at him until he glanced over. His face looked placid, only registering slight concern. "I haven't," she admitted.

George, Sarah thought, was the closest she'd come to a real message from her mother, along with all the other Sarah Joneses arriving in her life the moment she moved. There were so many signs that Sarah was finally in the right place at the right time, Ainsley's hand guiding her shoulder, maybe not to safety, but to something bigger and more meaningful than she'd had in her twenties.

"I don't know why she hasn't made contact," Sarah admitted. "I mean, there's the possibility that talking to dead people is actually unfeasible, right?" They both chuckled. "But I also think I've, like, felt her presence. Sometimes there's a feather tickling my face when I wake up." Sarah put a hand to her cheek. "I think that's her. Does that sound crazy?"

"It doesn't. Not at all."

"Really?" Brian had also assured her she didn't sound crazy, but she could tell he thought otherwise.

"Remember Henry O'Neill?" George asked.

"Of course." Sarah had googled him. She'd read about the Birdsong Woods. She'd held a chunk of amethyst and wished for peace for the family and for George.

"This is going to sound *really* crazy," George said, "but I have two of his Pokémon cards."

He sounded sad, but not too sad. It was like Sarah felt when she was talking about her mom—an implicit wish that she hadn't died, but a fervent desire to remember, as well. "Did you steal 'em?" Sarah joked.

But George's jaw dropped. "How did you know? Wait—" George pointed his index finger at the roof of the car, indicating the heavens. "Did he just tell you that? Like, from beyond?"

Sarah burst out laughing, and then George did, too.

"No," George said. "Well, I kind of stole the cards, but it's more complicated than just stealing."

Sarah poked her finger into his forearm. "You stole his Pokémon cards, and now you're stuck with them forever."

George sighed. "They do seem to weigh more than ordinary cardstock."

"Which characters are they?" Sarah asked.

"You know your Pokémon?"

"Absolutely not," Sarah said, "but like your parents, my job is making conversation with strangers. I can be interested in anything."

"Well, you can take a peek at them." George reached into the wheel well and handed her his money clip. "Right after my driver's license."

Sarah glanced at his ID. "Whoa, your middle name is Morris?"

George swatted her arm. "Hey!" he said. "This wallet investigation is limited to trendy children's collectibles of the early 2000s."

Sarah ran her finger over the cards' soft edges. "Not mint condition, though. Don't you have to keep these in plastic sleeves?"

George's eyes wrinkled in a smile again. "They're more like a talisman than an heirloom." At the mention, Sarah thought of the stolen yellow necklace, but she decided to let thoughts of Fed Sarah go for the weekend. Instead she breathed in George: the Old Spice, the scent of Tide detergent. She put the cards back in the clip and handed over the wallet without glancing at anything else. George was the investigator; she was just along for the ride.

"Here you go, Morris," she said, and they both laughed.

In the final minutes of the drive, Sarah glimpsed Lake Whitehook for a split second when they crested the last hill, the sun hanging low on the horizon. And then George turned left into a gravel driveway, and a man who had to be his father stood under the garage light.

"Here we go," George whispered to her. "We've got this." Sarah appreciated the "we." They'd driven through Jimmy John's for dinner about an hour from camp, and Sarah tried to look casual as she brushed the chip remnants from her jeans.

Paul Nightingale was at the car door before George had even put both feet on the ground. "I'm so happy to see you." He held both arms out, and Sarah was heartened to see a full-body hug. The Nightingale men held on, Paul's fingers spread wide over George's back.

"Dad," George said when he pulled away, letting one arm linger as he gestured toward Sarah with his other. "This is Sarah Jones."

"It's lovely to meet you, Sarah. And how wonderful that we knew your mom! We pulled a few old photos of her to show you."

Sarah's limbs flooded with the same feeling she'd had when she'd taken her first selfie next to Oldenburg and van Bruggen's *Spoonbridge and Cherry* sculpture, the Minneapolis classic. Right place, right time.

She hadn't even taken a full step inside the Nightingale cabin when George's mother approached with her arms out, gray hair braided into thick ropes over each shoulder. "Sarah! Welcome! I'm Sylvia, and I can't believe George met you at the gym! And that Ainsley Montague is your mother!"

"She is!" Sarah confirmed, liking Sylvia immediately. *Camp people.* Sylvia and Paul were in their midsixties. Sarah's mother, if she'd lived, would be fifty-four. Sarah had been born just two years after Ainsley worked here for the Nightingales.

"Let's get her some tea or a glass of wine." Paul clapped Sarah on the shoulder. Sarah wanted to stop and study the framed school photos of George and his sister, but the large lakeside window took her breath away. A lawn stretched ahead toward a stone fireplace, and then the giant, silvery lake filled the horizon. The water sparkled in the sunset.

"Wow," Sarah said. *Understatement.* She touched her cheek, thinking about her mother's hand on her head at bedtime, the times they sat together on the deck of a pool or put their chairs in the water on a beach vacation.

"Never gets old." Sylvia pointed at an armchair facing the water. "Sit here," she said. "You can watch the sun disappear into Whitehook. Your mother would have done closing campfire right there." She pointed at the stone hearth and patted Sarah's shoulder.

The conversation flowed easily as they got to know one another, and Sarah found herself laughing a lot. Sylvia told a story about George as an eight-year-old inadvertently leading a canoe trip. With the insurance policy of George in the group, Paul and Sylvia had sent their worst counselor that summer on the voyage, a guy named Will who'd tried to take the boys in the exact wrong direction.

"We figured George could play backup," Paul snorted. "He was going into third grade."

"It was fine." Sylvia waved the air in front of her face. "No casualties. Everyone back in one piece. We didn't even have to do a pontoon rescue. Georgie's always been a natural camp person."

"I started working in the kitchen at twelve," George said. "I think that's technically illegal. Child labor laws."

"Totally fine," Sylvia said again. "You turned out great."

Sarah took a sip of chamomile tea and held a stack of curled photos of her mother in her hand. Sylvia had dug them out of the archive. George reached over and stroked her forearm, the intimacy of it leaving her skin tingly.

Sylvia said, "I remember your mom loved Tater Tot hotdish! George got good at making that eventually."

"We ate it on the regular," Sarah admitted. "At least every other week."

"Green beans on the side!" George interjected. "Can you imagine?"

"It's such an amazing coincidence that you two met each other!" Sylvia exclaimed. "And Bea told us that Sarah is actually helping you with a fraud investigation? Your work lives are intertwined."

Sarah tipped her head toward George. "I'm helping you with a *fraud* investigation?" she asked. *Cases.* He'd said it was murder, that their training appointment had been a coincidence. Sarah had been battling her intuition ever since that slip.

George's face went redder, and he shook his head. "No, Mom," he said.

"Oh, I was sure"—Sylvia persisted—"Bea said something about developing an ... what did she say, Paul? An informant?"

"Uh-uh. Different, uh . . ." George folded his hands in his lap and shook his head in an understated but insistent denial. "Other case."

"Hmm! I must have been mistaken." Sylvia stood up and grabbed the teapot from the counter, over which hung a laser-cut wooden sign that read, "In a world where you can be anything, be kind."

Sarah studied George. "See?" she said. "You said 'cases.'"

"I'll explain later." George reached for her hand again, but she kept it in her lap.

"Let me pour you another cup." Sylvia approached with the hot water. Sarah held out the teacup, vintage porcelain with a delicate handle, not unlike the one she'd dropped on New Year's Eve, and Sylvia tipped the liquid in. "It's really nice to have you here, Sarah," she said. "I don't remember a ton about your mom, but I know she was really lovely and adored. That I do remember."

A couple of tears migrated into Sarah's eyes. Whitehook had disappeared into darkness outside, and instead of the lake, Sarah could see their reflection in the window. George's mother stood over her left shoulder and Paul leaned toward them from across the coffee table. Sarah half expected to see her own mother's image in the window, too, though she wasn't there.

"This feels magical," Sarah said to the room, putting George's extra case on the back burner once again and surrendering to the joy that swelled behind the suspicion. "I think my mom would like it that I'm right here."

Text Messages between Sarah Raquel Jones (17) and Sarah Elizabeth Jones (30)

May 26, 2023

17: Ok, so I know you're busy. But, this is a gd emergency.

17: ????

17: Srsly, have you ever heard the word "emergency" before?

17: Sarah! Come ON! I know you're out of town, but this is a big deal. I'm calling.

17: I've called four times, because my GOD!

30: I'm here. What's wrong? Are you okay?!

17: Finally. Yes. But something wild happened. 27 is NOT who we think she is.

30: What do you mean?

17: She's a lunatic. And she basically threatened my life.

30: OK. Slow down. 27 did what?

17: She called me a "little bitch" and threatened me.

30: I'm having a hard time processing this. OUR 27? What did you do to her?

17: What did I do to HER?! We were in a coffee shop. She threw a frickin' chair.

30: She threw a chair?!

17: Well, it fell over.

30: Okay, listen. I'm at Birdsong. I'm with George and his family. I'm learning about my mom. Is this actually an emergency? Because I'm in like a heavenly dreamlike experience. Srsly.

17: I get that, and I'm sorry.

30: Thx.

17: But don't you think it's weird that our so-called "friend" asked me to come to a coffee shop so she could yell at me and then threaten me? And don't you think it's weird she waited until you were OUT OF TOWN to do it?

30: Why did she yell at you?

17: You know that envelope you picked up for her? How many packages, btw, have you secured for that woman? And do you have ANY idea what's in them?

30: Wait, what? What about the envelope? Did you take it??!!

17: I opened it.

30: You opened the woman's private mail? You do know you're not an ACTUAL detective, right? And that's actually against the law?

17: Why do you think she asked you to get that stuff?

30: She's busy? She's new in town? She needs a friend? Not everything is nefarious.

17: I can't find her brother online. Have you tried?

MAKING FRIENDS CAN BE MURDER

30: You're not making sense. Is this because I'm friends with her now? People can be friends with more than one person. I'll still be there for you. And also, I'm busy right now.

17: It was pictures of Fed Sarah's stolen necklace in that envelope. Documents about its sale. The MISSING NECKLACE.

30: Listen. She was a family nanny. She could have been helping them with something. She knows the kids.

17: But I messaged Ruby! And she didn't say anything about that! She said the necklace was missing and they didn't know where it was!!!!

30: Ruby might not tell you everything. I know you're upset, but we can talk about this when I get back.

17: I might not be here when you get back. I'll lock the doors, but . . .

30: I think you're going to be okay. Ok?

17: UGH!

30: I'm signing off.

Text Messages between Sarah Elizabeth Jones (30) and Gabriella Johnson (27)

May 26, 2023

30: Hey, did something weird happen with 17? She's texting me?

27: 😵 Ruby asked me to meet with her. She's feeling a little overwhelmed by 17.

30: Really? It seemed like her idea to come to TSJP?

27: I guess 17 has been messaging her a lot, asking about details, the necklace? Ruby is . . . well, you know.

30: That makes sense. So, 17 took it poorly, I'm taking it?

27: Not great.

30: This is going to sound crazy, but did you throw a chair?

27: Throw a chair? Um, no?

30: I didn't think so.

27: How's camp?

30: Dreamy.

27: Enjoy it. 17 can wait until you get home.

30: Thx. Wait—one more thing.

27: Yeah?

30: Is there anything you're not telling me? Like, about Oscar or the necklace? I love you–I hope you know that. Anything I need to know?

27: xoxo We're good. See you on Sunday?

30: Yeah.

CHAPTER TWENTY-NINE

May 26, 2023

The Nightingales closed out the evening with a few stories about George—ramming the boat into the dock with seven staff trainee witnesses, misidentifying the distinctive red pine during a Tree ID class, breaking the dishwasher on the eve of a catered wedding. Unlike Sarah's own dad, who was reserved, Paul was gregarious in his storytelling, his laugh easy, his smile warm. His eyes crinkled at the corners just like George's did. Sarah could see why George had been torn about working for him or leaving to join the FBI.

Camp Birdsong held the essence of a happy childhood, but George carried the memory of Henry, who hadn't gotten to live it out.

Still, if Paul and Sylvia felt any anger over George's FBI choice, Sarah couldn't sense it. There were no mumbled or sarcastic mentions of abandonment. Instead, the peace of the place seemed to exude from these people. A sense of acceptance fell over Sarah. It was no wonder Ainsley had loved it here, too.

"At Birdsong," Sylvia said at one point when she was telling a story about a camper in Ainsley's Cabin Red-Tailed Hawk, "we say everyone is welcome and everyone belongs. You don't have to be good at something, or the best at anything. You just get to *be*."

Finally, when they were tired, Paul stood. "It's lovely to have you here, Sarah," he said, closing the conversation. "And don't worry. You don't actually have to get in the water tomorrow."

"But I want to be useful," Sarah said. "There's something symmetrical about working in the same exact spot my mom did before me. I think she'd like it."

Sylvia said, "I'll certainly pull a wet suit in your size, but I think Ainsley would be just as pleased if you took a hike in the woods and left the moorings to these yahoos."

"We thought you two would be more comfortable in the AD's cabin," Paul said, patting George's shoulder. "It's open."

Sarah and George grabbed their duffels out of his Civic and headed to the building next to his parents' house, the log siding identical. Sarah held her breath for a moment, imagining the sleeping arrangements. It was hard to picture anyone else's body but Brian's next to hers. She'd wondered more than once how George's broad shoulders would feel under her resting head, whether he'd throw a leg over hers, where his hands would land. She put her own hand against her hip, wrapped her fingers over the bone, and pressed into the flesh.

Paul and Sylvia had already turned the lights on in the assistant director's cabin. They'd opened a lakeside window, and George closed it against the evening chill after he'd grabbed them each an IPA from a cooler he'd yanked from his trunk.

"Planned ahead?" She was glad. They sat in twin chairs facing the water, though they couldn't see Whitehook in the dark.

"How do you feel?" George asked.

"So good," Sarah said. "My mom kept notebooks, you know? So, I've read a little bit about this place." Ainsley had written a two-sentence summary of her first date with Sarah's father, who worked at a boys' camp nearby: the way he smelled of lake water and pine, how she found herself holding a T-shirt he left behind in her car one night over her face as she fell asleep.

"I like having you here." George reached for her hand across the side table.

Sarah's fingers felt warm in George's. Goose bumps rose on her forearms. She thought about the piece of raw rose quartz—good for connection and openheartedness—she'd slid into her backpack. "There's a lot I know about my mom because of her notebooks, but it's nice to be with people who can just talk about her." She sighed. "I guess that's why I stayed with Brian for all those years." Her eyes flew open, and she dropped George's hand. "Oh, shit," she said. Talking about her mother was one thing, but she hadn't planned to mention her ex-fiancé, not to her new maybe-boyfriend.

"Brian?" George grinned. "Is that who chased you out of Vermont? I've been wondering about that."

"You have?" Sarah picked up his hand again, her heart still thumping. "In between bench presses, or what?"

George shrugged, and his closed-mouth smile looked extracute. "Not everyone just decides to start over. I think it's brave. And"—he pointed at her ring finger—"you've got a divot where the ring used to be."

Sarah rubbed it. "I keep wondering when that will go away." She looked over George's head at another decorative sign affixed to the beam separating the living room from the kitchen. "Be a Daymaker," the laser carving read.

"But you are starting over, too," Sarah continued. "And it's so idyllic here. I know why you left. But I'm still wondering, why exactly did you leave?" They laughed a little.

George shrugged and threaded his fingers between hers. She wanted to turn her chair and grab the other hand, to trace her fingers up his forearms and over his jaw. "I know it seems strange," George said, "but it's not that big of a leap to go from camp director to FBI."

Sarah let her hand go heavy in his. It felt nice to rest a little, to be in someone else's space. "It seems pretty different," she said.

"They're both about connections and relationships." George ran his thumb over hers, and a thrill traveled up her leg. "And problem-solving and intuition..." Sarah followed his gaze, which seemed to settle over the window frame.

"And?" she prompted. She resisted the urge to push his hand back into motion, to move it to her waist or her thigh.

"And about doing the right thing," George said. "But the FBI is more about justice and answers, in addition to that other stuff. I mean, I hope it is. Sometimes we can't solve something." He exhaled. "Sometimes there's no ending, happy or otherwise."

There had been a few times Sarah thought she understood finality—Ainsley's death, her flight from med school, her breakup with Brian.

"I had to make a change," Sarah said, filling the silence. "It felt like a solution, moving here. I'd been in the same spot for so long, and I wasn't *choosing* anything. It was just happening to me, right? Like inertia? So... I left?"

George nodded. "I get that. One thing about Birdsong, this place is everyone's home, right? Their second home?" He looked at her, and she blinked, trying to follow. He must have seen her confusion, because he clarified. "Like, your mom seemed to feel like the most real version of herself here, right? That's why you're here?"

Sarah understood; she felt it. "It's amazing what you guys have created."

"Right," George said, "but it's my *actual* home. I don't have another place where I feel more real or better. This is the whole place.

It felt weird to be the anchor when everyone else left and came back all the time." He didn't look sad exactly, but there was an intensity to what he was saying that Sarah couldn't quite decipher. "Maybe I'll feel better about it after I've been gone for a little bit."

Sarah let his hand go for a moment to trace one of the rings on the coffee table. "I don't think I'll ever go back to Vermont." She gasped. And then she laughed. "I didn't realize I felt like that."

"All right!" George clapped his hands and laughed, too. "Birdsong truth serum strikes again! And so, this Brian guy. He's, like, really, really out of the picture. Coast is"—he swooped his arm along the dark horizon—"totally clear."

"I was ready to move on," Sarah said.

George's eyes took on a mischievous glint. "So, what was the deal with that guy?"

"Do you really want to know?" Sarah hadn't felt sadness over Brian since the moment she merged her U-Haul trailer onto I-90 out of Vermont. It was hard to believe she'd spent fifteen years with him.

"Why not?" George asked. "We're taking risks, right? I mean, I just introduced you to my parents on our first weekend getaway."

First. A potential for more.

"Brian and I met in elementary school," Sarah said. "We started dating in middle school, never broke up, got engaged, and then I just couldn't do it anymore." She breathed out. "How can you stay the same person all that time? It had run its course, and it was just over. I moved here. We're still friends"—she tipped her head back and forth, considering the truth of this last descriptor—"-ish."

"Why was it over?" George coughed, and his cheeks flushed. Sarah watched him roll his shoulders, an unsuccessful attempt at nonchalance.

Sarah knew the answer. She'd told a version to Grandma Ellie and to her father and to Twenty-Seven. She sipped her beer. "He didn't want me to grow. He wanted me to be the exact same person I'd always been." She looked back at the Daymaker sign. "And to be fair," she continued, "I never really gave him any indication that I wanted things to be different. I sort of suddenly realized I didn't want to live a mile from the house I grew up in." George's parents slept one hundred meters from where they sat. "I guess that's kind of like you?"

"Not so different," George agreed.

And then Sarah leaned across the table. She felt swept away by Birdsong, by the phantom memory of her mother at age twenty-one. "Can I just ... ?" She reached her arms out and touched each of his shoulders. His cheeks flared. She ran a hand down the side of his jaw the way she'd wanted to.

He put his finger under her chin and held it steady as he moved toward her and their lips met. Immediately everything was different from what she'd known for so long with Brian. The shape of his mouth, the slightly sour taste of the IPA, a remnant of the wintergreen gum he'd been chewing in the car. A shiver traveled from her chest and into all four limbs.

"Is this okay?" she asked when they parted. "Is this the weirdest come-on you've ever experienced?"

George laughed. It was deep and real, and Sarah could feel his whole body relax. "Well, I did invite you to a cabin in the woods."

They stood up and George enveloped her. He felt as big and as sturdy and as completely different as she'd craved, as she'd imagined.

CHAPTER THIRTY

May 27, 2023

Gabriella turned the shower from hot to freezing cold and forced herself to stand still in the stream for fifty-two seconds, up from the forty-seven she'd done for the two days before. Annabeth had espoused the health benefits of cold showering, things like boosting immunity and reducing inflammation. It had always seemed like torture to Gabriella, which was why she'd started doing it a few days after Fed Sarah died.

She died, Gabriella repeated to herself, as the seconds ticked down. *She fell. She died. An accident.*

She snuck a look at her watch as her teeth chattered. The cold never got warmer. Sarah never got less dead.

Gabriella added two seconds more, even though the freeze felt unbearable, and then shoved the faucet into the off position. She counted to ten as she stood dripping in the shower. *You don't deserve a towel.*

But eventually, she stepped out. Her face appeared in the mirror, her eyes dull and her hair stringy and dripping on her shoulders. It had been different, showering, getting ready for work when she'd been a teacher instead of a . . . what? What was she? A con artist sounded so base.

She was in the business of saving a life.

That was how she'd always justified it. No one was really getting hurt. No one was even facing financial ruin, not really. Until Fed Sarah. *She died.*

Gabriella looked at the shower, wondering if the right thing would be to get back in there, to let her fingers and toes turn fatally blue, but then she thought of Oscar. The photo of him with his face bruised and bloody. If the body count doubled—Fed Sarah and then Oscar, too—then it all would have been for nothing.

Gabriella grabbed her towel and scrubbed her face too roughly. The FBI circled. George Nightingale knew who she was. The Minneapolis police had called her twice last night. She'd let them both go to voicemail and listened to the detective tell her they had more questions for her. The second message was from Supervisory Special Agent in Charge Jane Vance, whose name Gabriella had seen in the paper. The fake address she'd given would only hold for so long. When Vance's call came in, she walked to her room, grabbed the hammer she kept in the side pocket of her suitcase, and smashed the burner. She was so close. She'd be out of town in thirty-six hours. The walk to the convenience store on the corner for a new phone had taken seventeen minutes. On the way home, she'd texted Oscar's people. New number, she said. But still here for Oscar. They hadn't answered.

Now, Gabriella squeezed her dripping hair into the sink and put on her favorite black yoga pants, old ones from the days before armed gunmen stalked her elementary school classroom. She got in the car.

Last one, she told herself. *This is the very last one.*

Sarah's weekend away at Camp Birdsong was the perfect opportunity. Gabriella bet that her personal laptop wasn't on the packing list, so the IP address would be the same for the transfer. The bank system shouldn't require additional security questions or verification via text. Gabriella wished she could wait a couple more days, but this? This was the opportunity. It wouldn't get better. Oscar's people had said she was out of time. The FBI and the Minneapolis cops were aiming to question her. They'd look now until they found her. She'd ghosted the Campbells after the coffee with Seventeen and tried not to picture Ruby's sweet face.

Gabriella had the account number and the requisite routing numbers on a folded-up sticky note in the glove box of her car, stuck in the "Oil and Maintenance" section of the Camry owner's manual. Now, she just had to decide how much she was going to take. All eight hundred thousand? Gabriella didn't know what Sarah had planned to do with the money. Something noble, probably, or important. Gabriella could just transfer the remaining fifty-two thousand she owed to the cartel people. Maybe an extra twenty to start somewhere else for good, and an extra fifty for Oscar's rehab. He'd need it.

She hadn't yet decided where she'd go, not daring to believe that this nightmarish part of her life could be over. Gabriella couldn't go back to teaching. She couldn't move back to Chicago. She couldn't be Gabriella Johnson any longer. People—Annabeth—knew everything she'd done.

She'd have to be a new person, a new version. *But only one more.*

And maybe in the next iteration she could make some real friends. Gabriella could shape an identity—a version of her old self, cheerful maybe, hardworking, trustworthy—and settle down. Maybe there would be someone like George Nightingale for her, too. Well, not a federal agent, but a genuine person with a forehead curl and broad shoulders.

Gabriella hadn't thought at the beginning about the burden of always hiding. She'd been open, transparent, before. Now, there would always be an entire vault of things she wouldn't be able to talk about.

She died. It was an accident.

Gabriella parked a block away from Sarah's. She'd been to the apartment several times, and she didn't want anyone to note the car. The task force might watch Sarah's apartment, but no—they were interested in the murder. *The accident.* Gabriella clenched her molars. She pulled a black baseball cap over her ponytail and walked with purpose toward the entrance. She'd swiped Sarah's spare key from a cutesy hook near the door, something undoubtedly crafted by Grandma Ellie. She ran up the stairs two at a time to the third floor.

In the beginning, these covert operations had made Gabriella sweat, heart pounding and nearly gasping for air. But as the months passed, it got easier. *Act "as if,"* she told herself, just like she had in her first days of teaching. *Act as if you know how to teach regrouping. Act as if you can lead a line to PE.* Don't know how to call a parent to convey a concern about behavior? Act as if.

Interloping in Sarah's postwar building, Gabriella would act as if Sarah had asked her to water plants or polish up a crystal or do a tarot reading. She scanned the empty hallway as she turned the key in the lock. A neighbor's dish clattered in a sink and a phone rang, but no one appeared. Gabriella opened Sarah's door a crack, slid through it, and closed it behind her.

"Okay," she said aloud, testing the volume of her voice in the space. The sun streamed through the window, the selenite on the sill glowing with it. The stone was meant to clean the energy, to add protection. Maybe it would work for Gabriella if it wouldn't for Sarah.

Gabriella went to the laptop Sarah had plugged in on the kitchen table. She'd asked to check her email the other day, knowing Sarah would provide the lock screen password. "Ugh," Sarah had said before she confessed it, Gabriella trying to hide her anticipation. "Don't judge, because I haven't had time to change it."

Gabriella had laughed. "It's Brian something?"

"Brian1224." She rolled her eyes as she said it, a little flush rising in her cheeks.

"He likes Christmas?" Gabriella had asked.

"It's too embarrassing to tell you. It's just been my password forever," Sarah said.

"Wait." Gabriella had paused before she logged into the Gmail she'd made for Sarah Christine Jones, graduate student in sociology and resident of Minneapolis. "Did you and Brian . . ." She tipped her head and wiggled her eyebrows.

"Yes, okay! Yes." Sarah had covered her face with her hands and collapsed onto her couch. "It's our sexiversary." She shook her head. "Twelve-twenty-four. Never tell anyone. I'm mortified."

"It's adorable."

"I was nineteen," Sarah confessed.

"You know you should change your password more than once every decade?" Gabriella had been amazed how easily people would hand over their data: details, tells, trivia. They served up all the information Gabriella ever needed. The women she'd met, everyone really, assumed danger came from bad-looking people—shady people—when actually a threat could be anyone.

Gabriella typed "Brian1224" into the box and watched the screen dissolve into a menu of documents and shortcuts. She opened a browser window, navigated to Fidelity Investments, and held her breath until Sarah's username popped up. People generally clicked "Remember Me" on these sites, which made Gabriella's job so much easier.

Unfortunately, the browser didn't populate the password field, so Gabriella tried "Brian1224" and winced when the red error message appeared.

Next, she added a special character: "Brian1224!" She hovered her finger over the return button. "Please," she whispered. And then she collapsed against the back of the chair with relief as Sarah's dashboard loaded. The account balance appeared in a stately font, all six digits. Fidelity had been Grace Smith's company as well. Gabriella remembered where the transfer commands were, the way she'd need to enter the account number for Oscar's captors, the routing number for the offshore bank.

Now the amount. Oscar's eyes had been glassy and vacant in the newest photo. One hundred and twenty-five thousand, she decided, not even a quarter of what Sarah had. She saw Fed Sarah's eyes in her mind then, too, the way they'd bugged out when she'd plummeted, her mouth open and gasping. Gabriella hadn't meant for it to happen.

She blinked several times, entered the numbers in the appropriate fields, and hit "submit." She held her breath as an animated circle appeared on the screen. "Processing," the site told her, just as it had when she'd taken Grace's fifty-four thousand. And then, suddenly, the circle was replaced by a green check mark. "Success." It was really almost over.

Next, she took out the new phone and sent the message. Transfer initiated.

She watched her screen for the reply. How long until it clears?

Tuesday, she said, hoping that was true.

We'll send instructions then.

That was it.

Next, Gabriella navigated to Sarah's open email tab and deleted the alert about the transfer. She looked at the table near the door from which she'd stolen the statement in the first place. Sarah had a bud vase there. A few white daisies poked out of the top, their yellow centers impossibly vibrant. She closed the browser window and lowered the laptop screen. She scooted her chair into the table, making a scuffing sound, and then just as she checked for her wallet, keys, and phone, someone knocked on the door.

Gabriella froze, her quads instantly tight. She held her breath.

"Hello?" A woman's voice. Gabriella's mind raced. She hadn't seen anyone when she'd come down the hall.

The person knocked again. "I know I heard something," she said. "I'm going to call the manager. We place a premium on safety here. Or maybe I'll just call the police . . ."

These would be the same cops who wanted to bring her in, just when everything was so close. Gabriella was almost, almost done. The last thing she needed was a nosy neighbor torpedoing the whole thing. She ran to the door and "acted as if." "Hello!" she said brightly.

"Oh," the woman said. "Are you one of the Sarahs?"

"Twenty-Seven." She'd perfected the art of feigning innocence over the last two years; she couldn't fail now.

"Twenty-Seven." The neighbor crossed her arms. "I've seen the newspaper photos."

"Right," Gabriella exhaled, lowering her shoulders, still forcing a smile. "I'm Sarah's friend."

"She's a woman living alone, so I keep tabs on her." The neighbor's brow furrowed. "What are you doing here?"

"I left my wallet the other night," Gabriella said. "We went for gin and tonics. First of the season? Anyway, I left my wallet, and so I just came to get it."

The neighbor cocked her head. "She gave you a key?"

Shit. "Yeah, well that was lucky, actually." There had been so many moments like this—near catches, almost slips, like the other night when she'd almost admitted to Sarah that Oscar was still alive. "I happened to mention to Sarah that I wanted to watch the game, and I don't have cable."

"Sarah has cable?" The woman wasn't buying it. "And what game?"

"Twins," Gabriella said. "Baseball. You know what? Between now and the game, I have a bunch of stuff..." Gabriella pushed into the hallway.

"Sorry to chase you away," the neighbor called when Gabriella reached the stairs and started down them. "But also the Twins are off until Tuesday. So, that's kind of weird, don't you think?"

Shit, shit, shit, shit. Gabriella raced to her car.

CHAPTER THIRTY-ONE

May 27, 2023

"I feel happy," Sarah said.

"I'm so glad." George's hands felt warm and a little bit scratchy, just as they had on her rib cage the night before.

She shivered, remembering how he'd whispered in her ear as she'd fallen asleep. She'd already replayed what he'd said a million times over. First, she remembered it when she'd woken up in the night, his body still warm and sturdy beside hers, and then again when she'd shuffled into the kitchen that morning in stocking feet and his oversized T-shirt, the one he'd discarded by the bed.

"How did I get so lucky?"

That was what he'd asked her. She smiled so hard against his chest she worried about grazing him with her teeth.

When they cleared the thicket that separated the administrative cabins from the camp buildings, George stopped, tugging her hand and pointing with his free one at Lake Whitehook. The water spread out before them, mostly still and gray. "This view," he said, like his mother had the night before. "It never gets old."

Sarah wondered whether she might see this again and again, whether she'd be back with George when they were much older. Whether this was just the beginning of something huge, like the lake itself.

George led her into the dining hall, letting go of her hand only when she passed him on the way into the building. As soon as she was inside, Sylvia handed her a mug of coffee and a map labeled "Camp Birdsong Hiking Adventure."

"Good morning," she sang, "and I'm just so sorry!" She winked then. "But I couldn't find a wet suit in your size. Paul says he can do the docks without you."

Sarah glanced at the paper in front of her, the trails with avian names like "Plumage Pass" and "Flight Path." "Oh," she said, a tiny bit disappointed, "but I actually want to be useful."

Sylvia leaned in. "I haven't seen George so happy in quite a while." She smiled as she stood upright, and Sarah felt a warmth settle across her shoulders. What would her own mother have looked like at Sylvia's age? Would she have had silver hair like hers? A lovely trail map of wrinkles next to each eye? "So, you *have* been useful. More than you probably realize. It was hard for him, you know?" Sylvia bumped a shoulder against Sarah's, instantly familiar. "Making the decision to leave? And telling his father, especially. It's really nice that he brought you back here." Sarah followed her glance across the room at Paul, who had a hand on George's shoulder, both of them grinning.

Sarah's breath caught as she thought of the rumpled sheets in the AD's cabin, the shower they'd shared that morning, laughing too hard when she'd knocked the squeegee from its hook near the door. She wondered if Sylvia could see the evidence of it on her, could sense that she'd fallen asleep on George's shoulder, the breadth of him as homey as she'd hoped it would be.

"It's so cool to be here." Sarah aimed for casual. Behind her, three young people with bed head sat at one of the round tables, wet suits piled on an empty one next to them. "I can't believe you all run this place."

"All jobs seem mystifying until you do them, right?" Sylvia asked. "You're a personal trainer?" She flexed her biceps. "No way I could do that. Not that these guns don't scream, 'Which way to the beach?'" Sarah giggled. "Anyway," Sylvia continued, "Paul will lead the dock crew. George will be his first mate, which will make him happy. And between you and me, the job kind of sucks. I quit doing it years ago." She raised her eyebrows at the workers, indicating their coming suffering. "It would make *me* so happy if you'd explore the trails and relax a little. You can have some time to yourself."

Sarah's cheeks felt heavy all of a sudden. If she'd let them, the tears would come quickly. Grandma Ellie took care of her—always had—but to have this mother, George's mother who had known Sarah's *own* mother, taking care of her? "That's lovely," Sarah said, her voice thick. "You're lovely. Thank you."

Sylvia turned toward the serving counter, where another staffer had placed platters of food. "Get some breakfast," she said. "We like to eat here."

George appeared at her shoulder and leaned down to her ear, his stubble against her face. She raised her hand to his cheek and squeezed her eyes shut, remembering the way he'd pulled her T-shirt up to her rib cage and then over her head in the living room the night before. "Saved you a seat," he whispered.

After they cleared their plates, the staff and Paul headed down to the shores of Whitehook. George hung back with Sarah as the others began to wiggle into their wet suits. "See you at lunch?" he asked.

Sarah pulled the folded trail map from her pocket. "I'm headed to Plumage Path," she said, "and I'm so excited." She flung her right arm out toward the road, toward the trails, and then tucked her hands into her sweatshirt sleeves. George pulled her against him.

"You'll see the tree house Bea and I built last summer on that path." George sounded proud. She breathed him in.

"You know how to build a tree house?"

"I have mad skills that no one can deny." Sarah laughed. She kissed his cheek, and then watched him jog toward the water. She spun on her heel and headed toward the trails Ainsley had wandered all those years before.

Sarah wasn't sure how long she spent in the woods, the leaves thick and the trail narrow and damp. The forest seemed to close in on her in places, and then open back up. She could imagine kids and counselors playing tag games and sitting in circles. She could picture her mom in a high ponytail and soccer shorts, the outfit she'd been wearing in one of the photos Sylvia and Paul had shown her, traipsing along in worn running shoes and those socks with the balls on the heels that she'd always loved.

It wasn't until Sarah had touched the support beams on the tree house George and Bea had built, its platform more than a story high and with a tree trunk growing through it, that she followed the map back down to the lakeshore. She stopped to observe the dock crew, a pod of floating heads that sometimes disappeared with a shout from Paul. They left a trail of pilings in their wake.

When she got back to the AD's cabin, Sarah thought to check her phone. Red alert, the text from her neighbor Jeanine read. Sarah rolled her eyes and scrolled down. The woman was prone to exaggeration, the definition of "busybody." Did you give the Sarahs keys to your apartment? One of them was here today. *Keys to my apartment?*

What? Sarah typed as she walked toward the lakeside window. She reached a hand in her pocket and felt the polished serpentine crystal there, good for new beginnings, protection, and flexibility. She looked out over the water as Jeanine replied.

27 was here? she wrote. In your apartment. I thought I'd check because I haven't known you to give out your keys.

Sarah squinted at the phone. *Twenty-Seven was in my apartment? I didn't*, she said. Wait, are you sure someone was there?

I'm not known to hallucinate, Jeanine wrote. I heard a chair scuff in your kitchen, and I knocked.

A chair scuff?

Yeah, and I knew you were gone. Was gonna call the cops, but I knocked instead, and there she was.

A hollow opened in Sarah's chest. She'd packed crystals for the weekend, a collection supposedly good for enhancing psychic ability to entertain Ellie's idea about a supernatural visit. And not only had Ainsley been typically quiet, but also Sarah'd had no sense of anyone in her space at home.

Okay, Sarah typed to Jeanine. Thanks so much for letting me know.

What are you gonna do? Also? 27 lied about a Twins game.

Sarah needed to think. There had to be a reasonable explanation. Thanks so much for the heads-up, she typed. I'll investigate.

Will you keep me posted? Jeanine asked.

Sarah reacted to that with a heart and glanced at the clock on the microwave. Lunch would be served in twenty-five minutes, maybe enough time to figure out what was going on.

She texted Seventeen, just to check in, to make sure nothing more had happened. How's it going today? she asked.

The thumbs-up emoji reply came almost immediately, and Sarah felt relief. She'd been right not to be overly concerned. I'll have more for you in a few hours, Seventeen said. We're on it. Sarah wasn't sure what that meant, but it didn't seem like an emergency.

CHAPTER THIRTY-TWO

Video Transcript Recorded by Sarah Jones, Age Seventeen

May 30, 2023

Believe it or not, I'm very familiar with people ignoring me. It's not like I'm overwhelmed with IRL friend requests. So, though it worried and frustrated me, I wasn't totally surprised that Thirty disregarded my texts about Twenty-Seven.

Still, we were—are—real friends. I wanted her to be able to count on me, and I felt like something bad could happen to her. She was BFFs with basically a confessed murderer.

So, after I survived the night, just as Thirty said I would, I decided to figure out for myself what Twenty-Seven was up to. I started with the other members of TSJP. "Has anyone been to Twenty-Seven's apartment?" I asked in a modified group chat. I added an excuse. "I want to bring her a treat. She seemed so stressed at our last meeting."

"Nice try," Sixty-Nine texted back. "You're being nosy." Then, she texted me separately. "What's really going on?" she asked.

And immediately, I realized the grandma should have been my next contact all along. I called her right then and told her every single thing that Twenty-Seven had said and done, and unlike Thirty, she believed me right away.

"Something is way, way off," she said. "And it's maybe an emergency. I'm picking you up."

I'll admit it, I almost cried with happiness. A normal seventeen-year-old would have real friends, and instead I had a fake grandma. But Sixty-Nine is a grandma who was funny enough to roll down the window of her Elantra when she cruised into the condo driveway, push her plastic sunglasses down her nose, and say, "Get in, loser, we're going sleuthing."

I laughed so hard that I could barely buckle my seat belt.

"I thought a lot about this," Sixty-Nine said, patting my knee, "and we definitely need to go to the University of Minnesota. Because what are the chances she's actually a student there?"

"Zero!" I practically shouted it.

"I agree, and I think it's weird," Sixty-Nine said, "but the prettier someone is, the more likely that everyone will just listen to them and believe them. That's how we all got taken in."

"It's the patriarchy," I told her. Sister Mary Theresa would totally agree with me. Why else would the bosses of the church be men when the religious women were so unequivocally badass? Who's even doing the contemplative prayer over there in Catholicism? It's the nuns saving the whole darn world.

"I'm guessing your supervisor, Sister Mary Theresa, taught you about the patriarchy?" Sixty-Nine asked.

"Yeah," I agreed.

"That's why we need her, too. Let's stop at Sacred Heart and pick her up."

I was shocked. First of all, I wasn't sure Sister was allowed out of there. It was a cloister and all that. And second, I hadn't told Sister about this iteration of the project. She'd ordered me to quit, and I hadn't.

"I think it's a bad idea," I said.

"Well, I'm driving, and I'm old, and I already called her," Sixty-Nine said. "She's coming."

My mouth hung open. "You—what—like googled the phone number and called the *monastery*?"

"The number is listed on the website," Sixty-Nine said. "Someone called the Portress answered? Honestly, I thought I was being punked."

My breathing went shallow. "The Portress is a place and a person," I whispered.

"Anyway, I asked for your Sister Mary Theresa, explained the situation, and she's going to be ready when we get there."

"I think this is a bad idea," I said again.

"Nope, we need her." Sixty-Nine navigated toward school. "She was a police detective. She'll have the training to make this investigation go."

When we pulled into the drop-off circle at Sacred Heart, Sister was standing outside in dark blue slacks and a short-sleeved button-down, her cross dangling in front as usual. I opened my door and vacated the front seat before Sixty-Nine had stopped.

"You haven't been truthful," Sister said, "and we'll deal with that later."

I felt sweaty. I think I made a grunting noise, but she cut me off.

"It'll be good to flex my detective muscle." She slid into the front with Sixty-Nine. "I really enjoyed your latest post on Season Nine, Episode Six," Sister said. "'Night of the Coyote'?" Sixty-Nine put her hand to her collarbone, clearly honored. Sister gushed: "Excellent treatment of the postcolonial issues involved in the visual conception of the Old West."

I wish I were kidding. But these two were basically made for each other.

"We're headed to the University of Minnesota," Sixty-Nine said, ostensibly to both of us, but mostly to Sister. "We need to find out if she's actually a student."

"Good call," Sister said. "We can probably con it out of a student worker in the library."

"Con it!" I exclaimed, shocked by Sister's plans to manipulate. But she held up a hand between the seats and didn't look back at me.

"We'll park near Dinkytown since she's in sociology," Sixty-Nine said.

"Are you an alum?" Sister asked.

"Class of 1977 undergrad, and then 1982 law," Sixty-Nine said. "You?"

"Nineteen eighty-six. I studied psych."

I couldn't picture Sister on campus as an undergrad.

"Not a bad field since you have to deal with the likes of this one." Sixty-Nine jacked a thumb toward the back seat.

"Indeed," Sister said.

And I had officially discovered my superpower: I bring together people who become best friends all around me, just not *with* me.

After we parked, the two of them speed-walked out of the ramp. Sixty-Nine looked back at me and made a hook of her arm like she was swimming, urging me to keep up. "I've got a plan," she said. I felt a little dizzy.

Sister walked into Wilson Library first and did a sign of the cross. Then Sixty-Nine slowed her walk to a shuffle. She linked her arm with mine and hunched her shoulders.

"What are you doing?" I whispered.

"I'm being a grandma," she said. "Now watch this."

Here's what happened: we walked up to the counter, where the student worker smiled up at Sixty-Nine over the top of her book, which I couldn't help but notice was called *Discipline and Punish: The Birth of the Prison.*

"Can I help you?" the girl asked.

"Oh, I certainly hope so, dear." Sixty-Nine's voice was higher—and, I don't know, dopier?—than I've ever heard it.

The girl set her book down, spine up, and looked earnest. "Let's give it a try."

"Well, I'm helping my granddaughter," Sixty-Nine said. The worker looked at me. I wasn't sure if I was supposed to be the granddaughter here, so I just smiled.

"Not her." Sixty-Nine dipped her chin and looked at the girl over the top of her glasses. "She's just my neighbor, my driver. I'm getting older, you know? It's harder to navigate the freeways?"

It was all I could do not to roll my eyes, but I have to admit I was hella impressed. This woman had just woven in and out of traffic and infiltrated the center of a major land-grant university without even batting an eye. I would have crashed five times over, and that's why I'm not allowed to get my license.

The library worker nodded aggressively. "I totally get that," she said. "We all have to ask for help, am I right?"

"You are," piped in Sister. "Help comes to those who ask, from earthly sources and from above." She pointed at the ceiling.

Oh, lordy.

"I'm so glad you see that." Sixty-Nine poured it on thick.

More nodding. The girl swiveled her head between Sixty-Nine and Sister, clearly wondering about the relationship between the two senior citizens, but neither of them offered an explanation. They probably hadn't worked that out in the sprint from the car.

"So, how can I help?" the library worker asked.

"My granddaughter is just *so* overwhelmed," Sixty-Nine said.

"She's doing a special project with a professor in the sociology department this summer, and she's just buried. Yesterday, she told me she'd forgotten to pick up one of her holds from—what did she call it?"

"Interlibrary loan?" the worker asked, her optimism oozing over the counter. "That's how most books come in from other places! I bet it was interlibrary loan!"

"So, can I pick it up for her?" Sixty-Nine asked.

And then the worker's face crumpled. "Oh," she said, "you need a card. Her library card."

Sixty-Nine's shoulders fell and she pitched forward, alarming me for a moment until she caught herself with her elbows on the counter. It was part of the schtick. "Is there a work-around?" Sixty-Nine whispered it. The student looked at me over Sixty-Nine's head, obviously hoping I might be able to do something to mitigate the situation, but I just shrugged. Sister rubbed Sixty-Nine's back, as if she'd just gotten a death sentence.

"Um, there's a policy?" the worker said.

"Certainly nothing we can't circumvent?" Sister pressed her palms together as if beginning to pray.

"But we drove from Woodbury," Sixty-Nine said, which of course, we hadn't. Lying. It seemed to come easily to almost everyone.

"Okay." The worker scanned the library entryway—a little frantically, I thought—and, not noticing any other employees or really *any*one on a Saturday on Memorial Day weekend, put her fingers on the keyboard in front of her. "What's your granddaughter's name?"

Sixty-Nine brightened, her shoulders back. "That's easy," she said. "Same name as mine. Jones-comma-Sarah."

The worker typed. "That's a common one," she said. "There are quite a few records, but..." Her eyebrows furrowed, a line descending from between them all the way to the bridge of her nose. "This is odd. There aren't any active Sarah Joneses for summer semester. What department did you say she was in?"

I held my breath. This could be proof—definitive proof—that I was right about something. That I wasn't jealous, or overreacting, or lonely. Just actually and verifiably *correct*.

"Sociology," Sixty-Nine said. "I'm one hundred percent sure about that."

"Um..." The worker typed, the keyboard echoing in the empty foyer. "I'm really, really sorry, especially since you drove all the way from Woodbury, but I've checked sociology and child development and psych and education and social work, and there isn't an active Sarah Jones in any of those this summer."

"Wait," Sixty-Nine said, looking at me with faux confusion. The woman turned out to be quite a good actor, which was a bit surprising. If there are any takeaways from TSJP, it's that people will absolutely blow your mind if you get to know them. "Is this the University of *Minnesota*?" she asked.

"Of course," the worker said. "Wilson Library, Minneapolis."

"It's Minnesota State." Sixty-Nine shook her head and took several steps backward, dragging me along with her. "Can you believe I made that mistake, Olive? Sarah goes to Minnesota *State*."

I was Olive in this scenario, and TBH, I was thrilled. Later I checked, and there are only 121 Olive Joneses in the United States. If I were an Olive, I'd be exponentially more interesting just by the fact of my name.

"You've done it again, Sarah," Sister said, shaking her head and looking at the ceiling. "Details!"

Sixty-Nine assumed her real walk, not the fake elderly one she'd adopted for the trip in. Sister took a couple of hop steps in front of us and held the door.

"But, Minnesota State's in Mankato!" the worker shouted after us. "It's an hour and half from here!"

As soon as we got outside, Sixty-Nine stopped and turned to me. She jabbed a finger into my chest. "Okay, think," she said. "What do we know?"

I felt a thrill, strategizing with someone who cared.

"We know she's not a student at the University of Minnesota." Sister jumped in, ticking this first revelation off on her index finger. "Let's walk." She made the swimming motion this time, hurrying. "I think we're missing something obvious," Sister said. "Seventeen told me about the necklace. Our suspect stole the necklace from her boss, with whom she got a job in part because they shared the same name."

This was true. Ruby had said that's what got Twenty-Seven the interview.

Sixty-Nine held her index finger aloft. "What if she's *not* a Sarah Jones?"

"What?" And, I'm telling you, this idea hadn't yet occurred to me even a little bit. Because if you could make up any name you wanted, why in the world would you choose boring old Sarah Jones?

"Come on." Sixty-Nine marched back toward the car, fast. I ran every couple of steps to keep up with her, and so did Sister, who seemed to be in remarkably good shape for a contemplative nun.

When she'd fired the engine and peeled out of the lot, Sixty-Nine told me we were headed for our usual Starbucks. "I'm used to that place. You brought us there, and it has good mojo."

I can't totally explain why this declaration made me so happy. I think I just felt appreciated.

"You have your laptop, right?" Sixty-Nine asked. "I've never done this before, but we're going to attempt something I read about once called a 'reverse image search.'"

And, yeah, duh. I should have thought of that a while ago, but honestly, what reason did I have to be suspicious before the confrontation in the coffee shop? I checked IDs! I made a club for people named Sarah Jones. Why would anyone *not* named Sarah Jones bother to show up? Especially if that person had been involved in the mysterious death of *another* Sarah Jones? That seemed like the definition of self-sabotage.

"You know what I think?" Sister asked. "I think it's going to be hard to find a good photo. Remember the newspaper picture? She's in sunglasses and there's hair blowing across her face."

"Damn," I said, thinking it through. And then, "Sorry, Sister."

When Sixty-Nine and I searched our phones for pictures of Twenty-Seven, we found we hardly had any. In group photos, she had a hand in the way or inadvertently-on-purpose ended up with her face to the side or behind someone's head. Finally, Sixty-Nine found a candid she'd taken from what I think was our second meeting. It was before Fed Sarah had even died.

Sister found the reverse image search directions, which were widely available and followable, even for the olds. We uploaded the picture, and Sixty-Nine held my hand as we waited for the results to load. Finally there was something: a school photo of Twenty-Seven with a brilliant smile, the mottled blue background the exact same one we'd had at Sacred Heart that year. Twenty-Seven's skin looked fresh and dewy, even under the harsh light the photographers always brought. She wore clear-plastic-framed glasses. Superchic. We clicked on the link. "Former Teacher," the title of the article read, "Wanted in Connection with Fraud."

"Holy moly," Sixty-Nine said at the same time I said, "Holy shit." Sister flicked me on the back of the head, but I know she didn't mean it. The caption read, "Chicago PD looking for any information on former elementary school teacher Gabriella Johnson, also known most recently as Catherine Anderson."

Catherine Anderson? Gabriella Johnson?

"See?!" I said to Sixty-Nine. "I totally told you so."

"Let me make a call to that police department," Sister said.

"You think they'll tell you anything?" Sixty-Nine asked.

"People have a way of divulging things to the religious." She pulled a cell phone out of her habit pocket.

CHAPTER THIRTY-THREE

May 27, 2023

While putting in docks had never been among his favorite camp tasks, that morning with his dad, George felt an unexpected sense of peace. Paul had more grays than he'd had the previous year, but he still commanded the crew. His abs looked defined when he peeled down his wet suit and toweled off for lunch. When he swiped his hair back over his forehead, George could see the shadow of the young man he'd been before George had been born.

"It was a good morning, team!" Paul said now, shivering a bit even with his Birdsong branded towel around his shoulders. "Lunch in"—he glanced at the pink Timex he'd had since about 2016—"twenty-two minutes."

George headed up to the AD's cabin, hopeful that Sarah would be back from her hike. He imagined her on the couch with a teacup, a book in hand. And for a split second, he wondered what it would be like to change his mind about the future, to end his stint with the FBI, and to run the camp with Sarah someday.

He'd told her there wasn't such a big difference between the two career paths, but one difference was duplicity. Sarah was George's Confidential Human Source. That was why he'd gotten to know her in the first place. Their professional relationship would end as soon as he handed Gabriella Johnson over to the US attorney.

But after last night? His stomach dropped. He remembered kissing her nose, her eyelids fluttering, her soft breath against his collarbone as he himself drifted off, safe from Henry's searching eyeballs, safe from everything. He'd have to find a way to build a bridge between how they'd met and the potential rest of his life. Wasn't it possible that she was actually perfect for him, in addition to being perfect for the case?

His whole body flushed as he opened the door of the cabin, anxious to see her. "Sarah?" he called. Instead of being curled up on the couch, she was pacing the kitchen.

"Something weird is going on," she announced.

He readjusted, felt his FBI armor slipping back on. *She's my informant.* He was supposed to sense "something weird" before she did. "What's happening?" He felt his mind fire back up, the peace of the morning, the focus required by the dock task overwhelmed by stray pieces of information about Gabriella Johnson.

"Two things have happened." Sarah held up her fingers like a peace sign, and even with his stress rising, George couldn't help smiling. She was adorable, and so earnest. "First," she continued, "Seventeen texted me a bunch of times last night before"—her face went pink—"well, before bedtime, you know." She shrugged then, loose and goofy for a moment, and George almost melted. She was just herself. He could see every emotion rolling through her, no artifice. She'd be a terrible con artist.

Con artist.

He glanced at his watch. It had been four months since Gabriella Johnson and Sarah had met. Gabriella never lasted longer than this in a city. Her earlier best-friendships had spanned twelve weeks or fewer. And before this time, she'd never killed anyone.

How could I have scheduled this weekend away with the clock ticking? But then again, George wasn't supposed to stop Gabriella this time. He was supposed to watch her. Document. Let the transfer happen. If it happened—if the transfer was initiated—he could have documentation of it right now. But none of that plan made sense to him any longer with Sarah pacing in front of him, her anxiety ratcheting up.

Listen, he told himself. *Listen to what she's telling you now.*

"What happened with Seventeen?" he prompted.

"She kept texting me. She had some crazy story about Twenty-Seven threatening her in a coffee shop? It sounded hyperbolic, frankly, and I was distracted." The familiar smile again, and then back to pacing.

George wanted to ask to see the text messages from Seventeen, but he couldn't. Not yet. Instead, he cleared his throat. "What did she say?"

Sarah shook her head. "It's hard to explain. She has this theory that Twenty-Seven stole the necklace from Fed Sarah. The missing necklace? You know the yellow diamond I asked you about?"

George felt his shoulders inch toward his ears. There were the photos Gretchen had told them about, the pending follow-up interrogations with Caden Campbell and maybe the girls, interviews he hoped to attend. Could he have both? Sarah and the case? Sarah and the Minneapolis Field Office?

"Yes, the necklace," he said, willing Sarah forward in her story.

"And anyway, Seventeen presented some evidence about it at our TSJP meeting, and then Twenty-Seven asked to meet her for coffee, and what did she say?" Sarah scrolled back in her phone, looking for the exact phrasing. "She said, and frankly I didn't quite process this or, I guess, really believe it?" She paused.

George summoned the patience he'd displayed in the Campbell-Jones residence, the way he'd let the girls self-destruct in the middle of the living room, let them chip away at their secret about their mother's involvement in their grandmother's death. He needed Sarah's secrets, too, and he needed them right now.

Sarah stopped fidgeting and looked right at him. A little something—fear, he thought—had crept into her eyes. "She said Twenty-Seven called her a little bitch and threw a chair."

"Wow." George's heart thudded. He wanted to call Vance, to confirm that they'd brought Gabriella in that day as planned. She'd killed once already. George had let his girlfriend be best friends with a murderer.

Girlfriend!

"And I didn't really do a good job, right?" Sarah went on. "Because in the same conversation, Seventeen admitted she'd stolen an envelope I'd picked up at the FedEx store for Twenty-Seven, and I kind of reprimanded her for that? For being nosy? But now that I'm thinking about it, because of what my neighbor just texted me... But Seventeen said she's okay."

George clenched his teeth. She was moving so fast. *Listen.* He knew about the packages. He'd seen the one at LifeSport. He shouldn't have let Sarah keep doing that, but he needed the paper trail, the reports. The case had to be airtight before they gave it to the US attorney. His job—Vance had been clear about this—was to watch it happen. Not to prevent it.

But now, it was all happening to Sarah, and he... he possibly loved her? *Stop it. Listen.*

"What did your neighbor say?" he asked.

"She said Twenty-Seven was in my apartment today. I guess she had some story about a baseball game? But this is crazy, and I'm not telling you this because you're in the FBI, okay? Like, I'm not informing on my friend."

Informing.

"My only friend," Sarah said, to herself then, and she shook her head a little. "Maybe this was all wrong?" She turned away from him toward the lakeside window. Whitehook spread out around her messy ponytail, light infusing its white-blond translucence.

"Wait," he said. "What did the neighbor say?"

"Between us?" she asked, back to him, still. "I want this to be separate. From work."

"Between us." He nodded, not even really thinking about how it was a lie, how if this relationship had a future, he would have to explain how nothing had been private between them. He'd kept a file folder filled with reports of their conversations, about Twenty-Seven's brother, about Gabriella's entanglement in the Campbell-Jones family.

He had documented everything she was willing to tell him. *Had*. Maybe this could be different.

"Anyway." Sarah turned back, and her whole face sagged with sadness. "I didn't give her a key. So she was breaking in. The game she said she wanted to watch? It's not even on today, and I don't have cable." George kept his face neutral while his mind spun with options and contingencies. "So," Sarah continued, "I don't know what she was doing in my apartment. And? That, combined with the fact that she apparently threatened a kid? I mean, Seventeen can be a little much, but a *bitch*? No."

She looked at George again, her blue eyes completely clear, her concern obvious. She kneaded her hands, the same hands that he'd held that morning, the same hands she'd spread over his chest last night.

George felt every muscle in his body tighten. He wanted to help her; she was already helping him. Maybe this case didn't have to blow everything up. "Can I ask you a personal question?"

Sarah blinked a few times. "What? Of course!"

"You have a trust fund?" George cleared his throat. "From your mother? I mean, do you?" He knew that she did.

"What?"

"When your mother died." *Slow down.* "Was there money?"

"Why would you ask that?" Sarah asked. "I mean, yes, there was money. But what could all of this have to do with my mother? We're talking about *Fed* Sarah, Lula and Ruby's mother."

"No," George said, shaking his head. "It's about your mother, too, Sarah." He stepped toward her, closing the distance. He wanted to hold her hand, but he had to be professional. At Birdsong, his job was to be real and caring, but also to hold professional space. He'd never felt that boundary with Sarah, he realized now. He'd been in too deep since the first time he talked to her, since the first time she'd spotted his back squats.

She put her hand out, and he took it in both of his. "What do you mean it's about my mother?" A line appeared between Sarah's eyebrows. He wanted to put his lips there. To pull her toward him, but the muscles in her arms had tightened. She held herself away.

"First," George said, slowly, "can you answer the question about the trust fund?"

He kept her hand, even though she tugged. "Yes," she said. "I have a trust fund. My mom had one. I was the beneficiary. My dad is a physician. Grandma Ellie was fine. So, it's mine." Sarah shrugged. "I've never touched it. It just—" She looked over her shoulder at the lake. "It feels like it's for later. I don't know."

"Is it a lot of money?" George asked.

"What?" Sarah took her hand this time, a big tug. "Why do you want to know? What *do* you know?"

George pursed his lips and breathed in. This part of it—the secret part—was over. If there was any hope of keeping her, of making her understand, he'd have to tell her everything. "Twenty-Seven isn't a Sarah Jones," he said, and immediately, his body felt heavier. The satisfaction of the morning's physical work evaporated. He wanted to sit down and put his head in his hands.

"What are you talking about?" Sarah asked. "How do you know that?"

George swallowed. "You know I'm on the fraud team, right? At the bureau?"

Sarah nodded. She held her hands on her belly, her fingers gripping each other so hard he could see the white of the effort at her knuckles. "You said '*cases*.' And you denied it! And then last night, your mom said I was helping you."

George swallowed. "There are two cases. One's a fraud case and the other's a murder case. Twenty-Seven's name is actually Gabriella Johnson."

Sarah's mouth dropped open. "Gabriella? Like from *High School Musical*?"

George coughed out a laugh in spite of the layers of tension. There'd been several summers at Birdsong where they'd held *High School Musical*–themed events.

"It's not funny," Sarah said. "Never mind. So her name is Gabriella? And how do you know this?"

Just as he was about to tell her, the bell rang in center camp, the clangs intrusive even up at the AD's cabin. "Lunchtime," he said. He turned to his room, the room he'd shared with Sarah. He'd pull on sweats. They could get there in time, even though he hadn't started changing clothes. Everything at Birdsong ran on time.

"You think I care about *lunch*?" Sarah held her ground. "This woman was in my apartment. She is my *best* friend. And you're telling me two things." She held up her fingers again, but this time all of the mirth was gone. "You're telling me I don't know her." She put one finger down, leaving the index finger hyperextended. "And then also that you *do* know her. Now you have to fill in the blanks."

George stepped toward the bedroom again.

"Now," Sarah said, and he stopped.

He squared his shoulders. "Okay." He breathed deeply. "Sarah Christine Jones is the latest in a long line of aliases of Gabriella Eleanora Johnson. And she's the target of my fraud case."

"Your fraud case?" Sarah took several steps backward. "That started before the murder? What are her previous aliases?"

George moved toward her, but Sarah held a hand up. "What are the aliases?" she repeated.

"Catherine Anderson," he said. "Grace Smith."

He could see her thinking. God, he could see it all. Her face was a collection of her memories, her ideas, her desires.

The lunch bell rang again, and George pictured his mom pulling the rope, wondering where they were. At Birdsong, if someone didn't show up, it triggered an emergency protocol. A search began from the water all the way up to the trails Sarah had hiked that morning. But George was grown now. He could take care of himself.

"They're all really common names," Sarah said.

"Yeah," George said. "It's actually pretty clever—"

Sarah rolled her eyes. "Of course it's clever. Have you *met* her? She's brilliant." George smiled in spite of the tension. Here Sarah was, still defending the woman who now threatened her entire livelihood. She kept talking, filling in the pieces herself. "She needs to have the same name because of the package pickup? What is that? Like, she can't appear on any security cameras? If someone traces a stolen good or whatever, it's not her on the video feed?"

George nodded. "Exactly. You could be in the FB—"

"Stop," Sarah said. "I'm not an idiot." She frowned and kept going. "And everyone with a name like that—Catherine Anderson, Grace Smith, Sarah Jones—" she said, her eyes on the ground. "We've all met other people with the same names. It's not weird or alarming when that happens. It feels . . ." She turned away from him toward the lakeside window again. "In fact, it feels sort of cool. Sort of magical."

George waited. The bell rang a third time, but the clangs felt half-hearted. His mom would give up on them, maybe snag a sandwich or two and let them cool on an empty table.

Sarah spun back around, and there was a hardness to her posture now, a tightness he'd never seen. Sadness flooded him. "You don't get to feel sad, Agent Nightingale," Sarah said, seeing it. "No way." She shook her head. "This is my life, and now that I'm thinking about it, how did you even come into it? It wasn't random." His lips felt tacky, glued together. "Your first appointment? You chose me."

She scuffed her foot against the floorboards, thinking again. "Okay," she said, getting it, "I'm here because I'm *a* Sarah Jones, but I'm not *the* Sarah Jones, is that right?" Her eyes flashed in the low light. "You needed someone close to Gabriella Johnson. You needed her next victim."

All of a sudden, George felt every hard effort of the morning. Every piling, every "down" dive called by his father.

"So how did you find me?" Sarah's voice was low, but piercing.

"Wait, no," George said. He shook his head. Vance would kill him for this. For last night. Well, she wouldn't *kill* him, but he'd be washed out like her previous two trainees. He'd move to Yuma. "I—this is real." His hand ping-ponged between them, his fingers spread wide and desperate.

Sarah rolled her eyes again. "Don't treat me like I'm stupid." A shield descended over her. Whereas his exhaustion felt like it would crumple him, she'd straightened, resolve coursing through her. "How did you find me?" she asked. "And what am I doing for you?"

"Can I sit?" He was doing it wrong. His job was to stand in the corner and observe, to collect information, to write it down. How could he capture what was happening now? How much could he keep from Vance? How had everything gotten so knotted together?

"Whatever." Sarah shook her head, incredulous. He walked past her into the sitting area, brushing her shoulder. She didn't react except to turn toward him. "Okay," she said. "You owe me, and I want my payment right now."

George had spent his life since Henry's kidnapping staving off panic, and he'd gotten quite good at it. It had started the moment his friend disappeared. Since his friend had stayed gone. Since his friend Glen had broken his neck in the football game versus Cornell. Since Bea had left Birdsong to go to physician assistant school.

But now, his heartbeat whooshed in his ears. His eyes took in too much light.

"Spill!" He'd never heard her shout, not even in the gym.

George pictured Vance in front of him. How would he summarize it for her? "Gabriella Johnson looks for people with common names in the obituaries."

"But I'm not dead," Sarah said.

"No," George said. "She doesn't look for the dead person, but rather the survivors. Catherine Anderson's paternal grandmother died. Grace Smith's father."

"But my mother died almost twenty years ago. Her last name was Montague. How did she find me?"

"You were a bonus," George said. And then he waited, wanting to give her a chance to figure it out like she had everything else. She'd be happier if it came to her, if he didn't have to impart the knowledge like some bastion of the patriarchy.

Sarah blinked at the floor. "Seventeen started her group," she said. "She used LinkedIn. That was the magic part."

"The magic part?" George said.

"Nothing." Sarah shook her head. "So it wasn't me. I'm not the target. That's what you're saying?" She held up a hand, not actually wanting him to respond. "Who else has a dead relative?" She straightened up and stared at him. She had it. "Oh," she said.

"Yeah," George confirmed. "It's Fed Sarah. Her mother died. She was also a Jones."

"I'm not an informant for the murder. I'm an informant for the fraud."

"I needed a target to follow. I had to watch Gabriella do her thing, so that we'd have it airtight for the US attorney." George had never talked so fast in his life. "But then Fed Sarah died when I first met you. That was unexpected. No one else had died, and then I found your trust fund."

"Oh wait, this is new," Sarah said. "Sorry, I was a second behind here, and now I'm with you. I see." Her eyes flashed, her anger spread out on her face in pink blotches.

"But it didn't turn out like that!" George's desperation intensified. The control he'd worked so hard to maintain, the rationality, the laser-cut puzzle pieces he'd put into place—everything went ragged. "This! Our relationship—whatever this is—is real to me!"

"Stop." She shook her head. "You don't get to have it all the ways. You can't both stay and leave, right?" She spun her arm over her head, indicating Birdsong. "You can't both care about me and use me."

"I know, but I never hid the fact that I was FBI. I told you—"

"Nope," she said, commanding. If George didn't feel so awed by her, he would have tried to speak again. "I just want to get one more piece of information verified before I—" She looked toward the driveway, and George saw her realize that he'd driven her here. There was no rural Uber. She didn't actually have a way to leave unless she went on foot. "Well, how convenient for you that you've trapped me here, three and a half hours from my adopted home."

"You're not trapped." George heard the pleading note in his voice.

Sarah rolled her eyes again. There was no trace of the encouraging personal trainer, the silliness, the curiosity about the world. Her whole body seethed.

And, George realized, a terrible and choking lump in his throat, it was the only rational response to what he'd done to her. How could she see it any other way?

"Just tell me one more thing."

"Okay," George said, wanting to tell her whatever she wanted to know, but also knowing he couldn't. *Maybe*, the thought flashed into his head, *maybe I'm not cut out for the FBI*.

Sarah squinted. "Your plan, right? Your plan, your mission, your assignment—whatever I am to you?"

George's breath caught, but he pressed his lips shut and willed himself to maintain eye contact.

"You are here just to watch it happen. You are going to let her— oh wait, you *did* let her! That's what my neighbor is telling me, right? You let her steal my mother's legacy and leave me with nothing? You were going to watch it and, what? Take notes? Deliver the case file to the US attorney? Let me walk into whatever shit storm you knew—you hoped?—was coming?"

George's shoulders slumped. The omission was another betrayal.

Sarah stood up and pushed past him toward the door. "Okay," she said, her coldness chilling his whole body. "I've got it."

"Where are you going?" His voice was a croaky whisper, not at all confident or official.

"The bell rang," she said. "Did you hear it? I'm going to have some fucking grilled cheese sandwiches."

CHAPTER THIRTY-FOUR

Video Transcript Recorded by Sarah Jones, Age Seventeen

May 30, 2023

After we did the reverse image thing, Sixty-Nine and Sister Mary Theresa and I did more research. Sister made the call to the Chicago Police Department. I tried to eavesdrop, but she gave me her death stare. I did hear her say something about "retired Crow Wing County" and maybe "O'Neill." I didn't realize how relevant that was going to be.

"They've already talked to the FBI," Sister said when she hung up. "A Special Agent Nightingale is working the case here."

I felt myself blinking rapidly. "Oh my God."

"Third commandment," Sister said. "But what?"

"George Nightingale," I said. "That's Thirty's new boyfriend."

"Oh, shit." Sixty-Nine gasped.

I looked at Sister, expecting a reprimand, but there was none.

"Okay." Sister bit her lip and squinted at her latte. "Do we think Thirty knows she's an informant?"

"She does," I said. "But I think that's about the murder case?"

"Nope," Sister concluded. "It's also about the fraud." Sister steepled her fingers over her nose, and her eyes welled up. I had never pictured Sister crying. She was the person who dealt with other people's tears.

"Are you okay?" I asked.

"I know a George Nightingale," Sister said. "From Minnesota. With a pretty good reason to go into national security."

"How do you know him?"

"It's a long story," Sister said. "But he was a kid—a witness—in the last case I worked before I quit the force and entered the novitiate."

"Wait," Sixty-Nine said. "You entered the nunnery because of Thirty's FBI boyfriend?"

Sister shook her head. "That's too simple," she said. "But kind of. I'd felt like I was in the wrong place for a while, but then Henry O'Neill... not solving that case..." She grabbed her cross. "And the public fallout."

It hit me. "That kidnapping kid?" Parents still talked about Henry O'Neill. It was like the biggest unsolved case in Minnesota history. "George Nightingale is a witness in the Henry O'Neill kidnapping?"

Sister nodded. "He was the last person to see him, he and Henry's father."

We were all quiet for a minute. "Does this seem..." I started.

"Ordained?" Sister ran her thumb over the etching on her cross.

"Yeah," said Sixty-Nine. "It's a moment, for sure. But do you know what we should do? We should regroup, find out everything we can about Gabriella Johnson, and then give Thirty a call. She needs to know everything and fast."

It was a relief to have a task. We went to work, and I typed up a list of what we found. Frankly, I was impressed by the old people's internet prowess.

We believe the following things are true about Gabriella Johnson, our Twenty-Seven:

- She was an elementary teacher at Forest Down School outside of the city of Chicago, Illinois, for four years beginning in 2018. So she has way more in common with Thirty-Nine and Forty-Four than she ever admitted.

- She graduated from the University of Wisconsin–La Crosse in 2017. She was in every kind of honor society and also sang in at least two a cappella groups. We found Instagram profiles for those groups, and her solos over the years included "Down" by Jay Sean and "Party in the USA." Iconic.

- While Twenty-Seven is objectively gorgeous, what with all the singing and the studying, she is also clearly a first-class nerd.

- On one of Gabriella's defunct classroom teaching websites, she says her favorite fruit is watermelon, and if she could be any animal, it would be a koala. Okay, but did you know baby koalas eat their mom's poop? And also that male koalas have two-pronged penises? I bet Twenty-Seven didn't know that when she chose the koala.

- She was the maid of honor in Annabeth Silver's July 2019 wedding. The bachelorette party seemed to have a sexy zombie theme, and Twenty-Seven's—uh, Gabriella's—makeup skills came in handy with the blood drips she painted under the right corner of her mouth. Her bio on the wedding website calls her "the most genuine and fantastic person

Annabeth has ever met in her life." Sixty-Nine and I both stopped at "genuine." Fat chance. Sister was too nice to comment.

- After her third-grade class had read 4,623 books one spring, an article in a suburban paper quoted her as saying, "Reading is like everything else. It's not about bigger, better, faster, more. It's about a little bit every day. One page after another." Okay. But, 4,623 is a shit ton of books.

- Based on my math, there's little chance Gabriella is actually twenty-seven years old. So both of the names we used for her were fake. My best guess, based on her teaching career, her best friend Annabeth Silver, and her college a cappella stints, is that Gabriella Johnson is at least twenty-nine years old. Not a big difference, right? But another big fat lie.

And that was about it. We did a massive search for Catherine Andersons, too, but there were too many, at least 2,200 in the US.

When I checked the Catherine stats, that's when I started to solve the case a little bit. That was Gabriella's con. Names that were common. Johnson is the second most common name in the United States, although Gabriellas are harder to come by. But not Catherine Andersons. They're a dime a dozen. Sarah Joneses, too.

Annabeth Silver is another story. There are only seven nationwide, and *that* was something to go on. I found the one who matched the wedding website on Instagram and sent her a DM. "Odd request," I wrote, "but can you give me any information about Gabriella Johnson?"

Before her response came in, Sixty-Nine said it was time to alert the others. "I'm texting them in the group chat. You, too."

"And Twenty-Seven?" What if we tried again? I wondered. What if we told her everything we knew and asked for an explanation?

"Not Twenty-Seven for now," Sixty-Nine said. "I think we have to make a plan or something. If she already threatened you, she was the last one to see Fed Sarah, and we know now that she tends to disappear." She pointed at the computer screen. "It might be time for her to go again."

"And I—" Sister said, still emotional. "I think I need to call George Nightingale."

I was relieved to have some adults in charge. Even I know my limits. And then, just as Sixty-Nine was texting the group chat, I got a DM from Annabeth Silver. "How did you find me?" she asked. "And where is Gabriella? I've been looking for her for years."

"She's Sarah Jones now," I wrote. "In Minneapolis."

CHAPTER THIRTY-FIVE

May 27, 2023

Sarah was an expert at pretending everything was okay. At age eleven, she'd watched her mother die. You don't survive that and become a reasonably functional person without a pretty solid ability to fake it.

"Sorry I'm late," Sarah said in the dining hall as Sylvia handed her a blue plate with two grilled cheeses on it.

"No problem." They sat together, adjacent the dock crew.

Sarah bit into her sandwich, the American cheese just slightly undermelted. "Delicious," she said, though it wasn't exactly.

"Did you enjoy your hike?" Sylvia asked.

"Very much." This was true. "The trails, the tree houses—it's amazing. You have so much history here."

Sylvia nodded. "It's a gift to be an anchor for so many people. It's been a good life, you know? I married Paul when I was twenty-two. My degree in education transferred perfectly to camp."

Sarah considered her own path, the clarity she'd had at twenty-two when she'd been accepted to three different medical schools. "It must feel pretty great to have that sense of purpose," Sarah said. "In my job, I meet a lot of people who want to make a change. That's why they work with me, right? I'm going to change their bodies, and then maybe also their attitudes and their options? People don't usually come to me when they know exactly what they want."

The next bite of the sandwich felt gluey. George's intake form had said he wanted to run a three-hour marathon. She'd bought it. She'd been flattered he'd chosen her. And all those workouts? Sarah wondered if he'd even registered for the Chicago Marathon like they'd decided. *Probably not.*

Sylvia's smile faltered a little, and something about the set of her mouth looked suddenly sad. "But purpose can sometimes be a burden. Too much? I'm worried about that with George." She shook her head. "Sorry, I don't know why I'm telling you this exactly. It's just, it's been a long time since we've met someone he seems to trust like he does you."

Sarah had elicited confidences from clients through the years, within the capacity of being a personal trainer, and then also because her own grief seemed to emit a signal of safety. People felt they could talk to her. Sarah wanted to tell Sylvia the truth about what she'd just learned about their relationship, to be the secret-*teller* for once, rather than the repository. But George's duplicity made her feel stupid. If she told Sylvia it wasn't that her son trusted her, but that he was using her for his own professional gain, it would confirm that Sarah was lacking, both in judgment and self-respect.

"It's okay," Sarah said instead. "People tell me stuff a lot." She put a finger on her sternum. "I'm a safe space."

Sylvia chuckled. "Well, George obviously thinks so."

Sarah kept her face neutral, her eyes sparkling.

"He probably told you about Henry O'Neill?" Sylvia asked. "That's part of the Birdsong history that's just—"

Sarah waited, pretending Sylvia was in the middle of a set of squats, that she'd continue telling Sarah whatever it was when her breath came back.

"—it's heavy," Sylvia said. "Knowing the last time that boy was seen was just . . ." She pointed toward the side of the building. "Here."

Sarah nodded.

"Anyway, is George coming down?"

Sarah had decided what she'd say. "He had a work thing to deal with." Not a lie. "I'm sure he'll be down in a minute."

And George did come in then, his shoulders tense and his eyes cloudy. Sarah watched as his father intercepted him at the door and handed him a plate. George stashed it on the nearest table and strode toward Sarah. In spite of her anger, Sarah felt a shiver zing from her navel all the way to her toes.

He doesn't actually like you.

"Hey," he said, as he approached the table.

"You made it," Sylvia looked back at the abandoned lunch plate. "You're going to eat something, right?"

Sarah grabbed a water cup and poured from the plastic pitcher.

"Yeah, but Sarah?" he said, jittery. "I just got a call from my supervisor? Jane Vance?"

"On a Saturday?" Sylvia said, her voice airy. "Well, I guess crime doesn't stop after five on Friday."

George pointed at Sarah and then turned apologetically to his mom. "Can I just have a minute?" he asked.

"Of course." Sylvia walked toward the crew.

"I know you don't want to talk to me," George said, "but I think things are going down today. Or, at least by Monday."

"Things?" Sarah asked.

"Yeah. My supervisor called, like I said."

"And she's what? Like a senior FBI agent? The one who reads the reports of everything you and I discuss?"

To his credit, George had ditched his hangdog expression and just answered her question. "Yes," he said. "She's in charge of the Gabriella Johnson investigation and also on the Sarah Jones murder task force. The stolen necklace. All of it. I'm, like, a very junior agent. A beginner on every level, which is why I have so massively screwed things up here with you."

"And so?" Sarah said, grim.

"So," George continued, "Vance got a call from Sister Mary Theresa Conaty. And then I got a call from Sister Mary Theresa Conaty."

"What?" Sarah asked, disoriented. "The nun at Sacred Heart?"

"She was with Seventeen and Sixty-Nine. They were doing some"—he waved his hand, and Sarah tried not to feel anything as the curl fell onto his forehead—"sleuthing. And they discovered the truth about Twenty-Seven."

Sarah felt her chest cave in. Those three? The yarn-bombing grandma, the impulsive teenager, and a cloistered nun figured out that Sarah was being used before she did?

"They figured out that Twenty-Seven is Gabriella Johnson. They found a news article about one of her previous marks. They convened the troops." He pulled Sarah's cell phone out of his pocket. "Can you look to see if there are messages? From her or from TSJP or whatever?"

Sarah looked at the phone and then at George. "You don't know the password to my phone?"

George's cheeks took on their familiar pink, the flush that Sarah had so recently found charming. "I don't—" he started. "I would never—"

"Save it," she said, and she caught a concerned glance from Sylvia across the room. Her immediate impulse was to give the woman a thumbs-up, but she stopped herself. It wasn't her responsibility to make George comfortable or to appease his mother.

"Can you check to see what's going on? Like, if the group is gathering? Or if Twenty-Seven is saying anything?" George spoke fast. "I realize this is terrible timing. She's known you for months, we left town, I gave her access to steal..." He shook his head. "I know it won't help to say I'm so sorry."

Sarah grabbed her phone and scanned the TSJP group chat. She had forty-nine notifications. George would know this. He could see it without unlocking her screen.

She read the messages. It had started with Sixty-Nine. Seventeen had called her with the same story Sarah had disregarded the evening before. A pit opened in her stomach. She'd wanted George, wanted those broad shoulders, when her *real* people were trying to tell her something important.

"What does it say?" George put his hand out for the phone, and then when she glared at him, put it in his pocket.

"It's none of your business." Sarah was sure of the sentiment even if the words felt juvenile.

George's eyes bugged, and Sarah felt satisfied. She'd been unknowingly compliant, but she wasn't playing anymore. She wouldn't give George what he wanted.

"There are consequences," George said, trying again, his face betraying his growing desperation. Beads of sweat appeared at his sideburns despite the cool temperature in the dining hall.

Sarah put her phone under her right thigh and took a performative bite of her tepid sandwich, the cheese harder than it had been before.

"Don't you care what happens?" George asked.

"Care?" Sarah said, her mouth full. "Do I care? About my own money? My own trust fund? Or whether or not you've let me buddy up to a murder suspect? Are those the things I'm supposed to care about?"

George stared at her, shocked by her outburst. He looked over his shoulder at his mom, as if Sylvia could boss Sarah into obedience like she presumably had with so many campers.

Sarah took another bite of the now rock-hard sandwich, but couldn't make herself chew it. She spit it into her open palm, and overturned that onto her plate. She pushed her chair back, shoved her phone into her pocket, and headed to the bussing station, behind which stood a Birdsong staffer in an apron and a hat. "Thanks," she said to the young woman.

Then, without looking at George or either of the senior Nightingales, whose eyes she could feel on her, she pushed open the dining hall door with both hands and marched out toward the lake. She stood there for a moment, letting her eyes close and feeling the light breeze on her cheeks. "Mom," she whispered aloud, hoping to feel something else.

But all that happened was that she heard George's voice. "Sarah!" he called from behind her. "What are you doing?"

She kept her eyes closed and felt for her phone. She pictured the members of TSJP: Sixty-Nine with her ball of yarn, Seventeen with her fresh face and dripping wet hair, Thirty-Nine and Forty-Four with their matching shirts and selfies. These were real people. They had a real connection. That hadn't changed.

"Sarah?" George asked, his voice closer now, maybe just a foot or two behind her.

Sarah breathed the cool air in through her nose and exhaled it through her mouth, just as she'd instructed clients through the years.

"Sarah," he said again. And she wondered whether they'd taught any classes in patience at the FBI. She breathed again and tried to access her mother's face. She'd read it was normal to forget over time, but if she went deep into her memories, she could see the wisps of hair, the freckles across the bridge of her nose, the wrinkles next to her eyes, her light eyebrows. *Hello,* Sarah said to her memory. She had an impulse to reach out toward the water, but George was watching.

"Sarah," George said for a third time, "what are you going to do now?"

Sarah's phone buzzed in her pocket, and then again three more times. "I'm going to read the messages from my friends. And log into my bank. Obviously." Sarah opened her eyes and surveyed the grounds. She headed back to the benches that made a semicircle in front of the dining hall.

"Can I?" George asked.

"No," Sarah said, holding the phone close. "The messages are mine." She sat at the bench closest to the water, farthest from the door of the dining hall.

"But you know Gabriella is also a murderer, right? Who do you think killed Fed Sarah?" She didn't look at George. "If you protect her now, you're protecting a killer."

Sarah tried to imagine Twenty-Seven killing someone. How well did she really know her? And then she let Twenty-Seven enter her mind's eye. She remembered the sadness that had radiated off of her as she'd told them about Oscar's death, the tears, the shaking shoulders. It had felt real. Could someone fake that?

How many questions had Twenty-Seven answered, compared to the number she'd asked? She'd been a perfect friend. That, Sarah guessed, had been the point.

"If you know she did it, then why isn't she arrested?" Sarah asked. "You guys just let murderers walk around free?"

"We need evidence," George said. "And we still—" He pointed at her phone. "This is one of the reasons I wanted you to look. We still don't know exactly why Gabriella's dinner with Sarah was late on the night she was killed, what happened in that intervening ninety minutes when they'd ordinarily have been out. And now—" George made a sound like a whimper. It seemed like he felt as miserable and exposed as she did. "We can't find her."

They can't find her? Is she gone already?

Sarah felt herself shrinking as George spoke, his desperation right on the surface. "But, those girls. Their mother was murdered. You can help them."

"I know how I should feel." Sarah felt frozen, rooted, to the ground. She knew how she should feel, but not what she should do.

She could sense George gearing up for another run at her. But then a truck pulled in the camp drive. They both watched it. A tall but hunched man hopped out of the driver's seat.

"Oh, shit," George said. Sarah felt a prick of curiosity, but stifled it. Whatever difficulty George was facing, he deserved. She swiped up on her phone, opening the text thread that had continued to buzz. As she started to read, she overheard George and the man.

"You ready?" the man asked. "Do you have the files? Have you read—"

"Andrew." George's voice transformed to the professional one, the calm one, that Sarah had been so familiar with up until she'd rattled him.

"This was the weekend, right? Docks going in?" Andrew pointed at Whitehook.

The dining hall doors opened just then and the rest of the crew stood on the steps outside of it. Sarah watched as Paul scanned the premises, a practiced move on his part that he'd surely performed multiple times per day when other people's children were in his care. His whole countenance darkened when he focused on the truck.

He leaned over to Sylvia, and they spoke quietly to each other before Paul seemed to gather himself, straightened his spine, and skipped down the dining hall steps.

"Andrew O'Neill!" Sarah heard him say, and then she gasped. Henry's father. The man with no answers and a missing child, a person even more miserable than Fed Sarah's daughters. More miserable than Sarah herself. "What can we do for you today?"

Phone Transcript Between Agent George Nightingale and Sister Mary Theresa Conaty

Recording Provided by Agent Nightingale

May 27, 2023

George Nightingale: This is George Nightingale.
Sister Mary Theresa: Oh my goodness. You're a man.
GN: I guess that's true. And my boss says you're a nun?
SMT: It's not as weird as it sounds. Not all that different from being a cop.
GN: For real?
SMT: Well, I guess it's a little different, what with the four-times-daily prayer and the devotion to our virgin mother.
GN: [*laughter*] I'm not sure what to say to that. But I should let you know, I'm recording this conversation, okay? The O'Neill file is still open.
SMT: I'm well aware. I'm the spiritual advisor to the task force.
GN: Sister, I really, really wish all of that prayer had found Henry.
SMT: Prayer doesn't find the missing, Agent Nightingale, but it can bolster the people that are engaged in the search.
GN: I guess. I can't believe I'm talking to you again after all these years. The connections . . .
SMT: Sometimes, when I'm in prayer and remembering those days, I see your face as it was. There was an earnest wrinkle above your eyebrow. I bet it's still there.
GN: I couldn't say.
SMT: I suppose not, but I can hear your smile. That's reassuring.

It's been hard, hasn't it? People can't quite understand something like what happened to you. No resolution.

GN: For you, too. It sounds like not finding Henry really . . . it changed your whole life.

SMT: In a world where there are no answers, I had to devote myself to a higher power. It was a form of hope, I guess.

GN: I had to change my life, too.

SMT: I'm hoping you know, Agent Nightingale, that being on the *side* of right doesn't always ensure a right outcome.

GN: I wish it did.

SMT: We all do. But that's not the way it goes. Doing good and trying hard and working on yourself . . . it doesn't make everything turn out.

GN: Why not?

SMT: Well, theologically? Or philosophically?

GN: Do you ever think about justice?

SMT: Oh, honey. I think about it all the damn time.

GN: I have to go because I'm . . . well, Supervisory Special Agent in Charge Vance probably told you.

SMT: She did, but she didn't seem to know that Thirty is with you.

GN: Oh, shit.

SMT: I didn't tell her. But, you? You're probably going to have to.

GN: Can we talk later?

SMT: Anytime.

Group Chat of The Sarah Jones Project

May 27, 2023

69: This is a group chat for all of TSJP except for 27. Quick update: 27 asked 17 for a private meeting. (17 is currently with me.)

44: Wait, what?! We do private meetings? I thought we were all friends together.

39: We ARE all friends, but sometimes there are sidebars, right? Like us? At school? We're BFFs?

44: Oh, right. Well, that makes sense. Anyway, what's up?

69: Remember earlier when 17 asked if any of us had been to 27's apartment? Of course you do. It was this morning. Well, anyway, the reason she asked that was that she was suspicious about that place. Like, thinking it wasn't a real home.

17: Because she took me to a coffee shop and called me a bitch, and I accused her of stealing that yellow diamond necklace (which she totally did), and she threatened me and threw a chair.

44: She THREW a chair?

39: Like, why? And she stole that necklace? From those orphan girls?!?!

17: I think I was getting too close . . . I'd opened a package 30 had picked up for her, and there were pictures of the necklace. The same pictures I showed you all the other night.

69: So anyway, we picked up Sister Mary Theresa from 17's school, we did some investigating, and we discovered some things.

17: For one, 27 is NOT in graduate school.

69: And more importantly, she's not one of us.

44: What do you mean, one of us? Like, she doesn't really care about TSJP because, tbh, I was thinking that maybe now that summer vacation has started, I might . . .

17: Don't even think about it, 44. No, we mean SHE'S NOT ONE OF US. Meaning, she's not a Sarah Jones.

39: Why would someone who isn't a Sarah Jones come to a meeting of Sarah Joneses?

44: And how do you know that?

69: Long story, but we did a reverse google image search.

39: Oooh fancy!

69: The directions are literally on google.

17: Anyway, her name is Gabriella Johnson.

44: She's a JOHNSON? That's even more common than Jones! She's REALLY not one of us.

17: But Gabriella sets her apart.

39: Ok, focus: why did she lie to us, and what's the deal, and what do we have to do, and also where is 30?! Wouldn't she want to respond to all of this?

17: I tried to tell her, but she was very distracted by her new hot FBI boyfriend, who is also the star witness in Sister Mary Theresa's last detective case.

44: What?

69: Let's simplify: focus on 27 for now.

69: So, now we know that 27 has the stolen necklace that belonged to the dead Sarah, and she was the nanny for those girls, then . . .

44: Oh Holy Mary, she's a murderer, isn't she? She's THE murderer?

17: It's definitely possible.

39: So, where is she? Have we called the cops?

69: We called the FBI, actually.

39: A regular person can, like, call the FBI?

69: Sister Mary Theresa did it since she has the history in law enforcement, but it turns out anyone can. It's also on google.

44: AND?

17: It took a minute or three, but eventually, we got a call back from the special agent in charge of the Gabriella Johnson investigation.

44: Who is he?

69: It's a SHE and her name is Vance. I felt like I was in a movie.

17: She took us seriously.

39: What's going to happen now?

30: Hello?

69: THERE you are.

17: Are you okay?

39: Oh, thank god.

44: Are you actually with the FBI?

69: Are you okay?

17: Has your jewelry been stolen? Do you have any jewelry?

30: I'm okay. I'm up north with George. I guess I AM with the FBI. Anyway, can we talk about this once I get home?

17: Yes. Emergency meeting tomorrow.

69: Usual spot? 7pm?

30: Can we do the morning? Maybe 10? Since it'll be Sunday?

44: I'll stick around for this.

39: Confirmed.

17: Because in addition to everything else, now I'm in contact with 27's real best friend. Former. Her first victim, as it turns out.

CHAPTER THIRTY-SIX

May 27, 2023

Gabriella felt awful, transferring the money and then scramming like a common criminal. And there was the added stress of finding someplace to go. The in-between weeks exhausted her, especially if she hadn't yet found another mark. She drove to a medium-sized city: Des Moines. Fort Wayne. Cedar Rapids. Then she scoured obituaries in all of the papers. She'd had to pay a little for subscription fees, but it had been worth it. Catherine Anderson. Grace Smith. Sarah Jones.

The last one had paid double.

And she was done. She'd expected relief, but instead it felt like her body didn't fit into her skin anymore. In the beginning, her whole life had been over. She'd had to leave everything behind. Annabeth. Her students. Her mother. Her shabby-chic apartment, the distressed curio cabinet that had been her grandmother's, the pink-striped couch cushions, the sage metal bed frame. She'd just abandoned it all, no time to even sell.

What she should do now, especially after the run-in with Sarah's neighbor, was get in her car and leave the city limits immediately. But she felt so tired. She had no place to go.

Gabriella did fold her clothes, did put them into the two large duffels and haul them, one over each shoulder, to the car that had been her grandmother's back in the day.

She slid the key to the Airbnb apartment under the door and texted the owner. They'd been week to week via Venmo. And now, she'd leave. Delete the account. Go.

In the car, she tried to force herself onto the interstate, but she just couldn't. She'd be looking over her shoulder forever.

Instead, she steered toward the River Road, eased the car crookedly into a spot a block from the bridge.

It was an accident.

She left her new phone in the glove box and walked toward the path where the body had landed. Gabriella hadn't been able to look that night. The sound was watery, clunky, and completely foreign. What she'd done instead of looking, instead of calling anyone, was walk across the bridge in the opposite direction from which she'd come. She'd walked calmly away. Gabriella hadn't seen a single person between the scene of the scuffle and her car. She'd been lucky, if one could call it that.

They'd been late for dinner. Sarah had said it was something at work, but that had been a lie. Her calendar, to which Gabriella had access for the purpose of slotting her in for extra time with the girls, was empty.

Gabriella had been alone in the Campbell-Jones house when Gretchen had gotten there that evening. At first, Gabriella had thought it was an actual intruder. She'd hid in the powder room off the kitchen as Gretchen padded up the stairs, a burglar so polite she'd removed her shoes.

Gabriella had peeked out of the doorway and then tiptoed up the stairs herself. She slid into Ruby's room at the top, just catching sight of Gretchen as the woman ducked into the primary suite.

Gabriella paused a moment at the doorjamb, listening. She was used to being quiet. How long had it been, she wondered, since she'd actually drawn attention to herself?

Four days before the night of the accident, Sarah's "quarterly lunch" with Gretchen had appeared on her work calendar. The previous one had been in late January, just weeks after she'd started, and it had made Fed Sarah irritable. Gabriella recognized an opportunity.

"You have an aunt?" Gabriella had asked the girls once after school.

"She's a hag," Ruby had said.

"Not a hag," Lula countered. "That's just what Mom says when she's annoyed."

Gabriella had left it there, letting the girls' conversation meander to what they'd had for lunch and the ridiculous homework load from the meanest of the English teachers.

But later in January, when Gabriella had started lingering after work, she'd picked up the topic again. Sarah had invited her to stay for a screening of *The Bachelor*, and she had poured them both rosé.

"Cheers," Sarah had said, clinking their glasses. Gabriella didn't even like rosé. She didn't like wine—or really any alcohol at all—but everyone felt better if you just agreed that their favorites were your favorites. Gabriella had learned this back in college, way before she'd ever had to use her powers for manipulation.

At the first commercial break, Gabriella had said, "You have a sister? I saw the lunch pop up on your calendar. She lives in town? That's nice."

Sarah gulped her wine. She tended to. One large pour almost always turned into two or three. "I have a sister." Gabriella could hear the bitterness at the edges of her tone.

"You don't get along?" A drone shot of the *Bachelor* mansion gave way to a scene of six girls piled on an overstuffed velvet couch.

"It's complicated. But in general, no. Sometimes, I wish—" She held up a finger, and Gabriella bit her lip, waiting. She'd seen this episode already, with Thirty. The girl named Juniper would open the envelope and they'd all pretend to be happy for the brunette who'd get that week's first one-on-one date with the smarmy lead.

"You were saying?" Gabriella kept her eyes on the screen, just disinterested enough.

"Oh. Well, I didn't plan to be back in my hometown. Of all of the branches of the Federal Reserve, of all the government banking jobs, the one I get has to be here. I thought I'd escaped, you know?"

"Yeah. I get that." Gabriella tucked her knees up into her chest, wine resting on her knee.

"Families are so hard," Sarah said. "Anyway, Gretchen and I just never agreed on much. She thinks I'm a bad mom."

There was a little hitch in this revelation, a tinge of insecurity. "I've only been here for a couple of weeks." It had been ten days. "But things seem to be going great. The girls are happy. They love spending time with you. Seems like you're doing pretty well."

It did. That wasn't a lie. "Thanks for that," Sarah said. "Anyway, I'll get through the lunch with Gretchen. She's one of those uber-moms. Gave up everything for her kids."

Gabriella nodded. She wondered where she would fall on the mom spectrum or whether she'd ever get to have kids at all. Whether her own life was ruined, whether she'd ruined it herself.

Gabriella spent the next eleven weeks subtly questioning Sarah about her sister. Gretchen was the harsher one, stern with their father's nurses and bordering on unkind.

Though Sarah had never confessed anything to her, not even after Gabriella told her about Oscar, Gabriella got the sense that Sarah believed Gretchen suspected her of something. "Gretchen holds everything over my head. She thinks she knows everything," she'd said one night when Gabriella stayed late. She'd kept doing that, taking a long time to clean up dinner, folding an extra load of laundry.

Once, in the hometown episode of *The Bachelor* when the suitor met a grandmother, Gabriella asked about the necklace in the photo in the living room. "It's so beautiful," she said. "Striking. An heirloom?"

"My mother gave it to me." Sarah sipped the wine Gabriella had refilled twice already. "Gretchen hates that. She gets my father's watch. But he's not dead yet."

There was enough strife between the sisters to buy Gabriella a week after she stole it.

When the second lunch with Gretchen had appeared on Sarah's work calendar, Gabriella swept into the walk-in closet and draped one of Sarah's signature scarves over the bust on which the gold necklace rested. It had happened before, a scarf landing there. Gabriella had noticed it after she'd started taking a daily detour into the closet before she picked the girls up for school. Gabriella had taken photos of the individual stones and sent them to her contact in Connecticut.

After the scarf had stayed in place for a full eighteen hours, she tipped the bust toward the wall away from the light, not enough for anyone to consciously notice it. Maybe she'd get a few more hours, another evening, after it disappeared. On the day of Sarah's lunch with her sister, she took it. Gretchen would be in the house and could be a suspect.

The lunch had been a week before the final night, the late dinner, the bridge.

Gabriella had listened from Ruby's bedroom as Gretchen rummaged in the walk-in closet, and Gretchen's gasp was audible. *What?* Gabriella wondered. She must have already known the necklace was gone. The girls had told Gabriella of their mother's suspicions, that Gretchen had taken it "hostage."

And then when Gretchen raced down the stairs and out the door, the keypad locking behind her, Gabriella walked into the closet, looking for whatever had caused the gasp. It didn't take long to find it. A photo. Gabriella from the waist up, her arm at ninety degrees to her hip, bare chest thrust forward. The necklace glinted in the photo, an effect she'd added before she sent the picture to Caden as an insurance policy.

So Sarah knew. She knew about the photos, about the texting with her husband. She knew who had really taken the necklace, and she hadn't said anything. They'd had a cocktail the day before.

And tonight was their regular biweekly dinner.

I'm going to be late, Sarah texted as Gabriella left to get the kids. Push back an hour?

What could Gabriella say but yes?

CHAPTER THIRTY-SEVEN

Video Transcript Recorded by Sarah Jones, Age Seventeen

May 30, 2023

Just hours after we got home, Sister called me back. "We have a loose end," she said.

"One?" I asked. My head hadn't stopped spinning. "One end?" There were about four hundred, all tangled up.

"Well, more than one," Sister said. "But this is a lesson I learned a long time ago and frankly one I've been trying to impart to you—"

"One thing at a time," I said.

"Yes." I could hear Sister's smile through the phone. "That's it. And now Sixty-Nine is picking us up. It turns out we're not done for the day. We have to go see about the timeline."

"What timeline?"

"The bridge. The dinner. The missing hours. It's not adding up. Also, can you bring the photos you stole from the perp?"

"Perp?" Sister had morphed back into a cop.

"Gabriella. Twenty-Seven. The stuff from the envelope with the necklace. We're missing something. There's gotta be a spark for the kind of rage that sent Fed Sarah off the bridge. And actually... no, never mind."

"Never mind what?"

"I was going to ask you to call Ruby, but that's a terrible idea. Leave the girl alone. Sixty-Nine will be there in ten minutes, and then you're coming to get me, and then we have an appointment with the head chef at the restaurant."

She hung up before I could ask any questions, but let's be honest: I called Ruby. Well, first I texted her and then she called me back.

"I don't know what kind of clue we're looking for," I said to Ruby as I waited in the lobby for Sixty-Nine. "Something about the reason their dinner was late?"

"I think I know," Ruby said. "It's something Aunt Gretchen told me about."

"Aunt Gretchen? You're speaking to her?" The last I'd heard, Gretchen was on the suspect list, a "hag" who'd potentially had a fight with their mom at the exact right time to kill her after stealing the necklace.

"She's been over. The FBI questioned her, and something happened? She's been—good. Anyway, she's been here. And I overheard her and my dad talking about some photos."

And then Ruby told me: there were topless photos of Twenty-Seven. Topless! That Twenty-Seven sent to Caden Campbell. Photos of Twenty-Seven's naked chest with the necklace!

"Aunt Gretchen thinks she wanted to perhaps make Dad into a suspect, too? Like an affair with the nanny would make people think..."

That made sense.

Sixty-Nine pulled up in the circle, offering just the smallest toot of her horn as impetus for me to hustle. "But that didn't happen? They didn't have an affair?"

"No," Ruby confirmed. "It was just the pictures. And do you know what else?"

"What?" I asked as I slid into the passenger seat, a spot I knew I would vacate as soon as we picked up Sister.

"Now, no one can find Twenty-Seven."

"What do you mean?"

"Her phone is offline. The FBI can't find her. They called looking for her here. They found the Airbnb she'd rented, and it was empty. She's just gone."

"Do you think? I mean, I think she might have killed . . ."

"Yeah. Lula and my dad and Gretchen and Agent Vance. We all think it."

"She's the one?"

"Yeah," Ruby agreed. "It feels so bizarre to even say it, but the evidence . . ."

"I think she murdered your mom," I whispered as Sixty-Nine merged onto the highway toward Sacred Heart.

"I trusted her." It sounded like Ruby was crying. "I'm so stupid."

"No." I had to make her feel better. "I don't want to promise anything," I said, "but we're working on making sure she pays for it." TSJP had actually figured out a lot of stuff already. If we'd done it just a couple of days sooner, maybe Gabriella wouldn't have ditched her phone and skipped town.

"Call me later," Ruby said.

"Okay?" Sixty-Nine asked when I hung up. She looked worried and also totally alert. She wore her oversized tortoiseshell glasses and a scarf. Very Jessica Fletcher.

I'm embarrassed to report this part, but my first words to Sixty-Nine were, "I have a friend. She wants me to call her later."

But Sixty-Nine didn't act like it was weird. "Solid," she said. "I have one, too." And when we pulled into the monastery for the second time in a day, I realized she meant Sister.

I told them both what Ruby had said as we drove downtown.

Sister wasn't even that mad that I'd decided to call. "You know her best," she said. "And I have some news, too. The restaurant Gabriella and Fed Sarah went to that night is called Mill City Café. I looked at the menu online, and let's just say the patrons have not taken a vow of poverty."

"I've never been," Sixty-Nine said.

"Yeah," Sister continued, "you'd have to be a millionaire."

Sixty-Nine coughed.

"Oh my God," I said, and Sister reached into the back seat to swat me. "You ARE a millionaire?"

"I just finished a dynamite career in corporate law, and I spend almost nothing," Sixty-Nine said. "Of course I'm a millionaire."

Man. TSJP will just never quit with the surprises.

At the restaurant, the chef greeted us by the door, wiping her hands on her apron.

"Thanks for taking this meeting," Sister said.

"It's not often I get a call from a religious detective," the chef said. "You're here about that woman? Sarah Jones?"

"Do you remember seeing her on April 17?"

The chef nodded. "I do, and so did the host and the server. She's here a lot, and she's the chair of the Fed. One of our more notable customers. I'm happy to talk to you, but the police did ask about all of this."

Sister nodded. "We're double-checking some things."

"Sure," the chef said. "And you're official? Or are you like amateurs making a podcast or something?"

"Something like that." Sister leaned toward the chef. "Before I became a nun, I was a policewoman." She didn't leave time for questions. "You said Sarah Jones, the deceased, was a frequent customer?"

"Yeah. In here all the time."

"So can I assume she sometimes dined with her family? Her husband?"

"Sometimes," the chef agreed, "though more often with colleagues, friends, the girls' nannies. That's what she was doing here that night. Over the years we've become friendly. I try to stop out at her table if things aren't too busy."

"That's nice."

"This is a tough business," the chef said. "You start to appreciate the loyalty, you know? A lot of places don't make it. Or they stop making it. It can happen to anyone, especially after the pandemic."

"Speaking of, did you know Sarah's mother died in the pandemic?"

"I did, yeah. People had a lot of sadness during that time."

Sister took a long breath in and squinted over the chef's shoulder at the jewel-toned liquor bottles. Nuns didn't drink, I was pretty sure, except for communion wine.

"Did Sarah seem like an angry person?" Sister asked.

The chef grabbed the rag attached to her waist and kneaded it. "I didn't know her *all* that well. It was limited, you know."

"But did she lose her temper? Was she prone to point out mistakes? That night when she was here with the nanny?"

"She was busy and important," the chef said. "And society is really misogynistic, as I'm sure you know, Sister."

"So"—this was Sixty-Nine, also a trailblazer—"you're saying her behavior might be characterized as 'bitchy' if we weren't so feminist?"

"You got it," the chef said, "but I appreciated her, to be honest." She looked back toward the kitchen.

"I know you have to get back to work," Sister said. "But that night. They were late, and was there tension?"

"I told the police this. It was late, Sarah had a few drinks, and both of the women left in tears."

"Okay," Sister said. And I felt some of the loose ends tying, but not in a way I could understand. "Did the host say, or the server say? Were they angry?"

"I've described it as 'charged,'" the chef said. "There was tension, but honestly we couldn't tell what was going on. And we definitely thought about it after the news broke the next morning. A shame." She stood.

"Indeed," Sister said. "You have to go." The chef nodded. "Thank you so very much for your time."

We filed out and walked in silence toward the car, when Sister seemed to remember something and turned on her heel. "What?" I asked.

"Yes!" Sixty-Nine said. "Let's walk the route."

"We're going to the bridge?" I knew it was morbid, but I felt excited. I'd promised my mother I wouldn't, but I was here with my fake grandmothers, and we were all going, tracing the route from the restaurant to the bridge where the murder happened.

FBI Interview with Caden Campbell

Investigator Present: Supervisory Special Agent in Charge Jane Vance

May 26, 2023

Caden Campbell: You have to find her. I can't believe I didn't realize it was her right away.

Jane Vance: That's the thing, Mr. Campbell. You've left something critical out of your testimony thus far.

CC: It was embarrassing. It was nothing. I wasn't involved with her.

JV: But she sent you nude photos? What did you make of that?

CC: Nothing.

JV: Nothing? Do you regularly receive topless photos from household employees?

CC: When you put it like that... but honestly, it seemed temporary.

JV: How long had your nanny been sending illicit images?

CC: There were only a few. Over the months. She was almost done working for us. Our regular nanny is back from Budapest in June. It seemed harmless.

JV: It seemed harmless? I find that hard to believe, especially given your history at UVA. Wasn't there a student—

CC: That was a misunderstanding. I was cleared of all wrongdoing. I never touched her. I never touched the nanny.

JV: What did you do when you saw the necklace in the photo? Did you consider your wife's heirloom might be stolen?

CC: I checked Sarah's closet. Made sure it was there. It didn't occur to me she'd actually steal it. Why do that? She couldn't get away with it, having sent that picture, right?

JV: Unless she was convinced you wouldn't implicate her. For some reason.

CC: Listen. I'm innocent here, so I'm going to level with you: it was exciting, okay? The photos arriving at random intervals. Are you married, Agent Vance?

JV: Yes.

CC: So, a young and beautiful woman takes an interest in me? A couple of photos? It was a *fantasy*. I never even sent her any back. I never initiated anything. It was . . . it was nothing . . . Sarah and I were together in more of a business partnership. It was amicable. A lot of marriages go that way. It's not like we could split, not with her career goals. [*pause*] I wish you wouldn't look at me like that.

JV: I'm thinking.

CC: You've seen the phone records. You know I didn't do anything. I just . . . I just *looked*.

JV: And since you have two daughters to raise on your own now, and since your alibi is confirmed by cell data and by your daughters . . .

CC: We can forget it?

JV: Not quite, but I think that's enough for now.

CHAPTER THIRTY-EIGHT

May 27, 2023

Gabriella pulled her hood up. It was an old Forest Down Elementary sweatshirt, one she'd worn on her last day in every city. It had been a different woman who'd worked there, who'd taught third grade, from the one that stood here now. The thought of that change made Gabriella miserable. And this departure felt especially awful. Fed Sarah was dead. Accident or not.

Accident.

The first time she'd been at this bridge, it had been the culmination of a series of events that had begun one afternoon after Lula's tennis practice. There'd been that day, the photos, the theft, the bridge. Had she only been thinking of Oscar? Or had things gotten more complex?

That afternoon when it had all started, Ruby was busy with schoolwork in her room, with her precalc tutor on Zoom.

Gabriella had then been the nanny for six weeks, long enough to figure out some of the family secrets. Long enough to let a shoulder slip in front of Caden Campbell, to "inadvertently" brush a breast against his arm while they carried bags in from the car, long enough to send him the first selfie taken in his bathroom mirror.

She hated that part of it, but in the end, she needed some collateral in these cases, some secret that she could expose if she were backed into a corner. Telling someone's wife about an affair, hinting that there was some harassment involved. That was the kind of firepower she required.

In the end, the best collateral had come from the girls themselves. Gabriella had thought that Lula was in the shower when she'd wandered into Sarah and Caden's bedroom that afternoon for the first time and picked a dirty towel up off the floor.

The necklace had been on an actual stand in Sarah's walk-in closet, the size of a single dorm room, designed with multiple racks for shoes, a vanity, and an ornate mirror. When Gabriella hit the overhead light, the chandelier-style fixture reflected in both the glass and the metallic mirror frame. The Fed chair kept her jewelry to the right of that, on organizers that looked like they belonged in a boutique, little fabric rods and faux fingers for rings. Gabriella had never owned a ring. Her mother had promised her her grandmother's engagement ring, but they'd had to sell that, along with everything else, when Oscar needed rehab for the second time.

Fed Sarah's necklace had its own perch on a beige mannequin bust. She ran a finger over each of the stones. It was only after she'd lifted her finger off of the piece and tipped her head, trying to estimate the size of the diamond in the center, that she realized Lula was in the doorway. Gabriella jumped, pulling her hand back from the necklace and shoving it into her pocket.

"It's amazing, right?" Lula said.

"I mean, yeah." Gabriella accessed all of her "act natural" strategies. She wasn't in the closet to look at the necklace. She was here to pick up the spare towels, to gather the clothes from the hamper in the corner, even though she'd never done Sarah's laundry before. "I've never seen a closet like this except on TV." Gabriella walked back toward Lula. She planned to flick the light off, to flounce down the hallway and start the washer.

Lula blocked the door. "The necklace was my grandmother's." She slid down the wall until she was sitting on the artfully distressed paisley rug, her legs crossed. Her cat-ear headband sat slightly crooked on her head.

Gabriella glanced at her watch. It was only 3:45. Neither parent would be home for several hours. There was no chance she'd have to explain why she'd had a heart-to-heart in Sarah's private closet. Gabriella studied the girl, her blondish hair hanging in one big chunk over each shoulder, her hoop earrings glittering under the chandelier. "Does it make you sad?" Gabriella asked, as she sat down on the stool Sarah kept tucked into her vanity.

"The necklace?" Lula made the face that normally accompanied Gabriella's suggestions that she start her homework or take a "screen break."

"Or," Gabriella clarified, "your grandmother?" The woman was why Gabriella was here, after all. Based on the tributes she'd found online—the official obituary and a couple of website features about her dedicated and notable philanthropy—she was a model of old Midwestern money. There were two daughters, not too many to split the inheritance. Her husband was in a home. He had his own family money.

Gabriella had considered Gretchen as a mark. The sister. But there were far fewer Gretchens. It would be harder to pull off a name coincidence. And Gretchen's only daughter was twenty-two. Gabriella was the wrong age to befriend either of them.

Fed Sarah had been perfect, except that she was a genius. Gabriella had underestimated the Ivy League degrees and the fancy job. The woman actually deserved those accolades. She was insanely quick and intuitive. Gabriella considered cutting and running once she realized the extent of her intellectual abilities, but she was in it now. It had been six weeks. She didn't have forever. In a battle of wits, she'd eventually lose, but she only needed to stay ahead for a tiny bit of time.

"My grandmother was a total bitch," Lula said. Gabriella's eyebrows shot toward the chandelier. "Sorry," Lula added. "But it's not like you've never heard the word before, right?"

"Right." Gabriella gathered herself. She'd perhaps also underestimated the conversational agility of teenagers.

"So, no. Thinking about my grandmother doesn't make me sad exactly, but . . ." Lula trailed off, and Gabriella's antennae went up. She had people skills. That was why this whole thing worked in the first place. Lula had a secret, one she could possibly use.

Gabriella put on her most empathetic expression, the one that coaxed third graders to confess their playground transgressions. "But what?" she prompted.

Lula's face went dark. She pulled her headband off, holding one ear between her thumb and forefinger. "You know how sometimes when you're little, you don't realize what's actually going on? And people don't try as hard to hide things from you?"

Gabriella did know about that. It had happened when she was about Lula's age, when her father's mental illness could no longer be passed off as moodiness or some kind of offbeat quirk. She started hearing the doors closing harder than they needed to and catching wisps of conversations between her mother and her aunt. "I know that exactly." Gabriella slid onto the floor then, letting her toes touch Lula's. "But then you *do* see things and hear things."

"I know." The tears came fast. Lula's whole face was slick with them. "I wish I could go back. I never wanted to know that, never wanted to see it. Mom told me to leave. We snuck back in. We weren't meant to be there."

Gabriella scooted closer. She kept one hand in her lap, and with the other she rubbed Lula's shoulder the same way she had for Oscar before he got too old. "What happened?"

Lula looked back toward the closet door, checking to be sure they were alone. Gabriella took little sips of air, sensing the breakthrough she needed.

"I was visiting Gran in the home with Mom. During Covid." Gabriella kept her hand moving on the girl's back, same pressure, same cadence. "They said mean things to each other like they always did. We went to the vending machine. Ruby was there that day."

"Mean things?" Gabriella prompted.

"The usual," Lula said. "'Selfish,' 'shrewish'—whatever that means—'obsessed with money.'" She raised a hand from her lap and dropped it again.

Gabriella wanted to stop here, to ask if Fed Sarah had continued this cycle, had started with Ruby or Lula, calling them names and accusing them of being bad daughters.

"And then?" Gabriella asked. There was more. As was often the case with Gabriella, she couldn't tell whether she wanted to know because she needed the information to pay the people who were torturing Oscar, or if she thought she could actually help.

You can't be both, Gabriella found herself thinking. *You can't both help and steal.*

Lula was in her own emotional cave, her head bent all the way over, her hair grazing her knees. "And then, we snuck back in as a joke. It was a joke! It was my idea to surprise them, but then there was the pillow over her face. And Ruby grabbed me. And we slammed the door from the hallway."

Whoa. Gabriella's hand stopped its arc over Lula's back.

"She—" Lula started again.

Gabriella felt her fingers curl into a fist over the girl's T-shirt. A swirl of horror and hope began in her gut. This information, this woman—her power and influence—this could be the end of Gabriella's problems. She could maybe go back to Annabeth. Maybe there was a chance she could start over.

"She held the pillow over Gran's face. That had to be what happened. Because then she was dead." Lula's voice was a croak. Barely discernible. But Gabriella got it. And as soon as she'd processed the information that Fed Sarah had killed her own mother, Ruby appeared in the doorway of the closet, her cheeks aflame.

"What the fuck did you do?" Ruby said to Lula, who folded all the way over on herself and rolled onto her side.

It had taken Gabriella a full hour to get them out of there, to convince them that everything was going to be okay, that she understood, that she wouldn't tell. And then she'd kept her word. She hadn't told.

A week later, though, their mother was dead.

An accident.

Now, Gabriella stared at the base of the bridge. There was nothing there, but she imagined she could see the outline of the pool of blood, the imprint of the skull in the asphalt. Bright sun reflected off the Mississippi River. A stream of runners and bikers passed between Gabriella and the stairs to the bridge, the ones she'd climbed with Sarah that night.

She'd been so stupid to walk with her this way. It had been obvious at dinner that she'd have to cut and run, that Sarah knew everything.

"I know about you and Caden," she'd said first, over salad. "He's such an idiot."

Gabriella was surprised. Caden seemed like such a lightweight, not like the type to start something over nothing with his wife. All he ever did was heart the pictures, smile a little more awkwardly in the kitchen. One time, he'd written, "Very nice," and she'd screenshotted that. Gabriella took a sip of her drink and waited, not sure where this was going.

"I found the photos on his phone." She shook her head. "Well, my security guy did. I just met with him. He thought he'd have it this morning, but he was late."

"You met with your security firm?" Gabriella tried to process what this meant.

"If you have aims at federal office, you have to watch stuff like this. You can't trust anyone." Sarah finished her drink, the second she'd ordered. "In case you were wondering, I never trusted you, either. I'm not an idiot."

Gabriella blinked. Security guy? She hadn't had to fill out anything. There'd been vague mentions of a background check, but she'd been off and running with the girls. She'd made life easier for Sarah. She'd grocery shopped and picked up rosé. Everyone just went with it. And it had only been a couple of months. She was short-term, a sub for their regular nanny, who still FaceTimed the girls once a week from her study abroad in Budapest.

"So yeah." The server came back. They ordered entrees, Sarah first. Gabriella folded her menu and thought about making a break for the door, but she felt Sarah's hand on her knee, the nails digging in just a little bit. Gabriella swallowed and then choked out an order for seared scallops, her usual.

A silence persisted, but Gabriella couldn't speak. It had been a long time since she'd really considered what it would feel like to get caught.

"At first, I was distracted by the idea of an affair," Sarah continued like they were recapping *The Bachelor*, "but then I realized it couldn't be about him. You're beautiful, smart, young. You wouldn't want anything to do with a guy like Caden. His money is all tied up in mine."

Gabriella forced herself to suck in a breath, held it for a beat, and then let it out.

Sarah tipped her head. "So then I had the security firm dig. And guess what? You're not who you say you are. Nonexistent academic record. They found the teacher photo from—what was that elementary school?"

Gabriella looked at the door. She'd have to leave, yes. Tonight. But how? Would Sarah have already called the police? She peered past their reflection in the restaurant windows to the outside. It had started to drizzle. She could see the water droplets in the dispersion from the streetlights.

"Here's the deal," Sarah said. "I'm not stupid. I'm a good judge of character, always have been. You're not a terrible person, except that you kind of are."

Gabriella blinked. Annabeth had said something similar. She hadn't given Grace and Catherine the chance to indict her in person. Tears clogged Gabriella's lower lashes.

"So, tell me why," Sarah said. "I feel like you owe me—you owe my family—at least that."

Their dinner came, and Gabriella told Sarah some of it. "I have a brother," she said. And then the story overwhelmed her. How could she tell Sarah about the way their father always targeted him and made him feel small? How Gabriella's own coping mechanisms—to acquire as many gold stars as possible—made things worse for Oscar? How she knew that was what would happen to him, and she kept compulsively achieving anyway?

The entrees came, and despite the emotional distress, she bolted her dinner and drained her wineglass. They each had a refill.

"The girls like you," Sarah said. "I liked you. I was actually starting to think of you as a friend." She paid the check without speaking to the server, and Gabriella felt like a kid in detention, trapped at the table and out of options. "You're good at this con artist job," Sarah said, folding her napkin. "How does that feel?"

Gabriella couldn't answer. She used to be a decent person, a teacher, in a helping profession.

When they got out to the sidewalk, the drizzle had turned into a light rain. Sarah pulled an umbrella from her purse and held it over her own head while Gabriella's hair dampened.

"What are you going to do?" Gabriella asked, finally, as they walked past Sarah's Mercedes E-Class.

"First we're going to look at the river in the rain," Sarah said. "It'll give me a few minutes to sober up for the drive."

It wasn't until they stood on the bridge, looking east toward the iconic Stone Arch, that Gabriella remembered she had ammunition to shoot her way out of this after all.

CHAPTER THIRTY-NINE

Video Transcript Recorded by Sarah Jones, Age Seventeen

May 30, 2023

When we turned the corner from the restaurant and saw the river, I threw both arms out to the side to stop Sister and Sixty-Nine from walking past me. I couldn't tell for sure, but I had a spidey sense. A woman in a gray hoodie jogged across the road toward the Hennepin Avenue Bridge. It looked like Twenty-Seven.

What is she doing here? Her phone was gone, her apartment was empty. Everyone thought she'd left town. But as the woman's hood fell from her head, revealing the characteristic waves, Sixty-Nine whispered, "It's her." I grabbed my friends' hands and pulled them toward the side of the building to our right, hiding us.

Sister whipped out her phone and dialed. I could hear the voice on the other end.

"Agent Vance," Sister said. "It's Sister Mary Theresa Conaty. I'm calling with an urgent update. We traced the route from the restaurant to the murder scene, and we found her." Pause. "Yep. She's there, looking at the water." Pause. "How many minutes?" Pause. "Roger that."

Sister put her phone away. My whole body tingled with fear and excitement. Sister zipped her jacket to her neck. She looked like a regular senior citizen with her blue trousers and orthopedic sneakers. You couldn't see her cross. No one would look twice, probably not even Twenty-Seven. Sister held a hand up to us, indicating that we should stay put, and then she walked toward the River Road, calm and cool. When she got to a bench across the street from where Twenty-Seven stood on the bridge, she stopped there.

"What do we do?" I whispered to Sixty-Nine.

"I think we just wait," she said.

So we did, for a good seven or eight minutes. Twenty-Seven didn't do much in this time. At one point, she started walking toward the other side of the bridge, one hand to her temple. Sister stood up when she got far enough away and approached the sidewalk, but Twenty-Seven turned back. Then she rested her head on the guardrail in front of her.

And finally, a boxy sedan parked on the street next to us. A woman in a black blazer sprang out. Her hair held a slight wave. She wore aviator sunglasses, and as she strode toward Sister on the bench, I knew it was Supervisory Special Agent in Charge Jane Vance.

CHAPTER FORTY

May 27, 2023

Gabriella thought about jumping. She tested the barrier. She could hoist herself up and over and maybe land in the exact spot Sarah had that night.

The news articles had hardly mentioned Sarah's blood alcohol content, though it had to have been through the roof. Instead, the coverage was bloated with euphemism and hyperbole. "Dedicated," "selfless," "unflagging," everyone said about her.

People like Oscar, on the other hand, got merciless treatment, if they got any press at all. *Another addict died alone, another addict overdosed.* Their deaths weren't individual tragedies, but rather social problems. Nobody ever wondered about their survivors.

On the bridge that night with Sarah, when Gabriella had realized she could save herself, she felt the corners of her mouth turn up.

"Why are you smiling?" Sarah had demanded, slurring. "You're a thief and a con artist, and your name isn't even Sarah Jones."

"But I have some information," Gabriella said.

"What you have is a one-way ticket to federal prison." Sarah's sarcasm didn't quite fit her demeanor, her St. John suit, the Hermès scarf she'd tied around her wrist.

Gabriella had taken a step away, letting her back rest against the guardrail. "Lula told me what you did to your mother."

Sarah shook her head. "I didn't do anything to my mother."

Gabriella squinted. "Pillow to the face? Argument about inheritance? Ruby confirmed? Gretchen suspects? The girls would feel better if I helped them tell Gretchen what they know."

Sarah's blow stunned her, a knee to her groin as if Gabriella were a man. "Ow!" she said, but she laughed, too. "Cute! Did you take self-defense classes at the office, or what?"

"You're such a bitch," Sarah hissed.

"But I'm going to walk away, okay?" Gabriella pointed at the far side of the bridge. "I'm keeping the necklace, and I'll never bother you again."

"There's no way you're just walking," Sarah said.

"I am," Gabriella said, "because I also have text messages from your husband. You didn't print those with the photos, but I know what he said. Everyone else can, too." The replies were minimal, but the threat would give Sarah pause. It was like all of Gabriella's mojo had returned, an adrenaline surge that might be just enough to propel her out of town. She wouldn't have time to get to Thirty's trust fund, but she'd be closer than ever to her final payment. One more town. One more time.

Just as Gabriella started walking, Sarah launched herself at her, the force of her body another surprise. Gabriella held her forearms up defensively for a few seconds and felt like she was watching the fight from above, the middle-aged woman rapid-firing blows all over Gabriella's upper body.

First, she stepped away from the rail. Then, she tried to prevent the onslaught by grabbing Sarah's biceps. "Stop it," Gabriella said. "It's not dignified."

"Dignified!" Sarah took a step back toward the guardrail and unbuttoned her blazer. "Are you fucking kidding me?" It was when the Fed chair bent to take off her shoes that Gabriella pushed her hard, her head slamming back against the metal of the railing. She slid down to her knees, holding her head. When she brought her hand around, blood spread from the base of her fingers toward her wrist.

She sprang to her feet, and the sound was like a growl when Sarah lunged toward Gabriella's middle.

"No," Gabriella grunted, kicking her in the chin, her head snapping back again.

Gabriella had known in the split second before she delivered the next hit that it could knock the smaller woman up and over. The angle was just perfect. She drove into her like a linebacker. In the daylight and on the weekend, joggers and families milled all around that park. That night the women were alone.

As Gabriella stood there now, her vision grayscale despite the late spring sunshine, all of the images flooded her: Sarah's shocked expression, the jagged sides of her mouth, the smear of eyeliner on the left.

How could Gabriella have become the person who did this kind of thing?

She lifted a leg to the railing. She'd jump fast. And then she heard the voice.

"Gabriella Johnson?" It was a woman. Gabriella put her leg down and gripped the guardrail with both hands.

"Put your hands up, please, and turn around."

Gabriella opened her eyes and looked at the pavement below. "Can you just shoot?" she asked.

"That would cause me quite a bit of trauma," the woman said. "Why don't you just turn around, and then we'll see."

Gabriella spun with her palms up at chest height. The woman

had sideswept bangs. Instead of a gun, she held an FBI badge. "I'm Supervisory Special Agent in Charge Jane Vance of the FBI."

"Okay," Gabriella said.

"It's time to come in," Agent Vance told her. It didn't sound like a threat. It sounded like an offer, a chance for something besides death.

Vance stepped toward Gabriella with her own palms out. "I'm going to pat you down. And then we're going to get in the car."

CHAPTER FORTY-ONE

May 27, 2023

"Do not say you're sorry again," Vance told him over the phone as George held up a finger indicating that Andrew O'Neill should wait for him. He sat on the office porch while Andrew leaned on the picnic table far enough away to avoid overhearing.

George's boss didn't sound angry, but then again Vance never really did show any signs of emotion. It was all matter-of-fact, one day at a time, one detail at a time, one case, one conviction at a time.

"I can come back right away," George said, as he had twice before.

"Tomorrow is fast enough," Vance said. "It's Saturday, and one of my kids' birthdays."

George thought about having a kid and doing this job, his gun on his hip and a million secrets weighing on him like a backpack of bricks. Birdsong was literally an open book—a shelf of them, a collection of spreadsheets, files in the basement. He'd traded all of that transparency, all that organized history, for a life of deception and cageyness.

"I'm having MPD put Gabriella in custody and charging her with manslaughter, fraud, and extortion. We have enough for that, right? In the file? I don't have a confession on the manslaughter yet, but she's pretty vulnerable. I think we can get it."

"Yeah," George said, calculating. "For sure on hearsay, anyway. I'll need a day . . ." His head spun. What he'd need was for Sarah to make an official statement. He'd have to talk to her neighbor, too, the one who'd interrupted the break-in, and then also to Seventeen.

"It's enough to hold her." Vance sounded sure. "I'll call the others—Catherine Anderson and Grace Smith—and have them verify a photo. That'll do it."

It would, George knew. If they didn't need the airtight file for the US attorney, it would have been enough a while ago.

"I'll be back no later than tomorrow afternoon," said George, "and then—"

"And then pick up Sarah and bring her to the MPD. We'll need her statement, too."

George put a hand on his damp forehead and closed his eyes. He wasn't sure he could ask Sarah to do anything right now, and he really, really didn't want to tell his boss it was because he'd accidentally, maybe started falling in love with her. But Vance picked up on his reticence immediately.

"What's going on with your informant, Nightingale?" He heard a ringing phone in the background on her end. George imagined her in the police department, the excitement buzzing through the task force over an arrest.

George thought about trying to hide the truth about Sarah. But Vance was smarter than he was, savvier. She'd know, or she'd find out. And then she'd send him to Yuma. Plus, George liked her. "I screwed it up," he admitted.

"Damn," Vance said, still calm. "How badly?"

George thought about Sarah's hair spread out on the pillow in the AD's cabin, the way her waist felt when he ran the bar of soap over it. "I actually started to really like her."

"Oh, for fuck's sake," Vance said. "And so you've started to *act* like you really like her? We've gone from running together to . . ."

"She's here with me this weekend," George admitted, cringing. He sat down in one of the metal chairs on the office porch and rested an elbow on his knee. "But we got in a fight." He squeezed his eyes shut.

"Good lord, Nightingale," said Vance. "What am I? A high school guidance counselor?"

"I'm so—"

"*Don't* say it!" Vance admonished. "Just *fix* it. I'll figure out what to put in your file later."

George didn't want to imagine the addendum to that folder. The stuff in there about Henry seemed like enough baggage. And this? The mistreatment of a Confidential Human Source? That would leave a mark.

"I'll see you tomorrow," Vance said, steady as always. "Call if there's an emergency." She coughed. "Another one, I mean."

They hung up, but George held the phone to his ear for another moment, collecting himself. He wasn't used to making big mistakes. And this mistake, with Gabriella's arrest and Sarah—well, he didn't even know how to quantify the higher stakes. Never mind his unsanctioned questions about Henry O'Neill, plus the resurfacing of one of the detectives who'd been crucified in the media for not solving it.

George turned his attention back to the grieving father, and something about Andrew's posture there by the picnic table, the way he muttered to himself, reminded George of Little League. It was a memory he hadn't replayed in ages.

Sylvia had been the coach of his and Henry's third-grade team. Henry's throw from shortstop to first had all the snap of a limp noodle. Andrew had paced the sidelines, mumbling to himself just like he was now. After one particularly error-ridden game, the whole team had gone to the Dairy Queen, but not Henry. The next day, Henry had told him he'd gone right home to do push-ups and practice throwing with his dad.

George put his phone in his pocket and walked toward Andrew. "Sorry, Mr. O'Neill."

The man's fists were clenched and pressing into the tops of his thighs. "There's always something more important happening at the bureau, right?"

George rolled his shoulders back. Customer service was an aspect of both of his jobs. "Not more important." He shook his head. "It's just, it always seems like there are a bunch of things converging at once. You know?"

"And you're up here," Andrew said, still no lightness to his countenance, "doing docks? When all the stuff is, what, *converging*, back in the cities?"

George squinted, trying to get a good look at the man's face, but Andrew kept his chin down. "Doing docks," George confirmed. "Hey," he said, taking another run at it, "I've been looking into Henry's case. I pulled the files on the summer workers. I'm running down alibis. I haven't forgotten."

Andrew lifted his head and stared into George's eyes. His skin seemed gray, though George could see a bit of blotchiness rising from his neck. "I had no idea it would take this long," Andrew said.

"I can only imagine." George had repeated this line before, at the vigils and at the 10Ks.

"You were little boys." Andrew's eyes focused over George's shoulder, and George turned, checking. Paul stood there, under the white oak that George and his class had planted when they were second graders. "And I never imagined it would take this long. After raising him alone."

George turned back, desperate to say the right thing. "I'm here, Mr. O'Neill," was what came out. "I'm here for you and Henry, and I promise I'm trying my best to close this."

Andrew put his hand on George's forearm.

"Can you let it go, Andrew?" It was Paul, quiet but intense. "Can you find some peace now?"

George blinked at his father. *Find some peace?* What could he mean? How could anyone find peace when Henry was still out there? "Dad," George said, "we haven't found him yet. But I'm hopeful that we will."

Andrew pressed down on George's arm. He swayed a little, leaning into George. George put a hand on his waist.

Andrew stared at Paul. "Do you know where he is?"

George recoiled, but Andrew gripped his arm even harder. George gaped at his father.

Was this an accusation? George thought back on the day, the bikes, the way Henry had disappeared into Birdsong Woods, the transcript of their interrogations. Paul Nightingale had been in the wrong place at the wrong time, but certainly he didn't have anything to do with Henry. The family had devoted generations to helping kids become the best versions of themselves. He'd never raised a hand to George or Bea. There was no way.

George braced for Paul's self-defense, but there wasn't one. "I think I might," he said. And George felt his eyelids start to flutter. His cheeks felt numb. "But," his dad said, "I'm wondering if we can just make peace."

Andrew released George's arm then, each finger leaving its own indentation, and the man walked down the steps and back to his truck. George glanced at his father once, his mouth hanging open. But Paul just shook his head. "I don't know anything for sure," he said, finally. "I've never known *for sure*." George collapsed onto one of the steps to the office, confused. "I've never had that sense of absolute certainty," Paul continued. "Do you know that feeling?"

George thought about it. Had he ever known anything for sure? He'd had a gnawing feeling, an impulse, a gut sense. The first time he'd seen Sarah, that smattering of freckles across the bridge of her nose, the wisps of white hair at her temples, he'd felt something he'd attributed to making the right choice about the FBI. "I'm not sure." George blinked.

Paul sighed with his whole body as Andrew's truck circled the turnaround and headed back toward the main road, out of camp. "When I started to suspect," Paul said, "I stopped letting them search the land." He shrugged. "Henry was always happy here. I just thought maybe everyone would be better off if no one ever knew. But"—he gestured at Andrew's retreating pickup—"it's obviously killing him."

George felt his head shaking no. "Wait." He straightened his arms at his sides and flexed both quads, pressing the balls of his feet into the step. "Are you saying you think Andrew O'Neill is responsible for Henry—" George's vision blurred. "You think he did it?"

Paul backed toward the marina. "I never planned to tell you," he said. He raised his arms and dropped them again. "But then you joined the FBI because of it. And it seems like Andrew . . ." He trailed off and looked toward the road where the truck had disappeared.

"It seems like Andrew what?" George asked.

"It seems like he's trying to tell you." Paul's face sagged. "I made the wrong choice." George didn't have time to decide if he agreed before Paul said, "Let's finish the docks, yeah? One more session?"

At first George couldn't believe his dad had suggested it, working on something like the docks at a time like this. But then he followed him back toward the waterfront. He couldn't fix Sarah right now. He couldn't keep Vance from handing down discipline. He couldn't complete the Gabriella Johnson file. He couldn't interrogate Andrew O'Neill without alerting Vance. But he could put in the docks. He'd done it a million times before.

HENRY O'NEILL CASE FILE

Crow Wing County Sheriff's Office Interview with Andrew O'Neill

Investigators Present: Deputy Stephanie Granger and
Deputy Theresa Conaty

April 18, 2001

Stephanie Granger: We're recording this, okay, Mr. O'Neill?

Andrew O'Neill: Why are you even asking me that? Of course it's okay. Nothing matters except that you find him.

SG: I appreciate that, Mr. O'Neill, and I can assure you that we're working with the FBI to get the case closed as quickly as possible.

AO: You didn't say to find him. No one thinks we're going to find him.

Theresa Conaty: We are hoping for the best, Mr. O'Neill, but time and circumstances are against us. You're a smart guy. You know the statistics, right? But I can assure you, I'm not going to give up on this until I uncover everything I can. I want nothing more than to reunite you with your son.

AO: My dead son.

TC: I sincerely hope that's not the case, Andrew. May we call you Andrew?

AO: Don't ask me any stupid questions. You can call me whatever the hell you want.

SG: I want to go way back, okay, Andrew? I want to get as clear a picture of your son as I can. We don't want to miss anything, to miss any possible connection that might lead us to him. Okay? Can you bear with me while I ask some background?

AO: Okay.

SG: Let's go back. I know this is sensitive, but I'm aware that your wife passed.

AO: She did.

SG: I can't imagine how difficult that must be. I'm so sorry.

AO: People keep saying that, that they can't imagine. But that's your job, right? You talk to people who've had the absolute worst happen to them. Surely, you can imagine.

SG: Can you tell me how your wife died?

AO: She died in childbirth.

SG: That's heartbreaking. I'm so sorry. And I understand Henry is your only child?

AO: She wasn't supposed to die. It was a fluke. I didn't even want children. She wanted two.

SG: The adjustment must have been hard.

AO: Hard? It was fucking excruciating. People still remember my wife. Emily was spectacular. An artist. She said the lake was an inspiration. She liked the Northwoods. That's why we moved here.

SG: She wanted to be a mother? That's why you had Henry?

AO: She said she felt a yearning. I was worried . . .

SG: About?

AO: I was worried that if I didn't give her what she wanted, then she would . . .

TC: She would . . . ?

AO: Leave, I guess? I can't explain it to you. She had a light. She was . . . effervescent. I've never met anyone like her.

SG: Thanks for this, Mr. O'Neill. I'm going to keep going, okay? Detective Conaty is going to give you a tissue.

AO: I've never stopped grieving her.

SG: And then she died when Henry was born?

AO: Yes. An embolism. I left the room and she was alive, and then when I came back, it was just him.

SG: It was just Henry. Your son.

AO: Yes.

SG: And, Mr. O'Neill, stay with me here. Can you tell us about your relationship with Henry?

AO: I was his father.

SG: Right. I'm going to have Detective Conaty pour you a glass of water, okay? How was your relationship with Henry lately?

AO: He was a fifth grader. What kind of emotional depth do children have in their relationships at that age?

SG: Did you feel like Henry told you about his problems? I know this is an odd question to ask about a child, but did Henry have any enemies? Bullies at school?

AO: Henry was light on recess skills. His grades were okay. I can't believe anyone was threatened by him. He was just a kid.

SG: Recess skills?

AO: You know. He couldn't throw and catch very well. He wasn't the fastest. Oh my God, I'm talking about him in the past tense already.

SG: Were sports important to you?

AO: It was something I shared with my own father. Like I said, I never really envisioned having children, but when I finally accepted—no, that's wrong. When Emily was pregnant, I let myself imagine a little.

SG: And what did you imagine?

AO: I played high school baseball. My team was state runner-up in Delaware during my junior season. My God, I don't even know what I'm saying.

SG: So you were hoping that Henry would take after you? That he'd have a similar athletic experience? And instead?

AO: Nothing was how I wanted it to be. I know I'm not making any sense, Detective. I'm just—it's just been so sad.

SG: A missing child is a major trauma. Let's just take our time and see if we can uncover anything that might be useful, okay? Can you stay with me?

AO: It's just been so sad since the beginning. Since Emily died. Nothing at all has ever been the way I wanted it to be. And now this.

CHAPTER FORTY-TWO

May 27, 2023

Dinner was pizza, a celebratory order from the shop closest to camp. George had been dispatched to pick it up, and Sarah insisted she'd go, too.

"You really don't have to," he said. He looked less sorry than he had before.

"I want to see the town," Sarah said, not lying. Ainsley had been in Pine River, too, and her mother had been the impetus for the whole trip.

They were quiet as they walked to the car. So much had changed in less than twenty-four hours. "Can I ask you some questions?" Sarah had spent the afternoon wandering the grounds, peeking in the buildings, making a list.

She'd stopped in the office and Sylvia offered her some archives to peruse. Sarah sat at a table in the outer room with the photo albums. She cracked a window and let the chilly breeze in, the perfect temperature for pulling her knees up to her chest and tucking her hands into her terry-cloth sweatshirt. The photos showed happy kids and counselors. George featured in many of them: there was a younger George, still with the curl on his forehead, holding a clipboard at the marina. George with an apron serving burgers to a gaggle of eight-year-olds. She'd softened a little, but she was still livid.

"You can ask some questions," George said now. He opened the car door for her. He'd never done that before.

Sarah sat in the front seat, and George took his time walking around. He swung his arms a little wider. He stretched his right triceps across his chest. Twenty-four hours ago, she would have found this behavior adorable—adorkable, she remembered thinking the first time she'd trained him at LifeSport.

George finally slid into the car, in one fluid movement. He was nervous. Sarah could feel it radiating off him, and she was glad. He was a conniving asshole, maybe, but at least he cared? Sarah said nothing until he'd backed out of the driveway and pointed the nose of the sedan toward the big hill they'd descended when they'd first arrived at Birdsong, back when she'd felt nothing but glee and serendipity. And then, sensing his nerves again and feeling preternaturally calm herself after her afternoon of reflection, she waited for him to speak first.

He cracked after they'd crested the hill. Sarah looked out her window and saw a pod of antlerless deer communing in the middle of a field. "Um," he finally ventured, "you said you wanted to ask me some questions?"

"Yeah." Sarah had rehearsed while George and the crew dove down to secure the pilings. "My first one is, why does Gabriella Johnson do it?"

She'd tried to text Gabriella herself to ask this. Sarah had sent four messages that afternoon, but they'd gone unanswered.

"Like her motive?" George asked.

"I know she's a con artist and everything, and that she became my friend to steal my trust fund, but she's . . ." Sarah paused. She thought back to just the other night at drinks, how miserable Twenty-Seven had looked, her head heavy against the café wall. "I think she's really sad," Sarah said.

"She's sad?" George sounded surprised.

"Aren't you supposed to think about that? Like, her motive?" George had empathy, Sarah knew it. It had driven him into the FBI.

"Yes." George kept his eyes, bloodshot from a day under freezing water, on the road. "It's just that I've spent more time thinking about the victims. About you. About the woman she threw off a bridge." He coughed and glanced over for just a second.

"She's not a sociopath," Sarah said, sure of it.

"But," George said, calm, "she did kill Fed Sarah."

Sarah shifted in her seat. She replayed the moment when Twenty-Seven had asked whether intention mattered, whether killing was better if it were an accident. "How do you know she killed her?"

George coughed again. "She got arrested this afternoon."

"Arrested?" Sarah pulled her phone out of her pocket. There weren't any messages in the group chat. "Are you sure?"

"Vance called a while ago, right before we finished the docks." He scratched his neck—a tell, Sarah now realized. There was more he was hiding.

Her anger flared. She could keep some secrets, too. "I don't think she killed her on purpose," Sarah said.

"Does that make it better?" George asked. "Can you really do anything to atone for taking a life? You've met Ruby. She deserves to be motherless?"

They looked at each other. She got sucked in, for just a second, into his brown eyes. Sarah imagined them open under the water in Lake Whitehook. What did he see down there when he was drilling into the lake bed? What was he looking for? "Ruby doesn't deserve a dead mom." Sarah felt like she couldn't think straight. It was too complex, her being here, her best friend in jail for murder, the two girls who'd lost their parent. "People have to keep going, even after the worst happens." This she knew for sure, and better than anyone.

George gripped the steering wheel. She could see the tension in his arms. She'd trained them, after all. It occurred to her that maybe they'd already had their last session together.

"Are you even registered for that marathon?" Sarah asked. "Do you even want to run a marathon?"

George's mouth twitched. He opened it and closed it again, and Sarah's heart sank.

"Okay," she said before he could answer. "I get it." She wondered where the truth ended between them and the federal investigation began—if she would ever have the chance to know. George was the same as Twenty-Seven in so many ways. They were both blends of authenticity and manipulation. But still, only one of them, as far as Sarah knew, was a murderer. Her best friend was a killer. And had stolen from her and lied about too many things to count.

"Have you found Gabriella's brother?" Sarah asked next. "Is he actually dead?"

"Oscar Johnson," George said. "He has a rap sheet a mile long." He snorted. "Oh my God, I sound like a bad cliché."

Sarah leaned back against the headrest. "She said drugs." Could she put these pieces together? "Said he died from . . ." She hadn't actually said. Drugs, was what she'd said. "Well, now that I'm thinking about it, she didn't say exactly. Maybe an overdose."

George continued, "He wasn't dead when she told you, but he did die last week. Vance told her when she made the arrest. They found his body in Eau Claire."

"Wait." Sarah sat up straight. "How did Vance find her? Couldn't you have moved in a while ago? And"—she gulped—"did you ever consider that she might—" Sarah couldn't imagine Twenty-Seven hurting her. She didn't really think she'd been in mortal danger, but then Twenty-Seven had shown signs of violence in the coffee shop with Seventeen. By waiting on the arrest, George might have risked their safety. *Doesn't he care?*

"Believe me, I considered it. But the recidivism rate is minuscule for crimes of passion, and then things fell into place only this week. And *then* we thought we lost her." George breathed out before continuing. "She'd destroyed her phone. But we got a call from Sister Mary Theresa. Or, Vance did. I was here."

"Sister Mary Theresa?" Sarah asked. "Again?"

"Yeah," George said, "I actually know her—well, never mind. Anyway, the nun and Seventeen and Sixty-Nine, they found one of Gabriella's best friends, her first victim, a woman named Annabeth Silver. Then they decided to retrace the walk from the restaurant where Fed Sarah and Gabriella had dinner, and then they got lucky." George picked up a hand and let it drop again on the wheel. "I'm not totally sure how it all went down, actually." He seemed defeated, but Sarah laughed in spite of everything. "What's so funny?" George asked. She looked at him again and fought the impulse to trace his cocked eyebrow with her thumb. Was being so handsome seen as an attribute in the FBI? Was there a note in the file about his looks? How well he could use his wiles?

"What's so funny is it worked!" Sarah said. Seventeen had been so earnest. She'd had that clipboard, the notebooks, the social media account. They'd all wanted to help the weird kid be whimsical.

"What worked?"

"TSJP! The plan to investigate the murder. They solved it, right? They got Vance to the bridge at the right time?"

George's lips twitched, and then he grinned. And then, without thinking too hard about what it meant, Sarah found herself laughing again. George, too. "My first case with the FBI," George said, gasping a little, "and it was solved out from under my nose by a teenager doing a stupid school project that was supervised by a cloistered nun."

"Really makes you think, huh?" Sarah swiped beneath her eye, which had started to tear. "About your purpose in life?"

"Oh my God," George said. He took a left then, off the highway, and the downtown emerged. He pulled up outside of a storefront with a neon pizza slice in the window. "Are you saying my whole life's work—that it could be done by a kid on school probation? That's depressing." He turned the key and slid out of the parked car. "You can wait here." He almost slammed the door, but then caught it and peeked back in. Even though she was angry, she caught her breath when they made eye contact. She remembered the smell of his neck, the taste of his skin there. "I mean you can wait if you want to. I'll be right back."

Sarah felt herself smile a little.

It was when they were halfway back to the camp, the smell of hot bread and melted cheese pleasantly filling the car, that George spoke again. "I've been thinking," he said.

"That's pretty much all I've been doing," Sarah admitted. She kept her eyes on the darkening road even as she felt his glance on her.

"Well, I've been thinking, if it's possible you can see goodness in a murderer who also stole money from your trust fund—can you check that, by the way?"

"I did, as soon as you told me. There was a transfer in the works. I canceled it."

"I need the information about the transfer. The routing numbers, the amounts, all that stuff." He sounded all business, all of a sudden, as if they were sitting across a conference table from each other rather than driving back for dinner with his parents.

"I'll give that to you when and if I want to," Sarah said. She'd already thought about it. She'd made every wrong choice so far. She'd trusted every wrong person. She needed some space to think about how much she wanted to help the FBI and what it all meant.

"But we need that. *I* need it to close the case. Yours was the one—" George sounded nervous.

"Right," Sarah said. "And there's the problem. No matter how cute you are, or how much of the truth you told me, or whether you do actually, like, *like* me."

"But I do like you." George crested the hill near camp. This time, Sarah knew to look for the water at the horizon. It was gray under the cloudy sky, but she saw the sliver of lake there, just as Ainsley had all those summers before.

"Then you shouldn't have just stood by and watched and waited while I got hurt. Even for your job." That was the truth of it. She'd been trying to escape it all afternoon.

She saw that he couldn't argue. George sighed and pulled into the driveway. Sarah opened the back seat and grabbed half of the pizza boxes. Tomorrow morning, they'd drive home, and she'd have to rethink everything.

Group Chat of The Sarah Jones Project

May 27, 2023

17: WE SAW HER GET ARRESTED.

69: Sister called Agent Vance, and she took her in the car, we assume to the police station.

30: I feel bad, kind of. Is that weird? Her brother died, too.

39: We already knew her brother was dead. He died that one day she came wasted to the meeting, remember?

30: I guess he wasn't really dead that day. But clearly, he was on his way to being dead.

44: She LIED about her BROTHER being DEAD?

17: That's like the fortieth or fiftieth thing she lied about. She's like a literal con artist. Lying is the whole shebang.

30: I know. I can't believe I so misjudged her.

69: Don't blame yourself. That's her whole thing. It's to manipulate and take advantage of people's good qualities.

17: Do we know what the charges are?

30: Manslaughter, fraud, and extortion. They're holding her until they finish securing some evidence.

17: You're telling us every detail when you get home, right? Emergency meeting?

30: I'll keep you posted.

39: Wait a second. You guys.

44: I know what you're going to say, and yes, it's totally unbelievable.

69: What?

39: It worked! Our group worked! We solved the murder. We alerted the FBI.

69: The detective nun alerted the FBI.

44: Yes, and she was one of us.

30: She was our supervisor.

17: It worked!

CHAPTER FORTY-THREE

May 28, 2023

When the first crack of thunder woke him that night, the muscle memory of storm watching flooded George. As a camp director, he'd never had the luxury of curling up under a blanket and waiting for the lightning to stop. Instead, the radar required constant vigilance, like everything else at Birdsong, like everything else in the bureau.

George leapt out of bed and surveyed the lakeside window before the next rattle. Whitehook's waves had picked up. The newly installed docks would be an issue, but at least there weren't any kids in camp. He didn't have to think about the storm shelter.

Paul appeared in front of the window then. George had last seen him at dinner, which had gone smoothly despite the tension between him and Sarah. She was a pro at pretending everything was fine. On their way back to the AD's cabin, she lightly touched his forearm and told him she'd made up the second bedroom for herself.

On the next lightning flash, George raised a "one-second" finger, and his dad grinned. Paul loved a good storm. George paused at Sarah's closed door on his way to grab a slicker and his shoes. All quiet. He jogged down the hill toward camp after his dad's red rain jacket.

"How's the radar?" George asked when he'd caught up.

"It's a big cell, winds high in the middle." Paul turned to him and grinned, his eyes flashing. "Can you believe it? We just put the docks in? And now we're going to have to catch 'em!"

"No boats, at least," George said. That was a whole different level of mess, with lifts coming off the bottom of the lake and watercraft disappearing around the point, taken by the wind and waves. All they'd have to do tonight was get any unmoored dock platforms to shore.

Paul and George stopped at the top of the marina, surveying their work, which was holding for now. A giant lightning strike illuminated the rolling spread of water.

"Pretty, though, right?" Paul asked.

"Yeah," George said. "Why is it always breathtaking?"

"Not much like that in the FBI?"

Before George could answer, thunder unfolded above them, reverberating for seconds. One of the dock platforms creaked, straining against a piling. The waves crashed over the tops of them. If the boats were in, the dinghies would already be swamped.

"I'm not sure," George answered. "Maybe it's breathtaking to see the arrest of someone you've been investigating? Or to recover a missing child?"

"Maybe," Paul said, just as the dock platforms closest to the shore tipped up with the wave and slammed down again.

Without a word, the men jogged down the cement stairs to the waterfront. George followed his father into the lake. The platforms escaped the pilings, and they caught them and guided them to shore.

"Should have waited to put the platforms on," George shouted.

"But the crew wanted to see them!" Paul yelled back. "A good reward for all the work, you know? You have to have perks!"

George laughed as he braced against the water, spitting the remnants of a wave as he half floated on a section of dock. It was just like Paul to think of "looking at finished docks" as a perk for putting them in. George and his dad both turned their heads toward a large crack onshore, followed by a thud.

Tree down. There'd certainly be more. George held a hand in the air, measuring the wind speed. Fast enough to fell small ones, for sure, and if the lightning hit any of them right, a big tree wasn't out of the question.

"Strikes are kind of close!" George yelled as a long trident hit somewhere in the middle of the water.

"Yeah." Paul pointed toward the shore where all of the dock sections sat on the bank. They could get out and pull them far enough uphill that they wouldn't wash away.

They didn't speak while they did it. Every time he caught docks, George was amazed at how much heavier the wood was on the shore. His forearms and lats screamed as he backed away from the water with each section.

He hauled himself up the marina steps and had just exchanged a high five with his dad when they heard another tree fall somewhere on the east end of camp. Paul's mouth gaped, and just as he had earlier in the afternoon, George could see his dad's age. At some point, the ADs were going to have to do this stuff, the night storms, the docks. George hoped Owen was up to it. He reached out and slapped his dad's slickered shoulder. "I'll go make sure the cabins are fine. You can probably head back up, yeah?"

Even if the storm raged for a little longer, they wouldn't be able to fix anything else before morning. "I'll walk you past the office and check the power cords," Paul said.

George smiled. This was an old task, obsolete with the electrical upgrades of the recent decade. But it was nice, doing the work of the place together. Paul would wait for him while he circled the boys' cabins, making sure all was well.

They walked in silence, George splashing through the low spot on Birdsong Green that always filled with water first. "No sense trying to stay dry," Paul said. George responded by dragging his feet through another puddle.

Paul laughed. "Remember Bea out here?"

George snorted. His sister had a lot of skills—nobody did activity sign-up better or faster—but storms were a stretch. Her own tears of frustration always mixed with the rain on her face. Once, George had found her hiding in the swim dock shed behind a forest of pool noodles. Paul trotted up the office steps, lighter on his feet than he had been a moment ago, and unzipped his pocket for the key. "I'll be here," Paul said.

George gave a thumbs-up and jogged toward the lakeshore, weaving between the buildings. Everything looked okay. Lots of branches, but no damaged cabin roofs, no broken windows. Finally, when he'd made a left and headed toward the woods that separated the cabins from the point, he saw the first tree down. A white pine, good size. There seemed to be a glow at its roots, and George crouched down, reaching toward it. During outdoor ed, he'd told kids the roots could glow, the phosphorescence—one of his favorite words—caused by a fungus. But George had never seen it. He instinctively felt his pocket for his phone, but he'd left it on his bedside table. Phones and storms were a losing combination. At Birdsong, they often told kids to take mental pictures, a tech detox strategy. George circled the exposed roots and gaped at the green glow. He pretended to hold an old-fashioned thirty-five-millimeter camera and "clicked" the button.

Looking back on it later, George would think he'd maybe heard the footsteps behind him, but in the moment, he didn't register anything. It was just the glow from the roots, the wind in the new leaves, the crash of the waves, slightly less intense now than they had been an hour before, when he and his dad had first gotten out here.

The voice was low and scratchy. "It's caused by fox fire," he said. George's whole body reacted, recoiling.

When his eyes refocused as the adrenaline subsided, he saw Andrew O'Neill standing in front of him, one pocket torn almost all the way off his dirty cargo shorts.

"Andrew." *Slow down*, George commanded himself. He felt his right hip for his holster, but of course, he hadn't worn it down to the water. It was locked in a gun safe in the garage.

"Bummer," Andrew said. "No Glock on storm night?"

George forced his shoulders down, dropped both arms and breathed. He touched each finger on his right hand with his thumb in succession as he studied Mr. O'Neill. The man's T-shirt stuck to his body, the left sleeve pushed up to reveal his biceps. A streak of dirt followed his jawline on the right. What was Andrew O'Neill doing out here?

"Nice weather we're having?" George tried. Andrew let out a rough chuckle.

"Henry was deathly afraid of storms," Andrew said. Lightning flashed over the lake and Andrew turned toward it.

"Was he?" George asked. "My sister, Bea, hates them, too." He tried to smile. "Part of the job here, for better or for worse."

"You don't remember that about Henry?" Andrew asked.

George held his breath. Henry's eyes flashed in front of him, between himself and Andrew. He saw Henry drop a ball on the recess field, Henry fall off his bike, Henry miss a slide and get tagged out at second.

Andrew went on. "But you always seemed to like the kid okay. I remember you'd wait for him at the end of the high-five line.

Sometimes you gave him a sip of your water bottle. But how many errors did *you* have in all those years of Little League? Certainly not one per game, like he did."

George thought back to that last day he'd spent with his friend, to the Pokémon cards in his cubby, the way George had slid them into his own pocket. And then, how he'd tucked them into his pillowcase afterward and kept them there until he'd graduated from high school.

"I always liked Henry," George said. It was true. "I miss him all the time."

Andrew backed away from him, and George looked around, wondering where he'd come from. Where had he parked his truck?

George let him put some distance between them. The rain slowed. Thunder rumbled, but softer, farther away.

George forced his legs forward, following. Another shot of adrenaline sizzled through his torso. Vance would tell him not to engage without backup, but here he was in the Northwoods, at the end of a storm. There was no backup to be had.

Andrew staggered left. That was when George saw the shovel, its blade encrusted with mud. George glanced over his shoulder and could just see the light in the office. His dad would wonder soon what had happened. *Don't come out*, George thought, though he couldn't decide whether he wanted that or the opposite. "Do you know something? I never wanted kids," Andrew said.

George strode faster, trying to catch up, but also not to alarm Andrew or interrupt him. "I read that," George said, "in the transcript of an interview you gave. It was in the investigative files."

"I gave a number of interviews," Andrew said. "They never seemed to ask me the right questions."

George's fingers tingled. "What do you want me to know?" They started deeper into the woods. A layer of last year's leaves, wet now and mixed with pine needles, attached themselves to George's sandals.

"My wife," Andrew said. "Emily."

George kept his eyes down as he followed Andrew through the thicket. "I know you always missed her. Henry kept a photo in his cubby."

"Right. I made him have that." George couldn't read Andrew's tone. "I wanted him to develop a little gratitude. I mean, she gave everything"—his voice broke and he pitched forward—"everything for him."

George tried to remember every detail of the interview he'd read, but so much of his brain space was taken up with following and maneuvering. "Did you have a lot of help with Henry?" George asked. "Raising him when he was little?"

Andrew cough-laughed again, a rattly sound that chilled George. "We were new in town when he was born, when Emily died."

George thought about Sarah's mother then, also dead. Sarah's sister dead, too. At least Henry survived?

"I was alone. Emily's sister came to town. She stayed a week, rented a room at the Country Inn & Suites. Henry cried all the time."

"It must have been very difficult." George meant it. He couldn't imagine caring for an infant while grieving a wife.

Andrew turned back toward Whitehook. "And then, he couldn't do anything."

"Anything?" George echoed.

"He walked late. He read late. He was a bad swimmer. He couldn't throw or catch. It felt—". Andrew stopped walking and faced George. George tried to stay neutral. "It felt like a bad fucking joke." George breathed in through his nose and held it, his chest straining his rain jacket.

George's mind spun. He thought back to all the news coverage, of Andrew crying at the vigils, of Andrew calling the FBI. That whole time, whom was he really grieving?

So many details from that day clung to George, surfaced any time he got too comfortable. He'd been wearing Heelys, the shoes with the wheels. His teacher had handed the axles back at the end of the day per policy. George remembered sliding out to Henry's dad's car. He'd braked against the door of the Ford Escape. He'd been wearing a green hoodie with the Birdsong logo on the front.

He'd given it to Henry halfway through the afternoon. He'd gotten cold at the park. The green hoodie had been on every news broadcast, mentioned in the Amber Alert. It had tied George to the case from the beginning.

Andrew stepped to the left and George turned, too, away from the lake. Over Andrew's shoulder he could see a hole, the edges messy, something white stuck in one of the sides. "No," George said, passing Andrew, jogging toward it. And then he saw, on the front edge, the fabric worn and torn, but the color unmistakable. Kelly green. The hoodie.

"What did you do?" George said. He wasn't supposed to. This wasn't a line they'd practiced. But this was Henry. He'd lost him. He'd let him go. All these years, George had known intellectually that Henry was gone. The statistics, the case histories, the profiles all told the same story. But without the proof, there'd been a tiny spark of hope.

"It was an accident." Andrew wasn't crying this time. He sank to the ground, the mud sucking at his body. "I didn't mean for it to happen."

"What do you want me to know?" George asked again.

Andrew looked up at him. "He fell off his bike on the trail. *On the groomed trail.*"

The trail went behind the office and looped around the basketball court before heading back toward the road.

"There wasn't a rock or rain or *anything*." Andrew lifted a hand and let it drop on his muddy pants. "And he was crying again, just like he did all the time, just like he had from the very beginning, and I wasn't thinking about what I was doing, and I just *wanted it to stop*."

CHAPTER FORTY-FOUR

May 28, 2023

Sarah had heard the storm the night before, had heard George leave the cabin, but she'd stayed in bed under the covers. She'd drifted off again, and then awoke when the whole place seemed to light up—sirens, floodlights, and then, finally, sunrise. The moment the morning light lifted from ash to gray, she threw on her shoes and ran down to camp.

She could see the mob of law enforcement near the office and, not for the first time, started to worry. As she jogged past the dining hall she could see Sylvia's and Paul's gray heads, but not George.

All of this—the trailers and the devices on tripods and the drone that buzzed over the trees behind the whitewashed office—could be for George. He hadn't come back after he'd left around midnight. *Why didn't I come down sooner?*

She ran faster, and when she made it to the office steps, tempted to put her hands on her knees and catch her breath, George stepped out. "Oh thank God," she blurted, loud enough for him to overhear her. George paused on the steps to hand documents to an officer standing there. He wore a blue FBI windbreaker. Had he packed that? Did he travel with his uniform in addition to his gun? He scooted around the officer on the steps and came straight toward her.

She sat, a relief that embarrassed her weakening her limbs, on a railroad tie across from the office steps. "What's going on?" she asked, pushing her hair behind her ear.

"You're not going to believe it," George said, "but Andrew O'Neill is in custody. We found remains. Well, he led us to remains."

Sarah tried to process what George was saying. The father? The father in jail for the murder of George's friend? "You found Henry?" she asked.

"We found Henry," George said. His voice cracked. An excavator rumbled down the gravel road through the center of camp, and Sarah couldn't believe she'd made herself stay in bed for so long. She'd thought she'd be in the way. She was still mad. George sat down next to her. Sarah could smell lake water on him.

"I'm so sorry," Sarah said. "Or, congratulations? Tell me what happened?"

George held her gaze and she could see that he was both sad and sorry. "I'm going to tell you every detail."

The drone banked left above them and a gaggle of agents followed it. And then a striking woman with a sharp jaw stopped in front of them. She wore black lug sole boots, dark jeans, and her own blue field jacket.

George pushed himself to standing. "Sarah," he said, "this is my boss."

The woman put her hand out. "Supervisory Special Agent in Charge Jane Vance." Sarah shook her hand and then let her own drop back to her lap, still sitting, recovering from the adrenaline rush of worry. "As you know, Ms. Jones, we've got a couple of things going on at once. Yesterday, I arrested Gabriella Johnson, whom you know as Sarah Jones."

"I heard," Sarah said.

"While the O'Neill kidnapping is obviously critical, so is the

Jones murder. I need to take your statement before the two of you leave, which will be imminent." Sarah caught Vance's pointed look at George. Was he in trouble? *Probably,* Sarah thought. *He deserves to be.*

"I'm not ready to give a statement." Sarah shook her head and looked at the lake. She put her hand back on the damp wood and made her legs support her as she rose.

"The timing's important," Vance told her. "There are victims who need closure. There are constraints. Protocol."

Sarah walked toward the shore, toward the steep bank. Her mother had been here. Her mother's adult life had started here. What would her mother do if she'd been betrayed by both her boyfriend and her best friend, if she'd made nothing but mistakes and misjudgments since the moment she'd broken that teacup and said goodbye to her life in Vermont?

"I need more time to think." She didn't look over her shoulder, but she could sense someone behind her. She kept walking away toward a pavilion, the roof held up by pillars of stone. The sun had started glinting in the water, the clouds clearing. "Mom?" Sarah whispered, though she knew she wasn't there. At least not in the way Sarah and Grandma Ellie always hoped she would be.

She turned her head and looked at Vance, who'd followed her. She looked nice, her eyes dark and sympathetic. She tilted her head and squinted a little. Sarah noticed that her eyebrows were groomed. She wore no makeup.

"What time did you have to get up?" Sarah asked, thinking about her arrival. She hadn't put her watch on, but it had only been 5:15 when she'd run out of the AD's cabin.

"Nightingale called at 12:52 a.m. I was in the car by 12:57."

"Gosh," Sarah said. "My job isn't like that."

"We're closing two big cases today," Agent Vance said. "A lot of people are going to be able to start healing. The whole community up here, if you think about it."

Sarah turned and looked at Vance again. She noticed a couple of gray strands of hair stretching from her temple to her ponytail. "I've been wrong about everything so far. I don't know what I'm doing."

Vance clapped her on the shoulder. "You probably haven't been wrong about *everything*."

Sarah laughed a little. "Most things?"

"You're in a weird spot," Vance conceded. "In terms of George and Gabriella Johnson, you didn't know a lot about what was going on in your life. That never feels good."

"It's a lot to take in that my boyfriend was dating me under false pretenses," Sarah agreed. "And my best friend could be a murderer." She felt as if she were submerged in the lake before her, bobbing around on the waves, only her nose above water.

"But I will need to take your statement," Vance insisted, "and then I need to send you and George back to the cities. This is going to be a shit show here—" She gestured toward the woods where they could hear machinery and shouting. "The media will converge any second. It's national news. And it's my own kid's birthday party."

Sarah watched her shrug, resigned already to missing it. "How old?" she asked. As much as she didn't want to, she cared. The birthdays she'd spent with her own mother—she wished she remembered every detail.

Vance sighed. "Eight."

Sarah regarded her, watched as the woman bit her lower lip and extended her fingers. It was a tactic. She wanted Sarah to comply, to make things easier. But all Sarah had done was cooperate, and here she was: miserable and alone.

"Whether I give my statement now or not," Sarah said, "you're not getting home today." The two of them looked at each other. Sarah swallowed. Stalling the FBI wasn't anything she'd imagined herself doing.

"That's right," Vance agreed. "I'm fucked either way."

Sarah felt her shoulders drop. She could wait, look out the window on the way home, meet with the Sarah Joneses, get back to her apartment, decide at that point what to do.

"If you need time," Vance said as she turned back toward the camp office, "that's fine. But I'm going to make you take it in an interrogation room at the precinct until I get back. I'll have Agent Nightingale set you up."

"In jail?" Sarah asked. "I'll wait for you in jail? Is that legal?"

"For a few hours?" Vance shrugged. "Yes."

CHAPTER FORTY-FIVE

May 28, 2023

"She won't talk," Vance said to George.

"She won't give a statement?" Sarah had been furious with him, but she didn't seem furious now. He didn't know why she wouldn't answer their questions. They could move forward once these investigations were closed.

"No. She needs 'time.'" Vance did the air quotes and rolled her eyes. "I told her she could take it in a holding cell until I get back."

"We're arresting her?" Any hope George had harbored about making things right between them would fizzle when he clanged the metal door shut and locked it from the outside.

"Probably not," Vance said, "but we need the statement and the bank info." Without her cooperation, they'd sacrifice at least one charge. Vance continued, "And, for the sake of *your* future, as a rookie and someone in more than a little bit of hot water, you need to close this."

Damn. George had hoped that his break in the O'Neill case, the elicited confession, might save his career. And it still might? Though what had he really done? He'd lucked into a connection with Andrew O'Neill and had happened to be on-site when it broke. But still. *Serendipity.*

Murder was relatively easy to get away with. Almost half of

perpetrators achieved it. Andrew had. In the end, Henry was not more than a quarter mile from the spot George himself had last seen him. Camp kids had likely played woods tag over his grave hundreds of times since he'd disappeared. All that time, George had felt he owed something to Andrew for some imagined mistake he'd supposedly made in the fifth grade. In reality, Andrew had spent all of those years seething with his own guilt.

"Hello?" Vance said, waving a hand in front of George's glassy eyes. "You with me, Nightingale? I'd love to clear this fraud case. Let's bring it home."

"I'm not sure—" George started. "Couldn't someone else . . ."

"You developed her. You did the reconnaissance. You have the data. Let's finish this. Put her in the interrogation room and let her stew. I'll take her statement when I get back." She answered her buzzing cell phone and walked away.

In the time since Andrew had led him to the remains and George had activated the FBI, there'd hardly been a moment to debrief with his parents, even though they'd shared the burden of Henry's disappearance with him from the beginning. Finally, George sat with them while Sarah packed her bag in the AD's cabin.

"Dad," George said, his voice thick. "You knew."

"I didn't know it would end this way." Paul dropped his head into his hands and George's mom rubbed his back. "I never considered you'd have to see everything. Again." George could hear the tears in his voice. "Or that you'd be in danger."

George wasn't sure what to say to that. He wanted to absolve his father completely, but then again, Paul had kept his suspicions to himself for years while national security kept the case open. George might have chosen an entirely different career path if only

Paul had suggested a thorough search of the woods. And now Sarah was refusing to talk as well, for who knew what reason.

George felt lost in a swirl of emotions. "I'm just happy it's over," he said, finally. "We'll talk more later?" He grabbed his mom in a hug first, and then his dad.

They walked out to the car and met Sarah. Sylvia hugged her and then grabbed George for a second embrace. "I want to see her again," she whispered as she let go. "I have a feeling." George didn't have the heart to tell her he had probably already ruined everything.

They headed up the hill, past a line of law enforcement and media vehicles, and they didn't say anything for a while. George had started to feel tired, the adrenaline finally waning. He turned on the radio, and the classic rock station filled the Civic. Bon Jovi, the heavy guitar out of sync with their mood.

"You're going to talk to Vance, right?" George asked finally, already dreading leaving Sarah at the Minneapolis police station. He'd go home, shower, call Bea. And Sarah would be in jail.

"I honestly don't know what to do," Sarah said. "I just need a pause."

George understood the impulse, but neither of them would be afforded one. "You could start by just corroborating your neighbor's story about the break-in," he suggested.

He heard her breath catch, a little hiccup. And then: "Are you sure she's a terrible person?"

"Gabriella?" George remembered the photos of the blood pooled on the concrete under the bridge. "Sarah," he said, "she *killed* someone. Like, on purpose." The broken neck, the body abandoned. "She threw her off a bridge."

"Yeah." Sarah's head dipped toward her chest.

"Even if you can imagine how it might happen, what she might have done..." George shook his head. "You and I—most people—we would never do something like that."

"Are you sure?"

George glanced at Sarah. Her eyes were clear, sad. The blue matched the sky out the window behind her.

He was completely sure. Both Andrew and Gabriella had lost control in a way that most people would never. You can accidentally slam a car door too hard or kick a railroad tie with more force than you meant to. Some people might even punch a hole in a wall. But the kind of force it took to kill someone? Not to pull a trigger or even plunge a knife, but to actually break somebody with your hands? *No.* "Totally sure," he said.

She turned her body toward the window and pulled her foot up to the seat, her arms around her knee. It was quiet until George turned into a gas station parking lot thirty miles down the road.

"Oh good," Sarah said. "I could use a snack and a drink."

"I'll get it," George said, but she stopped him.

"I put my foot to sleep. It'll be good for me to go." She shook her right leg, the one she'd held against her chest, and then as she started to walk toward the store, she stumbled. Her arm shot out, and she caught her whole weight against one of the concrete poles that held up the overhang.

"Oh!" she cried. Sarah was usually so sure of her physicality. George took a step toward her. She steadied herself and turned her palm up. She'd scraped the heel of her hand. Beads of blood rose to the surface.

Sarah took a step back and sat down on the curb next to another gas pump, the customer there eyeing her suspiciously. She started to lower her head to her knees. But then, just as George got to her, just as he put his hand on her shoulder, ready to catch her, she sat up straight and tilted her head.

"Are you okay?" George pulled a paper towel from beneath the windshield washer fluid and handed it to her.

"It's blood." Sarah looked at it again. "And I'm still here."

"You usually faint?" George confirmed. She'd told him about the day Seventeen had helped her recover.

"I always faint." Sarah blinked at him. "But I guess not today."

After she ate her Peanut M&M's and twisted the cap closed on the bottle of root beer, Sarah turned toward the window and fell asleep. He heard her soft snoring, and his whole body melted, his hands sliding down the steering wheel toward six o'clock. When she woke up, he found himself rambling about Henry, little memories that bubbled to the surface. She held his hand and listened.

And when they hit the city limits, he thought about driving her to his condo, offering her a bed inside, bringing her a cup of the same tea she'd had with Sylvia at Birdsong. But George knew that Sarah wouldn't want to come home with him. And also, Vance had ordered him to take her to the station.

"I'm really sorry about this," George said as he parked in an employee spot at the precinct.

"Is Twenty-Seven—uh, Gabriella—here?" Sarah unbuckled her seat belt and pressed her scraped hand against her thigh.

She was. George nodded. In fact, Vance had added that to his task list. He could take a run at questioning her before he went home. She'd told him to drop the fact that Sarah was in a holding cell and see if that shook anything loose.

"I don't suppose I can talk to her?" George couldn't tell from Sarah's tone whether she actually wanted to. He shook his head.

"So how's this going to work? Do I—" She stared at her hand again. "Do I get cuffed?"

"You're not under arrest," George said. "We're just going to walk in there, and you're going to wait in a holding cell until Vance gets back to question you."

"Which will be?"

"Morning, at least." George hadn't wanted to tell her, but wasn't it obvious? She was working the biggest break in a decade. Vance had warned her it would be easier if she'd talked up north.

Sarah sighed. "And there's nothing I can do now to avoid that? Like, could I run?"

"I don't think so," George said. "You have me in good enough shape. I'd catch you." He felt his shoulders slump, and they both trudged inside. He told the desk agent what was happening, and led his girlfriend by the elbow to interrogation room six.

CHAPTER FORTY-SIX

May 28, 2023

Gabriella was aware of her own stale smell, her bad breath, the remnants of the grainy coffee they'd given her when they'd brought her in.

The cop across from her appeared to be about twelve years old. "I'm Officer—uh, I'm Detective Hurley."

Gabriella blinked. "New promotion?"

The kid looked at the ceiling for a beat and brought his shoulders up toward his ears. "It's been about a week. They fired the last guy for not—uh—the photos—" He coughed. "Never mind."

"Okay." Gabriella felt a little lighter, despite the news about Oscar and the fact of her arrest. If they were bringing in the new kids for this one, maybe they didn't have anything. But then she realized that couldn't be true. They had Annabeth and Grace and probably Catherine. And Sarah? Plus, the bridge. She'd been standing on the bridge when they'd arrested her. Gabriella closed her eyes and dipped her head toward the table.

"Where's the FBI woman from last night?" Vance had been, well, not kind exactly. But getting arrested hadn't felt like Gabriella had imagined it would. There was no yanking of her wrists into handcuffs or smashing her head against the side of the cruiser.

"Are you gonna run?" Vance had asked as she guided Gabriella toward the car with a hand on her lower back.

"No." The truth was, Gabriella could barely pick up her feet. Vance's hand seemed more for support than for exerting force. The agent had just opened the back door of her unmarked Dodge Charger, and Gabriella had let her head collapse against the window.

The kid across the table from her raised a hand to his mouth and coughed a little. He glanced at the camera in the corner. Not exactly the picture of confidence.

"She's otherwise occupied," the detective said.

"Vance is otherwise occupied?"

"Can I ask you a few questions? I mean, I'm going to ask you a few questions."

Gabriella followed his eyes to the camera. "Questions about what?"

"Can we start with your real name and your aliases?" The detective's cheeks were pink and he tugged at his collar, nervous as if their roles were reversed. She looked at the camera again. If she weren't actually guilty of the crimes for which she was being held, she'd think she was being punked.

Gabriella felt queasy. She'd eaten some crackers the evening before, had pulled the aluminum lid off a plastic container of apple juice. She ran her tongue over her teeth and thought again of the bridge. If only she'd had a few more seconds, she wouldn't be here. "I think you already know that stuff, Detective Hurley." It occurred to her to smile, but her face felt too heavy.

"How about your whereabouts on the evening of . . ." He flipped his notepad back several pages, and then a few more. Gabriella couldn't help it. She rolled her eyes.

"April 17?" She finally supplied. "Where was I on the evening of April 17?"

"Yeah," Detective Hurley said, stabbing his notepad with his index finger. "Wait. How did you know the date?"

He squinted at her, and Gabriella looked toward the door. Surely they weren't actually letting this guy go it alone?

"You know what, Detective Hurley?" Oscar popped into Gabriella's head again then, his fuzzy little-kid hair, the way he'd leaned against her shoulder while she'd read him Percy Jackson. She clenched her teeth. He was really gone.

The detective's eyes widened for a moment, and he almost smiled.

"I'm going to need a lawyer," she said.

"A lawyer?" The guy's voice squeaked. "Are you sure?" He pulled at his collar again. "Wouldn't you like to just—"

The door opened then, and the kid detective startled. "She just asked!" he blurted. "Just a second ago—" He stopped talking when he realized it wasn't a member of the MPD in the doorway but George Nightingale. "Um," the kid said. "And who are you?"

Gabriella felt her shoulders relax, of all things. At least this was predictable. "That's Special Agent George Nightingale of the FBI."

"But"—Detective Hurley stood up, his chair skittering backward on the floor—"the task force got pulled for the O'Neill—"

George held up his hand, stopping the kid. "Nope," he said, "I'm here for *this* task force. My case."

Hurley sat back down. "Well, I'm here, too."

Gabriella raised an eyebrow at Nightingale. Now she had two rookies in the room. "Wait," she said, realizing. "The O'Neill case? Like, the unsolved kidnapping?"

"Yeah." Hurley lay his hands flat on the table. "Can you believe that's blowing up at the same time as—"

"Nope," George said again. "Detective, uh, Hurley? Is that right?"

The kid nodded.

"I've got this, okay? Coffee?" He held an open palm toward Gabriella. She pressed her tongue against the roof of her mouth, feeling the dryness there. What she wanted was water, but she'd take what she could get. And, oddly, she wanted a few minutes with George. He would be able to tell her about Thirty, maybe what she was thinking.

But Gabriella knew what she was thinking—that she'd trusted everything to a criminal. *A murderer.*

"Yes," she said, weakly. "Coffee."

George nodded at Hurley. "Get that, please."

"Get the woman some coffee?" The kid hesitated. He glanced at Gabriella, who kept her own eyes down, watching the interaction surreptitiously. Hurley turned back to George, his mouth half-open in protest, but George pressed his lips together and blinked, the shake of his head barely perceptible. Hurley drew a breath in, ready for another effort, but then seemed to think better of it. He pressed a code on the door's keypad—7528, Gabriella couldn't help noticing—and walked into the hall. She relaxed a little now that he was gone.

George perched on the corner of the table and crossed his arms.

Since Annabeth, she'd read about how the FBI builds a case. It was a lot of surveillance, a lot of reconnaissance. Not a lot of action. Until now. She'd thought she had enough time to get out of town. And she had, but then she'd faltered.

What Gabriella still didn't know was whether George had gotten what he needed in terms of Sarah's financials. Probably, he had. George had been with Sarah when she'd initiated the transaction. George cleared his throat, but still hadn't spoken when Hurley came back with a Styrofoam cup that sloshed over the rim onto the metal table. He dropped a packet of nondairy creamer in the splash and stood at George's elbow.

Finally, George turned toward the young detective. "That's all for now," he said.

"But she asked for a lawyer? So ... doesn't that mean ... ?" He leaned toward George and started to whisper. Gabriella felt a chuckle rise in her throat despite her stress.

George held up a hand, his fingers nearly touching Hurley's face. "It means I'm going to need a couple more minutes," he said. And then, anticipating Hurley's forthcoming protest, he added, "I have Vance's permission."

"Supervisory Special Agent in Charge Jane Vance?" Hurley asked. "But she's up north with the O'Neill break."

"Yep," said George. "You want to see the texts?"

Hurley opened his mouth to say yes before he realized it wasn't a real question. "Okay," he said, finally. "I get the picture."

As the door clanged shut behind him, George moved to the corner and pulled the wires out of the camera. Gabriella scanned the room, sure that the bulky aughts-era wall unit had to be a decoy for the real thing.

George read her mind. "Budgets here aren't that big," he said. "This is a local office. We're not in Washington, DC. And besides"—he pulled the chair out from the other side of the table across from her—"none of this would be admissible. You asked for an attorney. We're off the record."

Gabriella rolled her eyes. "Forgive me if I won't trust you on that."

"I'm sorry about your brother," George said. Gabriella's stomach turned. She was ready to deal with whatever else he wanted to ask, but she couldn't think about Oscar. It was his little-boy face that had kept appearing to her overnight, his holey first-grade smile, the plastic baggie filled with quarters she'd helped their mother put under his pillow so he'd believe in the tooth fairy.

"That was the whole reason," she said, not expecting to. She wasn't planning on saying anything, but all she could think about was Oscar. If only there'd been something else she could have done, another solution she could have explored. But she'd tried everything. "I tried everything," she said.

"Why?" George asked.

"What do you mean?" Gabriella thought of Oscar's tired adult eyes then. The ones that hadn't been able to find respite. He'd tried everything, too.

"Why did you try so hard to help him? Vance said he'd struggled with addiction for years?"

"Years," Gabriella said. "Since high school, really. Do you know anyone like that?" Most people did. People had a cousin or a family friend who'd been ensnared and couldn't get out, no matter what, no matter how hard anyone tried.

George nodded, but didn't say anything.

Gabriella thought of the photos again, the ones Oscar had shown her in the restaurant, her students on the rug, the threat of a school shooting. She hadn't told anyone but Annabeth about the threats. She'd just taken action.

"There were really bad people," Gabriella said. The words sounded naive and futile. George pulled a notepad out of his back pocket. "I know that sounds ridiculous, coming from me."

"Bad people?" He didn't seem to be making fun of her. Gabriella could see why Sarah liked him. There was an earnestness to his brow line. He pushed the curl off his forehead as he began to write.

"When did you first find out about them?"

"Oscar asked to meet me," she said. "He told me he was in trouble. They—the people—they threatened to shoot up my school."

"Where you taught?" George asked, writing.

"Yeah. That's why I left."

"And," George asked, "did you ever talk to these people?"

"Text messages," Gabriella said. "A series of burner phones." As Gabriella told it, it seemed crazy. She'd shouted a bit of it at Annabeth before she'd left Chicago, but since then, it had just been her. Her secret, overtaking her entire life.

"We'll need the phone numbers you've used," George said, scribbling, "just in case."

He was so determined, so potentially helpful. It made Gabriella question all the times she'd decided not to call the police. Once she'd started the project—once she'd conned Annabeth—it just seemed like she was trapped. She'd be arrested herself. Now Oscar was dead, too.

Then again, she realized, George was like her—using people for his own gain. He'd been using Thirty. She really liked him, her eyes sparkling and cheeks pink when she mentioned him. Thirty thought whatever she had with George was real. She'd been so thrilled to go to his family's camp.

"Where's Sarah?" Gabriella asked. She remembered the time in the café when she'd almost told the truth. There'd been so many times, like with Annabeth, that she'd been tempted to confess. George swiped at his curl again and didn't look up.

"She's, um . . ." he stalled. Gabriella stared at his pencil. He'd stopped writing but kept it on the page, tapping it slightly as he thought.

"She must have come back with you, right?" Gabriella asked. "She was so excited to go up north. I, uh—" Gabriella smiled then, remembering the teasing she'd done about meeting George's parents. "I gave her some shit about making a good impression on your family."

George blew out a breath, deflating a little. "As if she could ever make a bad impression," he said, surprising Gabriella with his openness.

"Right?" Sarah's approachability had made her a perfect mark, one that Gabriella hated homing in on. "So it went well, then?"

George shifted, moving the notepad from one knee to another. It hadn't gone well. "Oh," Gabriella said. "How did you screw it up?"

"What makes you think it was my fault?" George kept tapping the pencil.

Gabriella raised an eyebrow. "Well, I know it wasn't hers."

George looked up at the dismantled camera in the corner and tucked his pencil behind his ear, pure Clark Kent.

"I've been investigating you, right?" he said. "Like, since Grace Smith?"

Gabriella swallowed, her doom feeling more real as he said it.

He continued, "But Sarah didn't know exactly what I was doing. She thought she was an informant on the murder case; she didn't realize there was fraud." He gestured between them.

"And she found out," Gabriella said. She would have heard of the arrest; she knew about the bank transfer. The neighbor would have texted. So did Seventeen, after Gabriella had lost her cool in the coffee shop.

"And, so... what? Your ruse fell apart on Saturday? Right before your boss arrested me?"

George coughed, seemingly coming back to himself.

"I think maybe I've said too much," he said. "Let's go back to you?"

Gabriella bumped her knee against the bottom of the table. They wouldn't need Sarah—not really. They had Grace and the others. And the photos of her in the necklace, the auction documents. Even if they couldn't make the murder stick, they had her on fraud. Those charges would put her away.

CHAPTER FORTY-SEVEN

Video Transcript Recorded by Sarah Jones, Age Seventeen

May 31, 2023

Okay, we're caught up now. A few installments ago, I told you that Thirty was in jail. She was. And now, she's not. So, we're all feeling much calmer, as people do after solving a murder or two and putting the perpetrators behind bars.

That Sunday, though, the day after the O'Neill case broke, it was still really tense. Thirty *was* in jail, in an interrogation room, unable to come to our emergency meeting, which was a giant bummer since she'd been so central to the whole thing as the informant. Also because you don't want somebody like Thirty in jail. She's just too good for that.

Sister Mary Theresa took a call from Supervisory Special Agent in Charge Jane Vance in the car on the way back to the monastery after the emergency meeting. Sixty-Nine and I exchanged looks in the rearview mirror. Sister knew everything about the O'Neill case, and that's where they'd started. Sister fired off details about interrogations and evidence tags, and referred to, like, file numbers. It was the kind of pitter-patter you saw on cop shows.

"Honestly, this is going to take a while to set in," she said at one point, wiping a tear from her eye. As far as I knew, not a single student at Sacred Heart had ever seen Sister cry, and now I had seen it twice. "I had a hunch about Andrew," she'd said at one point, "but to be honest with you, Agent Vance, it was so grim—" Sister bowed her head then and grabbed her cross, nodding even though Vance clearly couldn't see her through the phone.

"Yes," she said finally, after what seemed like a monologue on the other end. "I left the force just shy of the one-year anniversary of Henry's disappearance." And then she laughed. It was a guffaw so loud that Sixty-Nine and I both startled as we pulled into the drop-off circle at Sacred Heart. "I can see how it might look like that," Sister said, gulping. "But no. It just seemed like a call that had always been there had gotten stronger as Henry's trail went cold. It's turned out that I'm meant for little mysteries, not big ones."

Another pause.

"Well, the Holy Spirit *is* mysterious, yes, Agent Vance. I'm glad you can see that. We just pulled up at the monastery. I'll call you back?"

I wanted to come inside with her, to hear whatever else she was going to say to Vance, but Sister held up her hand as she got out of the car.

"Sarah," she said to Sixty-Nine, "this has been an absolute pleasure. And Sarah"—she looked at me—"I'll call you later, too. I'll need to speak to your mother. The lying wasn't great."

She nodded at both of us, and then sort of half ran inside.

I didn't hear anything back from Sister that night, or from Sixty-Nine or Thirty. I checked the jail roster online, and Thirty wasn't there. Gabriella was.

In the morning, though my mom was in the middle of a gigantic work deal, I still caught her misty-eyed at the kitchen table watching the footage of a backhoe in the Birdsong Woods up north.

"Can you imagine?" she said to me without looking. "Twenty-two years of not knowing? And the news anchor is saying the father is in custody?"

I'd seen that the night before. And it all happened when Sarah and George were there. The next news story that morning was about Fed Sarah. The anchor reported that a person of interest was being held, a person I knew to be Gabriella Johnson.

"So," I said to my mom as I sat across from her at the breakfast nook, "did Sister call?"

Mom put her pen down and peered at me over the top of her glasses. "Yes. I know you've been working on the project all this time, even though you were supposed to stop."

I launched into the defense I'd thought of. "But I haven't posted on social media," I said. "I haven't recruited any new Sarahs—"

Mom held her palm up. "I figured you were working on it." She shook her head and flipped to a fresh page in her notebook. "I'm not *so* clueless. I'm not the worst mother in the world."

That statement surprised me. "What?" I said. "You're not even *close* to the worst mother in the world. Did you know that Serafina Jones's mother suggested she get Botox between her eyebrows? In HIGH SCHOOL?" It was true. She'd confessed that in Mrs. O'Leary's class when we were discussing self-esteem.

"That's insane," my mom said. "Anyway, I've been relieved that you've been busy with friends. And am I crazy, or do you seem happier?"

I thought about it. After the basketball disaster, I hadn't wanted to admit that I was sad, but obviously I was. I had no friends. My reputation was in the toilet. My future at Sacred Heart, even though I'd been a student there forever, was hanging in the balance.

But the Sarahs had stepped in. Sister had stepped in. Ruby had stepped in, and I'd even FaceTimed with her the night before as she cried over Gabriella. These people, they seemed to actually like me.

"Yeah," I said. "I think, objectively speaking, I'm happier. So does that make sneaking around okay?"

"Okay that you totally lied to me and also to the representative of the church who supervises you and controls your future?" Mom rubbed the bridge of her nose. "I mean, it's not ideal."

I felt bad for her then. Let's be honest, I'm not the easiest daughter to deal with. But I'm also not the worst kid in the world. "I think it could look good on my college applications to continue the project when I'm not required to," I said. "Did Sister tell you that she was an actual police detective before she joined the convent? The possibilities for Season Three are endless."

"Let's not get ahead of ourselves," Mom said. "Sister and I both agree you seem happier and more well-adjusted." She smiled. "And neither of us really care about your college applications." I put my arms around my mom's shoulders from behind and squeezed.

And then, Sister called *me*. "Come with me to the jail?" she asked. And I'll admit that was not a line I ever imagined her saying. But the only possible answer was, "Hell yes." Without the "hell," obviously.

"What are we up to?" I asked as I hopped in the Sacred Heart van. I noticed right away that Sister had on her full wimple, a look she hadn't rocked in years. Usually, her gray hair was out for all to see.

"We're visiting the Sarahs," Sister said. "Vance put me on the list."

"The FBI put you on the official visitors list for criminals?"

"Remember I was a police detective," Sister said. "I remain a member of the O'Neill Task Force to this very day."

Right away, I noticed the wimple afforded a significant advantage in, like, getting people to do what you want. Merging onto the highway? People backed way off. Parking? Swear to God, people waved Sister into a closer spot. And the officer at the desk? He looked sort of crabby and disgruntled as he pecked at his keyboard, but when he looked up he became eager to please.

Sister raised her hand as if blessing him. "I'm here to see Sarah Jones," she said. "You'll find Supervisory Special Agent in Charge Jane Vance has authorized my visit. I'm Sister Mary Theresa Conaty."

The officer bounced in his chair a little bit, clicked something with his mouse, and then looked panicked.

"The thing is—" the desk guy said. His cheeks had started to get red. "The thing is," he repeated, the flush spreading to his neck, "I don't see? And, I mean, I'm not authorized to . . ."

Sister grabbed her cross and whispered something unintelligible toward her belt.

"Sorry, uh, Sister," the guy at the desk said. "I didn't quite hear that."

She blinked, still looking at her belly. "Oh, I wasn't talking to you," she said and smiled huge. "I was just privately entreating our heavenly Father to make his way into your heart to accommodate my mission." I couldn't help it. I rolled my eyes and blew a big breath out. Sister elbowed me subtly without letting go of her religious artifact.

"The thing is—" said the guy.

"You know what?" Sister interrupted. "I've just been having a word with *my* superior." A chuckle escaped my throat, but I think I effectively covered it with a cough. "Perhaps," Sister continued, "I could have a word with yours as well?"

The officer looked behind him. We followed his gaze over a couple of desks with dividers between them. The cops looked busy. A few were on the phone. A woman in the corner with a headset spoke in short, furious bursts.

"Unless," Sister said, "unless bothering them seems like a bad idea."

The guy clicked some stuff on his screen and looked over his shoulder again. We heard some indistinct shouting in the background, and then, no shit, George Nightingale walked up to the desk. He looked sweaty and upset.

"Sister Mary Theresa?" he asked.

"George." Without asking, she pulled him into a hug. "I can't tell you how often I've thought of you in the last twenty years. And now, now it's all over."

"You look different," George said.

"I'm older and more devoted to our Lord and Savior Jesus Christ." She smiled, and George pulled away.

"Can I ask you something?" George seemed to collapse a bit, that forehead curl a little stringy as it shifted.

"Did I know about Andrew?" Sister gripped her cross with both hands. "I told your boss I had a hunch, but it was never something I could make stick. It was, I think now, too horrible to keep pushing after he denied any involvement. My failure."

"Not just yours," George said.

"No," Sister agreed. She hugged him again, and he closed his eyes as he held on.

When they parted, Sister asked to see Thirty.

"Vance is finally in with her," George said, shaking his head. "But do you know who you *could* talk to?"

And that, my friends, is how Sister Mary Theresa got in the room with Gabriella Johnson. And what did I do? I sat in the chair next to the intake desk and wrote as much of this down for you as I could remember.

CHAPTER FORTY-EIGHT

May 29, 2023

"Wait," Gabriella said as the nun sat down across from her. "Sister Mary Theresa? Are you from Seventeen's school?" Gabriella's head felt as fuzzy as her mouth. She reached for the water the nun had placed on the table. It felt cool as it went down, and Gabriella shivered.

"Sacred Heart, yes," Sister said. "The last girls' school in the state."

Gabriella wasn't sure what to say about that. Instead she pictured Seventeen in the coffee shop where they'd met just the other day, her wide eyes and slightly greasy hair, the genuine fear in her expression as Gabriella dumped her coffee. Gabriella had been desperate. She hadn't cared who got in her way. It had been the same with Fed Sarah. Remembering, she put her head down on the table, the cold metal of it against her forehead, and let the tears come. Gabriella felt the nun's hand on the back of her head. The heaviness felt good. Sister moved her hand to her shoulder and squeezed.

"I'm so sorry for your loss," she said, and Gabriella cried harder.

"Sister," she said, "I'm not religious."

"That's okay, honey." No one had called her that since she was little. There'd been a grandmotherly babysitter. Gabriella couldn't even remember the woman's real name.

Gabriella sniffed and kept her head down. "I've made some

pretty definitive choices," she said. "Things that seemed right in the moment that put me in a spot..."

Gabriella felt the woman's hand moving slowly against her shoulder blade. What she was experiencing, her eyes closed and cheek against the table, had to be what people saw at the end of their lives, an accounting of all her sins. The faces of Oscar and her mother, and then Annabeth, and Catherine and Grace, and then Fed Sarah, Thirty, and Seventeen.

"Forgiveness is always a possibility," Sister said. But it wasn't. Gabriella knew this. Some choices were irreversible. She thought of Ruby and Lula, of the necklace that was supposed to have been theirs. And the dead woman at the base of the bridge. She'd done all of that.

Gabriella sat up and wiped her face, not for the first or second time, with the sleeve of her shirt. She was dirty and tired. Her hair felt stringy and her head hurt at the spot where she'd fastened her ponytail. "I'm not sure about a way out of this," she said.

"No way out but through." Sister had a solidness about her, something to hang on to as Gabriella felt like she'd lift into nothing. "What do you want me to know?"

"I broke into Thirty's apartment last weekend," Gabriella said, admitting it for the first time out loud. "Well," she qualified, "I had the key, but she didn't give it to me."

"And then—" Sister steepled her fingers, and Gabriella wondered why she was saying anything at all. Except that this seemed like an opportunity. Like a sign that she could be finished. That everything could maybe be, if not okay, then really, really over. "I logged into the account for her trust fund and transferred some of the balance. Not all of it."

Sister nodded. "It seems like you regret this," she said. It was the most obvious statement in the world. Of course Gabriella regretted it. She deceived people and hurt them and sometimes ruined their lives. Oscar's life. Fed Sarah's life. Ruby's and Lula's lives.

"I do," she said, like a vow.

Sister looked at her, waiting. Gabriella realized that nuns were probably pretty skilled at patience, what with their contemplative lifestyles. "Do you spend a lot of time in silence?" Gabriella asked, impulsively.

"I work in a high school," Sister said. "You know Seventeen, right? Life with people like her is not exactly quiet."

"But when you go home?" Gabriella wondered if she could also join a convent. Could she do her penance inside? Tucked away, praying her way out of it?

"Yeah, it's quiet," Sister said. "Lots of prayer. Contemplation. Different from when I was a police detective."

There was something about this woman's eyes, grayish in color, but sparkly. She was curious about Gabriella. She believed there was something worth knowing about her.

Was there? Was there anything good? Gabriella heard the thud of Fed Sarah's body on the bike path. She swallowed as she remembered the walk-in closet with Ruby and Lula. She'd used the kids, too.

"How do you, like, make something right again?" Emotion choked Gabriella's voice.

"It's complicated," Sister said, "and then, on the other hand, it's insanely simple."

"How do I do the simple part?"

Sister rolled her eyes. "Well, I can't do it because we need a priest for that, but you can start by looking within, being honest with yourself. This is what I tell the girls, right? 'Oh what a tangled web we weave . . .'"

"'When first we practice to deceive.'"

"You know your Scott," Sister said.

Gabriella remembered her high school infractions. She'd copied some physics homework and had it confiscated. She'd smoked a Marlboro Light in the alcove off the soccer field, and a teacher—probably on his own smoke break—walked by and took names.

"Can I do house arrest in the convent?" Gabriella asked. "I know for sure there's time on the table. I've done worse things than steal money. I've done things I can't even believe—" The tears came again. "It's like I'm looking down on myself, and it's some horrible version of me. Someone I never imagined."

"We contain multitudes," Sister said. "And we can't escape, but this confession, this is your first step toward atonement."

"I want a lawyer," Gabriella said, remembering she'd asked for one before.

"We have one for you," Sister said.

The door opened, and George let Sixty-Nine into the room. The retiree carried a thermos of coffee.

FBI Interview with Sarah Elizabeth Jones (aka Thirty)

Investigator Present: Supervisory Special Agent in Charge Jane Vance

May 29, 2023

Jane Vance: I'm turning on the camera. Agent Nightingale says you're ready to give your statement.
Sarah Elizabeth Jones: You were up north for a long time.
JV: What has it been? Thirty-six hours since I've seen you? Not so bad considering it's the end of a twenty-two-year-old cold case.
SEJ: How does it feel?
JV: You're still asking me thoughtful questions after I've had you locked up for a day?
SEJ: They haven't really treated me like a criminal, although the bed was a little iffy.
JV: You're not really a criminal. You said up north you worried you'd made every wrong decision?
SEJ: Not just that. I've been *wrong* about everything.
JV: What do you mean?
SEJ: I've never thought of myself as someone with poor judgment. I've met people like that, you know? In my work? Or, like, in school? People who make one bad decision after another.
JV: And you think you might be one of them?
SEJ: I did. But now? I feel differently.
JV: Can we talk about your relationship with Gabriella Johnson?
SEJ: Do you want to go home—we both could—and I could do this in the morning?

JV: No, I want to have the DA file the charges right away.

SEJ: And you're sure this woman—Gabriella Johnson? She killed Fed Sarah?

JV: She confessed to that, actually. Earlier today. Your Sister Mary Theresa helped us out with that one.

SEJ: Sister did?

JV: Your project? The Sarah Jones Project? You've been remarkably successful crime solvers.

SEJ: That makes me feel good, actually.

JV: Makes you feel like you were right about something after all?

SEJ: I guess maybe? Anyway, what do you need from me?

JV: Let's start with the packages you picked up for Gabriella, then we'll move to the break-in, and then you'll confirm some account numbers and a transfer order.

SEJ: Was picking up the packages illegal?

JV: We're not planning to charge you with anything.

SEJ: Can I see her?

JV: She asked the same thing about you. But right now? Probably not.

CHAPTER FORTY-NINE

June 20, 2023

"Still okay?" Grandma Ellie asked on the phone.

"I'm okay. I'll call you in a couple of days," Sarah said. They'd talked twice a week since Birdsong, Ellie obviously concerned that Sarah's best friend had turned out to be a con artist murderer, or manslaughterer. And that her now-ex-boyfriend had been using her for information that she didn't know she was providing. And also that her closest noncriminal friends were senior citizens and teenagers. Oh, and *also* that she'd become friends with another of Gabriella's victims. Seventeen had given her Annabeth Silver's contact information. The two of them had been messaging. "It's not your fault," Annabeth kept saying. "Gabriella has always been really good at whatever she wants to do."

In the beginning, right after Sarah came home from jail, Ellie couldn't believe any of it. "I can't believe you waited so long to give the statement to the feds," Ellie had said.

"Neither can I." Sarah really couldn't. "But you know what? Looking back, I would do it again the same way. Well, not *all* of it. But it's not terrible to wait until you're sure."

"I guess," Ellie had said. "And no matter what, your mother would have loved this story."

Sarah had laughed. "I know." Ainsley would have relished the ragtag group of same-named sleuths, the imposter among them, and maybe most of all, the Clark Kent FBI love interest.

Where's your happy ending? The voice came to her in the silence, and Sarah held her breath as she stared at her mother's old photo, the joy infused in every inch of her body. She flashed on her mom in the Birdsong sweatshirt. In the memory, she was stirring eggs on the stove and singing a camp song. "I want to linger," it went, "a little longer, a little longer here with you."

A week after the arrest, Sarah had booked a ticket home.

"For good?" Ellie had sounded hopeful.

"Not yet." Though Sarah knew it would feel good to be back with her family, she didn't have the sense that she was finished in Minneapolis yet, even though she'd been wrong about Gabriella and George. They had seemed like LRFMs, but they weren't. George still texted her every other day. And had called several times. It wasn't that Sarah didn't still think he was smart and handsome, it was just that she didn't think a relationship that had taken flight on the wings of deception was one that she really wanted to invest in. Not now, when she was determined to be true to herself.

As she stirred eggs on her own stove a text came in from Seventeen. You're never going to believe this, she said.

Tell me it's not another mystery. Sarah glanced at her watch. She had to leave for the gym. She had a new client.

No, Seventeen said. It's a FOUR.

Four?

My AP Bio test!!!!!

No way. Four was better than passing. Four meant credit at most universities. Four was a friggin' miracle.

WE DID IT!! Seventeen sent a selfie, a giant smile and a hyperextended thumbs-up.

We worked really hard, Sarah wrote. And then she wondered when she'd be able to stop working so hard. Ever since she'd dropped that heirloom teacup and broken up with Brian, she'd been working. Her mother would say, *It's hard work, becoming yourself.* And Sarah guessed that was true.

Incredibly proud of you, Sarah typed. Celebrate this weekend?

Sounds good! Seventeen said. They'd go for coffee at their usual Starbucks and maybe peek into a crystal shop.

At the gym, Allison walked in and dropped her sling bag behind the fitness desk. "A new client?" she asked. "Your roster must be almost full."

"Joyce the racewalker is on a three-week hiatus." Sarah fist-bumped her supervisor. "And the moms are on summer schedule. I've got a little space." She and Allison had been out a couple of times since Sarah had gotten less busy with TSJP on hiatus and George actually not being her boyfriend. Allison had gotten them tickets to see a hot local band in a week. While it didn't feel magical, it was fun to have a new friend.

"You're killing it, Jones." Allison patted her on the head. "I'm subbing for Bryce with the bros, so wish me luck."

Sarah made the sign of the cross and thought of Sister Mary Theresa, with whom she'd had lunch twice at Sacred Heart in the Sisters' Dining Room together with Sixty-Nine, who'd become a close friend of the nun. The two of them planned to do jailhouse ministry together, a "natural outgrowth," Sixty-Nine said, of the *Murder, She Wrote* blog. Sarah didn't see the logic there, but it made her smile. TSJP really had impacted all of them in unexpected, whimsical ways. And that had been the whole point.

Sarah sighed and clicked into the system, looking at the intake form for her new client. Joe Smith. More common than her own name, and she felt a twinge of suspicion. She scrolled down.

Under fitness goals, Joe had written, "Fast marathon. I can't be mediocre."

Sarah sat back from the computer screen, her eyes wide. But before she could stand up, he was in front of the desk. He wore a threadbare Birdsong shirt, the nest above the letter *i*.

"Sarah, I need you to know how sorry I am," he said before she could speak. "I just had to try one more time."

CHAPTER FIFTY

June 2023

The text from Vance had come in at 6:45 a.m. a week after the O'Neill break and Gabriella Johnson's arrest. George had been at his desk, filing paperwork, evidence, and transcripts. He'd called the detectives back at the police stations in Peoria and Chicago, letting them know that they could close their cases.

Meet me in my office at 7:55, she said. This was the conversation George had dreaded since they'd stood together at Birdsong, the number and depth of his mistakes alarmingly obvious. It'd be Yuma. Or worse. Once he finished assembling the Johnson and O'Neill files, the Minneapolis Field Office could easily dispense with his services, call in another recent grad with less baggage and better judgment.

George drove slowly past the LifeSport on his way to the field office. He saw Sarah's Subaru in its usual spot. Before, he might have had an appointment with her around this time. But since he'd seen her in the jail, both before and after she'd been free to go, she hadn't wanted anything to do with him. He'd texted, and she'd said she needed time to consider. It had been the same language she'd used at camp. I've been wrong about everything, she wrote again. I need to figure some things out.

It's true I recruited you as an informant, George wrote back to her, hoping it might make a difference. I wasn't expecting us to make such a good team. That part of this was always real. He studied it for a reply ellipsis that never appeared. Bea had advised him on one of their many debrief calls to give Sarah what she asked for: time. However long she needed.

In Vance's office, George stood ramrod straight, just as he had that very first day.

"Well?" Vance said when she looked up from her screen. "The FBI everything you thought it would be?" Her face was placid, as usual. But she had to be disappointed.

George clasped his hands behind his back. He wasn't sure if anything he'd say would make any difference. He decided on, "It's a little more complicated than I thought it would be."

Vance turned all the way toward him, her shoulders relaxed and her hands in her lap. She didn't look like someone who was about to ship him to the border, but then again, Vance had mastered emotional regulation. She'd certainly never fallen in love with an informant.

"Why don't you sit?" He never sat. She always conducted their meetings with George standing halfway in the hall. He couldn't feel his legs as he crossed the office and thunked down into the chair.

"Let's start with the O'Neill case," Vance began. "I said in the beginning you're a unicorn. You really are, Nightingale. Join the FBI and immediately solve the one case that's been dogging you for twenty-two years."

She blinked at him, and he wondered what he was supposed to say. George hadn't given any interviews about the case, and he'd been told he wouldn't. The facts were classified for now, though the Freedom of Information requests had already flooded in. Everyone in the state wanted every detail of what had happened to Henry. And someday—probably after Andrew was sentenced, likely to life—there would be myriad tell-alls across every medium. George felt his mouth open, and he closed it again.

"How are you feeling about Henry's case?" Vance asked.

George felt the rain sliding down the back of his neck in the Birdsong woods, his hair wet against his forehead, the phosphorescent roots glowing in the waning storm.

How was he feeling? "I think I'm overwhelmed." His hand strayed to his pocket, to the edges of the Pokémon cards. He'd taken them out of the clip the other day and put them on his dresser, but it had felt disloyal, and he'd put them back where they belonged.

"I'm having you meet with our psych. You have an appointment tomorrow at eight a.m." Standard procedure for someone who'd interacted so closely with a perpetrator, for someone who'd seen the bones of their childhood friend in a muddy hole.

"Okay," George said.

"And then I'm going to put you on tips for ten days." Sorting inquiries and suspicions from the public was typically a job for interns and non–field analysts.

George nodded. She hadn't said anything about a transfer or a decommission.

"You screwed up," Vance said. "But so did I. You have potential—it's all over your file. From your first contact with a recruiter, the bureau has been invested in your future. But, for a first assignment? The Johnson case got too complex and too high-stakes. And I should have kept you far from the O'Neill documents. That wasn't fair to anyone."

George started to feel relief. "No Yuma?" he asked, timid.

"No Yuma. Tip desk. Then fraud. Maybe a nice embezzlement or a couple of stolen tax refunds." She smiled.

"Understood," George said. "Thanks, boss."

"I like you, Nightingale. We make a good team."

The "we" again. George felt his spirits buoy.

"Get your head on straight, okay? There are still a lot of O'Neill threads that need unraveling." Vance turned back to her computer and George moved toward the door.

"Your Sarah is nice, too," Vance said.

George paused, his hand on the doorframe as it had been so many times in the last months. "I suppose I should . . ." George trailed off.

"Call her and beg for forgiveness?" Vance asked.

George was surprised. "Should I?"

"Shouldn't you?" Vance's tone was back to borderline sarcastic. "I had a great conversation with her. She's brilliant and superfit, and actually? Has she considered the FBI?" Vance waved him toward the hall. "Only kidding," she said. "Kind of. About the FBI, not about calling her."

And George had called. Enough to show how much he cared for her, he hoped, and not so much to seem like a creeper. And he'd gone to the gym, but less often. Allison came over once and told him she'd been out with Sarah. That maybe Sarah missed him. That maybe he should make a training appointment. And that was how Joe Smith had been born.

CHAPTER FIFTY-ONE

June 2023

Sarah swallowed hard. George was still handsome, but his curls were less bouncy and his eyes looked tired.

"I'm sorry," he repeated. He'd said it lots of times. Another text had come in when she'd been out with Allison the other week.

"You broke up with Clark Kent?!" Allison had leaned across the table, her expression one of disbelief.

"It's not that simple," Sarah said. And then she'd realized exactly how not simple it was, how long the story would take to tell.

"I want to know as much as you want to tell me," Allison had said. And she'd meant it. Sarah had told a little then, and a little more the next time they hung out, and then a few more details over text. It felt good to get it out there.

And now, here was George. Right in front of her.

"I know I handled everything terribly," he said. "I know you and TSJP basically saved my career. I know you feel like I used you, but I want to tell you—I've never known anyone like you. I've never felt about anyone else the way I feel about you. None of it, not even any tiny bit—" He crossed his arms in front of himself and then separated them like a baseball umpire calling "safe." "None of it was manufactured or for work or *anything*."

And though Sarah remembered the sting she'd felt on that

morning at Birdsong, she also remembered the warmth of the night before, and also the moments in the mostly silent car ride on the way back to Minneapolis after the storm, when George had wept over Henry. She'd held his hand then and rubbed her thumb over his. She remembered the way she'd cut her hand at the gas station and not fainted. Had that been because George made her feel safe? Or because she'd finally found the right path? Could it be both?

Sarah grabbed her clipboard from the desktop. "Okay, Nightingale," she said, and as they smiled at each other, she felt a tingle in her fingers. "We'll do a session. That's it for now."

"Deal," George said.

Allison air-fived her from across the room.

***Crime Wave* Podcast Transcript**

Season One, Episode Nine

September 15, 2024

Ruby Campbell: I'm Ruby Campbell and welcome to—or welcome back to—*Crime Wave*, a true-crime podcast with me and my friend Sarah Jones. We're two first-year college students who accidentally solved a murder—
Sarah Jones: Actually, it was a manslaughter.
RC: And a yearslong con—
SJ: —all in the first month of our best friendship.
SJ: We did it with the help of a religious Sister and a mixed-aged group of women who all shared my name.
RC: It's a miracle when you think about it.
SJ: And now we're telling the story to you, from two different recording studios and two different states.

[*theme music*]

SJ: We've gotten really good at the intro, Ruby!
RC: Just in time for the final episode. [*laughter*]
SJ: You mean the final episode of our FIRST season.
RC: And maybe our only season—
SJ: Definitely NOT our only season.
RC: TBD. [*more laughter*] But anyway, today we've got mostly updates *and* an interview with Sister Mary Theresa Conaty, the

spiritual advisor to both the O'Neill Task Force and to this very podcast.

SJ: That's a stretch.

RC: Well, that's what we're going with.

SJ: I'll allow it. Spiritual advisor of *Crime Wave*, Sister Mary Theresa Conaty, coming up later in the show. So, Ruby, you teased some updates. Since our listenership spiked after the special O'Neill episode, should we start with George Nightingale?

RC: Sure. I gotta say, that Apple Podcasts ranking really revved my dopamine.

SJ: Mine, too. Rate and review, folks! Let's keep this train rolling.

RC: Yes, and as everyone will recall, George Nightingale is the special agent who was assigned to the Gabriella Johnson case as his debut in the FBI.

SJ: Do they call it "debut"?

RC: I'm pretty sure they do!

SJ: And since he closed that case, what has George been up to?

RC: Well, that's the trouble with having a job with security clearance. He won't tell us. But he's still working at the Minneapolis Field Office under Supervisory Special Agent in Charge Jane Vance.

SJ: Aka, the Total Badass.

RC: Totes. As listeners know, we filed Freedom of Information Act requests for all of the material related to the Johnson and O'Neill cases. But, well, the bureau is not known for its timely handling of such requests, even though Andrew O'Neill is in jail and never getting out.

SJ: We do have a sound clip from George, though.

RC: We do. We asked George how he felt when Gabriella Johnson was convicted and sentenced to five years in prison for manslaughter and an additional three years for fraud, time to be served concurrently.

SJ: More on that later, but here's the clip:

> [Voice of George Nightingale] *As an agent in the FBI, I always feel satisfied when people are held accountable for their actions and also when the public is objectively safer because of the fair punishment of crimes. I also learned in this case, though, that there is nuance and room for forgiveness. Some really smart people taught me that.*

SJ: He's talking about you, Ruby. You're the smart person.

RC: Well, me and Sarah Elizabeth Jones from Vermont.

SJ: Ruby, we've gotten a lot of questions about your feelings about the conviction. You lost your mom, which is a bigger deal than a podcast and a mystery. Some of our listeners feel like five years isn't a long enough sentence.

RC: We covered this in Episode Six, Sarah, but grief is weird. My mom wasn't perfect, but she was my mom. And I'm always going to miss her. Gabriella Johnson isn't perfect, either, but she is someone's sister. Someone's daughter. I've decided not to share too much about my grief right now. My therapist recommended boundaries.

SJ: Superhealthy.

RC: My therapist also said I could explore forgiveness.

SJ: And, with that, we do have an update from Gabriella Johnson, your mother's killer. God. That sounds so graphic. Sorry.

RC: It's been a while now. I can handle it.

SJ: Anyway, we have an update from Gabriella.

RC: Yeah. She sent us a letter. She listened to the whole podcast.

SJ: From prison.

RC: Right.

SJ: So, it's fair to say we're famous behind bars.

RC: Okay.

SJ: Read us the letter?

RC: It says, "Dear Ruby," and then in parentheses "and also Seventeen."

SJ: Nice! Even though I'm Eighteen now.

RC: "I've been meaning to send this since I heard the first episode of *Crime Wave*. Does it sound crazy and patronizing to say I'm so proud of you both? You sound old and smart and just, well, so funny and cool. I take back everything I ever said about your weird social skills, Seventeen. That was mean and petty."

SJ: It was mean and petty, but I also did have weird social skills.

RC: That's big of you to admit. Hashtag growth. Here's what she says next. "The decisions that led me to the bridge that night with your mom, Ruby. I regret all of it so much. I wish I could take back the harm I caused to you and your sister. 'Sorry' doesn't even begin to cover it. And—well, you two have done such a beautiful job of talking about this—I was mired in a terrible grief. While jail is not good, and that's an understatement, I've had a lot of time and space to think about what the rest of my life could be, and the ways I could make a positive impact going forward. I'm embarrassed to say more. But I will parrot Sister Mary Theresa if that's okay. I hope we're all just a lot more than an accounting of our sins. I believe you think we are, and I'm so grateful."

SJ: Wow.

RC: Yeah. I don't even know what to say, except to remind everyone that therapy is really good. My dad and sister and I have done a bunch of sessions.

SJ: That's awesome. And also, we don't have to know what to say to Gabriella. We can just sit.
RC: You're right.
SJ: We can cover it in Season Two.
RC: TBD.

EPILOGUE

October 13, 2024

The mile twenty-five flag at the Chicago Marathon loomed before them. The race had gone in a snap, a reality Sarah couldn't quite let herself believe. In all of the marathons she'd run, she'd never had a day quite as magical as this one. She'd heard about this kind of race, had told her clients about the possibility of it, where all the miles felt easy. But even in her fastest marathon, it hadn't felt like this, like she was in exactly the right place at the right time.

"I think we're doing it," George said as he went through the second-to-last water stop right next to her.

"It's happening," Sarah managed, though she was out of breath.

"I don't feel good," George said.

"People generally don't when they're seven minutes from the end of a marathon," Sarah said.

"But you do." George tried to smile, but it was a grimace.

"It's a miracle," Sarah allowed, trying not to gloat. "An LRFM."

"We never have to do this again, right?" George asked when they'd gone up the final hill and turned left to see the finish line. Most people sped up around them, but Sarah felt George slowing down.

"What are you doing?" Sarah asked, laughing a little. "We're there." She pointed at the banner over the road just a couple hundred meters away.

"Is it weird that I want it to last a little longer?" George asked.

"Yes!" Sarah took a couple of quick steps, daring him to match her. He picked it up, but the finish line photos show her crossing first, her hands in the air and George grinning behind her.

Afterward, they found Ellie, who'd flown in to congratulate them, and Sylvia, who'd driven with them from Minneapolis. They all hugged and then laughed at Ellie's wrinkled nose. Twenty-six miles of sweat was no joke. At least Ellie had met George before, on her own turf. He'd toured the crystal collection in Ellie's living room and answered Sarah's father's endless questions about national security. He'd almost hugged George when he mentioned Vance's suggestion that Sarah apply to the FBI.

"Dad," Sarah said. "Don't get your hopes up."

It hadn't been "no," she realized, and she caught the glance between her boyfriend and her father. Something she'd learned was that people aren't on fixed paths, and you should grab opportunities and connections whenever life presented them. A "whimsical internet extravaganza designed to explore authentic friendship" had taught her that.

And George's family? Sarah and George drove up to Birdsong at least monthly. Sarah loved to run on the trails, and George helped with whatever needed doing alongside his dad. Bea and Tilly had met them there in August, a sonogram photo proclaiming the imminent arrival of the first Nightingale of the next generation.

Over dinner in Chicago, George pulled out his phone to read a text.

"Who is it?" his mom asked.

"Vance." George smiled, his eyes twinkling.

"New case?" Sarah wondered.

"It'll wait till Monday." George lifted the deep-dish pizza, and suddenly Sarah couldn't wait to go with him back to their hotel, to rest her head in that large and warm crook of his arm, to call Ellie to thank her for coming before they set off for home.

Sarah's phone buzzed then, too. She scrolled and smiled.

"A congrats?" George asked.

"From Sister Mary Theresa," Sarah said. "And also the TSJP group chat is blowing up. They followed our progress, and they're very proud."

"You can celebrate at your next monthly lunch," George said. Sarah did those with the older members. The younger two, including Ruby, made cameos via FaceTime.

"George, maybe you can make a guest appearance?" Sylvia winked. George cringed. Every time they saw him, Thirty-Nine and Forty-Four made him photobomb a selfie for their Insta.

"And what adventures do you two have planned next?" Ellie asked.

Sarah glanced at George. "Well," Sarah said, "we have the memorial for Fed Sarah next week. Her sister planned it." It had seemed weird at first to go to the funeral of a woman they didn't know, but then again, the point of The Sarah Jones Project had been connection. Sarah and the Fed chair had both craved it, which had made them vulnerable to Gabriella in the first place. "And then when that's over, I hadn't planned on a big announcement, but we're going on a trip. New Zealand!" She'd finally, after all these years, decided to spend a little money. Besides the trip, she and George had their eye on a lakefront bungalow outside of the city with a firepit not unlike the one on the lawn at Birdsong.

"New Zealand is the birthplace of bungee jumping," George said.

"But we're not bungee jumping," Sarah added.

"That's sensible," Ellie said.

"Agreed," said Sylvia. And they all raised their glasses in a big, happy toast.

ACKNOWLEDGMENTS

Writing four books so far has been hard, but writing this one has been the hardest. There were a lot of starts and stops and resets. Finally, the sunny Sarah Joneses started to emerge. Although my brilliant and patient editor, Kerry Donovan, described an early draft as "optimistic, quirky, and fun," I felt like none of those things while writing it. It took the whole team to buoy me up through the process. But now *Making Friends Can Be Murder* is here. It's the most fun thing I've written! I'm proud of the work and excited to share it with everyone.

There are a lot of people to thank. The team at Berkley has been a dream to work with since the beginning with *Minor Dramas & Other Catastrophes*. Kerry is the best. She pushed me to make this the smartest, most readable, and most heartwarming book I could. With her help, it became more than I imagined. A giant thank-you to the whole team: Kalie Barnes-Young and Tara O'Connor, who helped the book find its readers; art director Emily Osborne, and artist Andy Huang, who made the perfect whimsical cover; production editor Caitlyn Kenny and copy editor Shana Jones who made it sparkle; and Genni Eccles, who took care of all the details. Finally, thank you to Craig Burke, Claire Zion, Jeanne-Marie Hudson, Christine Ball, and Ivan Held, who have all supported my work at Penguin Random House.

And, of course, my home team can't be beat: My agent, Joanna

MacKenzie, never doubted me, which, given the circumstances, is really something. Chadd Johnson and KK Neimann talked through a million ideas with me. They read messy preliminary drafts and said only helpful and empathetic things. As usual, Chadd figured out a lot of bumps in the plot, including who kidnapped Henry. My other early readers cheerled like crazy. They include Nicole Kronzer, Miriam Williams, Martha Pettee, Dan West, Nigar Alam, Stacy Swearingen, and Maggie Bowman. Maggie hauled me across the summer of 2023, pushing and pulling me through some of the hardest days. Thank goodness she was up to the task. I wouldn't have made it without her.

While writing, I worked with fantastic and fun kids at Visitation School in Mendota Heights, Minnesota. There were moments of joy every day at Vis, especially with my Annecy homerooms and my talented colleagues, including Nicole Sutton, Sarah Patterson, and Brian Burgemeister. In addition to teaching, the runners I coached at the Blake School inspired me with their heart and dedication. Finally, in the closing stages of this project, I moved to my new teaching and coaching home, St. Anthony Middle School, where my clear-eyed seventh graders have sparked a million new ideas, and my colleagues have welcomed me with their big hearts. Through everything, my friends Adriana Matzke, Erin Dady, Jordan Cushing, and many others continue to support me. I'm so grateful to you all.

My extended family—parents, siblings, in-laws—is still the best, and my children are just wonderful. Shef and Mac, thank you for being you and also for being so individually and independently great. My husband, Dan, is the most logical, steady, and loving partner I can imagine. Dan, it's a miracle to do all the things together for all these years.

Finally, readers, booksellers, and fellow authors: Thank you all so very much for sticking with me. Thank you especially to those of you who agreed to take a look at this thing early, to help shepherd me into a new genre with your time and thoughtfulness. Abbi Waxman, Stephanie Wrobel, Laura Hankin, Megan Collins, Tessa Wegert, Joshua Moehling, Colleen Oakley, Nigar Alam, Alison Hammer, and Bradeigh Godfrey—I feel so grateful.

I can't believe we did it! During the writing of this book, I withdrew far into myself. I'm glad to have come back to life, and I'm excited to laugh, read, and solve mysteries together, now and in the future.

MAKING FRIENDS CAN BE *MURDER*

KATHLEEN WEST

READERS GUIDE

DISCUSSION QUESTIONS

1. Which one of the Sarah Joneses would you most like to spend a day with?

2. Have you ever had a close friendship with someone from a different generation than you? What did you learn from each other?

3. Many of the characters are searching for a sense of belonging and purpose. How does this desire impact their decision-making, for better and for worse?

4. This is a story about mistaken identity and of finding oneself. At the start of the story, which character did you think had the best sense of themselves? Did that change for you by the end of the book?

5. George feels guilty for leaving the family business. Should he? Did he make the right choice? What responsibilities do adult children have to their parents?

6. What did you like about Sarah and George as a couple? Should Sarah forgive George for his deceptions?

7. Gabriella feels responsible for her brother's struggles. Do you think that siblings should feel that sort of responsibility to each other?

8. Seventeen falls into a social media trap, bullying another student at her school on Instagram. What are your experiences with social media and teens?

9. Many of the characters are impacted by grief. How does grief show up for them? How does it impact their relationships with others?

10. One of Sister Mary Theresa's core beliefs is that "people can grow and change." How did we see this in the novel? Which characters changed, and how?

11. Sarah isn't entirely fulfilled in her career as a personal trainer, though she likes it quite a bit. What do you think she does next? Why?

Keep reading for an excerpt from Kathleen West's

HOME OR AWAY

LEIGH MACKENZIE

May 2022

Leigh ran out of the blue house and flung open the back seat of Charlie's station wagon. "You're here!" she shouted. Gus, her nine-year-old, hadn't even had time to undo his seat belt as Leigh dotted his freckled face with kisses. "Welcome home to Minnesota!"

"Mom!" Gus laughed. He tapped the back of her neck halfheartedly, and Leigh remembered those toddler days when he'd dug his fingers into that same spot. Charlie had pried each digit up in order for Leigh to make it out the door for work.

And now, her son was already pushing her away. "Wait until you see the place with paint!" She spun toward Charlie, who enveloped her.

Charlie held his cheek against hers. "Three months is such a long time," he murmured. Their temporary separation had been practical. Leigh had started her new job at Lupine Capital in March as an ill-timed retirement left her boss shorthanded. Meanwhile, Leigh and Charlie both thought Gus would be better off finishing third grade in Tampa.

"It was too long," Leigh agreed as Gus threw an arm around her waist, "but it gave me time to get this place in shape. Come see your room!" She untangled herself from her husband and grabbed his and Gus's hands.

Leigh had been in the blue house for only a week herself after camping in an Airbnb near her parents'. Now, though most of the Mackenzies' belongings were still en route from Florida, they had updated bathrooms, a new kitchen, and fresh paint in every room. Plus, Leigh had just finished the hockey zone in the basement, a surprise she'd manufactured for both her son and her husband.

"I already know where my room is," Gus said. They'd looked at the house on a trip "home," as Leigh still thought of the suburb in which she'd grown up, the previous winter. As they crossed the threshold, Gus dropped her hand and scrambled up the stairs.

"Did you do okay on the last leg of the drive?" Leigh ran her fingers over Charlie's handsome stubble. They'd talked several times in the last few days, and Leigh knew the solo road trip had been taxing.

Charlie rubbed Leigh's biceps, and her skin tingled. "I skipped the Iron Furnace in Illinois, which was clutch," he said. "Turns out that even for me, there's a limit to how many historical markers I'm willing to appreciate."

Leigh laughed. Gus had complained loudly on speakerphone about stops at various roadside attractions. "I'm so happy you're finally here."

"Me too." Charlie kissed her. He tasted familiar, like coffee and peppermint.

"The green is awesome!" Gus bounded down the stairs. "Does Uncle Jamie say it's Lions green?" Gus had been obsessed by Liston Heights Lions hockey since he was a toddler. Leigh's brother, the boys' varsity coach, kept him well stocked in old practice jerseys.

"He says it's perfect." Leigh raised her eyebrows. "Speaking of perfect, are you two ready for your surprise?"

"Surprise?" Gus balled his hand into a fist and bit a knuckle, clearly excited.

"I did something cool in the basement." Leigh pointed at the door that led to the wide-open furnished space downstairs. Gus sprinted ahead and Leigh pushed Charlie's shoulder. "Go see," she urged.

"You didn't tell me about this." She could smell Charlie's Old Spice wafting behind him and felt overcome by a desire to snuggle in, to let him hold her as they watched something easy on television and sipped drinks. In all their years together, they'd never before spent so much time apart as they had that spring.

"Holy hockey balls!" Gus shrieked from below. She could hear his shoes squeaking on the synthetic ice tiles she'd installed.

"Whoa," Charlie said, catching up. Leigh had transformed the room into a hockey practice facility with a special shooting surface, net, and custom paint job. She'd even ordered decals of several Minnesota Wild players and adhered them to the walls. "When did you have time to do this?" Charlie asked.

Leigh worked a zillion hours a week at Lupine. Between the travel and the research, she had called in a favor from her brother to finish Hockey Zone. "Jamie," she confessed. Her little brother had spent several hours in the Mackenzies' basement, painting the baseboards yellow to simulate a real rink. Leigh had attached a shooting tarp over the net she'd ordered, a picture of a goalie printed on it. When she'd stood back to admire the setup, she had an unexpected desire to shoot on it herself although she hadn't laced up in twenty years.

"My stick is in the car!" Gus ran for the stairs, but Leigh stopped him.

"Jamie left you one of his old ones." She pulled the well-worn Bauer with fresh green tape from its place against the wall. "He also left you these pucks."

"Oh, sick!" Gus overturned the bucket she'd handed him, the

pucks scattering in a four-foot radius. "Mom, you can even bend your stick against this stuff!" He grinned at them over his shoulder as he pressed the stick into the tile. Pucks sailed.

"The wall," Charlie whispered, as the third shot missed the net entirely and thunked into the drywall.

"We'll repaint." Leigh shrugged, remembering the myriad holes she'd put in her own parents' basement walls. "It'll be a while before his slapshot is hard enough to do any real damage."

Charlie nuzzled her ear. "I love it when you talk dirty to me."

Leigh giggled and led him up the stairs, leaving Gus to practice. "Let me show you your new office. I said they had to finish the wallpaper before you got here."

"Did you use shark tone?" Charlie tapped her butt cheek as they climbed the second flight. That's what he called her work voice, the one she used for final negotiations.

"Sure did." Leigh pulled him into the empty room they'd decided would be Charlie's study. "I can see you in here, babe," Leigh said, "writing your great American novel."

She hoped Charlie could see it, too, could envision himself glancing up from his manuscript out of the row of south-facing windows at their spacious backyard. Charlie had spent so much time with Gus in the last decade, so much time managing the household and Little Lights Bookstore, where he'd worked for years. He'd hardly done any writing since Gus had been born, though it used to be his passion.

Leigh hoped the move back home would be a fresh start for all of them.

Charlie wandered over to the accent wall and touched the banana-leaf pattern, the same he'd used at Little Lights. The wallpaper had become a mainstay on literary Instagram, with authors posing in front of it whenever they passed through south Florida.

Charlie grinned. "I love it." At forty-two, he was still a ringer for Matthew McConaughey, his double dimples every bit as endearing as her favorite movie star's. Leigh's stomach flipped, and she blushed although they'd been together for more than half their lives. She'd missed him.

"Good spot for your desk?" she asked.

Instead of answering, he pulled her toward him again and put a palm against the back of her head.

Leigh was so relieved that he was finally here that she felt like crying. "Thank you for doing this," she whispered. "For moving back here, for driving Gus all the way. I have a really good feeling about Minnesota, especially now."

"Are you kidding?" Charlie kissed her temple. Leigh melted against him. Months of tension—the stress of starting her new job and coming home to an empty house—dissolved. "You were right about Liston Heights," Charlie said. "It's an amazing opportunity. For all of us."

"Good hockey setup, right?" As she rested her head on Charlie's shoulder, she imagined Gus in his new jersey, celebrating his first goals with his new team.

Sometimes, Leigh still couldn't believe that she had managed to raise a hockey fanatic. When she'd learned she was pregnant, she decided she'd keep her child from skating, an insurance policy against the heartbreak she had experienced at the top of the sport. But her brother had gifted Gus a pair of toddler skates without giving her a heads-up. Her parents had once again installed their backyard rink, and no one could get Gus to come inside on their winter visits home, even with the promise of Santa.

Regardless of her best intentions, by age five, Leigh's son was a superstar in the Tampa Junior Lightning House League. In the most recent season, he'd averaged more than a goal per game.

Gus was clearly talented (a prodigy, his biased uncle said), but Leigh and Charlie balked at the more intense Florida programs that required national travel to find top-level competition for the kindergarten set. In Minnesota, hockey was different. So many kids played the sport that you could find great competition at every park in the Twin Cities metro area.

When an offer of a managing director position at Lupine Capital materialized, Leigh found herself yearning for home. She imagined Gus in a Liston Heights Hockey uniform just like the one she had worn. Though the end of her athletic career had been miserable, the beginning had been magical. Hockey was Minnesota's hometown game, with whole suburbs turning out to cheer on the high school stars. Youth associations like Liston Heights fielded ten teams per age group. There was so much room for Gus to grow here.

As she had described the possibilities to Charlie, he caught her enthusiasm. He'd experienced the culture, too, although from the outside. Leigh had taught him the game when they'd watched her brother's high school team. And after ten years in Florida, Charlie was eager to ditch the unrelenting heat. There were bookstores and coffee shops in Minnesota, too, he said. He could finish his novel anywhere.

"The basement is awesome," Charlie said now, still holding her. "Did you work on finding him a summer team?"

Leigh flinched. This was the hiccup. Moving back had left Leigh with the uncomfortable task of getting in touch with her old teammates and hockey contacts. Leigh was counting on their loyalty, even though she'd left the sport behind on the same day she'd flown home from the Lake Placid Olympic Training Center in 2001. Not six hours after the final cut for the Salt Lake team, she'd catapulted her Minnesota Gophers duffel from the top of her parents' basement stairs onto the concrete below. She'd javelined her stick down there, too, the blade bouncing against the floor. Leigh wished the stick would have at least splintered, if not snapped.

It had been twenty years since Leigh had ghosted everyone after being cut from the team, including Susy Walker, her former best friend, and also their old coach, Jeff. Instagram told her they both lived in Liston Heights. Leigh had thought moving home would be worth it—Lions hockey was the best, and Gus deserved his shot—even though she'd been so careful about keeping her old life separate from the one she built with Charlie and Gus.

Now that she was here, they were all so close to the truth of her past. She had her first moments of doubt as she pulled away from Charlie and led him back to the main floor of their new home.

"Too late for a real summer team," Leigh said over her shoulder. "But Jamie and I got him in with that hotshot coach. First session is next week."

Charlie nodded and walked into the kitchen. From there, they could hear Gus's stick tapping in the basement, the regular thuds of pucks against the shooting tarp. "Last night, I was checking out the Liston Heights Hockey Association page," he said. "You know that your old coach is on the board, right? Jeff Carlson? It says he coached the national team when you were on it, but I didn't really recognize him."

Leigh turned away from her husband and opened the refrigerator. She'd done the same Google search and had read the article about Jeff and Susy coaching together. Jeff had been quoted as saying he "just wanted to pass on the life-changing love of the game to the next generation."

That line had triggered a sudden surge of rage. The game had changed Jeff's life, and he'd so casually ruined hers. If Leigh had known what the end of her hockey career would bring—darkness, self-doubt, a band of regret that she could still feel tightening beneath her diaphragm whenever she stepped inside an ice rink—she wasn't sure she'd ever have started playing. The joy had only just started coming back in the stands, watching her son participate in the sport he loved so much.

Last season, Gus had been obsessed with the spiral notebook that his uncle Jamie had customized for him. In "Gus's Hockey Bible," as the cover read, her son tracked his points, his hours on the ice, and the quotes he'd internalized from coaches. He wanted to be the best. In order to have a legitimate chance, he'd have to adapt to the intensity of Liston Heights, the hotbed of Minnesota hockey.

Although they hadn't talked in years, Leigh knew Susy coached year-round here. She'd seen the Instagram posts. Her old friend and rival stood on the bench, towering over the players, her arms crossed. Leigh had never coached her kid's team. Though she could watch games from the stands, she'd never been able to get back on the ice after the Olympic selections. Jeff and Susy knew exactly why that was.

"Damn," Leigh said as she stared into the fridge. "Charlie, I meant to pick you up some IPAs and I forgot."

"It's no problem—" Leigh spun around and caught her husband's look of disappointment. She had ordered pizza for the three of them to be delivered in forty-five minutes. After the road trip, Charlie certainly deserved a beer alongside his pepperoni.

Leigh cut him off. "It's five minutes away," she said. "And I'm almost out of gin, too. I'll be right back." She pointed at the new sectional she'd ordered for the family room. "Take a load off."

Photo by Ann Marie Photography

Kathleen West is a veteran schoolteacher who writes fiction in the mornings and on the weekends. She lives in Minneapolis with her A+ human family and three B– dogs. *Making Friends Can Be Murder* is her fourth novel.

VISIT KATHLEEN WEST ONLINE

KathleenWestBooks.com
 KathleenWestAuthor
 KathleenWestWrites

Ready to find
your next great read?

Let us help.

Visit prh.com/nextread

Penguin
Random
House